"I still can't believe you don't decorate for Christmas," Miranda said.

Simon held Hudson and Harper on his lap while she put a green hat on Hudson. His little Santa's-helper suit and Harper's matching elf outfit would go nicely with Zig and Zag, the dogs Miranda adorably still thought of as twins.

"What would be the point? It's only me and the dogs, and they don't care that it's Christmas."

"Hello, Christmas spirit, where are you? What happened to getting in the mood for all things merry and bright?"

Simon snorted. "When have you ever known me to be merry and bright?"

But sitting here cross-legged with both the twins on his lap and Miranda zipping around with unflagging energy and excitement, he thought he might be as close as he'd ever been to those feelings.

There was just something right about the four of them being here together. He wanted to tell her. But the words wouldn't come. They got all tangled up in his head and never made it to his lips.

A *Publishers Weekly* bestselling and award-winning author of over forty novels, with almost two million books in print, **Deb Kastner** enjoys writing contemporary inspirational Western stories set in small communities. Deb lives in beautiful Colorado with her husband, miscreant mutts and curious kitties. She is blessed with three adult daughters and two grandchildren. Her favorite hobby is spoiling her grandchildren, but she also enjoys reading, watching movies, listening to music—The Texas Tenors are her favorite—singing in the church choir and exploring the Rocky Mountains on horseback.

Carolyne Aarsen and her husband, Richard, live on a small ranch in northern Alberta, where they have raised four children and numerous foster children, and are still raising cattle. Carolyne crafts her stories in an office with a large west-facing window, through which she can watch the changing seasons while struggling to make her words obey. Visit her website at carolyneaarsen.com.

Family Christmas on the Ranch

Deb Kastner

&

Carolyne Aarsen

2 Uplifting Stories

Texas Christmas Twins and
The Cowboy's Family Christmas

LOVE INSPIRED
INSPIRATIONAL ROMANCE

LOVE INSPIRED®

INSPIRATIONAL ROMANCE

Recycling programs
for this product may
not exist in your area.

ISBN-13: 978-1-335-42990-2

Family Christmas on the Ranch

Copyright © 2022 by Harlequin Enterprises ULC

Texas Christmas Twins
First published in 2017. This edition published in 2022.
Copyright © 2017 by Debra Kastner

The Cowboy's Family Christmas
First published in 2017. This edition published in 2022.
Copyright © 2017 by Carolyne Aarsen

For questions and comments about the quality of this book, please contact us
at CustomerService@Harlequin.com.

Love Inspired
22 Adelaide St. West, 41st Floor
Toronto, Ontario M5H 4E3, Canada
www.LoveInspired.com

Printed in U.S.A.

CONTENTS

TEXAS CHRISTMAS TWINS

Deb Kastner

What can I give Him, poor that I am?

If I were a shepherd, I would bring a lamb.

If I were a Wise Man, I would do my part.

Yet what I can I give Him: give my heart.

Through Him then let us continually offer God
a sacrifice of praise, that is, the fruit of lips
that confess His name. Do not neglect to do good
and to share what you have; God is pleased
by sacrifices of that kind.

—*Hebrews* 13:15–16

Chapter One

Miranda Morgan wouldn't even know what hit her.

He was here in front of her cabin, preparing to make certain of that. After he was through with her, the powers that be would want to name a tempest after him.

Hurricane Simon.

It didn't matter that he hadn't seen Miranda since high school, or even, as his best friend Mason's kid sister, that she'd bared the occasional brunt of his pranks and mean jokes. In another situation, he might be considering how to make amends and not additional strife. He was a new man, a man of faith. The Lord had changed his heart, and now Simon's goal was to change his life to match what had happened internally.

But try as he might, he fell short of being able to forgive Miranda for ignoring her responsibility to the sweet nine-month-old twins now in her care.

If this was a spiritual test, a trial in his bumpy new Christian life, it was a doozy.

Miranda was an eminently successful celebrity photographer. But he couldn't care less about movie stars and the la-di-da lifestyles of the rich and famous. He was a simple ranch owner and dog trainer and he liked his solitary country life.

What he *didn't* like was Miranda. She couldn't even be bothered to fly home to Texas long enough to attend her own twin niece's and nephew's christening, and she was not only Hudson and Harper's aunt, but had also been named their godmother.

And yet she hadn't managed to spare even one weekend for them.

Even Simon had been in church that day, though at the time he hadn't been a churchgoing man. He remembered feeling uncomfortable, but he'd *been there*. Simon was the twins' godfather, and to him, it was a big thing, a sacred duty, a promise that he'd always be there for Hudson and Harper in any way they needed.

Obviously, Miranda didn't feel the same way. Family obligations clearly meant nothing to her.

And now, through a cruel twist of fate, Miranda had been named the twins' permanent legal guardian.

How could that even *be*? The very thought of it was both confusing and infuriating.

It was painful enough that Mary, Mason's youngest sister, and her husband, John, had been taken from this world prematurely by the merciless act of a drunkard who'd made the deadly choice to drive while intoxicated.

But for Mary to name self-serving, high-flying *Miranda* as the twins' legal guardian, even after all she had done, or *not* done, for Mary and the babies—

Well, that made less sense than putting a Border collie in a room full of cats and expecting him to herd them.

What had Mary been thinking? How could she have considered her sister a worthwhile guardian, one with whom she could entrust innocent children? What kind of mother would a woman like Miranda possibly be?

Inconceivable.

Why hadn't Mason and his wife, Charlotte, been named the twins' guardians? They already had four children of their own with a fifth on the way. They were wonderful, experienced parents who *had* been there for Mary and the twins during every stage of their lives.

Mary might have sincerely believed that two more children would have been too much of a burden on Mason and Charlotte, and that they had their own family to think of and provide for.

But choosing *Miranda*?

Mary might have been sincere, but she'd been sincerely *wrong*.

However the future played out now that Miranda was the twins' legal guardian, Simon's determination to be a positive influence in his godchildren's lives hadn't changed one iota. They had always been a priority with him, but even more so now.

If Miranda was anything like Simon imagined her to be, Harper and Hudson would need all the protection and stability they could get.

He was going to step up for those two precious babies.

Unfortunately, that also meant he would, by default, be in contact with Miranda. She would have to let him into her world, whether she liked it or not. And likewise, he'd have to learn to work with her. They didn't have to be friends, but they would have to get along.

For the twins' sakes, he reminded himself as he removed his brown Stetson, combed his fingers back through his thick blond hair and knocked on the door.

"It's open" he heard Miranda call from somewhere inside the cabin, her voice muffled and distant.

Feeling awkward at having to let himself into a cabin he was unfamiliar with, he opened the door and stepped inside. He didn't immediately see Miranda, or the twins, either, for that matter.

His attention was instead captured by the insane display of Christmas decorations, red and green, silver and gold, everywhere his gaze landed.

It looked as if the North Pole had exploded in her living room.

An enormous eight-foot Christmas tree stood in one corner, the flashing angel topper just barely clearing the ceiling. Presents wrapped in colorful aluminum paper were piled high underneath the tree.

She'd arranged a large Nativity set, complete with a stable and an angel proclaiming Peace on Earth, on the end table.

Shiny red and gold garland adorned every wall, with evergreen garland gracing the fireplace where the stockings were hung with care, as the poem went. *Homemade* stockings, with Hudson and Harper's names written in flourishes of red and green glitter glue.

This woman was clearly obsessed with Christmas.

And apparently, shiny things.

It took him a moment to focus and find Miranda. He supposed he'd expected to find her changing a diaper or two, or feeding the twins their bottles—or whatever it was that nine-month-old babies ate—as the reason she couldn't answer the door. Instead, she was right there in the middle of the living room, stretched out on her stomach underneath a card table that she'd draped with sheets, holding a flashlight she was beaming on a picture book as Harper and Hudson cuddled on either side of her.

Of all the crazy, unexpected scenarios, this one took the cake.

Or the Christmas *fruitcake* as the case might be.

The tent was ingenious. She'd used stacks of hardback books to fasten the edges of the sheet to the sofa on one side of them and an armchair on the other, with the card table holding up the structure in the middle.

Lying on her stomach, jammed under a table only a few feet high, couldn't possibly be comfortable for her, with her tall, lithe frame, and yet she had an enthusiastic smile on her face and didn't look the least bit put out by the awkward position. He suspected her feet might be protruding out the back, although he couldn't confirm that from his current vantage point.

She shined the flashlight at his face, momentarily blinding him, and he held up a hand to block the light.

"Simon?" she questioned, surprise lining her tone. "Simon West?"

He was astonished she recognized him. He'd added a few inches to his frame in the years since they'd seen each other last, not to mention a few pounds. He'd stayed at the outskirts of John and Mary's funeral and hadn't spoken to anyone but Mason and Charlotte.

"*Uncle* Simon," he corrected her tersely, nodding toward the twins. "It's an honorary title."

Of which he was very, very proud.

"Well, *Uncle Simon,* you're more than welcome to join us." She shifted herself and the twins to the side to make room for him in the tiny strung-up tent.

"I'm welcome to—" he repeated. He'd walked into her house out of the blue. She had no idea why he was here, and yet she'd immediately offered him the opportunity to join in their...*adventure.*

"What are you doing here, by the way?" she asked curiously.

"I—er—"

Her offer completely threw him off his game, and for a moment he was fairly certain he was gaping and couldn't remember his own name, much less why he had come.

Eventually, he shook his head. There was no way he was going to get his large frame under that small table, no matter how hard he squeezed. And honestly, he didn't even really want to try.

"We can make it work," Miranda insisted, clearly not taking no for an answer. "I'm sure the twins will love spending quality time with their uncle Simon."

She couldn't possibly know it, but she'd just touched on his weak spot. He hadn't been spending as much time as he should have with his godchildren. If she'd been trying to give him a guilt trip, those words would have done it, especially given the reason he was here.

"Grab another sheet from the linen closet in the hallway, and grab a few more books from the shelf," she instructed. "Oh, and get a chair from the kitchen. Drape the end of your sheet across the card table and onto the chair. That'll give us all a bit more wiggle room. Believe me, these two are regular squirmy wormies."

By the time he'd followed all her instructions and lengthened the makeshift tent, she was fully absorbed reading the twins their book. He stood before them, wondering how he was going to get where Miranda wanted him to go.

She flashed the cover of the book at Simon, as if finding out what she was reading would somehow convince him to crawl in.

"We're reading *Little Red Riding Hood*. Hudson likes the wolf, don't you, buddy?" she asked the baby, making a growling sound and tickling his tummy.

Hudson squealed and giggled happily.

"Tell Uncle Simon you want him to come on down," she said to Harper, giving her the same affectionate tickling treatment Hudson had just received. "I think he's being a little bit stubborn, don't you?"

Simon balked at her words. He wasn't being stubborn. He was being practical.

And this was definitely *not* how this confrontation was supposed to go. He hadn't envisioned anything of the sort when he'd first knocked on her door, but then, how could he have? This whole scenario was mind-boggling.

He was losing his momentum by the second and he couldn't seem to do anything to stop it.

"But this is—" he started to say.

Ridiculous.

Humiliating.

Mortifying.

She raised a jaunty, dark eyebrow. There was no question about it. She was outright daring him to make a fool of himself with the twinkle in her pretty hazel eyes.

This was nuts. He was crazy just to be thinking about it.

There was no way he was going to get out of this with his dignity intact. But he'd never been the type of man to walk away from a challenge.

Not now. Not ever.

Grumbling under his breath at the ignominy of it all, he dropped onto his belly to army crawl into the mixed-up files of Miranda's imagination makeshift dwelling.

"Pirates or spaceships?" she queried as he settled himself in. Grinning, she passed him a handful of crayons.

"Uh—spaceships, I guess." Not that he had any real preference for one over the other. He'd honestly never given it any thought.

"So in your most secret heart of hearts, you long to be an astronaut and not a cowboy, right?"

Absolutely not.

He supposed he *had* imagined exchanging his cowboy hat for a space suit when he was a child—but his *childhood* had gone by in the blink of an eye, almost as if it had never really existed at all.

Reality was reality, and he was a cowboy.

Sort of.

"Yeah. I guess I did. When I was a really little tyke. Maybe three years old."

Back before his mother—a single mom herself—had gotten thrown into drug rehab one too many times. Before social services had gotten their hands on him and he'd been tossed into the pitiless foster system and left to sink or swim. His childhood dreams had morphed into a nightmare that he couldn't wake from.

"Coloring is another way of dreaming, you know."

Simon scoffed softly. He knew better. He had dealt with far too much reality in his life for him to imagine anything past the trials of the day. Scribbling on paper wouldn't change a thing.

And dreaming? That was a fool's errand.

He was a responsible man now. He colored black-and-white, inside the lines. But when Harper batted her hand at his coloring book and babbled her baby nonsense at him, he took a blue crayon and started filling in the page before him.

"So, you're not an actual, live spaceman," Miranda said with a mock frown of disappointment. "What do you do for a living, then?"

"I breed and train cattle dogs," he explained as he switched a blue crayon for red.

"I don't know why, but I assumed you'd grow up to be a rancher like Mason."

He shrugged. "I'm not really cut out to be a rancher," he explained. "I can ride a horse and rope a cow, but I didn't grow up in the country. I didn't live on a ranch until I was sent to the McPhersons in Wildhorn when I was a teenager. Training dogs is a better fit for me than herding cattle."

Dogs were reliable. They loved unconditionally. Not like people.

He didn't give his trust easily. Bouncing from one foster family to the next as a kid had taught him to depend on only himself. He wasn't much in the relationship department, either. He'd never really learned how to make a relationship work out. He was broken. Like the Tin Woodman in *The Wizard of Oz*, he was fairly certain he didn't have a heart.

It was hard enough to learn how to rely on God, never mind people.

He paused. "I do own an acreage with a few head of cattle, and I like the hat."

That wasn't exactly a rarity. Nearly all the men in Wildhorn, Texas, wore cowboy hats, from the time they were old enough to sit in a saddle until the day they were laid to rest. Even the local florist sported a Stetson.

"I remember when you moved to town," she admitted, her cheeks coloring under his gaze. "You were in tenth grade. I was in seventh."

He couldn't imagine why she would recall that, other than that he and Mason were such best buddies. He'd never been a popular kid and hadn't had many friends. The truth was, he hadn't made much of a mark in Wildhorn, then or now, and what he had done he wasn't proud of. He had a lot of ground to make up for.

"I never had a dog, even though I grew up on this ranch," she said thoughtfully, referring to the Morgan holdings, on which her cabin rested. "We only kept ranch animals. We had a couple of herding dogs and a mean-spirited barn cat, who never let me anywhere near him. Once I started my photography career, I was traveling too often to consider a pet."

"That's a shame. There are many reasons to have a dog, the least of which is that they are good for your health. And they are the perfect companions. They're easy for anyone to care for."

He probably sounded like a commercial, which he kind of was, since dogs were his life's passion.

She grinned. "Trust me, I'm the exception to that

rule. When I was about ten years old, my mom put me in charge of the garden for exactly one season."

Why was she talking about plants?

"Nothing grew but weeds. No vegetables thrived, and hardly any of the flowers bloomed. I took my mother's beautiful, colorful garden and murdered it.

"When I lived in my loft in Los Angeles, I experimented again and tried keeping a cactus. You know— the kind that don't need a lot of attention. Mary helped pick it out. She was the real green thumb of the family. She told me plants helped clean the air."

She stopped and swallowed hard. He didn't need her to tell him what she was struggling with, how fresh her grief must still feel for her. It was written all over her face, and tears glittered in her eyes.

Immediately, his innate masculine protective instinct rose in him, but he didn't trust female tears any more than he did the crying woman so he quashed it back.

Still struggling to speak, Miranda cleared her throat.

"Mary assured me a cactus was the easiest to keep and that even I couldn't fail, but I managed to strangle the life out of the poor thing within a matter of months."

"You forgot to water it?" He managed to keep his voice neutral, but he couldn't help but be concerned. If she was afraid of owning a houseplant or a pet, how was she going to get on with twin *babies*?

"Sometimes. I'd go weeks without thinking about it at all, and then I'd suddenly remember and overwater."

Her face flamed.

"Anyway," she said, taking a deep breath and swiping a palm across her cheeks to remove the lingering moisture, "at the end of the day, I destroyed it. What's the opposite of green thumb? Black thumb? That's me."

He chuckled despite himself.

"So you can see why I'd be concerned about owning a dog. Fortunately, I don't need a live animal to keep me healthy. I'm in good shape. I work out and eat clean, most of the time. Barring chocolate. Chocolate anything is my weakness."

She *wouldn't* be concerned about her physical condition. She was in really good shape—objectively speaking.

"You could use one for good therapy, then. Dogs make great listeners."

He didn't know why he was trying to sell her on the benefits of owning a dog. He wouldn't put one of his dogs in her care in a million years. She had more than enough responsibility with the twins.

She laughed. "I guess wc can all use a little good therapy from time to time, can't we? I imagine a dog is far cheaper than a psychologist."

"And a therapist isn't overjoyed to see you when you walk in the door at night like a dog is."

"Point taken." Miranda helped the twins change their crayons to a different color.

He didn't want to like anything about this woman, but he had to admit she did already appear to have somewhat of a handle on keeping the twins occupied and happy. Much better than he'd thought she would have, in any case.

"So tell me about *your* dogs." She propped her chin on her palms.

He raised a brow. Most people's eyes simply glazed

over when he tried to talk about his life's passion, yet Miranda was urging him to do so.

"My herding dogs are the way I make my main living," he said. "I own a few especially well-bred Australian cattle dogs with excellent working lines, and between all my females, I manage several litters of puppies every year. I train them and sell them to local ranchers in Texas and surrounding states. I've developed enough of a reputation that I've got a waiting list for my puppies. That's my bread and butter."

He didn't know why he was telling her all this. He hated talking about himself and didn't like to brag. But there was something about Miranda's personality that pulled the words right off his tongue.

Harper rolled over and stared up at him with her big brown eyes. He planted a kiss on her chubby cheek, making her smile and pat his whiskered face with her soft palm.

"I have a dog rescue on the side, and that's where my true life's work lies," he continued. "I take dogs from kill shelters and help them find forever families. That's the name of my shelter—Forever Family. But some of the dogs I pick up have health or behavioral issues and can never be rehomed, so they stay with me."

Her eyes widened. She was probably imagining how many dogs he sheltered. She would be surprised when she knew the truth, because she was probably guessing too few.

"I teach all my dogs—cattle dogs and rescues alike— to pass the American Kennel Club Canine Good Citizen program. That certification goes a long way into making the dogs more adoptable."

"How interesting," she said, and sounded like she meant it. "All the shelters I know just keep the dogs in cages and walk them from time to time. It's commendable for you to put in the extra effort to make them ready for their new adoptive families. And I imagine there aren't too many people who would be willing to take on a dog that they knew at the outset they couldn't rehome."

"No, I don't suppose—" Suddenly, he clamped down on his jaw and lowered his brow. Why was he continuing to yammer on about his work? It made him feel vulnerable that he'd shared a part of himself that he rarely revealed to others.

In general, he kept his thoughts to himself, and this—*this* was Miranda Morgan he was opening up to, telling her all about his life.

His guard snapped up. He sure as shootin' hadn't come to visit her on a social call, much less to put himself in the hot seat—or underneath a makeshift tent with crayons in his hand.

This was ludicrous. How was he going to turn the conversation around to the real reason he was here?

"No, no, Hudson," Miranda said when the boy started gnawing on the end of his crayon. "That's not your snack." She reached into a plastic bag she'd stored beside her and withdrew a hard cracker, replacing the crayon with the finger food.

Simon didn't want to be, but he couldn't help but be impressed.

Again.

The woman had actually considered that Hudson and Harper might want snacks before she'd arranged the twins—and herself—in the tent.

Miranda had been a single socialite and suddenly she was a mother. She couldn't possibly have adapted to her new role as much as it appeared she had. He must be seeing something out of the ordinary, catching her in an especially good moment.

But he had to admit she seemed to have thought of everything. He knew he wouldn't have fared so well, despite having known and interacted with Hudson and Harper since their births. He would have gone in with nothing and would have had to crawl in and out of the tent every time the twins needed something else.

He wouldn't have even thought of the *tent*.

He hated to consider the possibility, but apparently, despite that she'd just arrived in town and had only been the twins' official guardian for a few days, there was something Miranda could teach him about caring for babies.

Who knew?

Miranda handed Simon a cracker and gestured for him to give it to Harper, who'd pulled herself to a sitting position and was manipulating a toy cell phone, pushing buttons that made beeping sounds.

So Miranda had thought of toys, as well.

Simon tried to give Harper the cracker, but unlike her twin brother, she completely ignored his offering.

"What am I doing wrong?" Simon asked, his cheeks burning. He was glad his jaw was covered with a few days' growth of whiskers to hide the fact that he was flustered by his inability to get Harper's attention.

Miranda chuckled. "That's okay. Don't sweat it. You aren't doing anything wrong. Hudson will eat Harper's cracker if she doesn't want it. He'll graze all day if I let him. Snack after snack between meals. I think he's on a growth spurt."

"My godson's getting to be a big, strong boy," Simon said proudly.

"Typical guy, right?" she teased. "Eating everything put in front of him and then some. But don't worry. Harper can hold her own with Hudson," Miranda assured him. "When she wants to."

Typical woman, Simon thought, but did not say aloud.

"In general, Harper's more easily distracted by books and toys than food. It's one of the main differences I've noticed between the two of them. That and the way Harper babbles so much more than Hudson. She likes to look you right in the face and *talk*."

Also typical woman.

Simon filed that information away in the back of his mind. He welcomed anything that would help him get to know the twins better.

"How about you? Would you like a snack, *Uncle Simon*? Since we're camping out, we don't have as much variety as we would if we were hanging out in the kitchen, but I can offer you a cheese stick and a box of juice."

He grinned and shook his head, thinking she was teasing him.

"Your loss." She shrugged and handed Hudson and Harper sippy cups, then pushed a tiny straw into a box of juice and peeled a cheese stick for herself.

He thought she must feel silly chowing down on a toddler snack, but she didn't even appear to notice how incongruent she looked, gnawing on a cheese stick underneath a tent that was too small for her and then taking a long, noisy slurp out of a boxed juice.

"The first day here, I bought the juice boxes for the twins. Turns out they weren't quite ready, so this is my new go-to drink." She saluted him with the juice box.

It was as if she embraced her inner child or some nonsense like that. And yet there was something about her innocent actions that warmed Simon's heart—and then sent it scrambling backward in retreat.

Oddly, she made him feel like an old codger with his shirt buttoned all the way up to the neck, stiff and set in his ways.

He yanked on his collar, even though in reality he wore his chambray with the two top snaps open.

Her smile widened, as if she'd read his mind. "Sometimes I feel more like a kid than an adult."

She appeared to realize how that sounded the moment the words left her mouth. Her expression immediately turned apprehensive and she dropped her eyes so her gaze no longer met his.

"Um—that probably wasn't the best thing to admit, was it? Sometimes my mouth runs faster than my head."

He rolled to his side and couched his head in his hand.

"Probably not," he agreed as he schooled his thoughts to take advantage of this perfect opening. "We need to talk about that, actually."

Her gaze widened. "W-what?" she stammered, clearly taken aback, either by the sudden change in his mood or the way he'd narrowed his eyes on her.

"I'd prefer not to speak to you in front of the children," he said.

The twins might not understand the words, but they would probably pick up on the tension, because he already knew he was going to get flustered and he doubted his ideas would go down well with Miranda.

Her gaze widened. "Oh. I…see."

Clearly, she didn't. But she'd picked up on his change of attitude and her shoulders had tensed.

"It's about time for me to put the babies down for their naps, anyway."

She switched her attention to the twins and her expression lightened.

Harper snatched at the cracker Hudson was busy gnawing on, taking it away from him. Hudson howled in frustration. Miranda laughed and handed him another cracker.

Harper let out an ear-piercing screech, as if someone had pinched her. The guilty party, cracker crumbs on his chubby cheeks, darted forward, right out of the tent. The kid army crawled faster than any soldier Simon had ever seen.

Without thinking, Simon shoved his knees under him and went up on all fours, smacking the back of his head on the card table and sending it keening to the side.

Stretching to his full length, he grasped Hudson by the waist and scooped him into his arms on a roll, landing on his back with Hudson flapping on his stomach.

"Where do you think you're going, little buddy?" he asked, planting an affectionate kiss on the baby's forehead. "Did you pinch your sister? Gentlemen don't pick on ladies, even when they deserve it."

"Simon?" called Miranda, her voice sounding oddly muffled from behind him. "Harper. Ow!"

When he glanced back, it was to find the card table tipped completely on its side. Harper was sitting by Miranda, laughing and batting her arms as she pulled her fingers through Miranda's long chestnut curls.

Miranda couldn't stop the baby from yanking and tugging, even though it had to hurt, because somehow, she'd managed to get completely rolled up, cocoon-style, in a couple of the white sheets that had only moments before served as a tent.

"A little help here?" she pleaded around the cloth. She wriggled but only managed to wrap herself tighter and tighter.

"Ironic, isn't it?" he asked mildly as he placed Hudson next to Harper and started tugging at the sheets tangled around Miranda.

With effort, he gently unwrapped her.

"What?" Her brow narrowed in confusion when she noticed him staring at her.

He paused significantly.

"You're a *mummy*."

So not funny.

At least, coming from Simon West it wasn't. He'd been a callous teenager, and it didn't look like he was much better now. His mood had gone as dark as a thunderstorm.

After putting the twins down in their cribs for a nap, Miranda dragged her feet as long as possible before returning to the kitchen, where she was oddly certain a confrontation was going to take place. About what, she had no idea.

She'd never been the confrontational type. She preferred to keep the peace.

Simon had been nice enough for a while, but his surprise visit, especially the whole *we need to talk* thing, definitely had the edge of tension around it.

She serenaded the twins with an extra lullaby and lingered by their bedsides until they dropped into a tranquil slumber. She loved the sound of their deep breathing and cute little snores.

Here in the quiet of the nursery it was nice and calm, and Miranda's heart teemed over with serene warmth and love, the polar opposite of the crazy, uneven pulse-pounding her heart had taken with her surprising and unexpected encounter with Simon West.

Simon, the boy Miranda had crushed on for every angst-ridden day of her teen years, was now a man whose once soft adolescent face had been hardened by life but was no less handsome for whatever trials the years had given him.

Along with her brother Mason, Simon had picked on her incessantly when she was a soft-hearted, impressionable teenager, but that hadn't kept her from crushing on him. There was one prank in particular that had stayed with her that had, in a way, informed the woman she'd become when she'd left Wildhorn to pursue a career in photography in Los Angeles.

He probably didn't even remember the hurtful incident that had so mortified her, and if he did, it was probably only as a humorous blip on his radar.

She scoffed softly and shook her head. She'd just been a silly lovesick teenager. It had been a long time since high school, and she'd tucked her memories of

Simon, both the nice and the not-so-nice, deep into her heart and locked them away for good.

Or so she'd thought.

Naturally, she'd known when she'd moved back to Wildhorn that Simon would eventually cross her path. He and Mason were still best friends.

But she wasn't in any particular hurry to see him again, and she definitely hadn't expected the explosion of emotion she'd felt when he'd walked in the door of her cabin and she'd first met his sea-blue-eyed gaze. It was as if a boxful of fireworks had suddenly gone off in her chest.

Oh, she remembered Simon, all right. So much more than she wanted to admit. She still recalled every detail of her high school years, every single time she'd lingered by his locker in hopes of seeing him, or stared up at the ceiling in her bedroom, listening to sad songs and pining for the boy in the next room playing video games with her brother.

As an adult, she'd had her heart thoroughly broken by a man using her to further his career. She'd learned from that, and her trust didn't come easily anymore. She'd sealed up her heart and intended to keep it that way.

Which was all the more reason for this first encounter with Simon not to be an emotional explosion.

She'd been so *certain* she'd prepared her heart for the eventuality of seeing him again, now that she was home. That any silly teenage emotions she'd felt for him were far behind her.

Clearly not so much.

And anyway—why *had* he mysteriously shown up at her cabin, insisting that he wanted to talk to her?

She blew out a breath and straightened her shoulders. It wasn't doing her any good to hide in the nursery speculating over what he might be doing here. The only way she would find out what Simon wanted was to talk to him.

With a sigh, she gave the twins one last loving glance and quietly closed the door to the nursery behind her.

The first thing she did when she entered the kitchen was grab the baby monitor and place it on the table between them like a shield as she slid into a chair across from Simon. She'd brewed coffee earlier in the day, and he'd taken the initiative to pour them each a cup and warm the brew in the microwave.

"Cream or sugar?" Miranda asked, taking a fortifying sip of the hot liquid.

He shook his head. "Dark."

Kind of like the look he was giving her right now.

"I'm going to come right to the point," he said, moving straight past polite niceties and digging right in. "I have some concerns about Mary naming you the twins' guardian when Mason and Charlotte clearly would have been the better choice."

She choked on her coffee.

Of all the rude and unconscionable declarations he could have made…

His words were so blunt they hit her like a sledgehammer. She scrunched her brow and bit the inside of her lip in a desperate attempt to keep him from seeing how much his statement had hurt her.

"And this is your business how?"

He lifted his chin and narrowed his now ice-blue eyes. "I have a vested interest in them and have every intention of protecting them. I expect to have the opportunity to spend time with them and really get to know them. I'm their godfather, which you would have known if you had bothered to attend Harper and Hudson's christening."

"Wow. Judgmental much?"

"Just telling it like it is."

Miranda's first impulse was to argue with him, except for one tiny detail—

He was right.

She *had* missed the twins' christening, something that she now deeply regretted. If she could dial time back…but she couldn't. All she could do at this point was own up to her past mistakes and move forward from here.

"You're right," she admitted softly.

Simon looked as if he was about to speak, but then he cut himself short and stared at her openmouthed.

"I'm sorry. Did you just say I was *right*?"

Clearly that wasn't the response he'd expected. For a man who didn't know her, he certainly had his opinions about her firmly in place.

She couldn't help but be a little resentful, but she pressed back the prickly feelings in her chest and continued.

"I wasn't at the babies' christening, and I should have been. With John's schedule as a surgeon, Mary and John were only in Wildhorn for that one weekend. They couldn't change their schedule, so I should have. No matter what my reasons, I let my career take precedence over my family, and there's no excuse for that, so I'm not offering any."

Once again, he hesitated before speaking.

"Special client?" he guessed, curling his hands around the mug of coffee.

"A-list actors in a private ceremony." She sighed. "It wasn't about money or prestige. Both actors were and are close personal friends of mine. The wedding had been planned for a year in advance and I had committed to shooting it well before the twins were even conceived, never mind born. In any other circumstances, I would have excused myself from the shoot and found another photographer to take my place for them."

"That probably wouldn't have been a good move for your career, though, right? You wouldn't want to be seen to be reneging on your obligations," he said drily.

She couldn't tell whether he was beginning to see her side of the story or whether he was trying to coax her into digging herself deeper into the muck of remorse and shame. Not that it mattered either way.

"Maybe. I had a reputation for being especially trustworthy. But I would have survived, even if my career took a hit. As it is, now that I'm stepping into my new role as Harper and Hudson's mother, my celebrity photography days are history, anyway. So in the long run, it didn't really matter."

She felt slightly nostalgic at the admission, but surprisingly not sad or regretful. She'd left celebrity photography in the past, where she now knew it permanently belonged. How could it be otherwise?

It didn't matter if she'd made the decision to forage into the realm of motherhood unaided by circumstance, or whether she'd been thrust into the role by a tragedy. She had done everything she'd desired to do in her career, and it was time to come home. Hudson and Harper's guardianship had simply given her a push in the right direction.

Home.

"This must be a jarring change for you, going from the lifestyle you've been leading to living in a guest cabin on your brother's ranch."

Again, she felt as if he was probing for answers beneath the surface and possibly trying to trip her up.

She shook her head. "Don't forget I grew up here. It's not that much of a culture shock for me to return to my roots."

And if it was, she most certainly wasn't going to admit that to Simon. She still had the feeling he was pushing her to justify the decisions she'd now made, just as she had put it all out there about her past and admitted her mistakes.

Well, her decisions were her own, and none of his business.

"You said you want to be a special part of the twins' lives. What, exactly, does that look like?"

She tensed for the answer. She didn't trust him as far as she could throw him, which wouldn't be far, big lug that he was. And she suspected he didn't trust her, either.

"Exactly?" he echoed. "I don't know. You let me in to your life. I let you in to mine. Maybe we can do things once in a while. With the twins, I mean."

He cringed. He literally, actually *cringed*, enough that Miranda could see it in his expression. Was he looking for reassurance that the twins were safe and loved with her? And was it really that distasteful for him to consider spending time with her?

He was certainly no picnic, either.

She narrowed her gaze on him.

"Like what?" she asked warily.

"Take them to the playground. Attend community events together. Maybe have them come meet my puppies. Simple country living."

If that was all it was—and if Simon was really serious about this…

The twins could use another good male role model in their lives. Emphasis on *good*.

If Simon started acting like a jerk, this arrangement stopped.

"I accept."

"Simple country living," he repeated, appearing surprised that she'd relented so easily.

"Yeah. I got that," she said sardonically.

"You won't miss your old life? The parties? The society? The dazzle?"

The truth was, she was tired of the limelight. Even being the one behind the camera, every aspect of her life was exposed to the public eye. A nice, quiet cabin on a remote Texas ranch didn't sound so bad.

Okay, so maybe not *quiet*, what with two babies who made their needs known loud and clear at all hours of the day and night. But private, in any case.

She stared at him for a moment, trying to read his expression, but he did a good job concealing his thoughts.

"I suppose I won't have many opportunities to wear any of the glitzy cocktail dresses I've accumulated, but I can still tote around my designer purses. I'll have the best-dressed diaper bag in town," she joked.

He didn't laugh. He didn't even crack a smile.

He didn't think she was good enough to be Harper and Hudson's guardian.

Well, join the club, buster.

He was going to have to stand in line to claim that particular conclusion, because she'd already tried that one on for size, and unfortunately, it fit.

She sighed wearily. "Look. I get why you're concerned. I don't know why Mary chose me to be the twins' guardian. I only know she did, and I'm going to do the very best I can with what I've been given."

His lips were pressed into a straight line and his expression didn't give anything away. She half expected him to tell her to give up now. That was what he was here for, wasn't it? To bully her?

She might not have as much confidence in her maternal abilities as she would like, but if he was going to press her, she would push right back. She wasn't a vulnerable teenager anymore.

She wouldn't let herself be trod upon by Simon, or by any other man. It had happened once, in Los Angeles. It would never happen again.

Her words were brave, but in the deepest recesses of her heart, the question continued to nag at her.

Could a woman like her really *learn* to be a mother?

Chapter Two

Simon waved as Miranda pulled her tulip-yellow convertible up his long driveway and parked next to his beat-up silver dual-cab truck—a considerably more reliable vehicle in a small ranching town. The tiny two-door looked incongruous next to his old truck and the red barn, which desperately needed a new coat of paint.

It had been a full week since they'd had their confrontation, such as it was. He was still reeling from that one. It hadn't gone anything like he'd imagined it would.

He hadn't expected Miranda to own up to her mistakes, or even to feel any remorse about missing the twins' christening.

But she'd not only felt remorse, she'd shown it, too, throwing Simon off his game. It took a strong soul to do that. At this point he didn't know what to think of her.

The jury was still very much out on Miranda Morgan.

But no matter how he felt about her, now that the twins were living in Wildhorn, he'd have the opportunity to get to know his godchildren better, and he wasn't going to pass up on *that* blessing, no matter what form it had shown up in.

He chuckled as Miranda maneuvered halfway into the backseat in order to release the children from their car seats and pass them out to him. He would never understand why rich folks always bought minuscule sports cars to show off their wealth. No normal-size person could fit comfortably behind the wheel, and Miranda was tall for a woman—and many men.

In all, it took her about five minutes of squirming and stretching to get the deed done. Eventually, Miranda had managed to unfold herself from the backseat and take Harper into her arms.

"I know, I know," she said before Simon could say a word.

He cocked an eyebrow.

"This car is completely inappropriate for the country," Miranda spouted, rolling her eyes. He didn't sense a hint of the annoyance he'd been expecting from her, given that the last time they'd seen each other he'd come at her with a baker's dozen of accusations. "Thank you so much for inviting us to your ranch today to see the puppies being born."

He'd been less than tactful that day at the cabin. He thought she might—or rather, ought to be—upset by their altercation, and his, let's face it, blatant rudeness at times, even if at the end of their conversation they'd come to an uneasy truce. But if anything, Miranda's voice was laced with pure excitement, the same kind of childlike attitude she'd displayed while stretched out underneath her make-believe sheet tent, reading fairy tales with the twins.

"Of course, I grew up on a ranch, so I've seen baby animals born before," Miranda said in the same animated tone. "But never puppies. Birth is such a beautiful thing. The twins will be so excited."

He didn't know about the twins. He suspected they were too young to appreciate the event, although they'd probably enjoy the new puppies.

But Miranda?

Her hazel eyes were sparkling with delight.

He was proud to be able to show off such a vital part of his work, and one of his most satisfying.

He didn't trust Miranda, but he wanted to make sure she trusted him, to see that he worked hard and was successful with his endeavors, that he was stable and dependable, so she would have no questions about him being around for the twins, about him being a good role model for them.

He wanted to *be* dependable and stable for the twins. Be their rock when the world floundered around them. Be the man he'd never had in his life when he was a child.

Of course, by nature his business was anything but stable, but she didn't have to know that.

"I own six female Australian cattle dogs," he explained as he led the happy group into the barn, Hudson in his arms. "All from top working lines. I think I've mentioned a little bit about how this works. I selectively breed them and then train the pups to work cattle using their natural herding instincts."

"I'm impressed." There was an awkward pause, then she smiled.

Her words inflated his ego and he couldn't help but grin back at her. That was exactly what he wanted to hear.

"I get by," he said modestly.

Barely.

Yes, he made a decent profit on the pups, but a lot of work went into preparing them for ranch work, not to mention the vet and feed bills. And it was a feast or famine kind of lifestyle. Funds came in when he sold a litter of puppies, and then he had to make that stretch until the next litter was trained and ready to go to their new owners. So it wasn't exactly like he was swimming in money.

Not like *she* must be. Famous photographer to the stars. Traveling all over the world. Living a lifestyle of glitz and glamour that no doubt made her feel a step above the rest of the world. She probably made more in one day than he made in a good year. There was no way he, a humble cowboy, could even begin to compare to her—not that he wanted to.

"That's Shadow." He introduced the blue heeler to Miranda as she knelt before the cattle dog about to give birth.

"Is it okay if I pet her?" she asked, shifting a now-sleeping Harper onto one shoulder. "I don't want to do the wrong thing."

He studied Shadow for a moment and then nodded.

"Sure. I don't think petting her will be a problem. You'll reassure her that she's got this. I generally tend to stay out of the way when the puppies come and let nature take its course, but I'm always nearby in case she needs help with her delivery."

"She's such a pretty color." Miranda softly stroked between Shadow's ears and murmured gentle, indistinguishable words.

"She's called a blue heeler. I've also got red. I breed for color, working lines, temperament and health."

Shadow stood up, turned around in her whelping box a couple of times, and then lay down and panted heavily.

"It looks like she's close." Simon crouched down next to the box.

Miranda reached out the arm that wasn't holding Harper. "Here, let me take Hudson so you have your hands free to help Shadow."

Simon didn't immediately hand him over. Unlike the peacefully sleeping Harper, wiggly Hudson was wide-awake and squirming to get down, his thick chestnut-brown hair tufting in every direction, reminding Simon of a rooster. Simon didn't want to set the active baby on the dirty barn floor, even if he'd recently covered the area with a fresh layer of hay.

But holding a sleeping infant and a squirrelly one at the same time would be quite the challenge for Miranda. Hudson was sure to wake Harper up, and she might not be happy about that. Then Miranda would have a vigorous baby and a fussy one.

What did Miranda do during all the times when it was just her and the twins? How on earth did she manage without going stir-crazy?

She hadn't said a word of complaint, at least to him, but she must be exhausted beyond belief. He was only now starting to appreciate her new set of challenges. Even if she was an expert and, as she'd framed it, a natural nurturer, raising twins on her own would be difficult. It was more than he could have handled, were he the one in that position.

He loved the twins, but he didn't envy Miranda. He

had to remind himself that she might be putting on a show for him. For all he knew, she was only displaying her good side when the truth was far from what he saw now.

"Hold on a second," he said, keeping Hudson in his arms. "Let me run up to the house and grab a quilt. Then we can put both twins down while we watch Shadow giving birth."

"Good idea," she replied with a grateful smile.

As he jogged up the hill to the ranch house, it occurred to him that maybe he could find some graham crackers or a banana to keep the ever-hungry Hudson occupied. Although a banana might get messy. He'd go with the graham crackers.

Simon found himself grinning and whistling a tune under his breath as he returned to the barn with Hudson in one arm, already munching on a graham cracker, and the rest of the box to share with Harper if she woke, but his joy was short-lived.

As soon as he entered the barn he knew something had changed. Miranda was standing, Harper was crying, and—

His new next-door neighbor, arms akimbo, was hovering over Shadow's whelping box, her expression dire.

This old biddy had caused him nothing but trouble since the moment she'd moved into the active-senior housing development that bordered the land across the south end of his small acreage.

She'd already complained to him about the noise when he'd let the dogs out for a run, both his cattle dogs and his rescues. Cattle dogs needed tons of exercise and the rescues needed fresh air and the chance to stretch their legs.

He usually rode his horse along with the dogs, covering the whole distance of his land, but after Blanche Stanton had lodged her first complaint with him, he'd made a point to drive the dogs in the opposite direction from the housing community.

He couldn't imagine what the old woman was doing here now. She was blatantly trespassing, for one thing. He hadn't invited her to visit his property. What did she think? That she could just nose around in his barn whenever she liked?

Simon's muscles tightened and Hudson made a squeal of protest.

"Sorry, buddy," he murmured before handing the boy off to Miranda and spreading the quilt across the soft bed of hay for the twins, giving him a moment to decide how to approach the unwanted trespasser as he and Miranda situated the babies on the blanket.

"Blanche Stanton," he said drily. "To what do I owe the pleasure of this visit?"

Miranda caught his gaze and her eyes widened. She hadn't missed the dripping sarcasm oozing from his voice.

Blanche obviously wasn't aware that waltzing onto someone else's property was considered trespassing. Or maybe she just didn't care. The hunchbacked, gray-haired old lady turned on him, brandishing her cane like a weapon. It was all he could do not to step back, but he straightened his shoulders and held his ground.

"*More* puppies?" she barked—her voice really did sound like a bark, all dry and coarse. Simon bit back a smile, recognizing that Blanche would be furious if she knew what he was thinking. "You justify bringing more dogs into this world when you already have too many running around this place as it is? This is outrageous. I've a good mind to call the animal control police and report you."

Miranda's brow scrunched over her nose. He could see the wheels of her mind turning as she tried to comprehend the incomprehensible.

"This is what Simon does for a living. He breeds herding dogs."

Miranda sounded genuinely confused, as well she might. In Simon's brief encounters with the old woman, she rarely made a lick of sense.

"What?" Blanche demanded, turning her attention to Miranda. "Who are you?"

"Miranda Morgan. And not that it's any of your business, but Simon raises and trains Australian cattle dogs especially bred for herding," she said, louder and slower, overenunciating each syllable as if somehow that would help Blanche understand what she was saying. "His dogs are supposed to have puppies."

Wow.

Miranda had really been paying attention to what he'd been telling her. His appreciation for her bumped up a notch.

Blanche cackled, but not in amusement.

"Obviously, you don't have the full story, my dear."

Miranda stiffened at the artificial endearment, but her voice was steady when she answered. "Simon has been completely up front with me."

She had no way of knowing that, nor did she have reason to trust him, and yet she was, thankfully, in his corner.

"Ask him what he does with the rest of his time here on the ranch."

"If you mean about his rescue endeavors, he's already told me," Miranda said calmly, tipping up her chin in a silent show of defiance.

Simon was grateful that Miranda was fielding all the questions because he was about to implode, holding back his fury and frustration.

Hudson rolled to the edge of the quilt, gurgling happily and reaching out his chunky arm to grab a handful of hay.

Simon and Miranda reacted at the exact same moment, diving down to rid him of the straw in his little fist before it made it to his mouth. Miranda grabbed the baby and Simon shook Hudson's fist until it was hay-free.

Miranda folded her legs on the quilt and pulled Hudson and Harper into her lap. That was probably a wise move, since Blanche would stand as judge and jury on everything she witnessed.

Simon stretched back to his full height to face his irate neighbor.

"This," Blanche said, her wave encompassing both the dogs and the twins, "is totally unacceptable. It's irresponsible for you to bring babies into this environment."

Simon had to bite his tongue not to snap back at her that this was the country, and that nearly every baby in Wildhorn was growing up on a ranch, many of which had far more animals than Simon, and more variety, at that.

"That's it." Blanche pounded her cane against the ground, but because it was dirt covered with a bed of hay, the tip of the cane didn't make a sound. It was probably not the dramatic impact Blanche had been going for. Simon's eyes met Miranda's and her lips quirked in amusement—at least until Blanche's next words.

"I've made up my mind. I'm calling animal control."

"You do that," Simon said, his voice an octave lower than usual.

He had had about enough of Blanche Stanton. His nerves snapped along his skin and a fire raged in his chest, but the only outward indication of his annoyance was the way his fingers kept twitching into a fist. He couldn't speak to his expression. He forced himself to relax his muscles and shoved his hands into the front pockets of his blue jeans, rocking back on the heels of his boots as if to put more distance between them.

"Now, if there's nothing else," he said through gritted teeth, "you know your way out. And I suggest you take it."

Blanche shook a finger under his nose. It took every ounce of his self-control not to brush her hand away. He stood stock-still, not even allowing air to enter his lungs. He'd probably breathe fire out of his mouth like a dragon if he so much as exhaled.

"This isn't over," she warned.

"I didn't think it was," he snapped back.

He knew as soon as he spoke that he shouldn't have taken the bait. A brief glance at Miranda's wide eyes confirmed that, even if he hadn't created the scene, he was at least an unwilling participant. All he was doing was playing right into the old woman's hands. He knew better than that.

Do not engage.

And yet he had.

It was hard to consider any other way than the way he knew, the defense mechanisms that sometimes rose before he could stop them.

Should he be turning the other cheek here, or was it okay for him to defend his home and his dogs?

Unfortunately, Simon knew all too well that this was only the beginning of his problems with his new neighbor. That Miranda had been there to witness the whole sorry scene only made him feel worse.

How humiliating.

Blanche turned away and stomped a couple of feet toward the door—or at least as much of a stomp as she could make with a limp and a cane—and then slowly turned back to address Miranda, rudely pointing her finger directly at her.

"You'd do well to avoid this one," Blanche warned, nodding her head toward Simon and sniffing loudly.

He stiffened. The nerve of the woman. Not that he and Miranda had a personal connection, but it wasn't any of Blanche's business if they did. No one had called her in to be judge and jury of his character, especially because she continued to malign him for no good reason.

What if Blanche put doubt in Miranda's mind? Enough to make her reconsider about him spending time with the twins?

He swallowed the gall that rose to his throat at the thought.

Miranda merely lifted an eyebrow. "I'll keep that in mind."

Simon couldn't tell, either by her expression or the

inflection in the tone of her voice, whether Miranda was agreeing with Blanche or merely humoring the old woman, but Blanche seemed content with the answer and made her exit.

"Okay, then," Miranda said as soon as Blanche was gone. "Do you want to tell me what that was all about?"

Miranda's naturally empathetic nature—even to a man who tended to be a bully and had issues trusting her—kicked in despite her best efforts to the contrary.

Poor Simon's face had turned a distressing shade of red, followed by an unhealthy yellowish-green color, as if he was about to be sick.

She could see no reason why the strange old woman had gone off on Simon the way she had.

Over a litter of puppies? What was with that?

Practically all of Wildhorn was working ranch land. Horses. Cows. Pigs. Chickens. Llamas.

Simon's endeavors might veer slightly away from the typical cattle ranch, but he was offering a much-needed product—if you could call a well-bred and well-trained cattle dog a product, or maybe a service—to grateful ranchers in Wildhorn and beyond.

Now that the elderly busybody was gone, Miranda stood and plunked the wriggling twins back onto the quilt in a demonstrative display of rebellion.

Take that, Blanche Stanton.

How *dare* the woman render judgment on her choices where the twins were concerned? The old lady didn't even know the first thing about her. And anyway, it wasn't any of her business if the kids were lying on a quilt in a barn.

Then again, Blanche might be right.

Simon might be right.

Maybe she *wasn't* good mother material. But she was bound and determined to do her very best.

Simon sighed in frustration and picked off his hat, scrubbing his fingers through his thick blond curls.

"Yeah. I'm sorry you had to witness that."

"Who is she?"

"My next-door neighbor. Or one of them, anyway. There's a small housing development and retirement community along the south border of my land. That woman, Blanche Stanton, moved in a couple of months ago, and she's causing me all sorts of trouble—as you witnessed today."

"Yeah. What is with that?"

"Evidently, she really, *really* doesn't like dogs."

"What kind of person doesn't like dogs?" Miranda asked, realizing even as she spoke the words that, although she didn't exactly *dislike* dogs, it would never have occurred to her to keep one of her own.

"Cat people," Simon joked drily, one side of his mouth kicking up.

"She's probably one of those old ladies who has a hundred cats living in her house. That's why the idea of a dog upsets her so much."

He chuckled. "Maybe."

"I still don't see how it's any business of hers what happens on your property, as long as it doesn't directly affect her. I can't imagine that you allow your dogs to run wild. Or do you secretly let them out on her lawn?"

Simon snorted. "Now there's a thought. But truthfully, I don't give her any reason to complain about me or my dogs. My property is well fenced, and I almost always ride along to supervise when the dogs go out for their runs."

Simon crouched before Shadow's whelping box and checked her out, then stood and scooped Harper into his arms. It was oddly comforting, watching the big man holding the infant against his broad chest.

"Come on. I want to show you something." He started toward the barn door and then looked back to see if she was following.

She quickly bundled Hudson into her arms. "Should I leave the quilt?"

He glanced at Shadow and nodded. "Yes. We'll be back shortly to attend to the puppies. But there's something I'd like you to see back at my house."

Curiosity swelled within her as she caught up with Simon and walked side by side with him up a small incline to where his ranch house stood. They passed by several dog kennels built underneath a lean-to, but all of them were empty.

When he reached the door, he slid her another glance. "This is, I believe, the real reason Blanche is kicking up such a fuss."

She could already hear what sounded like a dozen barking dogs, everything from a low *woof-woof* to the high-pitched yapping of the smaller dogs.

He opened the door with a flourish. Even though Miranda had some idea what was coming next, she couldn't have guessed at the enthusiasm with which the dogs—more than two dozen in various breeds and sizes—greeted Simon.

He laughed—really *laughed*—as the dogs ran around

his feet and nuzzled his hands with their wet noses, begging to be petted.

"These are my rescue dogs." He crouched briefly to accept doggie kisses as he scratched ears and wriggling tail ends.

Was this the same man who, in the past, had such a chip on his shoulder?

The twins gurgled in delight and flapped their arms so hard Miranda could barely keep control of Hudson. Simon tossed Harper into the air amidst much giggling.

Miranda had as many questions as Simon had dogs, but she started with the most obvious one.

"Where is Christmas?"

"I'm sorry?" His eyes widened.

"Thanksgiving was last week and you don't have a single decoration up yet. And no tree!"

"You almost make it sound illegal."

"It should be. Where's your holiday spirit?"

He laughed. "You make up for it at your house."

"That's truly sad," she said, her frown halfway between real and mocking.

He scoffed it off.

"I brought you here to meet my dogs, not critique my lack of Christmas decorations," he chided.

She gave in reluctantly. "You keep all of these guys in your house? I noticed you have some kennels out there, but they're all empty."

Evidently relieved that he didn't have to talk about Christmas any longer, he grinned and bounced up and down to keep a fussy Harper, who wanted to be thrown in the air again, happy.

"Mostly they live with me. They are all crate-trained

and I use the kennels we passed by when necessary, but for the rescues that I plan to rehome, living in the house with me helps them prepare for life with their forever families. And the ones who will never be adopted out for whatever reason, well, they *are* in their forever home."

A medium-size, wire-haired dog limped up and bumped Miranda's leg with his snout, and then sat prettily, waiting for her attention. It was only when she reached down to scratch his head that she noticed he was missing one of his front legs.

Miranda felt awkward, not only because she was seldom around dogs, but because this one looked as if it had suffered a major injury at some point. Still, she continued to tentatively scratch the dog's ears and pat his back.

"That's Cumberland," Simon said by way of introduction. "But I just call him Chummy. He was run over by a car on the highway and left to die. But he's a fighter. As you can see, he doesn't let a little thing like missing one leg get him down."

"So you think you will be able to rehome him, then?"

Simon shook his head. "Unfortunately, Chummy has other health issues besides his leg. He'll stay with me for as long as he lives. But to be honest, I've fallen completely in love with Chummy. I wouldn't adopt him out even if I could. He's *my* dog. I have a blind husky named Loki, too."

He whistled and a beautiful husky with gray and white fur trotted directly and obediently to Simon's side. Miranda could hardly tell the dog was blind until she looked into the husky's eyes, which were white and hazy.

"Extraordinary," Miranda murmured, then caught Simon's gaze and held it. "You're not a typical dog rescuer, are you?"

He ran a hand down his face as if he was embarrassed to admit the truth, although Miranda was impressed by the size of his heart. "No. Not really. I don't keep the dogs in kennels until they are hopefully adopted out to new families. I rarely have folks visiting the ranch. Instead, I train them to be AKC Canine Good Citizens and then hold adoption events at Maggie's Pet Store. I've found that trained dogs are easier to rehome, and they make better family members once they're adopted. As for Chummy and Loki—I suppose I just can't say no to an animal in need."

He swallowed hard. "When I first saw Chummy, he was all mangled, and yet his eyes were so hopeful. Even with as much pain as he was in, he let me approach him and take him to the vet. Most people would have put him down, I guess, thinking that was the most humane thing to do. But in my heart I knew Chummy wanted to live. Seeing him all bandaged up with an IV sticking out of him—I almost couldn't stand it. But Chummy recognized me and wagged his tail. He has more courage than I'll ever have."

Miranda's heart warmed. She highly doubted that. In her mind, Simon showed an exemplary amount of courage. She could see how devoted he was to his cause. He was as passionate about his rescue endeavors as she was to her photography, only the work he did helped God's creatures, ministered to those who couldn't help themselves, while hers...had been completely for her own benefit. Publicizing famous people who didn't need any more boost to their egos. The closest thing she got to true charity was photographing high-profile, black-tie charitable events, and even those had mostly been a joke, a way for rich people to feel good about themselves.

"Come sit down for a minute," Simon invited, settling himself on the sofa with Harper on his lap and patting the seat next to him.

Miranda tentatively made her way to the couch, careful to step around the dogs and not on them. She admittedly wasn't the most coordinated woman on the planet at the best of times, and the moving sea of fur made her feel like she was walking on a field of land mines with a baby in her arms.

She breathed a sigh of relief when she finally parked herself safely onto the couch and cuddled Hudson close to her.

"I brought you up here, not only to meet Chummy, but because I have a couple of dogs I'd especially like to introduce to Harper and Hudson," he said.

She flashed him a surprised look. He couldn't possibly think that with all she had going on, she'd want to adopt a *couple* of dogs, or even one.

"I appreciate what you do here," she said, trying to buffer her next words. "But I want to make it clear up front that I have no intention of adopting a dog. They're cute and all, but I've already got my hands full with the twins as it is."

Which was true, but it was more than just a matter of having time to take care of a pet. After seeing the way Simon interacted with his rescues and how excitedly they responded to him, she felt fairly certain she wasn't a dog person.

Other than Chummy, the dogs had mostly ignored her.

"Oh, no," Simon said, raising his free hand palm out. "You misunderstand me. I'm not pulling some sneaky stunt on you to try to get you to adopt a dog. It's just that—well, maybe it would be easier to show you than to try to explain."

"Zig! Zag! Come here, boys."

Immediately after Simon called, two identical small white dogs dashed to Simon's side, their full attention on him.

"Down," Simon said, and both of the dogs instantly obeyed.

Miranda looked from one dog to the other and a lightbulb went off in her head. She understood exactly what Simon was getting at, why she wanted Harper and Hudson to see these particular dogs.

"Twins!" she exclaimed.

Simon laughed.

"Not exactly. They're littermates. Someone dumped them off at the side of the highway, tied in a bag. A Good Samaritan happened to see the bag moving as she drove by and she turned her car around to investigate. Once she realized the bag contained puppies, she contacted the town vet, Aaron Grimes, and he called me."

He helped an overexcited Harper pet one of the dogs, and taking Simon's lead, Miranda helped Hudson scratch the ears of the other.

"Soft fur, see, Harper?" Simon said in the high-pitched tone of voice men tended to use with babies. "This is a doggie."

"Gentle, gentle," Miranda added when Hudson tried to grab a handful of the white dog's fur.

"Zig and Zag are Westies—West Highland white terriers."

"They're very obedient."

He grinned. "We're working on it. Terriers tend to have a mind of their own, kind of like cats. They are one of the harder breeds to train."

Zig licked Hudson's fist and he giggled. Both dogs seemed to like the babies, and the twins were clearly taken with the dogs.

But she'd meant what she'd said earlier. No matter how cute Zig and Zag were, or how much the kids liked them—no dogs allowed. At the moment, suffering cuteness overload, she even had to give herself a stern mental reminder.

She cast her eyes up to make sure Simon understood her very emphatic message, but he was busy helping Harper interact with Zag.

When he finally looked up, their eyes met and locked. A slow smile spread across his lips and appreciation filled his gaze. For a moment, Miranda experienced something she hadn't felt this strongly since, well, since high school—the reel of her stomach in time with a quickened pulse and a shortness of breath.

Either she was having an asthma attack, or else—

She was absolutely *not* going to go there.

Chapter Three

Back in the barn, the strain that had occurred between Simon and Miranda in the house—because he refused to analyze and recognize it as any more than that—appeared to have dissipated as their thoughts returned to Shadow and her puppies. She was still scratching around in her whelping box and the puppies hadn't arrived yet. The twins, worn out from their excitement with the Westies, were both sound asleep on the quilt.

"I usually exercise the dogs by riding around my acreage with them," Simon explained, gesturing to his sorrel quarter horse gelding Dash, who was set up in a nearby stall.

"Some of my rescues like to run more than others. I've got a few couch potatoes who don't want to leave the house, but they all need fresh air and exercise. There's a small lake on the northwest corner of my property that my Labs can't get enough of. They'd stay in the water forever if I let them, and I could toss tennis balls all day and they wouldn't tire of it. I also keep a few head of cattle for the herding dogs to practice on.

"But ever since my first run-in with Blanche, I've been avoiding the land to the south, for the most part. My dogs generally don't go anywhere near the south fences, although from time to time they slip away from me. But I've been more aware of it. No sense stirring up trouble if I can help it. That's why I was so surprised to see her today."

"You don't think she'll really follow through with her threat to call the cops on you, do you? She sounded pretty serious about it."

He shrugged. "She hasn't yet, and she's been making that same threat since the first time she confronted me about my dogs. But it wouldn't surprise me if she did call this time. She was certainly in a tizzy today."

"Yes, but what does she really have to complain about? Everything you do is on the up-and-up, and in my opinion, is a ministry to the animals. There's nothing for an animal control officer to find."

Simon's gaze widened on her and he suddenly had a hard time swallowing around the emotions that had clogged in his throat.

Miranda thought he was doing something special—something she even qualified as worthy of the Lord to bless.

"I do it for the dogs," he insisted, his voice gravelly. It hadn't occurred to him until this moment to give his work to the Lord to bless.

He crouched in front of the whelping box to see how Shadow was faring.

"Exactly," Miranda agreed pleasantly. "For the dogs. That's what makes what you do so wonderful. Plus, I don't know how Blanche can possibly go to the police about this. The woman was trespassing on your proper—"

She cut off her sentence in the middle of a word.

Simon grinned. She must have seen the roly-poly bundle of fur that had arrived when they were otherwise engaged.

"A puppy is here."

Indeed, there was one tiny, squirming puppy being groomed by its attentive mother.

Simon picked up a warm towel from a stack that he had at the ready, heated by a nearby warming lamp.

Gently, he scooped the puppy into his hands.

"Here," he said, handing the pup to Miranda.

"It's white," she exclaimed. "Is that normal?"

"All Australian cattle dogs are born white, but their true colors come on fairly quickly. Back when the breed was first started, Dalmatians were bred into the stock. Hence the white coat."

He put his hands over hers and showed her what to do. Her skin was soft against the calluses of his, and suddenly it felt as if his fingers had thousands of tiny nerve endings crackling.

"Dry him off a bit. Give him a gentle rubdown to help his circulation and breathing. Then we'll put him back in with mom."

"Is he sick?" she asked in dismay.

"What? No," he answered. "This one is healthy, as far as I can tell. We're just giving him a little extra triage."

"This one?" She smiled as her tiny puppy wriggled in her palm. "Does that mean there are more coming?"

"Four more, if the ultrasound was accurate. You can

put that little guy back in with his mama now, if you want."

Simon watched as Miranda gently returned the puppy to the warmth of the whelping box. For a woman who'd told him flat out that she wasn't a nurturer, she certainly looked that way to him.

Not just with the puppy, but with the twins, as well, if he was being honest. Maybe he didn't have so much to worry about, after all.

He turned his attention to Shadow, who had just delivered puppy number two, a girl.

He waited until Shadow had cleaned the pup off and then scooped her into a towel as he'd done with the first puppy and handed her to Miranda. Puppies three and four soon followed, and they repeated the process.

She was staring at him with an odd expression on her face that made his gut tighten.

"What?"

She shook her head. "I'm not— I didn't expect—"

She shook her head and didn't continue.

"One more to go," he encouraged Shadow, running an affectionate hand down her back. "You're doing great, Mama."

Shadow looked spent, but was it any wonder? Birthing was hard work. She flopped on her side where her puppies could reach her belly and lowered her head to the ground, panting heavily.

Simon waited in anticipation. Nothing happened.

Maybe there were only four puppies after all, but Simon's gut instinct, along with his experience, told him that Shadow wasn't finished, even if she wanted to be.

Frowning, he went from a crouch to his knees, pressing his palms against his thighs as he considered what to do.

"That's not good," he murmured under his breath.

"Is something wrong?" Miranda asked, concern lining her tone. She dropped to her knees beside Simon and placed her puppy back in the box, then laid a comforting hand on Simon's shoulder. "What can I do to help?"

Their gazes met and held, hers serious.

"Tell me what to do. We have to be able to do something for Shadow." His stomach twisted when he realized he'd made a terrible mistake asking Miranda to bring the twins and come out to watch the birth of the puppies. At the time, he'd been thinking about the excitement of new life, and he'd been anxious for the opportunity to show Miranda his ranch and the work he did here. But he could have introduced the twins to Zig and Zag at a more appropriate time.

Now, instead of joy, he was handing Miranda a cup full of sorrow, just after she'd lost her sister.

"I'm sorry," he said through a tight throat. "This may not end well."

"Is there anything we can do?" she asked for the third time, her voice calm and containing an inordinate amount of strength.

Shadow stood and turned around in a tight circle. Simon and Miranda looked on intently.

"Possibly," Simon answered softly. "Look—the fifth pup is coming now."

Simon suspected that, like him, Miranda was holding her breath as Shadow strained and panted.

The puppy was large—bigger than his sister. Usually it was the runt of the litter who ran the risk of not making it through the birth or the first few days, but this puppy was so large Shadow had difficulty bringing him into the world.

Simon didn't wait for Shadow to break the sac and clean up the limp puppy. He had a warm towel at the ready.

"Is he okay?" Miranda's anxious gaze was locked on the puppy.

Simon rubbed the pup's belly, hoping for a welcome wiggle, but the puppy's body sagged.

Lifeless.

Simon kept rubbing, clearing the pup's nose and mouth and attempting to heighten his circulation.

"Come on, boy. You can do it," he murmured.

He cradled the dog's head in his palm and dipped him down and back up again in an attempt to get him to breathe.

Still nothing.

"What can I do?" Miranda asked, her voice surprisingly calm and steady, despite the tears in her eyes. She so desperately wanted to help, and Simon wished there was something she *could* do.

Simon shook his head and continued to rub the puppy, tentatively throwing out a silent prayer. He still felt new and clumsy talking to God.

Please don't let this puppy die.

Losing animals was part and parcel of owning a ranch, especially because his ranch was unique. He took in rescues that he knew would never recover, and cared for them with all his might, giving them the best quality of life they could have.

And love. These animals needed so much love—as much as they gave.

Dog breeding and rescue was a series of heartache after heartache sometimes, but despite all the pain, the good outweighed the bad, and he couldn't imagine himself doing anything else with his life. There were four healthy puppies to rejoice over.

But Miranda was still freshly grieving her sister. She didn't need to see the hard side of his business.

Not now.

"Come on, boy," he whispered desperately. "Breathe for me."

He performed the same down and up motion but to no avail.

"Give him to me," Miranda said, still amazingly composed as tears silently streamed down her cheeks.

Simon's gaze widened on her but he did as she asked and handed the lifeless puppy over.

Miranda cupped the puppy in one palm and coaxed his jaw open with the other. Then, without hesitating, she put her mouth over the tiny dog's snout and gently blew a breath into his lungs.

She hesitated a moment, rubbing two fingers firmly over the puppy's chest. She blew a breath into his lungs, waited a moment and then blew again.

Nothing happened.

She looked up and her watery gaze met his.

"I'm not giving up," she said as she performed the same dipping motion she'd seen Simon use.

"Miranda." His voice was as dry and coarse as sandpaper as he laid a gentle hand on her arm. He didn't want to lose the pup, either, but—

"I'm not giving up," she repeated firmly.

He nodded.

She blew another breath into the pup's lungs.

Then another.

Simon wasn't positive, but he thought he saw—

Yes.

There it was again.

The puppy squirmed and made a little mewling noise.

"I think that is the most wonderful sound I've ever heard," Miranda said with a relieved sigh.

"Me, too," he whispered in amazement.

Only now did he see that she was shaking. Adrenaline and shock were probably overtaking her.

He took the puppy from her tender grasp and put him in the whelping box for his mother's ministrations, and then turned back to Miranda and took her elbow.

"Sit down before you fall down," he said gently.

She sank gratefully onto the quilt between the twins, both of whom were now awake and wide-eyed.

"Oh," she exclaimed, pulling both children into her lap for an enthusiastic hug, as if reassuring herself that the twins were alive and all right.

"I love you," she said, kissing Hudson's chubby cheek, "and I love you." She kissed Harper's cheek, as well.

"How did you learn to do that?" he asked, still thinking of the magnificent way she'd stepped in and saved the pup.

"What?" she asked, shooting the twins a confused look. "Love the twins? That comes surprisingly natural to me."

He chuckled. "That's fairly self-evident even to the casual observer. I meant what you did with the puppy. Blowing breath into his lungs."

"Oh. That," she said, waving her answer away as if it was nothing special. "As soon as I discovered I was going to be Harper and Hudson's guardian, I took an infant CPR course. I wanted to be prepared for anything."

"Brilliant." Simon wouldn't have thought to do that. Maybe Miranda wasn't as irresponsible as he'd originally thought she was.

"A puppy isn't a baby, of course, but I knew I had to try."

"Well, it worked. And I've never seen anything like it. I think, given that you saved him, that you should name the little guy."

"Really?" Her eyes lit up like firecrackers and her voice once again contained childlike enthusiasm.

He wished he could embrace life the way she seemed to do.

"Okay, then. Let me see." She tapped a finger on her chin. "He's so roly-poly. How about…"

Her gaze met his and her smile coaxed his own mouth into a grin.

"Pudgy."

Chapter Four

Miranda hadn't been to church in ages—other than to photograph the occasional celebrity wedding. She'd been too busy taking pictures and traveling to take time out for Sunday worship—or at least that had been the excuse she used.

And then there had been—she swallowed hard—Mary's funeral. She'd darkened the door of the church for that.

Today she was feeling especially grateful. She was happy for Simon's puppy, which, when he'd called her this morning at her request, he had reported now appeared no worse for the wear. The pup was evidently healthy and robust like his brothers and sisters.

But she was especially grateful for Hudson and Harper and the role she now played in their lives.

Even though they'd changed the vector of her life in a single second, she'd never considered them a burden. If anything, they'd offered her an escape from a life that had become burdensome. She might judge herself and come up wanting as a mother, but that didn't make the twins any less of a blessing.

Today she felt the deep-seated need to return to her spiritual roots, to Wildhorn's small community church, the one she'd been christened in as a baby and had grown up attending every Sunday morning.

When she'd first returned to Wildhorn she'd had no idea what she would find. But reconnecting to her past, to her brother and his family, to her mom and dad, had changed her somehow. Learning the many ins and outs of baby care, and even bumping heads with the handsome, if sometimes irksome, Simon West, she felt as if new life had come into her heart. For the first time in years she felt truly awake, and with that awareness came a reawakening of her heart to God.

She'd just finished bundling the twins in their coats, hats and mittens when Mason knocked on the door of her cabin.

"Ready to go, sis?" he asked, his typical enthusiasm pouring out of him. But she knew he was especially stoked that his little sister wanted to return to the fold.

The evening before, when Miranda had asked if she could accompany them to church, Mason and Charlotte had been overjoyed. Mason told her they'd been praying for her.

She still felt a deep sense of shame that she'd missed Hudson and Harper's christening, but Mason and Charlotte didn't hold it against her. And she knew Mary and John had forgiven her, as well, or else they never would have named Miranda guardian of the twins.

With Harper and Hudson safely strapped in to her sports car, Miranda followed Mason's enormous SUV to church. Even with the largest vehicle on the market, Mason and Charlotte's brood of four barely fit. And Charlotte was pregnant with number five. Talk about loading up a truck to the brim.

Which brought her back to thinking about her own vehicle. She'd loved her little yellow convertible from the moment she'd driven it off the lot. It was a gift to herself, a way to find joy in a life that was often rushed and empty. At least with her car she could control the speed, and she loved the feeling of the wind in her hair.

But a sports car with children?

Not so much.

She'd definitely given her tiny car careful consideration after that humiliating struggle to remove the twins from the backseat as Simon looked on, probably laughing at her under his breath.

She really didn't need flash and speed out here in Wildhorn. She had nowhere to crank it up unless she sped off down the highway out of town, and there wasn't much call for that right now, what with babies to care for. She was more likely to bend a rim on a deep pothole going up someone's wash-boarded dirt driveway than impress anyone with the zero-to-sixty in ten seconds flat capability of her convertible.

Now that she was Hudson and Harper's mother, she needed a sensible vehicle, one built for country living and something easier to get the twins in and out of.

One more thing of many to add to her ever-growing mental to-do list. She really ought to start writing everything down.

She pulled into the parking space next to Mason and proceeded to unload the twins, trying as hard as she could to maintain her dignity in the process. Thinking of her last foray into unloading them from her vehicle, she'd worn a practical pantsuit rather than a dress, which would have been a total disaster.

Miranda mentally nudged purchasing a new vehicle to the top of her list. She didn't want to lose out on the one opportunity that she had all week to put on a dress.

Miranda's other little nieces and nephews, freshly unloaded from the SUV, pointed at the front lawn of the church and burst into giggles.

She whirled around to see what they found so funny.

Instead of glimpsing whatever sight the gathering crowd was looking at, her gaze was immediately drawn to a broody cowboy on the outskirts of the lawn.

Simon.

He was scowling at whatever had captured the attention of the other onlookers, although she still could not see what, exactly, that was.

The frown that creased his face was almost as deep as the one he'd given her the first time they'd met.

Why was he frowning when everyone else was laughing?

What was eating at him now?

She shifted her gaze, trying to see what was causing such a commotion, but the crowd, snapping pictures with their cell phones and raising a ruckus, was so thick now she couldn't see through it.

She returned her attention to Simon, who was absently curling the brim of his brown Stetson. Miranda thought he might be bending it out of shape. He was so deep in thought, his brow so furrowed that—

"Well, now, that *is* interesting," Charlotte murmured,

taking Harper from Miranda's grasp and threading her free arm through Miranda's as if they were two friends in high school and not the mothers of enough children combined to create a basketball team.

"What's interesting?"

Miranda surveyed the area, but she still couldn't see what the gathering crowd was looking at. Maybe Charlotte had caught a glimpse of whatever was so funny and could fill her in on the joke.

"Simon," Charlotte remarked thoughtfully.

"Simon?" Miranda parroted, hoping Charlotte hadn't noticed she'd been staring at him. How embarrassing would that be?

Simon was Mason's best friend, and had been since high school. Miranda didn't want anyone getting the wrong impression about the two of them—especially Charlotte, who knew she'd been spending time with him.

"What about him?" she asked tentatively.

"He's here."

"And this is interesting because—?"

"He hasn't attended church in years, not even on Christmas and Easter. The only time I've ever seen him cross the threshold of a church is at weddings and funerals—and at Hudson and Harper's christening, of course, given that he was named their godfather. Otherwise I doubt he would have been there. Mason said they've been talking a lot about God, but I hadn't realized Simon has come so far in his spiritual life that he is ready to attend church."

Miranda found that kind of odd. For one thing, he didn't look as if he was ready to attend church. He looked like he was about to spontaneously combust.

For another, the first time they'd met after she returned to Wildhorn, he'd made such a big deal about being the twins' godfather, which was a spiritual obligation. Wasn't it?

At the time, she'd just assumed he was a regular churchgoer like Mason and Charlotte were, and that the obligations he referred to in such strong language had to do with his faith.

But if he wasn't here to worship—then what *was* he doing here now?

She'd seen a lighter side of him yesterday, but there was no sign of that man today.

"You and the twins spent some time on his ranch yesterday, didn't you?" Charlotte asked mildly.

"Almost the whole day," she admitted, suddenly reluctant. "He wanted to show us the work he does, and one of his Australian cattle dogs was having puppies."

She wasn't sure she liked where this conversation was going, nor the sudden mischievous sparkle in her sister-in-law's green eyes.

"Interesting," Charlotte repeated.

"Doesn't he look kind of angry to you?" Miranda asked, desperate not to go there. If there was any inkling of past feelings in her expression, a strange by-product of when she'd crushed on Simon as a teenager, she didn't want Charlotte to notice.

Simon was still glaring at whatever was making the rest of the Sunday worshippers laugh in delight and take dozens of pictures.

"Meh," Charlotte said. "Simon is always frowning, unless he's working with his dogs. It's the only time the man's face lights up."

Miranda nodded. She'd witnessed Simon's transformation firsthand. She'd even heard him chuckle a couple of times yesterday.

"That, and maybe the twins. He really cares for them," Miranda added.

"You're right about that. I think maybe you and the twins will be good for him. Won't you, Hudson, sweetheart?" Charlotte tickled the baby's tummy, resulting in a happy squeal and him holding his chubby hands out to Charlotte, who laughingly took him in her arms.

Mason herded his children toward the church entrance and Charlotte followed.

"We'll save you a seat," she tossed over her shoulder.

Miranda nodded.

She hadn't a clue what Charlotte had meant, nor did she want to speculate. The twins were good for Simon, no doubt about that. But why Charlotte had added her to the picture was a mystery—one that she didn't necessarily want to solve. While it was clear Simon wanted to be included in the twins' lives, she wasn't sure how far he would go to achieve this goal. In her experience, men often acted with ulterior motives—which was why she'd avoided serious relationships altogether, even before the twins had entered her life.

Los Angeles was like living on another planet, completely different from the hometown she'd come from. Everyone looked out for their own best interests in LA, and not so much for the needs of others.

Faith in God was rarely mentioned and practiced even less.

It was all fake. A bad veneer.

The one time she'd opened her heart to a man, it was

only to discover he was using her as a stepping stone to further his own career, to make new contacts out of her friends and hopefully get some auditions.

She'd learned her lesson the hard way.

Pastor Corbit stood just outside the red doors of the white chapel, ringing a bell and urging his parishioners inside so the service could start. The crowd dispersed and was heading into the church building, finally allowing Miranda to see what all the commotion had been about.

A life-size, light-up Nativity scene had been set up in the middle of the lawn, a bright, happy reminder of the true meaning of Christmas.

Someone, or maybe a group of someones, had added their own *bright and happy* artistic embellishments to the display.

Miranda put her fist up to cover her mouth as laughter bubbled from her chest. Each figurine in the crèche had been uniquely and colorfully dressed for the season. She was actually impressed with the effort, although she probably shouldn't admit that aloud.

Each of the three camels had different-colored scarves wrapped around their necks. Christmas colors—red, green and gold. The wise men, who no doubt weren't used to the chilly Texas weather during advent season, seeing as they were from the Far East, had been gifted with warm mittens. The usually barefoot shepherds worshipping at the manger now wore sturdy farm boots.

The wooly sheep didn't need much to complete their wardrobes, so they'd been outfitted with sunglasses.

The most humorous member of the ensemble was

the donkey, whose long ears had been covered with warm woolen socks.

Inside the crèche, Joseph had been wrapped in a heavy fleece-lined jean jacket, while the Holy Mother was draped in a beautiful royal blue shawl.

The infant Jesus's manger had been neatly covered with aluminum foil that shimmered in the sunshine, and he'd been covered by an old-fashioned homemade quilt.

With her background in photography, Miranda admired the artistry of whoever had pulled the prank. There wasn't anything haphazard about the display. Clearly, a great deal of thought had gone into it.

Pulling out her cell phone, she glanced at the time to make sure she wouldn't be late for the service and then, shifting Harper to her shoulder, began taking pictures from various angles, capturing each of the figurines in a different light. She wished she had her professional camera with her so she could document the scene with the justice it deserved.

As she snapped, she noticed twigs set up as a ranch brand just in front of the Baby's manger.

Three interconnected *H*s—Triple H.

The artists had signed their work, as all good artists did.

Were the pranksters perhaps three teenagers whose first or last names began with the letter *H*?

That was one guess, anyway.

From the corner of her eye she saw Simon staring at her. Or maybe *glaring* would be a more accurate description of his expression.

She stiffened and met his cool gaze with hers, and his disapproving scowl only deepened.

What was the man's problem, anyway?

When she arched her eyebrows at him, he punched his hat back on his head and stalked toward her.

Apparently, she was about to find out what was eating at him.

"Miss breakfast?" she guessed when he stopped before her.

"What?" His frown deepened, if that was even possible.

"You just seem a little...*sour* this morning."

"And I am absolutely *astounded* that you are actually lowering your standards to take *pictures* of this... this..."

"Artistic interpretation of the Nativity?" she suggested.

"I was going to say sacrilegious nonsense." He scoffed and shook his head.

"Frankly, I'm surprised this bothers you so much."

"Yeah? And why is that?"

"Charlotte said you aren't much of a churchgoer."

He caught his breath and jerked back in surprise.

"I'm not."

"Then why does this," she asked, gesturing toward the Nativity scene, "matter to you at all?"

"Apparently, you *do* go to church, so I'm going to throw that question right back at you. Why *doesn't* this offend you?"

She didn't bother to correct his false impression of how often she attended church services.

"Because I don't see any malice in it. It looks to me like it's the work of teenagers on a lark."

"Exactly," he said as if she'd just proven his point—whatever that was.

"Look. Whoever it was, they clearly put a lot of planning into it and coordinated it well. No harm done."

"This time," Simon muttered.

Miranda didn't even know what that meant. And she still didn't know what had brought on Simon's bitter mood. But she didn't want him to ruin her morning.

This was her first Sunday back at church, and she'd actually been earnestly anticipating it. Better to change the subject before Simon's attitude started rubbing off on her and she decided to scrap the whole idea.

As far as the Nativity scene went, Pastor Corbit could remove the coats and hats if he found them offensive. It wasn't as if any permanent damage had been done.

"Mason and Charlotte are happy to see you made it to church this morning," she said, hoping her statement would be taken as the peace offering she meant it to be.

She didn't add her own name to that list.

There had been the briefest of moments right there in the beginning, when she'd first spotted him standing by the side of the lawn, that her heart had sparked of its own accord, but that was before she'd seen that perpetual frown lining his face.

Always judging, that one, and as far as she was concerned, he was actively looking to find fault, even when there was none. Miranda. Blanche—although Miranda could sort of see his point there. But he didn't appear to have the capacity to see the good in people.

Only animals. And Mason, but that was kind of the same thing.

Such a shame, but not her problem.

Simon scoffed. "Well, I'm sorry to disappoint Mason and Charlotte, but I'm not here to attend church."

She raised her eyebrows. She didn't have to voice the obvious question—if he wasn't here for the service, then why *was* he here?

He reached into the chest pocket of his burgundy chambray shirt and pulled out a sealed white envelope.

"For the twins," he said, pressing it into her palm.

Before she could open the envelope and see what was inside, Simon had turned away from her and was striding back to his truck.

Miranda stared after him, dumbfounded.

He showed up at church, but not to attend the service?

What was with the man, anyway?

As much as she would have loved to have had time to ponder the answer to that question, or at least open the envelope he had given her, she could already hear the congregation singing the opening hymn.

Great.

Now Simon had made her late for church.

Chapter Five

Simon really *had* shown up at the church this morning with the intention of attending the service for the first time in…well, it had been a long time.

Too long.

But he couldn't very well go in now. Not with Miranda asking so many nosy questions, and then him blurting out that he wasn't going inside.

With a growl of frustration, he loaded himself back into the cab of his pickup and turned for home.

He had a feeling that Miranda was going to continue to be a major pain in his side—and worse yet, she was getting into his head. She could be so sweet, like with the puppy she'd saved, but then there were days like today when they were like oil and water. He never seemed to say the right thing when he was around her. His mind got all muddled up. It was all he could do to keep his boots clear of his mouth.

Women in general were a dangerous species where Simon was concerned. He'd had very few relationships over the years and they'd never gone well. He wasn't great at expressing his feelings, and the ladies he'd dated needed far more from him than he was willing to give—or even *could* give, if the truth be known.

Mason had teased him about becoming a hermit, and maybe he was right. Or possibly an ostrich, burying his head in the sand.

At least his life had been peaceful, before Miranda had arrived with the force of a whirlwind.

He didn't even know how to begin to classify her.

Like how she not only made tents out of blankets, but crawled right in with the children and read fairy tales with separate voices for each of the characters, too.

The way she giggled when the twins giggled.

And why on earth she could possibly think the utter desecration of the Nativity scene had been the harmless work of teenagers on a lark.

No.

More than that.

She thought it was…

Artistic.

He scoffed aloud, even though there was no one in the cab of the truck to hear his disdain.

While he admitted the possibility of it being teenagers joshing around all in fun, as Miranda had suggested, that whole scene was anything but innocent.

Oh, it might start that way, harmlessly goofing around, but Simon had seen it before—how quickly harmless pranks escalated into greater and greater dares and hazing, which eventually became reckless, even dangerous.

He was probably overthinking it, but he'd seen the really bad stuff. Gang initiations. Fighting. Guns.

All of which might very well have started out as an innocent lark.

Another thing that bothered him was that the miscreants who'd gussied up the Nativity scene had felt compelled to sign their work with their mark—a Triple H, whatever that stood for.

Teenagers on an innocent lark didn't tag their work.

Simon had been in enough brawls over the years to immediately expect the worst. He'd been a scrappy kid who'd been on the receiving end of "teenagers on a lark," which had, on more than one occasion, landed him in a Dumpster. He'd started pumping iron in high school and had grown into his height, and all that helped him do was get into more trouble. His reaction today was a defense mechanism, one that had served him well over the years.

Miranda had been born and raised in a good Christian family. Her mother and father remained happily married to this day. Simon supposed he couldn't really fault her for believing the best when she'd never seen anything except happiness in her life.

If he was only thinking of Miranda, he'd probably just let her go on living in her fantasy world, free of all unkindness and crime.

But it wasn't just Miranda.

It was the twins, and Simon had a responsibility to them. He was bound and determined to protect them from anything and everything that could cause them harm, making sure they remained innocent children for as long as possible before they had to deal with the realities of the adult world.

They would have a sweet, innocent childhood, as

Miranda had. And when the time came for them to step out into the world as adults, he'd make sure they were street savvy as well as book smart.

Harper and Hudson's uncle Simon would always be there to watch over them, even when they weren't aware he was there.

His heart filled with warmth at the thought of those two sweet babies. He was truly blessed to be their god-father.

As he pulled up his long driveway, his mind was so focused on thoughts of Miranda and the twins that he didn't immediately see that there was a white SUV parked in front of his ranch house.

An SUV—with writing on the side and flashing red and blue lights across the top.

"What were you and Simon talking about before church?" Charlotte asked as they shared coffee and do-nuts in the fellowship hall after the service had ended. "It looked pretty intense there for a while."

"*He's* pretty intense," Miranda replied. "It's like he has a swarm of bees inside him just ready to burst out. Or is it just me he's that way with?"

"No, Simon is serious with everyone, all the time—except maybe when he's working with his dogs. He had a rough life growing up. When his mother was forced into drug rehab for the fourth time in as many years, poor little four-year-old Simon was picked up by so-cial services and tossed into foster care, until he was picked up by the McPhersons here in Wildhorn when he was in high school. They gave him the only stabil-ity he's ever had."

"I didn't know," Miranda repeated, her heart squeezing in empathy.

"No. You wouldn't, would you? It's not like he's going to come right out and tell you about a past I believe he'd rather forget. He doesn't talk about his childhood," Charlotte continued. "The only reason I know anything is because he's spoken to Mason about it, and he only knows a little bit."

Miranda wondered if she should be hearing all this, if Simon was so private about his past, but it wasn't exactly gossip. Simon had made it crystal clear that he was going to be a big part of the twins' lives. Anything she could do to make her relationship with him easier had to be considered useful information.

"He's a complicated man," Miranda said on a sigh.

"With good reason."

"With good reason," Miranda agreed.

"What's in the envelope he gave you?"

Miranda had temporarily forgotten about the envelope. She was in big trouble if being in Simon's presence, or even merely thinking about him, sent her into a tailspin. She needed to be able to keep her head on straight.

"I don't know. Hold on."

She slid her finger under the seal and withdrew a single sheet of tri-folded printer paper. When she unfolded the blank page, a personal check fluttered slowly to the floor.

Bemused, Miranda picked the check up from where it had landed by her feet.

No explanation.

Nothing.

Just a check made out to her, signed with Simon's scrawled signature.

"What do you make of this?" Miranda asked, setting the check on the table and sliding it toward Charlotte. "He said it was for the twins."

"To help with their upkeep, I imagine. Although—whoa. Two thousand bucks. That's a pretty heavy chunk of change for Simon."

"Really? When I visited his ranch, I was under the impression that his herding dog business was doing very well."

"He's a proud man, but dog training isn't exactly Wall Street. He only gets paid when he sells the litters, so there's a lot of ups and downs, I think. He loves what he does more than making money," Charlotte informed her. "And as you can imagine, every spare cent goes into his rescue.

"There's always something that needs fixing, or they are low on feed, and he's always on credit for his vet bills. Donations cover some of it, but Simon puts in a lot of his personal money, as well."

"Then why would he give me this? I don't understand."

"Because he is the twins' godfather and he loves them. He's always felt a special responsibility toward them, and even more so now that Mary and John are gone."

"And he's worried because I'm their new guardian." It wasn't a question. "Simon doesn't trust me."

"He just wants to do his part, feel like he's contributing to Harper and Hudson's upbringing. I think giving you a check is a discernable, objective way for him to do that."

"There are plenty of other ways for him to be there for the twins besides giving me money, Charlotte. I have more cash in my bank account than I could spend in a lifetime here in Wildhorn. I've already started investment accounts for each of the twins for their college expenses."

Charlotte shrugged, but warning lights sparked from her eyes.

"You'll have to take that up with Simon. But don't be surprised if he throws it back in your face."

"I'd like to see him try. Surely he'll listen to reason. I'm giving it back to him as soon as I see him again."

"Give it your best shot" was all Charlotte could offer.

Simon might be a stubborn cowboy, but Miranda wasn't a slouch in that department, either, and she could hold her own.

She wouldn't have gotten very far in her ultracompetitive photography business if she'd taken no for an answer every time a door started to close in her face. It was because she'd learned how to coax noes into yeses that she'd been able to rise to the top of her field.

One tenacious cowboy wasn't going to get the best of her. If she had to, she would shred the check right in front of him, though she hoped it wouldn't come to anything like that. She had no intention of treading on his ego if she could avoid it.

But she had to make her point crystal clear—she didn't need his money.

If he wanted to help with the twins, surely they could work out some other way for him to be of assistance.

Like teaching them all about the dogs he trained, perhaps, or how to catch a football. Miranda couldn't toss a ball to save her life.

There were a lot of gaps for Simon to fill in, things Miranda had no interest in or didn't possess the required skill set for.

Sports—*all* sports—topped that list.

If Simon was even remotely more coordinated than she was, there was a lot he could teach the twins.

Like many girls, Miranda had dreamed of being a prima ballerina when she grew up, but she'd never made it beyond tiptoeing around the stage with a teddy bear and a tutu before she realized *that* wasn't going to happen.

Then, in second grade, she'd signed up for after-school gymnastics at her elementary school. The program was free and any child could participate—but that didn't, apparently, mean that every child *should*.

After a week of awkward cartwheels and multiple failed attempts at simply leaping over a two-foot-high vault, her physical education teacher had pulled her parents aside and—*strongly*—suggested that she not return the next week. He'd been afraid she was going to seriously hurt herself—and he was probably right about that.

Her teacher hadn't even had to mention how uncoordinated Miranda was. That was a given.

She had cried her eyes out when her parents had told her she wouldn't be returning to the gymnastics class. She'd been so embarrassed at the thought of being rejected. Even a second grader knew when she didn't measure up.

But then, in an attempt to redirect Miranda's thoughts and feelings, Daddy had placed a shiny new camera into her hands. Taking pictures helped her feel better about herself, and she'd discovered something she *did* do well.

At first, she'd photographed landscapes, but she'd soon discovered she was much more interested in turning her lens on people. Faces were ever changing, and capturing unique expressions was both a challenge and a pleasure.

She still couldn't Texas two-step without stomping on her partner's toes, but she *could* take pictures of the party that would last long after the music had stopped and the last decoration taken down.

She had a gift.

And because she'd been able to take advantage of that blessing, she had more money than she knew what to do with.

Miranda retrieved the check from Charlotte, neatly folded it back up in the blank printer paper and returned it to the envelope.

"If I follow you home, do you think you could watch the twins for me for a bit? I don't want to wait to do this. I need to talk to Simon about his check and I'm afraid it might get a little—er—messy. I wouldn't want to subject the twins to that. No need to see their new mama and Uncle Simon arguing over money."

"Maybe it won't come to that."

Miranda hoped not, but she didn't really believe confronting Simon would be as easy as all that. He was a proud man, and after his reaction today, she suspected he might want to take a bite out of her, chew her up and spit her out.

Chapter Six

With his hands fisted and jammed into the front pockets of his blue jeans, Simon reluctantly followed the animal control officer around as he toured Simon's facility.

Officer Kyle Peterson was scribbling in indecipherable chicken scratch on an oversize clipboard. Simon couldn't see what he was writing, but he could guess that the officer was making notes every time he encountered something that, in Kyle's opinion, needed to be addressed or changed.

Was he going to try to shut down the rescue?

And what about Simon's herding dog business?

Simon's lungs felt like sandpaper as he rasped breath after breath.

The animal control officer, whom Simon figured had been alerted by Blanche Stanton, was mostly keeping his comments and judgments to himself, occasionally muttering under his breath as he made his notations. The few times he did stop, point and make suggestions, Simon had to grit his teeth until his head ached.

He suspected Officer Peterson was one of those

guys who thought his uniform gave him the right to make personal decrees about a man's life's work, and it wouldn't do Simon any good to argue with him. He was biting the inside of his lip so hard he tasted copper. He'd had run-ins with the law when he was younger and had even spent some time in juvie, and though he considered himself a changed man with great respect for peace officers, this one was giving him hives.

After touring the barn, the officer had made his first few comments and suggestions, ones that had gone completely against Simon's dog handling methods. Simon had briefly attempted to explain his practices and policies, but he soon realized the officer wasn't the least interested in what he had to say.

After what seemed like ages of trailing behind Officer Peterson, the cop finally turned his full attention on Simon.

"Is there somewhere we can sit and discuss my findings?"

The man didn't give away one iota of his thoughts, neither in his gaze nor in his expression. Simon had no idea how bad this was going to be, only that, given the profusion of notes, this could take a while.

"Of course. Come on inside and I'll fix us both a cup of coffee."

Simon realized the gravity of his error the moment the words were out of his mouth. The officer had toured the barn and the grounds, but he didn't yet know what was behind Door #1, otherwise known as the ranch's front door.

"That will do just fine," Officer Peterson said.

Simon picked off his hat and shoved his fingers through his hair as he scrambled for a plan B.

How could he be so stupid?

Puffs of dust swirled through the air from far down his driveway, alerting Simon that yet another visitor was on their way—just exactly what he didn't need right now.

And when he caught sight of that garish yellow sports car bumping along the road, he groaned aloud.

He'd thought nothing could make this moment worse, but he'd been wrong. The *last* thing he wanted was for Miranda to witness this humiliating display.

Yet there she was, plain as day, unfolding her tall frame from the tiny vehicle and heading right toward him. Evidently, she'd left the twins behind, which Simon immediately interpreted as a bad thing.

The twins were the automatic buffer between their dissenting personalities, the oil and water that would not mix.

The officer dropped his clipboard to his side and was giving Miranda an appreciative once-over, which brought out a fiercely protective instinct in Simon that surprised him.

He and Miranda were always bumping heads, except maybe when they were distracted helping the puppies being brought into the world. Why should he care if another man found her attractive?

Because she was the twins' *mother*. That was why.

How dare the man?

"Officer—?" Miranda squinted at the officer's name tag. "Peterson. To what do we owe the pleasure of this visit?"

Simon was instantly aware of two facts.

First was the crafty way she flashed the peace officer a thousand-watt smile that Simon imagined worked on most if not all the men she used it on.

Quite the dangerous weapon.

But not to Simon. Her smile didn't affect him.

Or if he did feel anything, he was strong enough and wise enough to shove it into the back of his mind and ignore it.

The other fact, one which was less obvious but much more telling—she had referred to them, Simon and Miranda, as *we*. And she had purposefully, he thought, given the officer the impression that she was on Simon's side.

Given the fact that she'd drawn up before a police vehicle with its lights flashing, that was some choice she'd made.

She trusted him.

Officer Peterson. She'd said it so sweetly it immediately won him over.

Why hadn't *he* thought to use the man's name? Make it personal and hopefully a little friendlier. It wasn't like he didn't know Kyle's name.

Miranda had swept right up with her people-pleasing, outgoing personality and had taken everything all in hand within moments, changing the entire tenor of the situation.

Officer Peterson was still gawking at Miranda. If he'd been a cartoon character his eyeballs would have popped out of his head attached to springs and his tongue would have been lolling, but Miranda didn't seem to notice.

"Officer Peterson here just showed up for a surprise inspection on Forever Family," he explained, trying not to sound bothered by the fact. "I'm not sure what it was that precipitated the event."

He was fishing, but the officer wasn't even paying attention to him.

"Oh, I see," purred Miranda. For someone who wasn't a pet person, she sure sounded an awful lot like a cat. "It's such a lovely place, isn't it, Officer Peterson?"

"I—well—" Officer Peterson stammered, his gaze dropping guiltily to his clipboard. He cleared his throat. "You can call me Kyle."

Simon repeated the officer's statement in his mind in a cartoonish voice.

You can call me Kyle.

"Kyle here has just toured our facility. All of the out-buildings, that is."

Simon didn't know why he said *our*. Maybe he was unconsciously referring to the nonprofit organization under which he worked.

Forever Family.

Us.

Yeah, he'd go with that.

"Simon just invited me in for coffee so I can go over my report with him," Kyle said, pulling himself up to his full height, which still left him gazing up at the taller Miranda like a love-struck puppy. "I'm sure Simon wouldn't mind pouring a third cup."

"Inside the house?" Miranda's surprised gaze met Simon's and she raised her eyebrows.

Was he crazy?

She didn't have to say it out loud. He was thinking

the very same thing. What did he think he was doing, thrusting the officer into the mayhem of madness that was the inside of his ranch house?

Since Kyle's back was turned to him, he shook his head to let Miranda know he'd realized the consequences too late, and then he pointed a finger at his temple and mock shot himself.

Miranda rolled her eyes.

"You know," she said, linking her arm through Kyle's and giving him her full attention, "I have a much better idea. Simon has a beautiful little lake on his land just over the hill there to the north, and if I'm not mistaken, there's a picnic table with a nice view of the land. Isn't that right, Simon?"

Simon nodded in agreement as he realized where she was taking this. He let out the breath he hadn't even realized he'd been holding. He didn't know why Miranda was here, but he was sure thankful she was.

She pointed to the cluster of trees peeking up just over the rise. "It's too nice of a day for us to be cooped up inside. Why don't you and Simon mosey on down to the lake. I'll bring along a carafe of coffee and see if I can round up a treat of some kind and I'll meet you fellas down there in a minute."

There were so many things wrong with this scenario that Simon could barely start to count them.

Miranda had just enlisted herself in a solo mission to take on his very messy bachelor pad house, and worse yet, snoop around in his kitchen in order to find everything she needed to serve coffee and treats. He had far more dog biscuits than anything edible for a human, but he thought he still had some packaged chocolate chip cookies left in the pantry somewhere, which he hoped she would find.

He had no doubt that Miranda, maker of blanket tents and encourager of babies' imaginations, could rustle up something for them.

He wasn't worried about the dogs accepting Miranda, but he wasn't so certain about how Miranda would respond to his pack of mutts on her own. They became easily overexcited when visitors arrived, and that was with him there to keep them in line.

At least her gaze had promised him she wouldn't leave him alone with Officer Peterson for any longer than necessary.

Still—a woman poking her nose around his things?

The very thought sent a shiver down his spine.

But then again, she'd successfully redirected the officer away from what would have most certainly been an unmitigated disaster. How would the officer have taken a pack of dogs living in his house? That wouldn't be easy to explain.

Miranda was here.

The thought gave him courage. Unlike Simon, Miranda was gregarious and friendly. She clearly knew what to do and say to defuse even the most delicate of situations.

Well, except for when it was just the two of them alone together.

They sparked like flint on stone.

Regardless, when push came to shove, Miranda had stepped into the ring with him, and he was glad she was on his side, even if that meant she was charming Officer Peterson—Simon refused to call him Kyle—into ignoring, or at least modifying, the many notations on his clipboard.

Simon didn't have the foggiest notion why Miranda was here, sans children—especially since earlier in the day they'd been quarreling over their differing opinions on the defilement of the Nativity scene.

But as he watched her heading toward the ranch house, and hoping Officer Peterson wasn't likewise enjoying the view, Simon decided it didn't matter why she was here.

Only that she *was* here.

And she'd just saved his bacon.

A million conflicting thoughts had rushed through Miranda's mind when she'd drawn up in front of Simon's ranch house and parked her convertible behind a police SUV with the lights still flashing.

Evidently nosy Blanche Stanton had finally made good on her threat to report Simon to the authorities.

Unbelievable.

She and Simon might frequently lock horns, like earlier at church, but that didn't stop her from worrying about him, picturing him being driven off in handcuffs for who-knows-what reason. Her breathing increased into short gasps until she was nearly hyperventilating.

She'd seen him at his worst—with her, obviously— but she'd also seen him at his best, delivering his beloved puppies. She hadn't been around Simon for that long, but it was enough for her to know that he was a man who took honor and loyalty seriously.

She quickly realized he'd backed himself into a corner he couldn't get out of, at least not without her help.

Inviting Officer Peterson into his chaotic, topsy-turvy dog-filled house?

What had he been thinking?

Had he panicked?

Was he insane?

More to the point...

Was *she*?

She'd taken one look at the anxiety in Simon's gaze, like a beacon warning against sharp rocks just under the water's surface, and her empathy had immediately risen in response. It was a blessing and a curse.

She hadn't actually thought all the way through her brilliant solution to Simon's problem, but she had managed to divert Officer Peterson away from the house with the first idea that had popped into her mind.

Which would have been fine, except...

Now that Simon and Kyle were heading out to the picnic table by the lake, Miranda had a moment to reflect on what she realized was *not* one of her brighter ideas.

Yes, she had distracted the officer from entering Simon's dwelling, but now she'd effectively volunteered herself in his place.

Brilliant move, that.

An animal control officer at least presumably knew all about dogs and would know how to handle himself around them.

Miranda, on the other hand, knew exactly nothing.

She understood why Simon didn't want the officer to know he usually kept all of his rescues in his house, not to mention all the throw-away dogs who made their permanent home with Simon.

Even though Miranda knew next to nothing about rescue work, she was fairly certain Simon was the exception to the rule. All the dog rescues she'd ever seen—albeit only on television and not in real life—had dogs in kennels, sad eyed and lifting their heads to join the cacophony of barking. Foster families might get involved in individual cases, possibly, but she imagined there was no other rescue that worked remotely close to the way Simon ran his operation, with his entire pack of mutts making their home in *his* home.

That might be difficult to explain.

Which brought her to her second concern—she'd only been in Simon's house once, and she wasn't sure what his dogs had thought of her even then. She wasn't exactly a dog person, and she was pretty sure the canines knew it.

What if she walked in and they thought she was an intruder?

She stood at the entrance to his home, blowing out a breath and shaking out her tense muscles.

She was certain she'd read somewhere that animals could smell fear, and that trait was rolling off her in waves.

What if the dogs trounced on her?

But Simon had immediately agreed to her suggestion when she'd made it, so he must not have been too worried—or else he was so distracted, or so desperate that the officer not see the inside of his house, that he was willing to sacrifice Miranda.

"This is the stupidest idea I've ever had," she muttered aloud as she turned the doorknob. "Well, here goes nothing."

She took two steps into the house and froze as dozens of doggie eyes peered up at her expectantly.

For the first few seconds not one of them moved or made a sound, and neither did Miranda.

Ignore the dogs, get the coffee and get out.

She felt like she was participating in some kind of covert op for a spy agency, except that she'd already been made by every doggie in the room.

Then the chaos started—low woofs, high yaps, and dogs of all shapes and sizes bound and determined to get her attention by every means they had.

Wet noses bumped her palms and tiny paws scratched at her ankles. Oddly, though, even with the frenzy of movement and the cacophony of howls, yips and barks, Miranda realized she was not afraid.

These were Simon's dogs.

He'd taken them in. Trained them. Loved them.

And he trusted them enough to send Miranda into his house unaided.

Three-legged Chummy, the wire-haired terrier, and Loki, the blind husky, greeted her and she reached down to scratch the dogs' ears.

"All right, fellows—and ladies," she amended. "Let's find the coffee."

Chapter Seven

Simon's neck and shoulders rippled with tension.

What was taking Miranda so long?

It had seemed like hours since he and Officer Peterson had reached the lake and silently seated themselves on opposite sides of the picnic table. Simon had given Kyle the side with the lake view, not so much as a courtesy as that Simon would be able to see Miranda approaching.

He had no way of knowing how long they waited. He didn't wear a watch and he couldn't very well pull out his cell phone to check the time with a cop sitting on the other side of the table. It was probably minutes, but the ticking of seconds in Simon's head grew louder and louder with each passing one.

He had thought the officer would get down to business straightaway—delineating the notes on his clipboard for Simon, rather than waiting on Miranda.

Simon wished he would. It would be far less humiliating for him to face the confrontation alone, because he was well aware that Officer Peterson was about to give him a good dressing down.

Why else would he have made so many notes on his clipboard?

Yet Kyle, as he'd invited Miranda to call him, appeared to be lingering, waiting for her to return.

At long last Simon spotted Miranda jogging down the hill, a coffee carafe in one hand and three cups in the other, as well as a canvas bag Simon guessed carried chocolate chip cookies.

"Sorry for the delay," she said, her breath coming in gasps as if she'd run a marathon and not the short distance from the ranch house. Her cheeks were flushed a pretty pink and the smile on her face was contagious.

Simon's lips were curving upward well before he remembered Officer Peterson was still there. And a quick glance at that man confirmed that he, too, was taken in by Miranda's vibrant expression. The officer was grinning from ear to ear like a mule eating briars.

Simon lowered his brow. Officer Peterson had better stick to his official business and not go off flirting with Miranda.

After all, she was now the new mother of twins. She didn't have time in her life for frivolity and dating.

Simon had no idea how he would stop such a situation if it occurred, and if she knew he was putting himself up as her personal protector, she'd probably have more than a few sharp words to say to him.

Like that it was her life and he should keep his nose out of it.

But it wasn't just her life. It was the twins he was thinking of.

Mostly.

So he was going to keep his proverbial mantle of protection around all three of them—without ever saying a word to let on.

He wasn't foolish enough to risk his own neck.

Miranda passed out the coffee mugs and laid out the contents of the canvas bag—sugar and creamer for the coffee—for the officer, he assumed, as he knew he and Miranda both drank their coffee black. She'd found the chocolate chip cookies Simon had been fairly certain were in the pantry, and she'd included an assortment of fresh fruit.

"Now," she said as Simon poured each of them a cup of coffee, "what seems to be the problem here, Officer?"

To his credit, Officer Peterson's expression turned serious. Simon breathed a moment's relief before he remembered that *that* wasn't such a good thing, either.

"Let's start with your fences," Kyle said, addressing Simon, though his gaze occasionally strayed to Miranda.

"What's wrong with my fences?" He knew he sounded defensive, but really. He was meticulous about keeping his fences in order—metal posts reinforced by chicken wire, safe for the sake of the dogs as well as the cattle.

"I'd like to address the southern border in particular. The new retirement community's home owner's association requires eight-foot privacy fences between properties. Building your own will assure you of *your* privacy."

"I don't see how any of this has to do with me. My land isn't part of any HOA. There are already privacy fences on the houses. Why do I need to build one on my land?"

"You are right about the fences already around the houses, and you're also correct that you aren't under any obligations here. But I think it would be in your best interest to consider building one anyway. There's a perception—" he started, then stalled. "One of your neighbors—"

"Has been complaining," Miranda finished for him. "We already know that. But is a new fence really going to solve the problem? I believe the woman is a—how can I say this delicately?"

She grinned and tapped her finger against her lips as if carefully considering her words, although the glimmer in her eyes told Simon she already knew exactly what she was going to say.

"Busybody. Yes, that's the word I was searching for. She's complaining just to hear herself talk. I'm not sure a fence will help with that."

Kyle cleared his throat. "I'm not supposed to say anything, but—yeah. I agree with you," the officer said with a nod, stunning Simon into silence.

Miranda appeared equally as surprised, but she found her voice first.

"If Simon is willing to build this fence, Kyle," she said, nodding toward the officer's full clipboard and slightly emphasizing his name, "then do you suppose he will be able to run his business as he sees fit?"

It couldn't be that easy.

Miranda was really reaching, and yet shockingly, there it was.

The officer was actually nodding in agreement.

Kyle's gaze returned to Simon. "You have a clean facility and your horse and your herding dogs look well cared for. Your barn could use a little bit of a spruce up, but I'm guessing you know that already."

"Nothing a coat of paint can't fix," Miranda affirmed enthusiastically. "Aren't his dogs wonderful? They are Australian cattle dogs from the very best stock. Simon breeds and trains them and then sends them to their new owners. He even has a waiting list with ranchers from several states."

Simon didn't know what was more surprising—that Officer Peterson sounded like he might go easy on him instead of hitting him with the gazillion notes on his clipboard, or that Miranda appeared so animated about the cattle dogs.

She'd really been listening to him when he'd explained his operations to her, even though he knew he'd probably gone into far too much detail because of his natural passion for his business.

Most people's eyes started glazing over at some point when he really got into his subject, but not Miranda. She actually sounded proud of his accomplishments. His chest swelled just a little.

"I'll tell you what, Simon," the officer said. "You put up the privacy fence along your south border and we'll call it good."

Simon stared blankly at the hand Officer Peterson thrust out at him.

The officer was ready to call it good—except that it *wasn't* good. Simon didn't have the kind of cash lying around to build acres of a privacy wall.

What little money he'd had, he'd just given Miranda

to help with the twins' upkeep. Twins meant two of everything—and even though she had her own money and the insurance payout, he wanted to contribute. He was a man. He wanted to do something concrete to help. If he could ease her burden, he would. The twins were the most important thing.

But the fence—

Miranda reached out and shook the officer's hand, as smooth as could be, rescuing Simon from what could have been an extremely awkward situation.

"Done," she said in an overly cheerful tone. "And thank you, Kyle, for understanding."

The officer held on to Miranda's hand, and her gaze, just a little bit longer than Simon thought was strictly necessary. Long enough to make Simon uncomfortable and feel like a third wheel.

"Can I take you for coffee sometime?" Kyle asked Miranda. "That is, unless…" He nodded toward Simon.

"Oh, no, Simon and I aren't together."

Simon clapped Kyle on the shoulder, refocusing his attention before he realized Miranda hadn't actually answered his question.

"Can I walk you back to your car?" Simon urged.

"No need." Officer Peterson gathered his clipboard and tipped his hat to Miranda. "I've got to get back to the station and fill out my report. You know how it is with police work. Endless paperwork, it seems like. Anyway, you get that fence built and I think our problem is solved. In the meantime, you two should enjoy this sunset. It's unseasonably warm weather this evening, don't you think?"

Officer Peterson didn't wait for an answer, but turned

and headed back over the hill to where his SUV was parked. The sound of tires on gravel signaled the end of that particular confrontation.

And now Simon had a whole other one to face.

Miranda chose a chocolate chip cookie over a piece of fruit to assuage her sweet tooth, and turned around in her seat so she could view the lake.

The officer was right. It was a lovely evening.

Too bad she had to ruin it with the whole not-cashing-the-check nonsense. Simon had already had a stressful day, and now she was going to have to add to it.

Just what she didn't want to do.

For a moment she considered staying silent on the matter and tucking the check away somewhere for safekeeping, but that was only a temporary solution to a larger problem. Sooner or later Simon would realize she hadn't cashed the check, and then he'd have every right to come completely unglued on her.

No—it was better to be honest and up front about the check right out of the gate. Besides, he could probably use the money to help fund his privacy fence.

All the more reason for her to get this out in the open as soon as possible. Maybe it wouldn't be such a big deal after all.

Simon tossed his hat on the table and sat down beside her.

"I suppose I should thank you," he said in a voice as coarse as gravel.

"What?" Of all the things she thought he might say right now, that wasn't one of them, especially because he didn't sound particularly grateful. "Why?"

"Don't tell me you didn't see the way Officer Peterson was looking at you. Smart of you to distract him that way."

She must be out of practice, because she actually *hadn't* noticed. She wasn't in the market for a relationship, but she thought she'd know if a man was showing interest in her. Until Kyle had asked her for coffee, she hadn't been on that wavelength at all. Did Simon really imagine she would *flirt* with a peace officer to get out of trouble?

Or rather, get *him* out of trouble.

The nerve of the man.

"Well, thank you for working your charm on him. I was concerned there for a while."

"You're mistaken. This has nothing to do with me. I think Kyle admires what you're doing here at the ranch. He's just being nice, trying to help you fix the problem between you and old Mrs. Stanton."

"Hmmph. Being nice? *Kyle* was admiring *you*. He asked you for coffee."

If Miranda didn't know any better, she would have thought she detected a note of jealousy in his tone.

But of course that was ridiculous. Why would Simon care if another man found her attractive?

"Which I turned down," she pointed out.

He scoffed. "No, you didn't. You didn't answer him at all."

She clicked her tongue against her teeth. "Same difference. And honestly, does it even matter how it happened? The point is that we have a *solution*—and one that doesn't require any more interactions with Officer Peterson."

Why she thought she needed to reassure him on that point was quite beyond her understanding.

Simon lifted one eyebrow, then frowned.

"Not a *viable* solution."

She tilted her head and captured his gaze. "I'm not following. When you build the fence, your problems go away—and so does your nosy neighbor. The next time Blanche Stanton phones the police, they'll tell her to mind her own business."

"I don't—that is—" His face turned an alarming shade of red and he coughed as if he was choking on something.

She gave him three helpful thumps between his shoulder blades to dislodge his breath. Not exactly the Heimlich maneuver, but—

"I don't have the money," Simon mumbled, his voice so low that Miranda could barely hear the words.

She leaned in closer. "What did you say? I didn't quite catch that."

"I said I don't have the money to build the fence!" This time his voice was loud enough to be heard in the next county.

"You don't have to shout."

He growled. Literally, actually *growled*, and Miranda briefly wondered if maybe he was spending a little too much time with his canine companions.

"You don't get it, do you? You just put my head on the chopping block, promising Officer Peterson that I will comply with something that I don't have the resources to build. What's going to happen when that fence *doesn't* get built, huh? It won't just be Blanche breathing down my neck. My whole operation will be in jeopardy."

"I understand," she said. And she did—far better than he did right now. Because happily, she had the answer to his problem tucked away in her purse. He'd be so relieved that she intended to give him his money back.

Problem solved.

"Hold that thought for a moment."

She jogged back to her car and returned with her cute, high-end black clutch purse that was highlighted with a sparkling red rose.

"I have your remedy right here."

Laughing, she waved the purse under his nose.

He frowned.

Of course he frowned. What else did Simon West ever do? She wanted to roll her eyes in exasperation.

But he'd be smiling in a moment.

"Ready?"

She snapped open the clutch and then paused for dramatic effect.

"Miranda," he warned with a growl.

"Oh, fine, spoilsport. Here," she said, pulling out the envelope he'd given her earlier. "This is the answer to your problem."

She tried to hand the envelope to Simon but he just stared at it, unmoving, his expression as hard as stone.

"That's for the twins," he said after an extended pause.

"Is it?" Miranda took the blank paper from the envelope, laid the check on the table and exaggerated her examining of both blank sides of the printer paper. "I

don't see anywhere on here where this check is desig-
nated to the twins. No note or anything."

"You know well and good that's what it's for. Why
else would I give you money? I didn't think I had to
spell it out for you."

"You didn't. You don't. And I do know what you
were trying to accomplish here. That's very sweet, and
the twins and I appreciate it.

"But here's the thing—I don't need your money. I
made a very good living as a celebrity photographer.
A great one, actually. And since I'm really not the sort
of woman to spend huge amounts on myself, I tucked
most of that money away. I didn't know at the time I
would be able to use it raising Harper and Hudson comfortably, but God knew."

Simon flinched but remained silent, his scowl still
firmly set.

"And that's assuming I never use my photography
skills again, which I can't imagine. Even without my
savings, and even in a small town, I have a viable career."

He grunted. She didn't know which part of what
she'd said upset him. Maybe all of it. But he should
be thinking about his fence right now and not his ego.

"I've already set up investment funds for their college expenses. Their future is as set as their present."

She pushed the check in his direction.

"Keep your money. Build your fence," she urged.

He crossed his arms, and his jaw tightened until she
could see his pulse throbbing at the base of his neck.

"There are lots of other ways you can support the
twins besides using your checkbook," she said, trying

to soften the blow to his ego. "You can be their male role model. You know how important that is. A man to love them and give them guidance."

He didn't so much as blink.

"What?"

"Until some other guy comes along."

Miranda wasn't going to get into this with him. There was no other guy, and she doubted there ever would be.

Simon was their godfather—an important influence in Hudson and Harper's lives. That wasn't going to change.

But there was no point in telling him that, because he wasn't listening. He'd completely turned himself off to her.

She sighed. "I really, *really* didn't want to have to do this, but it appears you leave me no choice."

Picking up the check off the table, she held the top corners between her fingers and thumbs and tore it neatly in half.

He stood so fast that Miranda was glad the picnic table was secured to the ground with concrete. It was a wonder the whole thing didn't crack into sawdust with the intensity of Simon's movement.

He stalked away, muttering under his breath and shoving his hair back with his free hand. Miranda couldn't hear what he was saying, but she suspected it had something to do with her, and they were probably not very nice sentiments.

Suddenly, he swiveled back on her.

"I'll write you another one. Maybe you don't need the money, but I want to do something concrete to support my godchildren."

She shook her head. He wasn't getting it. She could see that he wanted to give sacrificially, and she didn't want to stomp on his ego, but she had to make him see her point.

"I'll tear up any check you write. You can't win this battle, Simon. The best thing you can do right now is build your fence so you have a business to sustain you and you can keep rescuing your dogs. That won't happen if animal control shuts down your operation. The twins need you around as a role model, not a banker."

"But—"

"Nope. End of subject. Now, I'm going to leave you to your nice sunset and get back home to Hudson and Harper. When you figure out what you want to do, give me a ring. You have my number."

She couldn't help but smile the tiniest bit as she strode up the hill. Simon might not realize it right now, but she'd done him a huge favor, because the twins really did need their godfather in their lives.

Together, they'd find the answer to this dilemma. In the meantime, it was—

Miranda: one.

Stubborn Cowboy: zip.

Chapter Eight

The next Saturday, nearly a week after the incident with Officer Peterson, Simon was working on obedience training with some of the rescues he hoped to find forever homes for at the upcoming Christmas adoption event, but his heart and mind weren't in it and the perceptive pups could tell. They were all over the place, just like his thoughts.

He'd reached for his cell phone to call Miranda a dozen times, and a dozen times his thumb had strayed from the call button and he'd ended up pocketing his phone.

He'd never been so frustrated in his life.

Just when he was starting to like Miranda, maybe even admire her, she had pulled the rug out from underneath him, exposing his weaknesses and vulnerabilities.

He hadn't always been the nicest guy. As a youth he'd floundered, because he had no foundation, no family to care for him. And he would do anything—anything—to make sure the twins never found themselves in a similar situation.

While he now conceded that Miranda may have been right about the money, he had his pride, and she had popped his male ego like a blade into a balloon when she'd ripped his check in half. He'd felt every tiny tear of the paper in his gut. His emotions had warred between humiliation and anger.

Even thinking about it now, a whole week later, made conflicting feelings swirl around in his chest like a whirlwind. He wanted to be the role model the twins looked up to. But even with his new faith, could he be that man? It seemed as if it was one step forward, two steps back in his life right now, especially since Miranda had arrived.

What could he offer the twins that Miranda didn't already provide?

And yet his concerns didn't negate his heartfelt conviction that he *needed* to contribute to the twins' well-being in a concrete way. Maybe he'd made a misstep with the check, but the reasoning behind his offering hadn't changed.

What had she said? That the twins needed his presence in their lives more than his money, a man to love them and give them guidance.

Lord, how can I be that man?

He needed a new game plan. Something that would work for all of them.

What he had to do, he realized, was make up with Miranda, set aside his pride for the sake of the twins. Be the one to step up and make the first move. If he and Miranda spent time together with Harper and Hudson, maybe they could find some common ground and learn to get along better with each other for the twins' sake.

Certainly, there'd been moments when they'd worked together successfully, but those didn't outweigh the number of times they'd butted heads over issues.

He needed to find things they could do together. Events that Miranda, Hudson and Harper would all enjoy. Keep it light and friendly.

He hesitated a second before dialing Miranda, and that was only because he didn't know what kind of immediate reception he would get.

Would she hang up on him?

He snorted. What was this? High school?

He felt like a teenager phoning a girl for a first date, only in this case, he and Miranda were adults who'd gotten off on the wrong foot.

Several wrong feet, actually.

Of course she wouldn't hang up on him. Technically, he was the injured party here. But he was going to let that go for the twins' sake.

Surprisingly, Miranda answered on the first ring, catching him completely off guard. He couldn't even stammer a hello.

"Simon. What's up? Is everything all right with the doggies?"

"The dogs?" Her question confused him for a moment. "No—yeah—the dogs are fine. I was just—"

He paused and cleared his throat, his nerves tingling from the tips of his toes to the top of his head.

"If you and the twins are free this afternoon, I thought we might take them to the Christmas carnival at church that the youth group is putting on. They do this every year and it draws most of the community, especially the children. They've got all kinds of little games and prizes, and the money goes toward feeding Christmas dinners to the homeless."

"I heard about that during church announcements last week and I was just bundling the twins up to take them."

Simon's spirit dipped.

"Oh. I see. Well—"

"But why don't we meet you there and we can hang out?"

He felt as if his heart was on a spring, popping back up again as easily as it had fallen.

"Yeah? That'd be—great." His throat tightened around his voice.

"Wonderful. See you there in twenty?"

Simon assented, then hung up the phone and headed for the house to wash up. As he splashed cold water on his face, he stared at himself in the mirror, for once taking stock of what he saw.

Debating on whether or not to change his shirt, he wet his hands and shoved his fingers through his curls, trying to tame them, but it was hopeless, and anyway, he had permanent hat hair from his cowboy hat. He ran his palm across his whiskers, wondering if he should shave, then scowled at his reflection and snorted.

Why should today be any different than any other day?

He was five minutes early from the time they'd agreed to meet, but Miranda's yellow convertible was already parked in the lot, sticking out like gold amongst coal. She really did need to get a more practical vehicle with all that money she'd said she had tucked away.

Miranda was waiting at the entrance with the twins in a double stroller. She waved as he approached.

"I thought since the carnival is interactive that we could leave the stroller out here and take the twins in together."

He grinned as he unstrapped Harper and pulled her into his arms. Together sounded good. Olive branches being extended both ways, it seemed.

With Hudson in her arms, Miranda gestured for him to follow her into the fellowship hall, which had been decorated almost as obnoxiously as Miranda's living room. Red, gold and silver garland everywhere. Wreaths at every booth, which were separated by tables.

"What should we do first?" Miranda asked. Simon wasn't sure whether she was addressing him or Hudson, so he merely shrugged.

"No deep-seated aspiration to throw darts at a balloon? I imagine it's quite therapeutic if you can pop one. And you get a prize."

"Shouldn't we walk around first?" he asked—not that he wasn't willing to display his dart-throwing skills. He had a dartboard at home and often spent evenings playing. It was one game a man could do without a partner or challenger.

Miranda assented and they walked through the aisles, taking note of the games aimed at the youngest children, and those more suited to adults. There was even a Wildhorn version of a kissing booth, where couples donated money to kiss under a sprig of mistletoe.

Simon made a note to avoid that booth. Trouble with a capital T.

Miranda slid her free hand into the crook of his elbow

so they could stay together as they walked through the crowd. It was oddly comfortable, even with the curious glances that were thrown their direction.

"Cakewalk?" she asked, her expression eager with anticipation.

"For the twins? They can't even walk yet."

She laughed. "No, silly. For us. I mean, for us and the twins. We can carry them with us." She turned her attention on Hudson. "What do you say, Hudson? Think we can beat Uncle Simon and Harper?"

"So not going to happen, is it, darlin'?" he responded, directing his comment toward Harper, though his smile was for Miranda.

The cakewalk alternated between older kids and adults, so they had to wait their turn, but it wasn't long before they were on their spots, ready to begin walking with the music, which was, appropriately, a lively version of "Jingle Bells."

Even laden with the babies, both he and Miranda laughingly caught chairs through the first few rounds, and before he knew it, it was just him and Miranda left, fighting over one chair. His competitive nature reared and he clutched Harper to his shoulder.

"This one's for you, baby girl," he whispered.

Around and around they went. The inky-haired teenage boy in charge of the MP3 player took his time about shutting down the music, but when he did, Simon leaped for the chair, which happened to be facing his direction.

He hit the seat just as Miranda rolled around, squealing in surprise as she made contact with Simon's knee and not the chair. She tipped to the side, clearly going down, but she had the presence of mind to press Hudson into Simon's waiting arm. He'd been reaching for Miranda but had no choice but to take the baby instead.

His pulse ratcheted as Miranda landed in an inglorious heap. For a moment she didn't move or speak, and he wondered if she'd had the wind knocked out of her. She'd landed pretty hard. But then he heard her groan as she rolled to a sitting position, favoring one knee.

He was kneeling beside her in a second, but he was limited in how he could help her with two babies in his arms—babies who were both clapping and giggling as if they wished for Miranda to do it again.

Hudson in particular thought being suddenly tossed into Simon's arms was great fun. At least Miranda's fall hadn't hurt the little guy, and he had to give Miranda props for getting him to safety before impact.

Simon definitely didn't want anything like that to happen again.

"Miranda?" he asked gently. "What hurts, honey?"

She groaned again, her face flushing. The teenage boy running the music was at her side, a concerned look on his face as he offered his hand to her.

"Only my pride. And possibly my knee, although it's not anything major. I may have twisted it a bit as I fell."

"Can you stand?"

She nodded and slowly came to her feet, carefully testing out her left knee before putting any weight on it.

"Yep, good to go," she said as much to the crowd that had formed around her as to Simon.

"Are you sure?"

"Of course. And thank you," she said to the teenager, who beamed back at her.

His brow creased. She was taking this far too well.

He probably would have crawled into a hole and not come up again. Ever.

But not Miranda.

She smiled at those surrounding her and curtsied, as if she had just finished putting on a play instead of flopping nose down on the concrete floor.

Curtsied.

People actually started chuckling and clapping, offering their support, while all he could think about was that it was a wonder she *hadn't* hurt herself more than she had.

Just another addition Simon could make to his mental list of differences between them.

While Simon admittedly took everything too seriously, Miranda was—

The truth was, he didn't know how to describe her. Emotions swirled around and knotted themselves in his chest whenever he even thought of her. But one thing was for certain. They were as different as night and day—in the way they perceived the world, as well as how they encountered it.

Before he'd gotten to know Miranda, he hadn't realized what a strong and dedicated woman she was. He'd misjudged her. But now that they were spending time together with the twins, he had the distinct impression it would be harder than ever to be the godfather he wanted to be.

He and Miranda were so different. He didn't understand her view of the world, and before long, she would get tired of his cup-half-empty outlook.

He'd made a mess of every relationship he'd ever been in, and Miranda was a complicated woman.

Could they be friends? He had a hard time seeing through their dissimilarities, and he was nothing if not practical. The more time they spent together, the larger their differences appeared. How long before the gap between them would be too far to cross?

Well, that had been humiliating.

When she was a kid, Mason used to tease her that Klutzy was her middle name. And she'd just proven that for the benefit of the entire town.

And Simon.

At least she'd provided a good laugh, after everyone was certain she hadn't actually injured herself in her inglorious fall. And the twins had loved it. They thought it was all a game, which was just as well.

Her knee hurt slightly but not enough to make a big deal of. She'd ice it when she got home. In the meantime, there were plenty of other booths to explore.

Simon threw three darts, popping the same number of balloons, and won a purple giraffe for Harper. He then proceeded to knock down bottles with a tennis ball and won Hudson a large red ball with white stars on it.

Miranda was glad for that, because she couldn't throw darts or tennis balls. She and Simon encouraged the twins to throw bean bags into buckets, which neither of them managed to do, not that it mattered. They each received small participation prizes—candy cane tree ornaments that the teens had fashioned into reindeer using pipe cleaners.

By the time they'd nearly finished visiting all of the booths, Miranda's knee was beginning to hurt in earnest, but she didn't want to cut the twins' fun short and Simon legitimately appeared to be enjoying himself for a change.

There were only two games left—the kissing booth, which Miranda was purposefully avoiding, and she suspected Simon was doing the same, and a big tin barrel filled with water and floating rubber ducks.

"Pick a duckie, win a prize," said the teenage girl, a pretty blonde with her hair pulled back in a ponytail.

"That sounds easy enough," Simon said, setting the giraffe on the counter and bracing Harper so she could lean over the barrel and grab a duck.

Harper being Harper, she tried to pick one for each hand.

"Easy does it," Simon said, gently returning one duck to the pond.

The teenager looked at the bottom of the duck, where the prize had been written in permanent ink, and handed Harper a six-inch dolly.

Simon shot Miranda a grin. "I'm glad we're getting to the end. I'm out of hands."

Miranda laughed and set the red ball on the floor so Hudson could have his turn at the duckies. His hand hit the water palm down, splashing it into Miranda's face.

She sputtered. "That's not how this works, buddy."

Taking his hand, she guided him to a duck, which he pulled out in triumph before it went straight for his mouth. Miranda was so busy trying to remove the duck without causing Hudson to wail that she didn't immediately see what Hudson had won.

The teenager stood with her arm stretched out, bearing a bag half-filled with water, a goldfish nervously swimming back and forth in its depths.

A real, *live* goldfish.

"Oh, dear. I don't—can we get something different?" she stammered.

The teenager shrugged. "Sorry. All we have left are dolls and goldfish."

Simon nudged her shoulder. "Come on, be a sport. As pets go, goldfish are a piece of cake."

Miranda cringed. "Says you. Remember the cactus? I have no idea how to take care of a goldfish."

"Don't worry. I'll set you up and show you the ropes."

That was what she was afraid he was going to say. Reluctantly, she accepted her live fish offering, but only because both of the twins appeared fascinated by it. They'd probably enjoy watching the fish, for as long as that lasted.

"I think we're finished here," she said, eyeing the ball at her feet. "But I can't pick up the ball and hold the fish at the same time, and you've got your hands full, too."

Mason appeared at her side, his mischievous brotherly grin causing Miranda some pause.

"I'll help with the ball and the fish," he said, picking up the ball, taking Miranda by the shoulders and pushing her *away* from the exit. "But you've missed one booth."

"Knock it off, Mason," she said under her breath. "I've been embarrassed enough today."

"Yeah, I heard about your little fall. Are you sure you didn't hurt yourself?" At least he sounded semi-concerned, though no less impish.

Big brothers. Can't live with them, can't shoot 'em.

"Nothing an ice pack won't fix," she assured him, not that Mason was going to listen.

Unfortunately, Simon was following them, probably not realizing he was a lamb being led to the slaughter. He really ought to know better, having been best friends with Mason for over ten years.

"Nothing that a little kiss can't fix," Mason amended, shoving Miranda underneath the mistletoe in the kissing booth.

"I don't have any more cash," she protested.

Mason grinned like a Cheshire cat and tossed the teen behind the table a five-dollar bill. "It's on me. Simon, the honor is all yours."

Simon eyed the booth—and Miranda—dubiously. He looked like a kindergartner, afraid of getting cooties. Miranda didn't know whether to laugh or be offended.

She chose laughter.

"A kiss to make it better," Mason prompted.

"Am I really that bad?" Miranda teased, handing Mason the goldfish and shifting Hudson to her right arm so she could offer Simon her left cheek.

"Yes. I mean no. I mean—" Simon stammered, looking like a deer caught in headlights.

Miranda raised her brows. "Is it yes or no? There'll be a foot of snow in Texas before you figure this out."

Simon scowled, intensely concentrating, clearly looking for a way out of this situation, and that only made Miranda and Mason laugh harder.

At length, he tipped his hat back with the arm that held the giraffe and dolly and sighed, the poor, long-suffering cowboy.

He first pressed a kiss on Harper's forehead, then stepped forward and kissed Hudson, as well. Last, he leaned toward Miranda, his lips hovering over her cheek as if in indecision.

But when his warm lips finally met her skin, it wasn't the hasty peck she expected.

He lingered.

Chapter Nine

Simon's mind lingered on that kiss far longer than it should have. Stupid Mason for making a complicated relationship even more thorny. Kissing Miranda reminded him once again that she was a woman, and not just the twins' guardian.

Part of him wanted to do what he always did when threatened—fight. Fight the feelings, and stay far away from Miranda Morgan. Or was that flight?

Instead, he called and made arrangements for them to take a day trip to the zoo. At least the zoo didn't have a kissing booth. In fact, it was specially decorated for the Christmas season, with zoo lights in the shapes of animals. The kids would love it, and it would be the perfect place for him and Miranda to walk on neutral ground—literally and metaphorically.

Something told him the zoo was a place that not only the twins would like, but that Miranda would delight in, as well. Anyone who enjoyed making play tents out of sheets would enjoy seeing all kinds of exotic animals.

And he didn't even want to get her started on special Christmas decorations.

When he arrived at Miranda's cabin and rang the bell, she only opened the door a crack and poked her head out.

"We're not quite ready yet," she murmured, and then shut the door in his face.

He didn't have to see what was going on to be able to imagine the scene from the ruckus he was hearing inside.

Squeaking and squealing and shrieking and giggling—and not all coming from the nine-month-olds.

It must be total chaos in there. He waited patiently for a couple of minutes, but finally, his curiosity got the best of him and he slipped inside the door.

Miranda squeaked when she saw him.

"If you can just hold on a moment more, Simon. I have to put these two in the bath before we go. We were making hard biscuits for snacks and a certain someone—" she coughed the name "Hudson" into her palm "—had both fists in the bowl the moment my back was turned. He got flour and sticky dough everywhere."

"Maybe if you hadn't left the bowl on his high chair where he could reach it," he suggested with a chuckle.

She laughed. "You're right. My bad."

Once again his opinion of her shifted, bumping up a few more notches. It took a brave soul to attempt to make homemade anything with two nine-month-old babies "helping." That sounded like way more trouble than it was worth to any sane person, but Miranda was all smiles and laughter.

The house smelled scrumptious, but her kitchen

looked like a powder keg had blown up in it—a keg of *flour*. Sticky dough dotted the counter, and Simon suspected more dough had gone onto baby skin than had made it into the biscuit batter.

To his amusement, the goldfish Hudson had won at the Christmas carnival was swimming around in a bowl on the far end of the counter. Miranda had managed to keep the little fish alive for a week.

"Can I help?" he asked, thinking he could wipe down counters or mop the floor or something useful.

Miranda grinned at him. "I thought you'd never ask. Can you grab me a couple of bath towels?"

He grabbed the towels—bright yellow, surprise, surprise—and followed her into the bathroom, stopping short as he entered.

The woman had an evergreen wreath in her bathroom.

In her *bathroom*.

And the toilet seat was decorated as Santa Claus. No shortage of Christmas cheer here.

Shaking his head, he turned on the bath water while she divested two wriggling babies from their dough-covered fuzzy footie pj's.

"This is so much easier with a second set of hands," she gushed. "Usually, my bathroom looks like a water bomb exploded in it when I have to give them a bath. These kids really know how to make a splash."

As if to prove Miranda's words, Harper started wildly kicking both legs, sending a wave of water over the side of the tub and utterly soaking one leg of Simon's jeans.

His gaze met Miranda's. She was desperately going

for a mortified expression, but he could see she was barely holding in her mirth.

She shouldn't be laughing at him.

And he ought to feel affronted. Would have, in the past. But oddly, he could see the humor in the situation.

It *was* funny.

He chuckled and the dam cracked.

Miranda clapped a hand over her mouth and began laughing uncontrollably, holding her stomach and rocking back and forth.

"Oh, Simon. Your face!"

"You're one to talk." He reached over and wiped his thumb across her cheek where a large smear of dough remained. "It looks like you three are wearing more dough than you baked."

"We learned fractions today," she informed him with a mock snooty sniff.

He lifted a brow. He didn't know the first thing about children, but wasn't nine months a little young for a baby to be learning math?

She snorted when he tipped his head and stared at her in confusion.

"One fourth of the dough gets on your clothes, one fourth goes on your face, and if all goes well, half gets into the oven."

"You learn something new every day."

"See? I'm a great teacher, aren't I?"

He definitely learned something new every day when he was around Miranda. She was teaching him loads without a classroom and never ceased to surprise him. Sometimes good, sometimes not so good, but always something different. He handed her one of the towels and slung the other one over his shoulder.

"I have a much higher learning curve than figuring out only one new thing a day," she informed him as she soaped down the two squirming babies and then scooped Harper into one of the plush, vibrant yellow towels. "I learn several *hundred* new things a day, usually by trial and error. Mostly error."

"I noticed you like yellow," he observed.

"Why wouldn't I love it? It's the color of sunshine."

Yellow wasn't just Miranda's favorite color. Miranda *was* yellow. Sunshine. Tulips and daffodils and other spring flowers. She was always so quick to move on from whatever conflicts they had. She didn't hold a grudge and just let go, rising new with every morning.

He was more like midnight.

Dark and broody.

Which meant what? Was *he* the instigator of conflict?

He didn't want to be that man. Not when he'd worked so hard to do more, to be different from the youth he had been.

He sent up a silent prayer asking God for assistance to be a new and better man. Without the Lord, he was nothing.

As he lifted Hudson from the tub and wrapped him in an identical yellow towel, he mentally resolved to do better.

It didn't matter what his past had been, or even if his natural predilection was to see the dark before the light.

If he could learn it, he could unlearn it, and hanging out with Miranda was as good a place to start as any.

He'd never be bright like sunshine, but at least maybe he could reflect her rays.

"Let's take my new car to the zoo," Miranda suggested as they dressed the babies in identical outfits.

"You got a new car?"

"The safest SUV on the market," she said proudly.

"No tiny bumblebee convertible anymore?"

"Royal blue. Unfortunately, the SUV I wanted doesn't come in yellow."

He couldn't imagine why that new bit of information caused him a moment of dismay. It was a practical decision on her part, but it was almost like taking away a little bit of her personality.

"If you can get the twins buckled up in their car seats, I'll get changed into something more appropriate for the zoo. If I go in these," she said, gesturing to her dough-covered baggy golden sweatshirt and battered yoga pants, "the lions, tigers and bears are apt to want to eat me for lunch."

Even in a bulky sweatshirt with her shoulder-length chestnut hair pulled back in a messy bun, Simon thought the lions, tigers and bears weren't the only ones apt to notice her. She was a stunning woman. Any man would take a second look.

He shook the thought away. He wasn't here to date Miranda. He was here to learn to get along with her for the sake of the twins.

And even if that wasn't his primary motivation, there were dozens of reasons any attempt at a relationship with Miranda would be a disaster.

Fire and ice, for one. Sunshine and midnight.

That she was Mason's little sister, for another. There

had to be something in the man code about not getting involved with your closest buddy's younger sister. Mason would have no choice but to take Miranda's side in a bad breakup and Simon would lose the best friend he'd ever had.

Was he willing to risk that?

And there was yet another wide chasm between them—even here in Wildhorn where she was the single mother of twin infants, in essence, she would always be the successful celebrity photographer with boatloads of money and a contact list full of famous friends, and he would still be the poor, simple country cowboy who could barely make ends meet, and whose existence was primarily working with dogs that would never have another chance at life were it not for him.

What sane woman would want that for herself? Especially because she came as a ready-made family. She would always have to put the twins first.

Not a chance.

He wasn't good for any of them.

The fact was, he had nothing to offer Miranda, or Hudson and Harper, so it was especially important not only for him to rein in any errant thoughts, but to also make it clear to her that he was in this for the twins and only for the twins.

"What about the kitchen?" he asked as Miranda slid behind the wheel and plopped a camera case in his lap. He felt guilty about leaving it such a mess, even if he hadn't been party to creating it.

She started up the engine and made a quarter turn in her seat so she could look him straight in the eye.

"What about the kitchen?"

"Don't you want to straighten it up a little before we leave? I should have offered to help," he said, although technically, he *had* offered to help.

"Zoo…messy kitchen. Zoo…messy kitchen." She paused and cocked her head as if deep in thought. "Nope. No contest. The zoo will win every time. Sticky dough can wait. I want to see the monkeys."

Simon probably thought she *was* a monkey. It certainly looked like a whole tribe of them inhabited her kitchen. And he had a point that she probably should have at least wiped down the counters before they'd left.

But she loved the zoo, and she knew Harper and Hudson would, too, especially with Christmas zoo lights. She couldn't wait to see their happy little faces all fascinated by the animals, hear the squeals and giggles when the polar bear swam by them.

And Simon—he'd made the first move, not once, but twice now, reaching out to her with a hand of friendship.

How great was that? She wasn't about to turn his overture away.

Hanging out with Simon was an adventure, to say the least, sometimes up the path, sometimes down. But even though it seemed like they often bumped heads, whether on purpose or as an accident…this was the *zoo*.

What could go wrong at the zoo?

She turned the corner and headed toward Tumbleweed Avenue, Wildhorn's version of Main Street. Running east and west, with only two streetlights at either end of the town, it was the primary shopping thoroughfare, such as it was.

About two blocks away from Tumbleweed Avenue,

Miranda's SUV came to a sudden stop behind a long line of other cars. It appeared there was some kind of commotion on Tumbleweed. It wasn't like Wildhorn to have a traffic jam, and it wasn't a holiday, so there shouldn't be anything blocking the road.

"I'll go see what all this fuss is about," Simon said before hopping out of the cab and striding down the street.

He returned minutes later, a frown creasing his brow. Miranda hadn't been able to move her SUV an inch, and now there was a line of bumper-to-bumper traffic behind her, as well as in front of her.

"Are we missing a Christmas parade?" she asked, even though she knew from Simon's expression that it wasn't anything as nice as that.

Ever since the moment Simon had exited the SUV, Miranda had been praying there hadn't been a terrible accident on the road. She'd rolled down her window, and while the murmur of voices was quite loud, she didn't hear any sirens.

Simon didn't bother answering her teasing question.

"Those kids—the ones who messed up the Nativity scene at the church? They've struck again, this time out on Tumbleweed."

"Really? What did they do this time?" Despite Simon's grave expression, she was more curious than worried. She hadn't thought the Nativity scene was such a bad thing. Not the way Simon had.

"It's town pickup this weekend. Folks are encouraged to bring out their bags of late fall leaves and the town disposes of them for free."

"Right. I remember hearing about it on the news.

The drop-off spot is in front of Duke's Hardware, as I recall."

"Well, it *was* in front of Duke's Hardware. Now it's the whole length of Tumbleweed Avenue. And it's an enormous mess."

"What do you mean?"

"Some *kids on a lark* dumped all of the leaves out of the bags and spread them from one end of town to the other. It's a huge disarray and it's got to be cleaned up as soon as possible because of traffic. As it is right now, no one can get through."

He pressed his lips into a grim line. "I'm sorry, Miranda, but the zoo is going to have to wait for another day."

"Of course," she immediately agreed. "Did you see what's being done to take care of the problem?"

"Lloyd Duke is handing out rakes and donating new lawn and leaf bags, and the townspeople have banded together to pitch in and clean up the mess."

Miranda glanced in the rearview mirror. "Well, this vehicle isn't going anywhere in the near future. Why don't we bundle the little ones up in the stroller and see what we can do to help?"

"Why am I not surprised?" He shook his head.

"About what?"

"That you'd want to pitch in, even though you have two active babies to look after. You amaze me. Hudson and Harper are just a natural part of your life. They don't slow you down at all."

"Why should they?"

He shook his head again and helped her unload the twins. The stroller became cumbersome as they hit the main street, which was covered with at least two inches of golden leaves.

Miranda gasped audibly at the sight. Multiple tones of reds, oranges, yellows and golds mixed to make the avenue look like the road leading to the gates of heaven. It was an absolutely beautiful sight to behold, leading from the far end of town all the way up to the life-size Santa's sleigh and wire-cast reindeer. Snow might have fit the theme better, but given that they were in Texas, golden leaves were a decent runner-up.

"What?" Simon asked, concern lining his tone.

"Can you watch both kids for a moment?"

"Well, sure, but—"

She was already dashing away, heading back to the SUV, where she'd left her camera bag.

She gently pulled the camera out of the case and quickly added one of the longer lenses, glorying in the feel of the weight in her hand as she slid the strap over her head and around her neck.

She took photograph after photograph of the leaf-lined street, along with pictures of the Christmas-light-decorated windows on most of the business storefronts, blinking holiday goodwill.

To her dismay, she realized she hadn't taken a single picture of the twins since she'd arrived in Wildhorn. It was all she could do to manage the care of two babies without trying to photograph them, as she should have done.

What had she been thinking? The twins grew and changed every day. She should be documenting it. Not to mention all the cute shenanigans they got into. Sticky dough pictures would have been adorable.

Well, she couldn't change the past, but going forward, she'd be taking such a variety and number of pictures of Harper and Hudson that everyone she knew would get tired of her showing them off.

She chuckled lightly. She sincerely doubted anyone could really get tired of seeing photos of that kind of cuteness.

She was short of breath by the time she returned to Simon's side. He started to ask her why she'd run off in such a dither, but she anticipated his question and lifted her camera.

"I wanted to document this, and my professional camera catches the light much better than my cell phone."

Simon nodded. "Great idea. I'm glad you think like a photographer. I would never have thought of visually documenting the crime scene, but it makes perfect sense to do so."

"Crime scene? What crime scene? All I see is leaves. A wonderfully colorful road of multicolored leaves."

"You don't think the culprits should be caught and taught a lesson?" he asked, sounding astounded that she couldn't see his point of view.

She could. She just didn't agree with it.

"At the very least, they ought to be given community service—picking up the trash by the side of the road for a hundred hours, since they made such a mess of it."

"This prank seems harmless enough. No worse than the Nativity scene, except that we'll have to clean it up. At worst, drivers will need to reduce their speed through the town, which in my opinion they ought to be doing anyway."

"And the townspeople have to stop what they're doing to clean up the mess." Simon held up the rake someone had passed him. "Doesn't that at least score them down for inconvenience?"

He sounded annoyed. Hopefully not with her, although she wouldn't be surprised if he was.

Miranda saw the scene completely differently than Simon did. She looked around and saw neighbors helping neighbors, all working together—some raking, others holding open bags in which to deposit the leaves.

Simon was right about one thing—people had had to change their plans. There was no easy way of getting through on the road until the leaves had been cleaned off it, and someone had to stick around to clean up the mess. The zoo was up in smoke for them today.

But the zoo would still be there tomorrow.

And as with the Nativity scene, Miranda was awed by the artistic workmanship of the pranksters who had strewn the leaves on the avenue. They weren't randomly dumped around, making messes of sidewalks and decorated storefronts, as she expected vandals would do.

No. It was meant to be a golden road. Miranda was sure of it.

She snapped a few more pictures and showed them to Simon.

"Don't you see the beauty here?"

"Don't you see the damage?" he barked back.

She snorted. "I wouldn't call it damage. It's just leaves. No person or property has been hurt by them."

"That depends on your definition of *hurt*, now doesn't it? The twins didn't get to go to the zoo today because of these vandals. I would call that direct damage."

"How do you know it was the same kids as the crèche, anyway?" she asked, although she suspected from the care and artistry that had gone into the project that it was the same group of teenagers.

"They tagged it." He pointed to a macramé-like rope dangling from one corner of the Duke's Hardware sign. "Triple H. Just like the last time."

"I wonder what it means."

He shrugged. "Trouble."

Miranda took Hudson out of the double stroller and plopped him down in the middle of a fresh pile of leaves.

"Look up here, buddy," she coaxed as she took snapshot after snapshot of the bouncing baby boy.

"Can you grab Harper for me?" she asked. "I want to do some single photos with her, as well, and then get some of the two of them together."

"I thought you were documenting the damage," he said as he got Harper out of the stroller and set her down next to Hudson.

Miranda sighed. "There is no damage, Simon. Not really. I was taking pictures of the golden road. Besides, if I have to document something, I'd much rather document people. There's a reason I was a celebrity photographer and not a landscape artist."

The twins were giggling and pelting each other with handfuls of leaves, and Miranda continued to photograph them, as well as taking pictures of others cleaning up the stretch of road.

Neighbor chatting with neighbor. Children taking running jumps into piles of leaves and happily undoing all the work the laughing adults had accomplished. The church youth worked as a group, methodically gathering bags of leaves and placing them back in front of Duke's Hardware while elderly neighbors looked on.

Not only had it become a community event, but it also wasn't long before Miranda found herself the center of attention. Folks were interested in the way she went about snapping pictures of them with her professional camera, and before she knew it, she'd promised at least a couple of dozen people that she'd get business cards made up as inquiries came in for weddings, pregnancy pictures and family photo shoots.

"That was the fastest, easiest business start-up I've ever seen." Simon appeared particularly pleased by that statement. He actually smiled as he crouched by the twins and showered them with leaves.

Then he looked up at her and frowned. "But you don't need the money, right? So why are you giving all of those people false hope?"

"It isn't about the money. I love photography and I miss doing photo shoots. Up until today I didn't realize how much."

"It's something you can do on your own time, as much or as little as you want, to fit your schedule with the twins."

"Exactly."

He smiled again.

She would never figure out this man.

"I can guarantee you that you'll have more business than you'll know what to do with, but it's all country around here. Won't you miss the glitz and glamour?"

Miranda dove for Hudson as he stuffed a handful of leaves into his mouth.

"Oh, pah, pah, pah! Spit it out! Spit it out!"

Hudson wailed in protest.

"Blech. Blech." She forced her finger into his mouth and scraped out the remaining foliage.

Simon tossed down his rake and snatched Harper out of the leaf pile before she could mimic her brother.

"Oh, gross, Hudson," Miranda groaned.

She'd thought she'd been doing better, getting a handle on the whole motherhood business, but every time she gave herself a pat on the back for a job well-done, something like this happened.

Maybe she really *was* the lost cause Simon seemed to think she was.

Her gaze reached his, but instead of the judgmental frown she expected, he held up his free hand in surrender and burst into laughter.

"What? I didn't say anything," he said when she lowered her brow.

"You didn't have to."

"You were the one who told me kids were gonna put stuff in their mouths that they weren't supposed to."

"Yes, but not an entire fistful of leaves."

"You should have gotten it on your camera for posterity's sake. You could have teased Hudson with it when he was a teenager."

"I was too busy trying to get the leaves out of his mouth." Miranda scooped Hudson into her arms.

"In you go, you little scamp," she said, strapping him back into the stroller. "And somewhere," she continued, digging through the designer purse she was currently using as a diaper bag, "I think I've got a package of crackers for you to nom on. It's much better tasting than leaves, I promise you."

Simon didn't immediately put Harper in the stroller with Hudson. He appeared to be waiting for something.

Oh, yes. The answer to his question.

In the whole panic of Hudson stuffing leaves into his mouth, Miranda had almost forgotten what Simon had asked.

"Will I miss the glitz and glamour of Los Angeles? Honestly? No, not really. I never did care for life in the limelight, even if it was mostly behind the scenes. I miss some of the friends I made out there, of course, but that's to be expected. I loved traveling, seeing new places and experiencing different cultures. But I've been there and done that, and as great as it was at the time, as Dorothy said, there's no place like home. Especially now that I have Hudson and Harper with me to love and to make my life complete."

Well, almost complete. Her life was full to overflowing with the twins, but she was suddenly aware of a tiny aching deep within her heart, something she hadn't noticed until the past few weeks.

He stared at her, taking her measure. He opened his mouth as if to say something and then closed it again.

"What?"

He shrugged as if he had no idea what she was talking about and then dropped his gaze, using his boot to leverage the rake back up to one hand. Still holding Harper, he busied himself raking leaves into a pile.

Whatever Simon had been about to say, the moment had passed now, leaving Miranda's imagination to fill in the gaps—gaps that zigzagged up and down and all around.

She'd always had an active imagination.

Chapter Ten

Simon marveled at Miranda's ability to see the good in everything. He'd looked at the street and had seen disaster, where she'd seen beauty.

And he supposed she had a point, although it had nothing to do with the prank and everything to do with the community.

Neighbors had gathered to help each other. Everyone from nine-month-old twins to Wildhorn's octogenarians had come together to make their town a beautiful place to live. Families were working as a unit. The church youth had jumped in to do their part. No one thought twice about chipping in to help.

This was why he loved living in Wildhorn. He knew what it was like not having a family. And he wouldn't wish it on anyone in a million years.

He kissed Harper on each of her soft, chubby cheeks and reluctantly returned her to her stroller.

Money couldn't buy what Wildhorn gave for free. And Miranda captured that through the long lens of her camera.

He wished he had more to offer her and the twins, personally speaking.

She had a wonderful network of extended family to support her. He wondered if she even realized how blessed she was. She had a faith in God that Simon envied. She didn't know what it was like to have no one—no family, no faith. To be knocked around by the world.

To be truly alone.

One thing was certain. He couldn't convince her that the work of these Triple H pranksters might eventually lead to something more serious. Something truly damaging, hurting people as well as property.

She looked through her camera lens and all she saw was light.

He just couldn't do that.

"It looks like things are pretty well in control here," Miranda said. "Folks are starting to get through. We'd probably better get back to my SUV now. I left it parked right in the middle of the street. People will be waiting for me to get out of the way."

"I'm going to organize a neighborhood watch committee," he informed her when they were buckled in and on their way back to his ranch. "I don't expect you to agree with me. I just wanted you to know."

He wasn't trying to cause another rift between them, so he was careful how he chose his words. Right now, more than anything, he wanted to get along with her—for the twins' sake, and also because, oddly enough, despite the fact that it drove him batty, he was starting to depend on her sunny outlook on things to keep him from sliding off the other end.

Her gaze flashed briefly in his direction.

"I think that's a good idea, actually."

"You do?" Whatever he'd imagined she'd been about to say, agreeing with him definitely wasn't it.

"I haven't changed my view on the whole thing. I still think it's just a bunch of harmless teenagers getting into some Christmas mischief—and they are artistic kids, at that. But I know there's a reason you have a different perspective and I want to understand where you're coming from, as well. I'm open-minded. I know you don't like to talk about what happened to you when you were growing up, and I don't want to pressure you to say anything you don't want to, but I would like to understand."

By this time, she'd pulled up in front of his house, but the twins were both sleeping and neither Simon nor Miranda moved to get out of the vehicle.

Simon inwardly balked. To say he didn't like talking about himself, and especially about his past, was an understatement. He didn't like to remember those times, much less dwell on them. He didn't like the person he'd been back then, the hotheaded kid life's circumstances had turned him into. But if he didn't speak now, she would never know why he was so adamant about the subject.

"I was a scrappy little kid. Skinny as a beanpole."

It was a start, but it was hard. Very hard.

She nodded but didn't interrupt his train of thought.

"The bigger boys, they picked on me a lot. It was about what you'd expect out of a group of bullies. I got a few black eyes. More than one awkward landing inside a Dumpster of decomposing food."

She wrinkled her nose.

"I know, right? So when puberty hit me in seventh grade, I started lifting weights. I was determined that no one was going to mess with me anymore.

"And they didn't. In fact, the guys who ruled the middle school recruited me into their gang. I was foolish and lonely, and I wanted to be accepted so badly that I didn't realize I was going to get messed with again, except in a different way."

Still, Miranda didn't speak, though her gaze brimmed with empathy and sorrow. She slid her hand across the cab and linked her fingers with his, silently giving him the courage to continue.

"Since I had no family, I desperately wanted to belong to something. I went right along with their hazing, allowing them to put me in all kinds of bad situations. But I didn't question it or complain about it.

"The first thing they made me do was dress up the school mascot—a big bear. I put a balaclava over his head and wrapped him in toilet paper. That wasn't so bad. I didn't get caught. The principal was mad, but all he had to do was take off the mask and TP and everything was back to normal. It wasn't like I permanently marred the mascot. Every student in the school had a good laugh and we moved on to other things.

"But then the next week they had me sneak into the school at midnight again, this time to tie pieces of string through the holes in everyone's locker handles so no one could open them the next morning. There were two hundred and sixty-five lockers—I still remember the exact number. It took me half the night, and I had two very healthy scares when the night janitor came around. My adrenaline was working overtime. But again—harmless, right?"

Miranda nodded. "Harmless, but not very nice. I've had a few experiences like that myself."

She paused. For a moment, it looked like she was going to say more about what had happened to her, but then she shook her head and closed her mouth. It felt as if she was waiting for him to say something to her, but he didn't know what he could say that would comfort her, so instead, he continued with his story.

"I doubled up the string on the lockers of the people I didn't like—the guys who used to pick on me. At the time I thought it was funny to watch them struggle to get their lockers to open."

He couldn't believe the depth of the narrative he was sharing with Miranda. Even Mason didn't know all the gory details.

But then again, Mason had never asked.

Miranda had.

"The next night I was supposed to siphon gas from some vehicles in a parking lot to fill up the tanks of a couple of the older guys' cars. I was having a hard time with it. Siphoning gas isn't as easy as it looks in the movies, by the way. Anyway, the cops showed up and the fellows I thought were my friends ditched me faster than you can say, 'You're under arrest.'"

"No. They didn't."

He groaned. "Let's just say orange isn't my favorite color, and I picked up a lot of trash on the side of the highway because of that one stupid move."

"Your friends weren't very courageous if they just deserted you."

"And it was stupid of me to break the law just to try to impress the jerks. They were never really my friends, but that's not something you realize until much later in life, when you can look back at it without all the emotions clouding the subject. Thankfully, soon after that I got sent to Wildhorn to live with the McPhersons. They were good to me. And I met Mason. His friendship is the real deal. I was still kind of a jerk for a while, but he pulled me out of the funk I was in and set me on the straight and narrow."

A shadow crossed her expression, but all she said was, "He's a good guy."

"Yes, he is."

"And now I understand why your view is so different from mine. I can see the obvious parallels between what happened to you and what's been occurring around here. Dressing up the bear and TPing it. But do you really think it's possible that Wildhorn has some sort of gang activity going on? That seems so unlikely to me, given what a small town this is."

He shrugged. "It could happen anywhere."

"Growing up, I don't remember much crime in Wildhorn at all, of any nature. I never even heard about thefts. No one locked the doors to their cars or their houses. I guess times have really changed."

Her brow knit in concern and he immediately back-pedaled. He didn't mean to frighten her with his theories, only open her mind to the possibilities so she wouldn't take any unnecessary risks.

"Like you said, it's probably nothing," he amended, adjusting his cowboy hat lower over his eyes. "Kids on a lark, right? Nothing dangerous. Wildhorn is still one of the safest towns to live in—in Texas, or the whole country, for that matter. Our crime rate is remarkably low across the board.

"The police would already be involved if they felt there was a viable threat," he continued. "I'll organize an off-the-record neighborhood watch, something casual, just to keep folks alerted to the situation. The sooner we catch the culprits, the sooner the pranks will stop, innocent or not."

"I'll talk to Mason and Charlotte, and mention it to Pastor Corbit. It won't take long for the word to get around. Shall I have anyone interested in being involved call your cell phone?"

"That'll work. It's best if we can catch the pranksters red-handed. We need to get some cold, hard evidence so we can convince them to stop what they're doing. But in the meantime, I want you to take extra precautions for you and the twins. Lock your doors. Keep your cell phone on you. And put my number on speed dial."

"And this is only because of the leaves on the street?"

Her words could have been laced with sarcasm, but when he met her gaze, he realized she was teasing him, and he let out a breath that released the coils of tension in his neck and shoulders.

He wanted her to be serious about this, but not too serious. He didn't want Miranda to lose any of the open, trusting vibrancy that made her the woman she was. But he didn't want her to be in danger, either.

He'd protect her and the twins, no matter what happened. He'd keep his eye on her, but he didn't want her to feel hovered over, like she wasn't a strong, independent woman.

She was. No doubt about it.

He was just an overcautious man.

"Unless you have another reason in mind for putting my phone number on speed dial?"

Which sounded like flirting.

Miranda must have thought so, too, because her eyes widened almost as much as her gaping mouth.

Suddenly the path they were traveling on had nothing to do with pranksters and everything to do with—

A place they could never go.

The next Saturday, Miranda was busy preparing the twins for the town Christmas party, her mind mulling over the last time she'd seen Simon. She had put his number on speed dial, but not because she was afraid of some random gang activity in the small town.

There was no gang. She was positive of that. Not in Wildhorn.

She understood why Simon saw things the way he did, and she was definitely aware of the striking parallels between his life and what was happening now, but that was his past, not Wildhorn's present.

She kept his number as the first spot on her contact list because—well, because she was starting to depend on Simon. For other things, not for his brand of protection. Even when they clashed, which was often, she still trusted that, while his methods left a little bit to be desired, he only acted the way he did because he cared.

About the twins, that is.

And lately, she wondered if he might even care just a little bit for her. She was hesitant to explore that thought, because she'd been so desperately wrong in the past when it came to relationships.

Which was why, even though she admired Simon and felt her heart jolt every time their eyes met, she was going to be very careful with him. Take it slow.

If there even was an *it*.

From the very first day they'd met again as adults, after she'd returned to Wildhorn to take up Hudson and Harper's guardianship, Simon's focus had been solely on the twins. As time went on, she and Simon had developed a friendship with each other, a bond she believed she could trust in.

She respected him.

But she was also wary.

She didn't want to get hurt again. He might not be the jerk who'd been so callous to her in high school, but she didn't trust her heart any more now than she had then. So Simon's number would stay safely on her cell phone and she would see where time and circumstance took them.

In the meantime, Mason and Charlotte were waiting on her.

She had a party to attend.

Wildhorn's community parties were nothing at all like the glitz and glamour of the functions she'd attended in Los Angeles, with catered food, professional string quartets and borrowed diamonds. There was no comparison whatsoever.

No—this small town *really* knew how to pull out all the stops. The band was local, the food was potluck and the clothing anywhere from casual to Sunday best, all the better for dancing in. No one stood around in penguin suits holding flutes of expensive champagne. They were too busy Texas two-stepping.

"Is there anything cuter than dressing up babies at Christmastime?" she asked Hudson as she adjusted the adorable little red bow tie that matched the red suspenders holding up his black pants. She'd tried to slick back his thick tuft of chestnut hair with gel but all she'd managed to do was turn it into porcupine spikes that stuck out in every direction.

Harper, with her green velvet dress, was a little easier to groom. Her identical thick tuft of chestnut hair had been corralled with a big green ribbon on top of her head—a style Miranda had promised herself when she was a single woman that she would never do to her poor daughter. But with Harper?

Adorable.

"You two look delicious enough to eat," she told them, and then, amidst much squirming and giggling, she nommed on their sweet necks and tickled their tummies.

Miranda's camera was never very far away from her these days, and she shot several pictures of the twins next to the glowing lights of the Christmas tree, sitting back-to-back, or standing supported by foil-wrapped Christmas gifts. She'd seen some photo shoots with babies holding large ornaments or wrapped up in lights, and she wanted to make sure and take the time to do a full session before Christmas came and went. But right now they were in a hurry. Uncle Mason and Auntie Charlotte were already out in their SUV waiting for Miranda to follow along in hers.

But that didn't stop Miranda from admiring her children.

Were there ever any two more darling babies in the world? Miranda didn't think so. And she couldn't even begin to imagine her life without them now. They'd changed her whole world, and all for the better.

The cuteness, it hurt. They were going to be the life of the party.

Miranda had fudged a little bit with her own wardrobe, and she knew she was bound to stick out from the crowd, as well, but she reasoned that it was one of the few times she could even remotely consider wearing a cocktail dress, so she was all red sparkles tonight, even though she knew she would be overdressed.

She'd expected to catch folks' attention, all right, but she had no idea how much until she met up with her brother.

Mason's eyes widened to epic proportions when he first caught sight of her, and his lips twitched as if he was holding back a guffaw, but Charlotte, dressed in a lovely pine-colored skirt with matching blouse, shot him a warning look and then linked arms with Miranda and told her how pretty she looked.

"She way overdid it," Mason murmured in Charlotte's ear. Charlotte pressed a cautionary finger over his mouth. Miranda wondered for the tenth time that hour if her dress was too flashy, but at this point she didn't have time to change.

When Miranda entered the church's fellowship hall where the party was being held, a hush fell over the room, followed by quiet murmuring. Every eye was on her, and it was only partially because of the two adorable babies she held in her arms.

She pretended to appreciate the decorations—columns wrapped like candy canes, red, green, gold and silver garland strung from the ceiling, and a gigantic evergreen in the middle of the room, glowing with lights and large bulbs and frosted with icicles.

"Told ya so," Mason muttered from beside her.

"Quiet, you," Charlotte reprimanded, swatting his arm. "Stop talking and help with the twins."

"I'm fine with them for now," Miranda said. Mason and Charlotte had their own brood to worry about, and she suspected many of the townsfolk would want to interact with the twins, which was her primary reason for attending the party in the first place. She could already see a swirl of movement headed in her direction.

"Honey, I think you're going to be way too busy to look after the twins tonight, and I really don't mind," Charlotte said. "And look—there's your mom and dad. You wouldn't want to deny the proud grandparents the opportunity to show off their sweet grandkids."

As Charlotte predicted, Miranda's mom wanted to take the twins for a stroll around the room, but Miranda's arms felt oddly empty without them, and she wasn't quite sure what to do with herself. She'd planned on having the twins with her for the whole evening.

She should mingle, she supposed. She hadn't had the opportunity to do that much since she'd returned to Wildhorn.

She sidled back up to Charlotte, who was straightening Mason's collar.

"The man can't dress himself," she teased mildly.

"If I had more than five seconds before being bombarded by children, maybe I could do a better job of it."

"You love being a daddy and you know it." Charlotte ran an affectionate hand across his stubbled jaw.

Mason grinned and shrugged, then placed a gentle hand against Charlotte's growing midsection.

"Dance with me, sweetheart?"

Miranda hadn't even noticed that the band had struck up a romantic tune.

"Go," she encouraged, waving them away.

"Your dance card isn't full yet?" Charlotte asked.

Miranda snorted. "No, I think I've pretty much scared off all the single men in Wildhorn with my over-the-top shimmer. I knew I had overdressed, but this—" she gestured to her dress "—is major overkill to the nth degree. There's not a single cowboy here who would dare to take me on."

Charlotte's eyes flickered with mischief.

"I can think of one." She nodded toward the door.

Miranda glanced back to see Simon entering with his foster mother on his arm and his foster father walking on the other side of him. Simon's head was tilted down toward Edith McPherson as she spoke to him.

He appeared relaxed and smiling, and Miranda silently thanked God that Simon had ended up in the McPhersons' care. From everything he had told her about them, they had significantly changed his life for the better.

She turned back to Charlotte. "You think?"

She wasn't nearly as certain as Charlotte seemed to be that Simon would display any interest in her. Not without the twins in her arms.

"I've never seen him so—*involved*—in a woman's life before you came along. He's a changed man."

"Yes, but that's because he's the twins' godfather."

Charlotte's eyes twinkled. "Is it?"

"You girls can gossip later. I want to dance." Mason made a face at Miranda and dragged Charlotte toward the dance floor.

Miranda crossed her arms, feeling suddenly very exposed and awkward, which wasn't like her at all.

She just needed to get over herself, she decided, heading toward the nearest group of people. Nothing that a little friendly chitchat with the neighbors couldn't fix.

Before long she was the center of attention the way she liked to be the center of attention—talking and laughing with a group of people.

A man's hand closed around her elbow from behind her and her heart leaped into her throat.

Simon.

Had he finally decided to ask her to dance?

She turned, a smile already forming on her lips, but it wasn't Simon staring down at her. Technically, no one was looking down on her at all. It was Kyle Peterson, and being as short as he was, he was staring up, his gaze full of blatant admiration.

Simon had accused her of using her charm on the officer last time they'd met, but she hadn't seen what Simon had seen.

This time, she did. Her heart sank.

"Officer," she said, trying to mask her disappointment. Instead, she sounded choked, like she had just swallowed a bullfrog whole.

"Kyle, please."

"You look different in plain clothes."

That was a dumb thing to say. She'd seen him out of uniform dozens of times before. He attended the same community church as she. But she'd never *noticed* him.

He tugged at his collar and cleared his throat.

"You look—that dress is amazing."

"Er—thank you," she said, uncomfortable with the way he was complimenting her—and with his almost gawking perusal.

There was nothing wrong with Kyle, exactly. He was handsome in his own way, if a little short for Miranda's taste. He just wasn't her type—

Or maybe it wasn't so much that he wasn't her type as that she was comparing him to the one man in Wildhorn who *had* caught her interest.

She couldn't help that her gaze trailed around the room, following her heart as she looked for Simon. She finally found him leaning against a post that had been decorated like a candy cane, wrapped in red and white ribbon.

He'd apparently lost his smile when he'd parted from his foster parents, because his expression now was as hard as stone.

She caught his gaze and smiled, hoping he would realize she needed rescuing and come ask her to dance.

No deal. He tipped his hat to her and his frown deepened.

She had the distinct feeling he was upset with her for some reason, though she couldn't imagine why. They'd parted on good terms the last time they'd seen each other.

But with Simon, it was always a toss-up. She ought to know by now that she could never gauge his mood. She'd never met anyone quite as unpredictable as he was.

"I was hoping to snag a dance with you," Kyle said, his voice rising. "We never did get that coffee."

"I—uh—" Reluctantly, she turned her attention back to Kyle. They hadn't gone for coffee because Miranda had never agreed to his request, although with the spark in his eyes, she wondered if he remembered it that way. Asking her to dance had caught her off guard, although she supposed it shouldn't have.

This was a party, and people were dancing.

Too bad the only man in the room she wanted to dance with was staring a hole through her back.

He wasn't going to rescue her.

Well, he could hang his stony expression on his beak.

She was going to dance.

"Thank you, yes," she told Kyle, feeling a little guilty when his expression lit up like the brightly decorated evergreen in the middle of the room. "I'd love to dance."

Chapter Eleven

Simon watched Kyle encircle Miranda's waist through narrowed eyes. He didn't move a muscle, afraid if he did, it would be to stalk over to where they were dancing and snatch Miranda out of Kyle's far-too-familiar arms.

"What are you waiting for, buddy?" Mason jerked Simon from his thoughts when hc bumped shoulders with him.

Was it that obvious?

Granted, Mason knew Simon better than most folks did, but he hoped his admiration for Miranda—and his sheer frustration that she was dancing with any other man besides him—wasn't somehow being publicly broadcast through his expression.

That was all he needed—Mason razzing him about Miranda.

He shook his head. He wasn't going to give himself away that easily. "Waiting for what?"

"Oh, come on. Admit it. You have a thing for Miranda."

Simon cringed. His feelings for Miranda, as confusing as they were, were bound to come out sooner or later. He ought to be appalled with himself, although he couldn't quite find it in him to feel it as much as he knew he ought to be. He was tearing the man code into pieces and he didn't know how to stop it.

"I don't—"

"Charlotte and I have been observing the two of you doing this crazy back and forth thing for some time now. You're clearly attracted to each other. Wouldn't it be easier to just admit how you feel and go get what you want?"

That was half the problem. Simon didn't *know* what he wanted.

Not exactly.

Whenever he thought about Miranda, his insides started getting all twisted up and his mind…

His heart…

He groaned softly.

"If I did feel something," he said tentatively, "and I'm not saying that I do—she's your little sister. How do you feel about that?"

Mason chuckled. "I don't know whether you've noticed or not, but Miranda is all grown up now."

"I've noticed," he muttered, not quite looking Mason in the eye.

"Oh, I get it. You don't want to date her because she's my sister, and guys aren't supposed to do that."

"I never said I didn't want to date her."

Mason pumped his fist. "Then you *do* want to date her. Ha. I knew it."

"It's complicated."

Mason slapped his back. "Isn't it always, where women are concerned?"

They chuckled in agreement.

"There's women, and then there's my best friend's younger sister," Simon felt obligated to point out. "That is not the same thing."

"Look. I'm cool with it. I promise I'm not going to go all haywire on you if you have a relationship with Miranda, if that's what you're worried about."

"And if it ends badly?" Simon couldn't believe he was actually having this discussion with Mason. Saying it out loud made it real. "What happens then?"

"Will it?"

"I hope not."

"Then don't borrow trouble. Nothing is going to come between you and me. Our friendship is too important. But so is what you feel for Miranda. For all you know you could be watching her walking down the aisle to you before long."

Married men always wanted single men to get married. Simon thought that was because they wanted them to suffer in the same way.

At any time in the past, Mason's annoying statement would have sent him running for the hills. But now...

"And the twins," Simon added.

"What?" Mason looked puzzled.

"When I picture it, the twins would be walking down the aisle with Miranda. They are a package deal."

Mason grinned like the Cheshire cat and punched Simon on the biceps.

"Now, see? That's what I'm talking about. That's exactly why you're the right guy for her. You see Miranda and the twins as a package deal and you want it that way."

"Doesn't Miranda have a say in this? She might disagree with you on all counts."

"She doesn't. Disagree with me, I mean. I can ask her what she thinks of you, but I already know what her answer is going to be." Mason gestured toward the dance floor, where Miranda was dancing a second song with Kyle Peterson.

"Look at her. She's miserable out there."

Simon had to admit he thought so, too. They looked ridiculous together. Miranda was clearly uncomfortable. She would have towered over the animal control officer even if she wasn't wearing heels. Which she was.

She needed a taller man.

She needed *him*.

He was plenty tall enough for her, heels or no heels. She fit right into the crook of his shoulder as if she was made for it.

"That doesn't look right at all, does it?" Mason scoffed.

"No, it does not."

And Simon was aiming to fix it.

Now.

Miranda couldn't have been more surprised when Simon took her hand right out of Kyle's, twirled her around and whirled her away without a word of explanation.

One second she was in Kyle's arms, and the next she was in Simon's. She ought to be affronted by his alpha-man tactics, but really, she couldn't complain.

She *wanted* to be in Simon's arms.

"You probably should go apologize," she said.

Kyle was still standing in the middle of the dance floor, stunned into inertia.

Simon chuckled. "You're right. I probably should. And I will. Later. Right now I want to dance with you."

"Really? Because I got the impression earlier that you were unhappy about something. Something to do with me."

"Was I? I don't remember."

"Well, you were smiling when you came in the door with Edith, but when I saw you later—"

"You were talking to Officer Peterson."

Miranda's heart warmed when he didn't offer more of an explanation than that. He hadn't liked what he saw. He made it sound like the only *right* place for her to be was—

In his arms.

And at the moment she couldn't agree more.

She leaned her head against his chest and he tucked his chin on top of her head, drawing her close and swaying softly to the music. He was a good dancer, a natural leader and easy to follow. Which was good, since Miranda was not as coordinated.

She'd always felt awkward dancing. But not now.

She knew things were far from settled between them, and if they were headed toward a real relationship, they were both taking teeny-tiny baby steps, but right here, right now, she was in his arms, listening to the quick, steady tempo of his heartbeat, and everything was right in her world.

Who would have guessed that ten years after pining for a boy in high school, a young man who had laughed at her and brought her down, she'd be dancing with that very same boy, now grown into a rugged, handsome man whose angry youth was a thing of the past.

The feelings she'd experienced as an angst-ridden teenager paled in comparison to the way her heart expanded with the most tender of emotions now. Every nerve ending snapped and crackled pleasantly like a warm fire on a cold day.

"Lookee here." From behind her, some guy's hand stole out and made contact with Simon's shoulder, knocking them both off balance. He pulled her closer and swung them around to keep them upright.

"The cowboy and the celebrity chick. How do you rate, West? What did you have to do to get her attention?"

"Knock it off, Russell," Simon muttered.

"Just ignore him."

"Yeah," he agreed, but his tension was palpable.

"Thinkin' about marrying up? Like way, *way* up. She's out of your zip code, buddy," another man said.

"Mind your manners, Alfie Redmond," she scolded, but that only made Simon's jaw harden more.

"She's so far out of your league, pal. Wishful thinking."

Miranda didn't even know the third man. Why did they all have to gang up and pick on Simon? She knew he had to be extra-sensitive to being bullied, even if it was all in fun—and Miranda wasn't sure it *was* all in fun.

The guys, who all had women in their arms and were sorta-kinda dancing, had maneuvered around Simon and Miranda, making a circle and blocking them in, the jerks.

Simon stiffened and Miranda leaned back enough to catch his gaze.

Clearly the men's razzing was getting to him, but she didn't see why it should. Either these guys were all friends of his giving their buddy a hard time, or they were grown-up bullies. And Simon knew what to do with bullies.

"They're not worth it," she murmured.

What they were saying was ridiculous. In her eyes, she and Simon were perfectly matched. It wasn't as if she was better than him in any way, just because she'd been a celebrity photographer and he'd stayed here in Wildhorn to pursue his own dreams. She admired what he'd done with his life. There were many qualities about Simon she wished were part of her own character.

And as far as personalities went, Simon definitely held his own when they were together, even when they clashed.

And yet clearly he was bothered by the men's words. Maybe it was thoughts of his past rising up to taunt him.

And all because of her stupid dress.

She now deeply regretted her choice of attire. She should have known better. Why had she ever wanted to wear a sparkly cocktail dress to a party in Wildhorn?

Because she didn't mind standing out in a crowd.

But Simon did.

"Don't you guys have anything better to do with your time than give us grief?" she asked, not quite able to keep the annoyance from her tone. "Your dates are going to abandon you if you don't pay attention to them."

Russell's date playfully slapped his chest. "That's

right, big guy. After all this nonsense, I'm thirsty. Let's go find the punch bowl."

Russell laughed and let his date lead him away, and without him, the other two instigators danced their dates off in different directions.

Good. Well, that was settled.

Simon stopped dancing and stood stock-still, his muscles clenched tight.

"Men just never grow up, do they?"

She hoped her flippant observation would bring a smile to Simon's face, or at least unravel the coils of tension in his arms and shoulders, but instead, his jaw tightened with strain and his gaze grew hard.

"What is it?" she asked, wondering if he now regretted cutting in on her dance with Kyle. If he hadn't been dancing with her...

"It's nothing." He started rocking them slowly back and forth, but he was so tense that the movement was awkward and arrhythmic.

"Maybe we should just go," she suggested, meaning that they should leave the dance floor. Get a snack, or find the twins.

His expression lightened in relief. "You should stay. Have fun. But only if you're sure you really don't mind if I skip out of here."

"You're leaving the party?" she asked, confused.

"Isn't that what you just suggested?"

"No. I only meant—"

"They're right," Simon cut in.

"What? The men? Right about what?"

"You're too good for me."

She snorted. "That is about the most ridiculous statement I have ever heard come out of your mouth. This is about this outlandish dress. It's over-the-top and draws too much attention. I should have known better and I wish I had never worn it."

"It's not the dress. Although let me say you are more beautiful than any other woman in the room."

"Thank you, I think. But I—"

She felt like she should apologize to him for something, but other than drawing attention because of the dress, she wasn't sure what that was.

Their gazes met and locked, and she reached out to him with her eyes, baring all the emotions she was feeling in her heart. His usual sea-blue eyes darkened like a tempest and his arms tightened around her.

Their attraction to each other was visceral. There was no way either one of them could deny it.

And she no longer wanted to.

"Simon," she breathed.

"Miranda, I—"

He dropped his arms to his sides, his fists clenching and unclenching, his breath coming in uneven puffs.

"This isn't going to happen."

It wasn't a definitive statement by any means. He sounded like he was trying to convince himself.

From her perspective, it *was* happening, and there was nothing either one of them could do to stop it. Their relationship was like a boulder let loose at the top of a high hill, gaining momentum as it tumbled down the side of the mountain.

Sure, they were polar opposites in every way, but if anything, that only made them stronger as a potential couple. He made up where she was lacking, and she liked to think she lent strength to him when he needed it, although she was clearly failing in that now.

He'd been through so many trials in his life. Surely a trio of overzealous testosterone-filled men wasn't going to trip him up from what could be a really good thing.

That wasn't the Simon she knew.

He was a fighter, a scrapper. He'd told her that himself. He stood up for what he believed in, and just now, when their gazes had met, she'd been certain he believed in *her*.

In *them*.

But then he was striding away from her with long, determined steps, headed straight for the door.

And he didn't look back.

Chapter Twelve

Simon hadn't run away because of anything the guys had said. He had *walked* away to give Miranda the opportunity to discover her freedom. To dance with other men and flutter around the room like the butterfly she was.

This was all about her. But he couldn't stand there and watch it.

He cared enough to walk away before their hearts became any more entwined than they already were. He'd felt the tug of his heart and the undeniable chemistry every time their gazes met, and he knew it wasn't all one-sided.

She cared for him, too.

Mason had encouraged the relationship. He might even have mentioned it to Miranda. But Mason was wrong.

And the guys at the dance, well, they were jerks, but they were spot-on.

Simon wasn't good enough for Miranda, and even

more so because she came part and parcel with that beautiful set of twins.

He was just a poor, simple cowboy.

What could he offer her?

Nothing but his heart.

And while that might work out in romantic movies, this was real life. Miranda might have her own financial resources and not need someone rolling in dough, but—especially because of the twins—she needed a man with a strong, steady lifestyle, which was the furthest possible thing from Simon's constantly-walking-on-a-tightrope herding operation and canine rescue.

His dogs used to be enough for him, but now his heart had grown to make room for Miranda and the twins, and when they weren't there, he felt all empty inside.

But that was his problem.

Miranda would probably be happier with a man who smiled when he saw the sun rise, and she definitely needed a man with a firm faith in God's goodness.

Simon had been privately working on that part of it—cracking open the Bible Edith McPherson had given him when he graduated high school, and taking baby steps in the prayer department.

His prayers weren't anything formal. They were more like a running commentary with God while he worked with his rescues or groomed his cattle dogs.

When he'd sent his first tentative prayer heavenward, he'd expected it to ricochet right back down at him. Instead, he'd felt a quiet acceptance in his heart. No fireworks. Nothing he could put a name to, or share in words, but a sweet, silent something nonetheless.

He had yet to talk himself into attending a church service, but he figured that was probably the next step down the line somewhere. In the meantime, he just kept talking to the Lord, mostly about Miranda and the twins, because he had no idea what to do next where they were concerned.

A little divine guidance would be great. But since that wasn't likely to happen, Simon just kept to himself.

Mason had called on Tuesday to make sure everything was all right. Apparently, Miranda had taken the twins home not long after he had left. Simon felt bad about that. He hadn't meant to ruin the occasion for her.

He'd assured Mason that all was well, even though his life was far from it. He had hunkered down at his ranch and had spent the entire week putting the finishing touches on the training of the rescue dogs who would be taken to the adoption event.

Only a week and a half before the Saturday event, and he still had so much to do—washing, grooming and making every pup look their best. Saturdays were always Wildhorn's busiest shopping days, even when it wasn't one week before Christmas. Of all the adoption events he sponsored during the year, Christmas was his best season. With a careful vetting of owners, a dog could be the perfect gift—one that would give years of love and joy to their forever family.

He was too busy to think about anything else besides the upcoming event—or at least that was what he'd told Miranda when she'd texted him about rescheduling the zoo.

The truth was, he didn't know how he was going to explain his actions at the party when he saw Miranda next, and he was dragging his feet because of it. He had to say something, but he didn't know what. He had answered her text with a cryptic one of his own, and from then on, he'd let her phone calls go to voice mail.

After a couple of days she'd stopped calling. He figured she'd probably given up on him. All the better for her.

But he was still the twins' godfather. He would have to face Miranda sometime, work things out and get over the awkwardness he was feeling.

Just not today.

He was elbow deep in soap suds trying to turn Zig and Zag back into the West Highland *white* terriers they had been before their most recent roll in the mud, when his phone buzzed in his back pocket.

It was probably Miranda again. He wished he had never insisted that she put his number on speed dial. She was punching that call button way too often.

At least this time he had a valid reason for letting it go straight to voice mail, and not just that he was pretending the phone wasn't buzzing at all.

But when his phone rang again five minutes later, Zig and Zag were towel dried and zipping through the house chasing each other.

Simon pulled his cell out and checked the screen.

It was Mason. No doubt calling to check up on him again.

Maybe Miranda had put him up to it.

He sighed and answered.

"Still fine," he said instead of hello.

"What?"

"I've been busy. I built an eight-foot privacy fence

across my southern border, and the big adoption event is next weekend. That's why I haven't been answering my phone."

Wow. And how lame of an excuse was that? It sounded terrible even to him.

"I have no idea what you're talking about, buddy," Mason said.

"Oh." Simon had just assumed Mason was calling on Miranda's behalf. "What's up, then? Are the twins okay?"

"You should really be asking Miranda that question, but yes, the twins are fine. I'm calling about the neighborhood watch."

"Someone caught the pranksters?" he asked hopefully.

Mason paused. "Not exactly. They've, er, struck again."

Simon groaned. "What now?"

"You have to see it to believe it. They've hit Tumbleweed Avenue again, and this one's a doozy."

"Nobody saw them?"

"Not to my knowledge."

"How is that possible?"

"Search me. But you need to see it."

"I'll be there in ten."

"Can you do me a favor and call Miranda for me? I'm sure she's going to want to see this, too. And tell her to bring her camera."

Simon knew he was being set up. There was no reason Mason couldn't just call her on his own phone.

"Is it that bad?" he asked.

"Not exactly," Mason hedged again. "Look. Miranda

isn't at home and I'm not sure where she is, only that she has the twins with her."

"Yes. Yes. I'll call her. I'm sure she'll want to be there. She's part of the neighborhood watch."

A *reluctant* part. She was more likely to want to see what the *artists* had done.

He hung up with Mason and punched in Miranda's number. He didn't expect her to pick up, since he'd been avoiding her phone calls all week, but the phone only rang once before he heard Miranda's warm alto on the other end.

"What's up?" she asked cheerfully.

Why was it every time he thought she'd be upset with him—like right now, for example, when she *should* be ready to rake him over the coals—she surprised him with her positive attitude?

He sighed. She practically beamed sunshine. He had such a long way to go.

"Mason asked me to call you."

"Oh." Her voice dropped. He thought it might be disappointment.

"I'm sorry I didn't call you back earlier in the week. The adoption event is next weekend and—"

"You don't have to explain yourself. But I am kind of right in the middle of something. I'm taking pictures of the church youth group. They're waiting on me. So if you've got something to say, just say it."

"Where are you?"

"At the park. Why?"

"Apparently, the Triple H pranksters struck again."

"You're kidding. What is it this time?"

"I'm not sure. Something on Tumbleweed Avenue. Mason said to make sure you bring your camera."

"Okay. I'm just finishing up here. I'll meet you on Tumbleweed."

"Are the twins with you?"

"Of course. Always."

Despite all the promises he'd made to himself throughout the past week, Simon's heart warmed at the thought of seeing his three favorite people again.

It was hopeless.

He was hopeless.

A lost cause.

He could no more stay away from Miranda than he could stop breathing.

Unless he moved somewhere far, far away.

Like Mars.

Miranda took a few more snapshots of the youth group under a large elm tree and then pulled them in for a meeting to let them know something had happened on Tumbleweed Avenue again and their assistance might be needed.

They responded as enthusiastically as they always did. Much of the youth group's time was spent doing service projects. They were always ready and willing to help.

As was Miranda.

She packed the twins up in her SUV and made quick time to the main street. Anticipating similar circumstances to the last time around, she parked a couple of streets down from the road, set up the double stroller for Harper and Hudson, and then set off on foot the rest of the way.

She was curious about what kind of prank had caused Mason to suggest she bring her camera, but mostly, she was just anxious to see and talk to Simon.

He couldn't ignore her if they were face-to-face, as he had done with her texts and phone calls. And she needed to speak with him urgently, because after much reflection, she thought she had figured out what had set him off so vehemently and caused him to leave the party in such a rush.

Well, she'd known what the problem was from the moment it had happened. But now she'd come up with, if not a solution, then at least a suggestion that would ensure they spent lots of time together *and* possibly help his beloved dog rescue to be even more success-ful than it already was.

She wasn't ready to give up on Simon yet, even if he apparently was ready to give up on her and the twins. She couldn't wait to share her thoughts with him and see if his reaction was as positive as she hoped it would be.

As she turned onto the avenue, her mind was dis-tracted with thoughts of how she was going to explain to Simon why they needed to work together, but as soon as she caught her first glance of it and looked around, she gasped in surprise.

Tumbleweed Avenue had been TP'd from one end of town to the other. Miranda couldn't even begin to imagine how many rolls of toilet paper the kids must have used.

But the work they'd done was breathtaking. Simply

and utterly amazing. It must have taken them most of the night. How no one had seen them was a mystery.

No wonder Mason had wanted her to bring her camera. The teenagers had strung toilet paper from one old-fashioned lamppost to the next, all the way down the street on both sides, carefully twisting and mimicking garland. The poles had all been wrapped from top to bottom to look like candy canes. Above the doors of every shop and business were enormous, intricately tied toilet paper bows.

The entire avenue was the epitome of warm, blessed Christmas spirit. It screamed merry and bright, highlighting the already-decorated avenue and bringing it to new heights of artistry.

She focused her lens on the artwork and started snapping photos.

"At least this won't take as long to clean up" came Simon's deep, clearly annoyed voice from behind her.

"But it's beautiful. Surely, we don't have to wreck it yet. No one else seems to be in a big hurry to do so."

Simon picked off his hat and shoved his fingers through his hair.

"I have to admit this is pretty impressive. They went to a lot of trouble. But I can't help but wonder what's next."

Miranda realized that would always be the question with Simon—what was coming next and would that something be worse than the last time?

"I think we can gather from this project that these kids mean no harm to the town," she assured him.

Simon didn't immediately reply. Instead, he busied

himself taking Harper out of the stroller and swinging her into the air, smiling when she squealed in delight.

"I've missed these little ones."

Miranda noticed that he didn't say anything about missing her.

But that was where her idea came in—making herself useful to him until they got over this bump in the road. Until he *did* miss her when she wasn't around.

"I've been thinking a lot about your adoption event," she started. "I want to help."

His gaze widened in surprise. "Yeah? How's that?"

"I think I may have come up with a new, possibly better way to advertise—not only for this upcoming event, but for the future."

"I have posters on all the public bulletin boards and in the windows of some of the shops."

"Do they have pictures of your dogs on them—or better yet, photos of dogs and children that suggest forever families?"

He shook his head, his gaze brightening with interest.

"Do you think that would help?" he asked.

"You know what they say—a picture is worth a thousand words."

"I can see where that would work," he said, but then frowned. "It's a little too late for this year, though."

"Well, if you would have picked up your phone…" she teased.

Even under the shadow of his stubble, she could see that his face stained red. "That was immature of me. I shouldn't have ignored your phone calls. I'm really sorry. I didn't know what to say. I wasn't sure how to explain why I left the party so suddenly."

"You don't have to explain anything. I get it," she assured him.

"You do?"

She nodded. "It's forgotten. And as far as advertising for this year's adoption event goes, I don't see why it's too late for us to do something about it."

"You don't?"

"You have a printer with a copy function in your office, right?"

"Yes, of course."

"Happily, technology has increased by leaps and bounds in the last couple of decades," she ribbed. "No, but seriously. It won't take me more than an hour to do a photo shoot of the adoptable dogs and put together new posters for you. Then we can canvass the area this evening. It's perfect timing, really."

"You can do all that in such a short time?"

"Of course."

"But why would you want to, after the way I've treated you, I mean? You say you understand, but really, there are no excuses for my bad behavior."

"Then I forgive you." She grinned at him.

"Just like that?"

"Just like that," she assured him. "Now, we ought to get going. But I have to run by my cabin first."

"Why?"

"To pick up Christmas outfits for Harper and Hudson. They're going to be your Forever Family models."

"That's an awesome idea. Did I mention how wonderful you are?"

He embraced her and twirled her and the twins in their stroller around and around.

She'd never *literally* been swept off her feet before. She liked the feeling.

As he set her back on solid ground, she felt dizzy and off balance and she pressed her hands against his chest to steady herself. Their eyes met and his gaze darkened and dropped to her lips. His heartbeat pounded under her palm.

With infinite gentleness, he lifted his hand to frame her face and tip up her chin. He moved slowly, giving her plenty of time to respond.

And respond she did. When he tilted his head so his mouth was aiming for her cheek, she turned hers and met his lips straight on.

Surprise flashed through his gaze before his eyelids dropped closed and he slid his hand to the nape of her neck to pull her closer.

This time he clearly meant to kiss her on the lips, and he did—so thoroughly and wonderfully that Miranda thought she might have discovered a literal cloud nine.

Every thought, every emotion, every nerve, was in tune with his. She'd never felt more alive, more connected to another person. This was life in Technicolor and she wished she had a way to photograph her feelings and keep them forever.

"PDA much?"

Mason's laughing voice drifted slowly into Miranda's consciousness. "This ain't no kissin' booth. Now, granted, Charlotte and I thought y'all ought to figure this relationship business out, but in the middle of Tumbleweed when there's a crowd around? Really?"

"Go away, Mason," Simon said, his lips still hovering over hers.

Mason held up his hands in surrender. "Just sayin', Simon. It's a good thing you're kissing the photographer or your picture would be spread all over Wildhorn's social media by tomorrow morning."

Miranda would happily have taken that photo—*and* posted it on every social media account she had.

Simon groaned and pulled away.

He didn't like to be the center of attention, and she respected that, but she didn't care who was watching.

She wanted the whole world to know.

Chapter Thirteen

Simon held Hudson and Harper in his lap while Miranda decorated the miniature tree he'd just bought for this purpose. She hung little bulbs and strung red garland around it, then checked the lighting through the lens.

"I still can't believe you don't decorate for Christmas," Miranda said, putting a green hat on Hudson. His little Santa's helper suit and Harper's matching female elf would contrast nicely with Zig and Zag, the dogs Miranda adorably still thought of as *twins*.

"What would be the point? It's only me and the dogs, and they don't care that it's Christmas."

"Hello—Christmas spirit, where are you? What happened to getting in the mood for all things merry and bright?"

Simon snorted. "When have you ever known me to be merry and bright?"

But sitting here cross-legged with both of the twins on his lap and Miranda zipping around with unflagging energy and excitement, he thought he might be as close as he'd ever been to those feelings.

There was just something *right* about the four of them being here together. Next year he might even go whole hog—cut down a real evergreen and toss around some tinsel. And of course, he would hang a sprig of mistletoe, maybe a whole bunch of them, which he'd be pulling Miranda beneath as often as possible for a long time to come.

"This publicity campaign isn't just about Christmas," she commented, as if reading his thoughts.

He situated Zig and Zag, and then Miranda sat the twins back-to-back just behind the little dogs. She lifted her camera and took as many good shots as she could in the short amount of time she had before the twins started crawling away and the dogs got distracted.

"What do you mean, it's not just about Christmas?" he asked when she had a moment to hear what he said.

"I'm picturing this as an all-year-round solution. Photographing one or both of the twins with each individual dog. You don't have a website, do you?"

"I'm not much of a computer guy," he admitted, feeling once again like a simple cowboy living in a world far too small for a woman like Miranda. "Forever Family has a social media page, but there aren't many pictures on it and I don't update it very often."

"Well, there you go. We take cute pictures of the dogs and the kids and get them up where people can see them. If we update the website and social media page every time you get a new dog, I think you'll see a real uptick in your rescue efforts."

"And you'll be the one taking the pictures?" He held his breath as he waited for her answer.

She laughed. "Unless you want someone else to do it."

Simon didn't want *anyone* else. And he was beginning to imagine how this might work out after all. Miranda could take pictures of the dogs and help him with the rescue. He could care for the twins when she had photo shoots to do.

Was the inconceivable possible?

Because there had been all kinds of possibilities in their kiss.

"I'd like to get a couple of shots of the twins with Chummy," she said. "I know he's your dog and he isn't going to be up for adoption, but I would love for the world to see how much you care about even the wounded animals."

She'd just given him a solid opening to say what was on his mind.

Speaking of caring…

Miranda, I care for you.

I want you and the twins to be part of my life.

But the words wouldn't come. They got all tangled up in his head and never made it to his lips.

He sighed and whistled for Chummy.

The photos of the twins with Zig and Zag had turned out even better than Miranda had expected, and it was a simple matter for them to make and distribute the posters.

She spoke to a lot of people as they canvassed. Simon, not so much. As usual, he turned introspective when there were others around. But that was okay. She talked enough for the both of them.

She supposed that was another way she could help him with his rescue efforts—spreading the word with, well, *words*. Maybe the Lord had given her the gift of gab for a reason after all.

As a surprise for Simon, she'd blown up the photo of the twins with Chummy into an extralarge poster and had added the Forever Family logo in big letters. She thought they could use it for all of the adoption events and then in between events he could hang it on his office wall.

There was another thing, also, that she'd noticed when she'd been going through her snapshots, although she hadn't shared the information with Simon yet—and wasn't certain she should.

She didn't really have any definitive ideas on what her discovery could mean, anyway, and she didn't want to come to the wrong conclusion.

But as she'd sorted through the photos she'd taken of the church youth group, she'd noticed something peculiar carved into the trunk of the elm tree the youth had wanted their pictures taken under.

Triple H.

But that was hardly conceivable, was it, that the youths from the church would be responsible for all the mischief that had recently gone down in Wildhorn?

These youths were the best of kids, the teenagers who were always first in line to help whenever it was needed. Were they the young artists who were pranking the neighborhood?

One thing was certain. She wasn't about to share

her random, wild theories with Simon, anything that he might latch on to and act upon.

She wasn't even sure she was right. Anyone could have carved that tag into the tree. It didn't have to be the kids in the youth group. The teenagers probably chose the location under the elm tree because it was the prettiest place in the park.

With that, she let it go.

On the day of the adoption event, Miranda bundled up the twins and headed for Maggie's Pet Store, which was located right next door to Duke's Hardware. All of the shops along the main street were hosting sidewalk sales in conjunction with Simon's event, so there would be plenty of foot traffic and browsing.

Everyone from age zero to one hundred would want to look at the cute doggies—and hopefully some of the onlookers would fall in love with one of the pups and want to take them home to be part of their families.

Miranda had agreed to meet Simon at the pet shop because she already had her hands full with the twins, and he had volunteers coming out to his ranch to help transport the dogs to and from the event.

By the time she got there, Simon had the dogs secured in a dog yard where people could interact with them.

Already in cahoots with Miranda, Maggie Jennings, the pet shop owner, had pasted the oversize poster of Chummy and the twins in the window as a special surprise to Simon—the icing on the cake for what she hoped would be his most successful event ever.

As soon as Simon saw Miranda wheeling the twins toward him, he broke into a big grin. That happened more and more often these days, and Miranda's heart warmed as she grew nearer.

"You continue to surprise me," he said as she approached. "That poster that you made up—"

He swallowed hard and didn't finish his sentence. He didn't have to.

"You're welcome. I'm glad you like it."

"And I'm glad you brought Hudson and Harper with you." He crouched in front of the twins and kissed each of their foreheads. "Of course, you always do, don't you?"

"To be honest, I almost took up my mom's offer to watch them for me today because I'm not sure I'll be much use to you with two wiggly babies to take care of."

"Are you kidding? They are the stars of the show. If the puppies don't draw people in, the babies definitely will."

"You can count on that. Now what else can I do to help?"

"Talk to people? You know that's not my forte."

She laughed. "Ah, yes. But it is mine, isn't it? See how well we complement each other?"

He grinned and tapped the clipboard he was holding. "Send folks my way when the twins have sold them on a puppy. And don't forget to remind them that we deliver Christmas morning. We're as dependable as Santa Claus himself."

"This is so exciting, to think that so many of these precious dogs will go to families who will love them."

She couldn't believe how invested she'd become in Simon's work. She wanted him to succeed, not only for his own sake, but also for the canines he cared so much about. She wanted all the dogs to go to happy homes.

He reached a hand into the dog yard and was immediately surrounded by wet noses and furry ears.

"That's what it's all about," he agreed. "Finding a forever family."

Chapter Fourteen

The adoption event was by far the most successful Simon had ever held, which he entirely attributed to Miranda and the twins. Among the three of them, they had made all the difference in the world.

It was as easy for Miranda to engage people in meaningful conversation as it was difficult for him. And Harper and Hudson just had to giggle and flap their arms and look cute to get people to cross the street to see what was happening. They'd had a crowded sidewalk all day.

Altogether, they'd received paperwork from fifteen families, and in the week since, Simon had done his due diligence on each of the families and visited every home to give suggestions and make sure they were dog ready.

He couldn't believe it was Christmas Eve already. Where had the week gone? Time seemed to be rushing by at the speed of light when he wanted to slow down and savor every moment.

Maybe because, for the first time in his life, he felt happy.

Truly happy.

And he was going to attend the Christmas Eve service tonight to thank God for all His blessings. The end of this year marked a complete change in Simon's heart, in more ways than one.

He had a new yet sound and deep-rooted relationship with the Lord, one that he believed gave him hope and a future.

And that future, he prayed, included Miranda and the twins.

He hadn't breathed a word of his faith to anyone yet, because he wanted Miranda to be the first to know how much God was a part of his life now, just as she and the twins were. He knew she'd be thrilled with the news. As with all things, Simon was a private person, and up until today his faith had been between him and God, and the occasional conversation with Mason. He'd given himself time to let it grow and flourish.

Tonight that would all change. He planned to give Miranda the surprise of her life when he waltzed into the sanctuary of the church as if he belonged there— which he did. It was nerve-racking to think about, but faith didn't happen in a vacuum. Mason and Charlotte would also be over the moon with the news. He knew they'd been praying for him for many years, and he would be happy to report that their prayers had been answered.

But even Christmas Eve wouldn't be as exciting as Christmas morning would be. Adrenaline pumped through him as he went over his plans in his head. He'd driven to another town earlier this week to purchase an engagement ring, knowing if he'd gone into the local jewelry store, the news would be all over town by the end of the day.

He'd kept the secret—and the ring—close to his heart, both literally and figuratively, in all the days following. Right in his shirt pocket. He might not be as creative as Miranda, but after much thought, he believed he'd put together a proposal she would never forget.

His affection for her had grown over the month and a half they'd been together. He'd only had to get out of his own way and be willing to put a label on it.

He was in love with Miranda.

He hoped and prayed she returned the sentiment. He would know for sure tomorrow morning. It would either be the best Christmas present ever or the worst holiday of his life. One or the other, and there was only one way to find out.

It was early in the day yet, but he kept checking his phone and glancing out the front window, anxious for Miranda to arrive at the ranch with the twins. They were coming over to help give all of the dogs a bath, and then the fortunate adoptees would be corralled out in the kennels until it was time to make Christmas morning deliveries.

He laughed when he thought of the twins helping with the baths. He remembered how wet his jeans had gotten with Harper in the tub. She might even be more enthusiastic as a "helper." He'd stocked up on extra towels, knowing his entire bathroom—and probably everyone in it—was bound to get soaked.

His heart warmed until he thought it might burst. How could a man possibly be as happy as he was right now?

After tomorrow he would have a real forever family

to care for and love, for as long as he lived. He would no longer be alone. And he planned to count his blessings every second of every day from now until forever.

Miranda honked as she pulled up in front of his place. He missed the high, piercing sound of her convertible, but he didn't think she ever thought about it at all. She'd adapted everything in her life to make room for the twins.

He counted to ten and then burst through the door and strode out to meet them. He didn't want to seem too eager, but he expected his expression was a dead giveaway.

Could he blame his joy on the holiday and the success of his adoption event, or would Miranda see right through him?

"I thought we'd better start with the adoptees," Simon said as he unhooked Hudson from his car seat. "If we don't get to the other dogs, it's no big deal. We can always wash them later. But I want the ones going to their forever families to look their very best."

"This is exciting," Miranda said enthusiastically as she took the helm of the bathtub, the sprayer in her hand. "I'm so happy for every one of these dogs."

"It's a good day for everyone," Simon agreed, handing her the first pup on the list. Miranda used the sprayer to wet the dogs and, with the twins' "helping" by splashing water all over the bathroom, soaped them up and hosed them down. Simon stood behind them with towels at the ready.

As he'd suspected, the water didn't exactly stay in the tub. Some of the dogs, like the labs, loved the water and didn't object at all to being bathed. Others, like the

Chihuahua, not so much. Taco looked like a miserable drowned rat when Miranda and the twins got through with him. But he was going to a wonderful forever home with a senior couple who had instantly fallen in love with him at the adoption event.

After the fifteen dogs were washed and kenneled, Simon brought Zig and Zag in for a bath.

Miranda's face fell. "They've been adopted?"

Simon nodded.

"Oh. I guess I was so busy I didn't see them at the adoption event."

"They weren't there. This is a private adoption. The family has a couple of kids who I think will really love the Westies."

She tried to smile, but it didn't quite reach her eyes. "I'm sure they will. The twins certainly like them. They'll be missed."

"Mmm."

He turned away from her. He just couldn't look her in the eyes right now. Her expression nearly broke his heart.

When Zig and Zag were bathed and were zipping through the house chasing each other in their usual method of blow-drying their fur, Simon pulled on his jean jacket. "I'm going to go feed the dogs and spend a few minutes with the ones leaving tomorrow. Do you want to come with me?"

"Very much. Just help me get the twins bundled up."

It took a few minutes to get the babies into their coats. Miranda was quicker than Simon and somehow managed to get Hudson's arms where they needed to go. Harper apparently didn't feel like wearing her jacket, because every time he got close to putting her arm in the appropriate sleeve, she'd pull away.

"Be a good girl for Uncle Simon and put your army through your sleevey," Miranda said, taking Harper into her arms. "You're just creating trouble so you'll get more attention, aren't you, little miss?"

Simon met Miranda's gaze and smiled.

"Remember that first day, when I told you I had concerns about you becoming Hudson and Harper's guardian?" he asked.

"It's hard to forget. You were pretty forthright with me."

"Rude, you mean."

"Your words, not mine." She laughed.

"I was also wrong. Very wrong. You are a wonderful mother to the twins. It's been a blessing for me to watch you bond with them, and they with you. Mary's and John's deaths were a terrible tragedy, but they made the right choice in giving Hudson and Harper into your care. There's no doubt in my mind that you three were meant to be together."

Four, perhaps?

Her eyes brightened. "Do you really think so? I still have moments when I wonder if I'm doing enough for them."

"You love them with your whole heart, and they love you right back again. The rest of it is just icing on the cake."

"Thank you."

She ran a hand down his arm and every nerve ending came alive as she squeezed his hand. When their eyes met, it was all he could do not to steal a kiss, despite the twins perched between them.

He didn't want to give himself away, but she was just too beautiful to resist. He leaned in, intending to brush his lips across her cheek, but her gaze widened and she moved away before he could make contact.

His pulse jolted in surprise.

Did she not want him to kiss her?

If that was the case, this was going to be the worst weekend of his life.

"It's going to be dark soon," she said, fussing with Hudson's jacket. "We'd best get out and see your doggies."

He took Harper back into his arms and followed Miranda out the door, his mind rehashing every moment since the time they'd kissed right in the middle of Tumbleweed Avenue. He hadn't attempted to kiss her again until now, but she hadn't given him any reason to think she wouldn't welcome his affection.

What if he was all wrong about this?

What if she didn't return his regard?

He continued behind her toward the kennels, his head lowered in thought and his gaze on the ground.

He'd been alone most of his life, but until now, he'd never been lonely. Not until now. Miranda and the twins had filled his heart in a way he never could have imagined.

"Simon?"

Miranda came to a dead stop and Simon's boots skidded in the dirt to keep from running into her.

The sound of her voice—

Surprise.

A note of panic.

He looked up, his gaze following the direction of hers.

"Did I misunderstand you? Are the dogs in the barn and not the kennels?"

His heart fell into his gut, which was turning like a combine.

Oh, Lord, please. Anything but this.

The kennels were empty, and the gate to his property was swinging in the wind.

His dogs had vanished.

"You put the dogs into the kennels, right?" She was trying to keep the alarm she was feeling out of her tone but she knew she was failing miserably. Her heart was pounding wildly in her chest and her breath was coming in short bursts.

How could this have happened?

Simon's mouth opened and closed but no words came out. Miranda watched his face blanch under his stubble.

"Where are they?" he ground out coarsely. "Where are my dogs? I know I shut the kennel doors. And the gate—"

From a distance came the sound of barking. At first it was just one or two dogs, but then the chorus picked up and howling filled the entire neighborhood.

Simon scrambled for the barn. The door was open there, as well. Dash was still stabled, but the cattle dogs were missing.

All of them. Even the puppies.

"Someone's been in here. They stole the dogs. What am I going to do, Miranda?" His voice was coming in sharp, staccato bursts, his tone somewhere between panic and tears. "My whole life's work. They're all gone. If I lose the dogs, I've lost everything. I've got to go after them."

She reached for his hand to steady him.

"Before we go off half-cocked, let's go back inside and think things through."

"There's no time for that." Simon's voice had risen an octave.

"It's better if we stop and make a plan," she said, taking his hand and urging him to return to the house. She placed the twins in a portable playpen so they couldn't get into too much mischief and turned her attention fully on Simon. "There's two of us. If we split up, we can cover more ground, as long as we're not crossing over each other. And I'm not positive the dogs have been stolen. With the cacophony out there, it sounds like your dogs are all over the neighborhood. I think they got out on their own somehow and escaped through the gate."

He groaned. "That's even worse. I don't know how that could have happened. I know I shut the kennels tight, and the gate was closed when I came back inside the house.

"If they're running all over town, I'll never get them all back. Think of all the kids who won't get their puppy on Christmas morning. And my herding dogs—I can't replace them. And even if I could, I was training a few ranchers' dogs for them. What am I going to tell them? That I lost their expensive cattle dogs?" He sank onto the couch and put his head in his hands. "I'm done for. Finished."

"I don't believe that." She had no idea how she was

going to fix this problem, but Simon was *not* going to lose his life's work in one fell swoop. She would do anything in her power to see that didn't happen.

She had to figure this out, and fast.

"The kennels were open. The barn door was open. And so was the gate. If it wasn't someone trying to steal your dogs, then—"

"It was the pranksters," Simon finished for her. "I told you things were going to get out of hand. I just didn't realize I'd be the victim."

His words could have been an accusation, but they weren't. They were more of a statement of fact, as if he had already given up.

"Simon, listen to me. The pranksters. I think I know who they are."

His head snapped up. "You *what*?"

Now she had his full attention. His eyes blazed into hers.

"What do you mean you know who they are? You're part of the neighborhood watch team. You were supposed to report them to me if you caught them in action."

"Well, that's just it. I didn't exactly catch them in action. I—"

She paused. "It will be easier for me to show you than to tell you. Can you watch the twins for a moment while I go get my camera?"

He nodded, his expression stony. Harper and Hudson were contentedly playing in the pop-up playpen Simon had bought for use at his house.

He was going to blame her for this—and maybe he'd be right in doing so. She *was* a member of the neighborhood watch. She should have told Simon about her theory as soon as she'd discovered it herself.

But she'd stayed silent, and now, because she hadn't spoken up when she first found out, Simon might be losing everything that was dear to him.

She couldn't imagine why the church youth group teens would play a cruel prank like this. They had to know how important Simon's dogs were to him, even if he wasn't a member of the church.

Simon was right. The pranks had gone from innocent to harmful.

But one piece of the puzzle didn't fit.

There was nothing artistic about letting dogs loose.

She stopped just short of Simon's porch and looked around for clues. What had the teenagers meant by this cruel act? Was it possible it was even the same people, or was it someone who'd taken advantage of the teenagers' mischief to do something harmful that they'd be blamed for?

"Hold on a moment," she said, racing outside to get her camera from the car. As she approached the porch, she took a determined look around. Her heart fell when she saw the evergreen wreath Simon had hung on his door. Inside, someone had placed a carved wooden Triple H.

So it was the youth group.

"I'm so sorry," she said as she reentered the ranch house. "This is all my fault. I knew who it was, and I didn't say anything."

"How *could* you?"

She understood why he was directing his anger at her, and she didn't blame him for it in the least.

She pulled up the photos on her camera and found the ones she'd taken of the youth group under the elm tree in the park.

"What am I looking for?" Simon asked. "Is this the bunch of kids who just ruined my life?"

"This is the church youth group," she admitted miserably.

"The church youth group?" he parroted. "I don't believe it."

"Neither did I. That's why I didn't say anything. But if you look at the trunk of the tree just above where the teenagers are standing, you'll see a carving of the Triple H brand."

"How long have you known? Why didn't you tell me?"

"Because I thought it must be a mistake. I rationalized my way out of my original conclusions. I figured that anyone could have put that mark there. It didn't have to be the youth group."

"Which is true."

"Yes, except they specifically asked me to photograph them under that tree. I think it might have been a joke to them."

"I'm not laughing."

"Neither am I," she agreed gravely.

"What now?" He shoved both hands into his hair. "We both go and canvass the neighborhoods looking for the dogs? Even if I find some of them, I don't see how I can recover from this."

"Not if it's just the two of us. Let me make a phone call. We need all the help we can get."

She went into the kitchen to call Pastor Corbit. She

had an idea, but she wasn't sure Simon would go along with it. She thought it was better that she just put the plan in motion and then tell him what it was.

She returned to the living room a minute later.

"The youth group is on its way over. We'll mobilize them to canvass the neighborhoods in cars and on foot. And Pastor Corbit has contacted the prayer chain. Everyone in town will know to look out for your dogs."

"You're bringing the *pranksters* over here to look for my dogs?" he asked, astounded. "Why would you do that?"

"Because despite everything, I think they want to help. There are some things that still don't add up. There is nothing remotely artistic about what they've done today. I want to hear their explanation before I call in a judgment."

"I'm not as kind as you. I want to call the police, except that I'd end up with animal control coming out and I'll be the one taking the brunt of all this. Fat lot of good building the privacy fence along the south border did me."

"You already are." She brushed her palm across his face but he jerked away from her, refusing to meet her gaze.

"Let me talk to the youths. I think I hear some of them approaching now." She was afraid he might lose his temper with the kids before she was able to find out what had actually occurred. Somehow, she felt like there was more to the story than a group of teenagers sneaking onto a ranch in the dark and freeing all the dogs from Simon's rescue so they would run off into the night.

That just didn't sound right.

It wasn't long before the entire group was assembled out in Simon's front yard. She could tell by the looks on their faces that they were as appalled by what happened as she felt.

"Who wants to tell me what's going on?" she asked gravely.

They all looked at each other without speaking. After a few seconds a boy with his hair dyed as black as night stepped forward. Miranda recognized him as Owen Blake, the son of a local rancher.

"It's my fault. We all let the dogs out of their kennels, but I was the last one out. We heard a noise and thought someone was coming, so we left in a hurry. I must not have closed the gate correctly. I didn't mean for this to happen, Miss Morgan, but I'm the one to blame. The rest of the group isn't at fault."

Another boy stepped forward. "I opened the barn door. I got sidetracked by the puppies. I must not have shut the door behind me when I left. You can blame me, too."

"Let's not point fingers here. We're running out of time. Do you want to tell me why you all were here sneaking around in the first place?"

"The dog adoptions," a girl with a short blond bob said. Her name was Wendy, although Miranda couldn't remember whose daughter she was. "We brought out Christmas ribbons to put bows around their necks, since they'll all be presents for little kids. We let the dogs wander outside the kennels because we thought Mr. West would be sure and notice them that way. We had some extra ribbon left over, and we thought it might be a nice surprise for Mr. West if we put bows on his cattle dog puppies."

"That's lovely," Miranda said. "I knew in my heart you all were trying to do something nice."

"Yeah, but I messed it all up," Owen said miserably. "Now all of Mr. West's dogs are gone."

"We've already got the prayer chain going to let folks around town know to look out for stray dogs. We're asking ranchers to saddle up and check out their acreages. How many of you have cars?"

Several of the teenagers raised their hands.

"Go in small groups. Park at the end of a street and canvass the neighborhoods by foot. Let's designate a couple of you to bring Simon's dogs back to the ranch as you find them. Who has a truck?"

Nearly everyone who'd initially raised their hands when Miranda had asked about having a vehicle raised their hands again. This was the country, and most of the residents of Wildhorn were ranchers. Folks tended to own trucks over cars so they could tow horse trailers.

They quickly organized who was going where, and who would be bringing the dogs back to the ranch. Miranda was staying at the ranch and playing point person. Everyone put her cell number on their phone before they left.

After a few final instructions, she walked everyone out past the gate and waved as they took off down the lane, then decided to check the barn.

As she entered, she thought she heard a sound from the far end of the barn. It was already twilight and it was getting more and more difficult to see by the minute. Soon it would be full-on night. Miranda prayed most of the dogs would be found before then. She didn't want to think about what would happen to the ones who got away.

She pulled the gate of the farthest stall open, looking for the source of the sounds, and was delighted to see five little roly-poly puppies in a box half-covered in Christmas wrap with a roll of tape nearby. Someone had clearly moved them from the stall nearest the entrance, but it was equally obvious that that person had left in a hurry, just as the other teens had done. The puppies were all bedecked in red and green bows, crawling over each other as their mama paced around the box.

"Shadow," Miranda said, crouching to pet the blue heeler's neck. "Boy, am I glad to see you. And all of your puppies, of course. Let's get you back to the stall where you belong, so I can bring Simon some good news."

Chapter Fifteen

Just when Simon thought it couldn't get worse, it got worse.

He was sitting on the sofa, watching the twins play and waiting for Miranda to come back inside and tell him why the youth group had ruined his life. He expected she'd probably have some kind of fancy story to tell, giving him some reason she thought he ought to forgive them for what they'd done.

Was this how Jesus felt in the Garden of Gethsemane, when His friends had turned their backs on Him and He had lost everything?

He had no idea what he was going to do next. He supposed that partially depended on how many dogs they managed to round up, and how many would be lost to him permanently. It made him sick to his stomach just to think about it.

What was he going to tell all those excited children on Christmas morning, when they woke up and didn't find their puppy underneath the tree?

And what about the ranchers whose investments in

their cattle dogs had now disappeared under his watch? He didn't have the money to pay them back for what they'd lost, although he'd find the way to do it somehow, even if it took him years.

Chummy bumped Simon's hand with his wet nose, demanding affection, but Simon barely noticed. Chummy jumped onto the couch and burrowed in his lap, determined to make him feel better.

He sighed. At least he hadn't lost Chummy. And Loki was lying down by the fire. Zig and Zag were around somewhere, although now all of his plans with those two had been completely dashed to pieces on the rocks. With his life in ruins, he could not possibly ask Miranda and Hudson and Harper to be a part of it.

He'd lost his reputation.

He'd lost his dogs.

And now he was going to lose Miranda and the twins.

He didn't even know how to start over, but whatever he did, he wasn't going to drag Miranda down with him. She was loyal to a fault, and he knew she wouldn't abandon him in his time of need. But she would never know about his true feelings for her, because he was never going to share them with her.

She deserved better, and though it would shatter his heart into billions of pieces to let her go, he knew that was what he had to do. It was the *right* thing to do. He couldn't tell her how he felt now.

His cell phone chirped and jerked him out of his thoughts, startling him so much that he almost dropped it.

Good news?

Had someone found one of his dogs?

"Hello?" he said tentatively.

"How dare you let one of your dogs loose to roam about in the streets in the middle of the night."

Blanche Stanton. Exaggerating as usual.

"You've seen one of my dogs?"

"I have it right here. I found it wandering around in my bushes. A little gray fluffy thing. It doesn't bite, does it?"

"That's Sasha, my senior toy poodle mix, and no, *she* doesn't bite. She's one of the sweetest dogs I have."

How had Sasha gotten out? She wasn't even outside with the rest of them. She must have slipped off when he'd been distracted.

"Well, I don't appreciate her nosing around my house."

"Look, Blanche, it's been kind of a rough day. I'll come get her as soon as I'm able, okay? But it might be a little while."

"Don't bother," Blanche said gruffly. "I'm bringing her back to you. And I'm going to stay right there at your ranch until the animal control officer arrives. I've already called in to report you. Do you hear me?"

Simon didn't answer. His breath had been punched from his lungs.

He was in trouble. Big trouble.

Even if they found most of the dogs, he'd still be accountable for having let them escape, as well he should be. At the end of the day, he was responsible for every one of his dogs. And if they got into any mischief, it was all on him.

None of his dogs was unfriendly. They'd all passed the AKC Good Citizen's certification. But he knew some people considered dogs in general dangerous. Officer Peterson had given him a break last time he'd visited, but there would be no bending rules this time, especially with Blanche Stanton looking on.

"Guess who I found," Miranda said as she came inside the house.

He was leaning on his elbows, staring at the floor, and he didn't even bother to look up. He couldn't stand to look Miranda in the eyes right now.

Not because he was angry with her. He didn't know why she had kept her suspicions about the youth group a secret, but he was sure she had her reasons. The truth was, he didn't want to let her see him with tears in his eyes, in his greatest moment of weakness.

He was heartbroken.

"I found Shadow and her babies in one of the stalls in the barn," Miranda continued animatedly, but Simon couldn't wrap his mind around her words. "One of the teens must have moved them to the back of the barn, but they're safe and sound. All five puppies. I made sure the door was shut good and tight this time."

Shadow was safe. That was good news. And her puppies. Could he make a new start with one dog and her puppies?

"Simon, did you hear me? I found Shadow and the puppies. Isn't that good news?"

When he didn't respond, she sank down next to him on the couch and put her arm around his shoulders.

"This isn't over yet. We're working on getting all the dogs corralled as we speak. I've got the entire youth group out looking for them, and the church prayer chain is spreading the word throughout town to be on the lookout for stray dogs. It hasn't been that long. They can't have gone far. We'll get them all back, Simon. I know we will."

He held his cell phone up for her inspection.

"One dog has already been found. I just got off the phone."

"What? Well, that's good news, too, right?"

He shook his head.

"No. It's not. It's my toy poodle mix, Sasha. She wasn't with the adoptees. She must have skipped out when I was preoccupied and frantic about the other ones. The poor little thing is a senior, so the chances of adopting her out were always slim. But now..."

He groaned and scrubbed a hand through his hair.

"She must be scared to death," he finished, thinking of the poor dog cowering under Blanche's typically sour mood.

"But you said someone found her?"

He lifted his head and groaned again.

"I just got off the phone with Blanche Stanton. Apparently, she found Sasha wandering around in her bushes."

"Oh, no."

"Oh, no is right. I told her I'd come get Sasha when I had a moment, but she's on her way over with the dog as we speak."

"Well, that is nice of her—I guess."

"Not so much. She called Officer Peterson and reported me, and she intends to stay at the ranch until the officer does his duty and shuts me down for good. Hopefully it's not an arrestable offense. I don't really want to be dragged off in handcuffs tonight."

He was kidding, trying to lighten the mood a little bit, but Miranda turned as white as a sheet.

"I'm joking. About being carried off in handcuffs. Not about Blanche Stanton and Officer Peterson being on their way."

Miranda's phone rang and she held up a finger as she listened to whatever the person on the other end of the line was saying.

"One of the groups is heading in with the first load of dogs. Four of your cattle dogs. So we only have one more cattle dog to go, right? You have four females and two males, counting Shadow?"

He nodded. At least Shadow was the only one who had puppies at present. "And four that belong to other ranchers."

"We'll have to keep looking, then. The group coming in says they also have a handful of other dogs," she continued. "I've had text messages from all around town. Your adoptees are being found and picked up one after the other, Simon. Everybody is out looking for them. It's going to be okay."

For one short moment, he brightened. It was so easy to get caught up in what Miranda was saying that he almost believed everything *would* be okay.

But then he remembered Blanche and Officer Peterson.

Even if the dogs were all on their way back, which was unlikely, he still had to deal with the consequences. This wasn't going to go away just because he wanted it to. The entire town knew his dogs had gotten loose. Officer Peterson surely would have heard that it was more than just Sasha. And members of the youth group would be in and out of his ranch house all evening, delivering his dogs back to him—he hoped.

How would he explain *that* to the officer?

"I have an idea," Miranda said as if reading his mind. "I think I know how to work this out so that Officer Peterson has other things to think about than where your dogs are, or why you've got the youth group swarming around your house. But I'm going to need your help, and we're going to have to work quickly."

She paused dramatically. "We're going to throw a Christmas party."

Miranda wasn't sure how this was going to work out in practice, but in theory, everything looked great. They'd had to improvise, since Simon didn't have many Christmas decorations. She'd sent him outside to collect any greenery that looked even remotely Christmas-like. She hoped he would also get a good breath of fresh air while he was at it.

Owen had shown up with what was left of the ribbon they'd used on the dogs, and he and his small group set right to work making the living room look festive. She found an old disco light in Simon's linen closet—she'd have to ask him about that sometime—and she cut out and hung up a fake mistletoe sprig made from colored copy paper in the doorway between the living room and kitchen.

It wasn't perfect, but hopefully it would be enough.

She'd called each small group and let them in on the plan. After they had canvassed their assigned neighborhood, they were to return to Simon's ranch for the party. Afterward, they'd all attend the midnight church service together.

Amazingly, at last count there were only two dogs missing—one cattle dog and one rescue. Miranda held out hope that both of the final two would be found.

She lowered the lamps and turned on the disco light to red and green, which threw soft outlines across the ceiling and walls. She'd just plugged in her cell phone to Simon's surround sound so she could stream Christmas music when someone banged on the front door.

It didn't sound like teenagers. Miranda held up a hand to Simon to let him know she'd answer it.

Blanche stood on the doorstep, Sasha cradled in one arm. Her expression was somewhere between annoyed and exasperated.

"Do you know how hard it is to drive with a puppy on your lap?" she asked, pushing past Miranda and into the house. "Are you having a party in here?"

"Yes, and you're welcome to join us. I can take Sasha. She's a senior, you know, and not a puppy."

"She is?" Blanche glanced down at Sasha, but made no move to pass her into Miranda's outstretched hand. "Well, isn't that interesting?"

Miranda dropped her arm. If she wasn't mistaken, Blanche had drawn Sasha nearer to her. She'd thought the toy poodle would be afraid of Blanche, but they seemed to be getting on very well.

"Why don't you come on over and make yourself at home in this armchair?" she suggested, gesturing to the most comfortable chair in the room.

For the first time Miranda was seeing Blanche as a different person—a tired, lonely old lady in need of company. Once she'd been seated by the fire, she looked rather content watching the teenagers mingling, with Sasha curled up and sleeping on her lap.

Maybe she'd misjudged Blanche.

Time would tell.

She looked for the opportunity to pull Simon aside, but two new groups of teenagers arrived with bottles of punch and packages of Christmas cookies.

"Great idea, guys," she told them.

She peeked outside. The dogs slated to go to adoptive homes the next day were all back in the kennels, still wearing their festive bows. A few of them were a little worse for the wear from their nighttime jaunt, but nothing a washcloth and a little soap couldn't fix. They could deal with that in the morning.

Her phone buzzed. A rancher had found one of Simon's cattle dogs practicing on his herd. Miranda texted back that she'd send one of the teenagers out immediately to pick up the blue heeler and bring him back to the ranch.

Miranda wanted to pump her fist. One down, and only one to go.

No—wait.

Blanche had brought in Sasha, and Miranda had forgotten to count the toy poodle.

Unbelievable. Every dog present and accounted for. She couldn't wait to share the good news with Simon.

She found him leaning his shoulder against the doorway between the living room and the kitchen, his arms crossed over his chest and a despondent expression on his face as he watched the teenagers interact. The twins were wide-awake, and some of the members of the youth group had taken them from the playpen and were sitting on the floor with Hudson and Harper in their laps.

Any misapprehension she'd felt earlier when Simon had tried to kiss her dissipated. Up until tonight, she'd still questioned her ability to trust herself and her choices.

Miranda was done second-guessing herself—and Simon. She stepped in beside Simon and slid her arm around his waist, filling up the door frame. When he glanced down at her, she smiled, but he didn't return the grin, nor did he put his arm around her as she'd hoped he'd do. Apparently, he hadn't noticed the mistletoe hanging above them—or maybe she'd done such a poor job creating it that he couldn't even tell it *was* mistletoe.

Bad or good, no matter what, they were together. If they could work through this, they could work through anything.

But this latest news?

This was beyond great. It was fantastic. God was good.

"I've been tallying up the dogs that have come back in. We have five of your cattle dogs back in the barn, as well as the four you were holding in training. A rancher just found number six out herding his cattle for him. I sent one of the teens for him."

She felt the breath leave his chest.

"That's good. Great. But we'll have to wait and see what Officer Peterson has to say about what happened tonight. I'm responsible for that. Despite all the work I've done on the south fence, he still may take the dogs away. I wouldn't blame him, really. I can't have my dogs running around the neighborhood unsupervised. And there are still going to be disappointed children tomorrow morning if we don't capture all the rescues."

"There's absolutely no reason for Kyle to go to any trouble whatsoever. As soon as he gets here, I'll send him on his way. I came over to tell you that *all* of the adoptees are back in the kennels. Most of them still even look like they've been bathed recently, if you can believe it. You're still going to get to be every bit as dependable as Santa Claus," she said, remembering what he'd once told her.

Simon slid down the door frame until he was seated, clutching his knees to his chest and breathing heavily.

"Thank God. Thank God. Thank God."

She crouched next to him, her heart warming and swelling in her chest. She loved this man so much. The intensity of her feelings surprised her.

"Thank God, indeed."

"Where is Blanche? I saw her come in earlier."

"She's sitting in the armchair by the fire."

"Do you think she's going to give us any trouble? I'm already in enough as it is."

Miranda smiled softly. "I think you should go look for yourself."

Simon's eyes widened, but he stood and walked over to the armchair. Miranda watched as he bent over the woman. She was surprised at how long they spoke. Usually their conversations were short and abrupt.

He was shaking his head when he returned to Miranda's side.

"What's the verdict?" she asked.

"Turns out we're going to have sixteen adoptees

ready to go home to their forever families. It appears that Blanche now has a new best friend."

"Sasha?"

He chuckled. "Who would have guessed it, huh? Blanche being a dog person? Maybe we misjudged her."

"I think you're right. She's just a lonely old lady. And the teenagers? They didn't mean to let your dogs out. They were trying to put Christmas ribbons on all of them when they were spooked by a noise. I hope you can find it in your heart to forgive them."

"I'm still trying to wrap my mind around getting all my dogs back. They really jumped to it. Maybe the teens really were trying to spread Christmas cheer. Which means the other pranks were probably made in good fun, as well. I wouldn't have given them the chance to make things right."

"Exactly. It's not easy to forgive."

He narrowed his eyes on her, taking in her measure.

"Why do I feel like we're not talking about the youth group here?"

"Do you know why I left Wildhorn?" she countered.

"To become a celebrity photographer," he answered promptly, looking at her as if she was one cookie short of a dozen.

"To get away from you."

"What?"

"I know, right? You probably didn't give me a second thought, did you? And yet I ran away from Wildhorn to get away from you."

"I have no idea what you're talking about."

"You aren't the only one who's ever been the butt end of a mean, hateful joke. I've never been thrown in a Dumpster, but that doesn't mean that I wasn't affected by jokes—mean pranks."

"I hate to admit it, but all I vaguely remember about you is that you were my best friend's kid sister. It wasn't until much later that I…well…continue with your story."

"You don't remember setting me up, leading me to believe that you had asked me to your senior prom? That you and Mason wrote a note to me asking me to be your date?"

She took a deep breath. Even though she knew in her heart that Simon was a different man now, it was still hard to talk about her impressionable past.

"I was so excited that you'd finally noticed me, and I was just foolish enough not to confirm that date directly with you. Maybe if I had, you wouldn't have gone through with it."

"Oh, boy," he said, shoving his hand into his hair. "I think I see where this is going, and it isn't good."

"Right. I spent all of my savings on the prettiest dress I could afford. I got my hair done at a salon, and even splurged on my very first mani-pedi. I wanted to look absolutely perfect for you."

"I was such a jerk." His gaze flooded with sympathy.

"Of course, I wanted to make a grand entrance. I wanted you to look at me and see only me, just like in the movies. I waited at the top of the stairs for an hour until I heard you arrive. And then—"

"Then you saw me walk in with my real date to the prom."

"Yes. I was halfway down the stairs before I realized you and Mason had set me up. I'd never been more mortified in my life. As I was running up the stairs in distress, you and Mason broke out into loud laughter that cut me to the quick. By that point, I'd been crushing on you for two years, you know."

"You were? You did?" His mouth kicked up into a heart-stopping half smile.

"Don't look so smug." She swatted at his arm.

"That was seriously the reason you left town? Because of me? You had two years of high school left. Surely you moved on from one stupid prank."

"You still came to my house to hang out with Mason. I couldn't avoid you, and it took me a long time to put the incident in my past."

"But you aren't like me. You don't hold grudges."

"It's a learned art, one that I mastered over time, because I realized that keeping those feelings close was hurting me, not you."

"Did you ever confront Mason about this?"

"Eventually. It was easier to forgive my brother than the boy who broke my heart."

"Wow. Just—wow. I am so, so sorry."

"Don't be. I'm over it. But I hope you won't be too hard on the teenagers. They really meant well, no matter how it looked to us earlier. There was no malice intended."

He cringed. "Not like me, you mean."

She squeezed his hand. "I forgive you. I forgave you long ago."

She would have said more, but at that moment someone knocked on the door. The teenagers had just been letting themselves in without knocking, and the final cattle dog had been reported as returned to the barn—with the door double-checked as tightly closed—so Miranda had a pretty good notion of who was pounding so firmly.

She started toward the door but Simon stopped her. "I've got this one."

He let Officer Peterson in and shook hands with him. "I've been expecting you."

"Oddly, I had a number of encounters on my way to your ranch. I had the distinct impression your neighbors were trying to slow me down."

Miranda tensed, holding her breath and praying for Simon.

"They were," Simon confirmed. "They were trying to give me time to get my dogs back after they got loose. I'm sure you've heard. It was pretty much chaos tonight."

Miranda was surprised that Simon was so open and honest about what had happened, but she supposed she shouldn't have been. He'd always been the type of man to own up to what he considered his mistakes.

"And did you?" Kyle asked. "Get all of your dogs back?"

"I did. Would you believe, with the youth group's help, that we found every last one of them?"

"I'm happy to hear that. I know you've worked hard to build up your business and the rescue shelter. How did they get out, anyway?"

Miranda's gaze shifted back to Simon. She didn't know what he was going to say, but she trusted him enough to know he wouldn't purposefully get the teenagers in trouble.

He merely shrugged. "The gate got left open."

That was all he said. Not how. Not who. Just that it had been left open. And that was the truth.

"Well, all's well that ends well, I guess. Except I haven't yet spoken to—"

"Officer Peterson." Blanche stepped forward, Sasha tucked up against her chest. "I'm the one that called in with the complaint."

He nodded and pulled out his pad to take notes.

"I know, Mrs. Stanton. Please go ahead with your complaint. I'm sorry, Simon, but I do have to formally report this," the officer said.

"No worries," Simon responded.

"Put that notepad away," Blanche barked, waving her free hand at the officer. "I'm rescinding my complaint."

Officer Peterson's eyes grew large.

"You are? But—"

"But nothing, young man. Now, can't you see we're having a party here?"

"And you're welcome to join us, Kyle," Miranda said, stepping into the fray. She couldn't hide her smile at the way Blanche had turned everything around as easily as she'd stirred things up. "Although we'll soon be leaving for church for the midnight service."

"I'll be there. But I'd rather change into a suit. So if you'll excuse me, I'll be on my way."

As the officer walked away, Simon swept Miranda into his arms and hugged her so hard her feet left the floor.

"You are amazing," he whispered into her ear. "I thought my world had ended tonight. How did you do this?"

"With a lot of help from our friends," she said, gesturing around the room at the kids gathered in social circles.

"Oh, stop it, you two," Blanche said feistily. "You'll set a bad example for the teenagers."

"Speaking of which," Miranda said, "it's time for me to gather them all up and get to church. I don't like leaving your house such a mess, though. I promise I'll come over tomorrow and clean it all up."

"No, you absolutely will not. It's Christmas morning. You are going to spend Christmas at home with the twins."

"We're celebrating at Mason and Charlotte's house. I'm sure they wouldn't mind if you came, as well. There's bound to be plenty of food," she said hopefully.

"I would, but I'm afraid I have plans of my own."

"Oh." She hadn't expected that answer, and she didn't know how to respond, so she turned to the teenagers and flickered the lights to get their attention.

"It's time for us to go to the midnight service," she announced. "But before you leave, I would just like to thank you for all your help tonight. Thanks to you, we got every dog back where they belong."

The teenagers clapped and hooted.

"That said, I would like to organize one more service project. I think you'll all agree that today was pretty chaotic."

There were many nods and murmurs.

"So, to make up for it, tomorrow morning, you all are going to gather in the same groups as you did this evening and make some special deliveries. Since you like being sneaky so much—now you're going to do it for a good cause."

The teenagers cheered and started gathering their coats.

The youths who were holding Hudson and Harper handed them to Miranda and Simon, and everyone dispersed.

Owen approached, looking ashamed of himself.

"I just want to say again how sorry I am," he said to Simon. "I was the last one out of the gate, and I should have double-checked that it was closed properly. I would have felt really bad if you hadn't gotten all your dogs back."

Simon clapped the youth on the shoulder. "But we did. It's forgiven and forgotten, son. Now get yourself to church."

"I do have one more question," Miranda said before the black-haired young man turned away. "Owen, what's with the tag?"

"Tag?" he asked, his confused gaze sweeping from Miranda to Simon and back again.

Miranda's gaze met Simon's and they both burst into laughter.

Simon had been thinking the pranks might be gang activity, and Owen, who appeared to be one of the youth group leaders, didn't even know what a *tag* was.

"The brand," she clarified. "Triple H."

Owen grinned. "I'm surprised more people haven't figured it out by now, seeing as it's Christmas and all."

He paused and bobbed his dark eyebrows. "*Ho, Ho, Ho.* Triple H."

Miranda laughed so hard she snorted.

"Clever," Simon said, having a difficult time controlling his own laughter. "Miranda's right. Y'all *are* very artistic."

"Thank you, sir."

"Now, get on your way. We've got to get the twins bundled up. It's time for us to head for church."

Miranda turned to Simon, her mouth agape.

"Us?"

"Do you have a problem with that?" he asked, grinning.

"No, of course not. It's just surprising, is all."

He kissed her cheek.

"Isn't that what Christmas is all about? Surprises?"

She pressed a hand to her cheek where he'd kissed her and nodded.

"Then Merry Christmas, darlin'."

Chapter Sixteen

After the chaos and confusion of yesterday evening, Simon was glad he'd still been able to surprise Miranda by accompanying her to church. Her look of sheer delight was worth every time he had to bite his tongue not to give away his secret earlier.

Mason and Charlotte were pretty stoked to see him darken the door of the church, as well. They introduced him to everyone he didn't know and many whom he did, they were so happy he was with them.

If he'd surprised Miranda, she wasn't half as astonished as he'd been by his first real church experience—how welcomed he felt by the parishioners, and most especially how wonderful it was to worship God with them and sing Christmas hymns loud and strong, if a little off-key. He was sorry he'd missed out all these years, but now he'd come home.

Speaking of home, he had a lot to do this morning. He had *tagged*—laughing at his own pun as he did it each of the adopted dogs, and the teenagers had arrived to make their special deliveries. He enjoyed watching the excitement in their eyes at the prospect and realized some of them might appreciate volunteering for the shelter.

He'd always been a one-man band, depending only on himself to do all the work, but now he was beginning to realize that being all alone wasn't necessarily best. He couldn't imagine his life without Miranda and the twins. And now he'd have extra help from the teenagers who'd agreed to assist him in grooming and training the rescue dogs. The kids would be doing something both useful and fun, and that felt good, too.

After making sure all of the dogs got where they were supposed to go, with each teenager checking in by text when their present was delivered, he showered and dressed in jeans and his newest red chambray shirt. He wanted to look his very best today, so he'd picked a festive color that went along with the Christmas season, knowing Miranda would appreciate it even if this was all new territory for him. He'd never before in his life thought about what he was wearing. Any shirt and jeans would do.

But not today.

That was what having a wonderful woman in his life did to a man. She made him a better person, inside and out.

Complicated? Yes. But worth every crazy moment.

Combing his hair in the mirror, he rehearsed what he was going to say. He'd actually taken the time to write his speech down and memorize it. He intended to do this only once, and he didn't want to mess it up.

That was going to be the hardest part of the day—speaking his heart. But this day wasn't very well going to go the way he wanted it to if he couldn't get the words out of his mouth. He ran a hand across his jaw and nodded.

If ever there was a time for a man to speak up, this was it.

He was fairly certain Miranda had no idea what was coming. She'd looked a little stunned when he said he had other plans for Christmas morning, and he hadn't been able to tell her otherwise.

He hadn't wanted to hurt her feelings, and he knew he had. He felt sorry about that. But he *did* have other plans, and hopefully, by the end of the day, any sorrow she had felt by his supposed rejection would turn to joy.

Miranda sat in front of the Christmas tree with Hudson on one knee and Harper on the other. They were tearing into their presents like nobody's business. Somehow even at nine months they seemed to grasp the gift-getting idea, although Hudson was more fascinated with the wrapping paper and the boxes than he was most of the presents she'd given him.

Harper liked the toys, especially the ones with lights and noises.

"You probably thought that baby drum set sounded like a good idea at the time," Charlotte said with a laugh, "but mark my words, you're going to be regretting that purchase in less than a day."

"Don't worry," Mason said with a shrug. "Hudson will break it in a week. That's how it goes during these first few years."

"I'm going to enjoy every second," Miranda assured them. "This is the best Christmas I've ever had. It's so much fun with children."

"Isn't it, though?" Charlotte agreed, pulling her own toddler into her lap.

Miranda sighed happily and leaned back on her hands. With all the presents open, she could just sit back and enjoy her twins. She wished Simon were here, though. He would have liked watching Hudson and Harper open their gifts. And he would have laughed when Hudson tried to stuff a wad of wrapping paper into his mouth.

She couldn't imagine where Simon could be on this Christmas morning, now that the youth group was delivering his dogs, but he'd said he had other plans. More likely he just wanted to spend a nice, quiet holiday alone, without all the fuss children would make. He loved the twins to death, but she suspected he'd had way more celebrating already this year than he was used to.

"I think there's one more present for the twins to open," Mason said, looking mysteriously around the room, "but I've forgotten where I put it. Hold on just a second. If I'm not mistaken, I think I left it in the spare room."

"Did you hear that, my sweethearts?" she asked the twins. "There's one more present for you. Yay!"

Miranda clapped, and Harper clapped with her. Hudson picked up the excitement, pumping his chubby arms and babbling eagerly.

"This is heavier than it looks."

A jolt of adrenaline shot through Miranda and her pulse leaped into overtime.

That wasn't Mason's voice coming from behind her—it was Simon's.

"Simon," she exclaimed, peeking over her shoulder to smile at him. "I thought you weren't going to make it."

"Yeah, well, I have a very special delivery to make. You didn't think I'd forget the twins, did you?"

He hefted a large foil-wrapped box onto the floor in front of Hudson and Harper.

"Here you go, kiddos. Rip off the paper to your heart's content."

"You were watching?"

Simon grinned.

"The whole thing. I've been standing in the hallway for near on an hour now. I about lost it when Hudson crammed the paper in his mouth."

"Why didn't you come on in here and join us?" Miranda asked, wondering why Mason and Charlotte hadn't considered the same thing. She felt like she was missing something.

Mason's face gave away nothing, but Charlotte's eyes were sparkling.

Simon crouched by the box, waiting for the big reveal.

"This is why I didn't bring their gift out until now," he said cryptically, his killer half smile making Miranda's stomach flip over.

The box was rocking back and forth so hard Miranda was afraid it might tip over onto its side.

"Hudson, go easy on the present. It might be breakable."

But Hudson wasn't pushing on the box. Neither was Harper.

"Simon?" she queried.

"Wait for it." He held up a hand. "Wait for it."

A moment later Zig and Zag came tumbling out of the box, a big green bow on Zig and a matching red one on Zag. The twins squealed in delight.

So did Miranda.

"I thought you said you'd adopted these two out," she said. "A special, private adoption, as I recall. Did the family back out on you?"

"The family," he said with a smile, "is sitting right here in this room."

"You kept them for *us*?"

"Now, before you say anything, I know you said you didn't want to have dogs in the house, but—"

Miranda leaped forward and flung herself into Simon's arms, bowling him over and knocking both of them to the floor.

"Easy, there, sweetheart," he said, his blue eyes glowing with affection.

"I'm just so happy. I had decided to ask you if we could adopt Zig and Zag, since the twins love them so much, but before I had the opportunity, you said they weren't available. I was so disappointed."

"I'm glad you like them."

"Like them? I love them."

And I love you, she wanted to say. But Mason and Charlotte were in the room, and Simon was a very private person.

Today, though. Sometime. Maybe after dinner. She'd pull him aside and tell him how she felt about him. It was frightening, putting herself out there, but love was worth the possibility of being rejected.

And if he didn't feel the same way?

Well, she wouldn't make the relationship between

them awkward, no matter what. He was Hudson and Harper's godfather, and the very best male role model they would ever have. She'd never take that away from him, or the twins.

But she hoped beyond hope that he would say he loved her, too.

She stood and stretched. Her legs had gone to sleep holding both babies on them simultaneously.

"Shall I set the table for dinner?" she asked Charlotte, who was laughing at one of her own children's antics as they all gathered around the overexcited Westies, who were wagging their tails so hard their entire back ends were moving.

"What? Oh, well, of course, later. But... I think there's another present that hasn't been opened yet."

Another one?

Nothing could *possibly* top Zig and Zag. They were the highlight of Christmas morning, one she would remember for the rest of her life. She hoped Charlotte wouldn't be too disappointed if the twins didn't show much interest in whatever new gift was about to be presented to them. She doubted they'd be interested in much of anything besides the dogs for the rest of the week, at least.

And then they'd grow up together. Hudson and Zig. Harper and Zag.

She reached down and scratched Zig's ear and he nuzzled her hand.

Cute little thing. She couldn't imagine how she ever thought she wasn't a dog person.

"I don't know why it's taken me so long to—"

She had been going to say she realized that she was

indeed a dog person and couldn't imagine why she hadn't had a pet before now, but when she turned, it was to find Simon on one knee, a red velvet box in his hand.

And in the box…

She never finished that sentence about the dogs.

"Simon?"

Yes. Her answer was yes. He didn't even have to ask her the question.

But when she held her left hand out to him, he shook his head.

"Not yet. I've got this speech I wrote and memorized and I'm going to say it before I lose my nerve."

He'd written a *speech* for her?

And even more surprising, he was going to give it to her in front of Mason and Charlotte and all the kids?

She knew what it took for him to do that. And yet for her, he was pulling out all the stops, getting out of his comfort zone to impress her. The warmth in her heart was the most wonderful feeling she had ever experienced.

"Okay," she said, dropping her arm to her side. "Continue."

He cleared his throat.

"As you know, I've spent most of my life alone, living what was basically a completely solitary existence, with the exception of my dogs. And I was fine with that, up until the day I walked into a room and saw the most beautiful woman in the world stretched out underneath a made-up sheet tent, reading a fairy tale to my two favorite godchildren, loudly sipping a box of juice through a straw and munching on a cheese stick."

"Your only godchildren, I think," Mason said with a laugh.

"Hush, you," Charlotte warned. "This is so romantic. Don't ruin it. *You've* never written me a speech."

Mason snorted.

Simon was still gazing up at Miranda, his face turning as red as his shirt.

"I think we ought to let him finish," she suggested. If he felt anything like she did, breathing was an issue right now.

"I was really hard on you when you first came to town. But it didn't take me long to realize how dedicated you are to Hudson and Harper, how much you love them, and how much they love you. And along the way somewhere, I realized—"

He stopped and forced himself to breathe evenly a few times, inhale and exhale. Miranda was breathing right along with him, afraid if she didn't, she might pass out from the sheer excitement of it all.

A speech was great and all, especially from a man who usually never put more than two words together, but she was anxious to get to the part about the ring.

"I—I realized—"

He stopped again.

"I love you," she blurted, letting him off the hook. "I've never known a man with as much loyalty and honor as you have. And I so admire how much you love Hudson and Harper. I feel like I should pinch myself to make sure I'm really here and not just dreaming this."

Simon cringed. "Please don't do that."

He stood and reached for her left hand, slipping the diamond solitaire on her finger. It glinted in the light as she showed it off to Charlotte. She couldn't wait to take some pictures of it. Simon would have to deal with having her joy posted on social media, just this once.

"I forgot the rest of my speech."

She framed his face in her hands, relishing the feel of the shadow of his beard under her palms.

"You don't need a speech. I only want to hear three little words from you."

"Marry me, please?"

She laughed and kissed him.

"That wasn't quite what I had in mind."

"I'll try it again, then." He placed his hands over hers and brushed his lips over her mouth.

"I love you."

"That works for me."

"I love you."

"You said that already."

"I love you. And I'm just getting started here. I love you." He chuckled. "You're going to hear that every day for the rest of your life, probably several times a day, now that I've got the hang of it. I'm going to do everything in my power to be the best husband to you and the best father to the twins that I can be, with the Lord as my guide."

"Oh, Simon," she breathed as he kissed her again. Then she turned and picked up Hudson. "Did you hear that, little man? Uncle Simon is going to be your new daddy."

"And you, sweet miss," said Simon, swinging Harper into the air and then kissing her cheek several times until she giggled, "aren't going to get to date until you're thirty. I never played baseball, but I have a bat."

"I say the same thing about my girls," Mason said approvingly.

"I'm so happy for you both," Charlotte exclaimed, embracing them in a big hug. "I've had a feeling about you two since the very beginning."

Miranda didn't know about the *very* beginning. Simon hadn't even liked her then. But she was looking forward to seeing what the future would hold for the four of them.

"Our forever family," she murmured.

Simon grinned and wrapped her and the twins in his big, strong arms, kissing each one of them in turn and lingering with Miranda.

"I like the sound of that," he whispered over her lips. "Our forever family."

* * * * *

THE COWBOY'S
FAMILY CHRISTMAS

Carolyne Aarsen

For my grandkids.
You've taught me a whole new huge kind of love.

But as for you, ye thought evil against me;
but God meant it unto good, to bring to pass,
as it is this day, to save much people alive.
—*Genesis* 50:20

Chapter One

It was a surprisingly balmy Tuesday for November.
Fall seemed reluctant to leave and Leanne Walsh was
fine with that. She had too much to do on the ranch.

Late afternoon sunshine softened the day, creating
gentle shadows on the Porcupine Hills of Alberta. A
chill cooled the air, a threat of winter coming. Leanne
hoped it hung off for at least a week. They still had
cows to move down from the upper pastures and then
had to process them.

Her son, Austin, sat astride the palomino mare his
grandfather purchased a half a year ago when Austin
was only two. Leanne had protested the expense but
George Walsh insisted that Walshes learned to ride a
proper horse as young as possible.

Now Austin was laughing down at her, his shock of
brown hair falling over his forehead, his chubby hands
clutching the saddle horn, the cowboy hat he'd gotten a
couple of weeks ago clamped firmly on his head. Since
George had given it to Austin, he'd worn it nonstop.

"He looks comfortable up there." George stood by the fence, his arms hooked over the top rail, his battered cowboy hat pushed back on his head. Though he was only fifty-eight, Leanne's father-in-law looked twenty years older.

Life had knocked a lot out of the man, Leanne thought, acknowledging his gruff comment with a tight nod. He'd lost his first wife to cancer and was left with a young son, then he was abandoned by the second wife, leaving him with another young son. Dirk, his eldest son and Leanne's late husband, now lay buried in the graveyard abutting the church in Cedar Ridge, and the son of his second marriage, Reuben was so far out of George's life, he may as well be dead.

"Is that mare favoring her one leg?" George asked, concern edging his voice.

Leanne watched more carefully as the horse walked, each footfall of Heart's Delight's hooves raising small puffs of dust in the round pen. "I can't see it," she said glancing up at her son again, the sight of him pulling her mouth into a full smile. "But I'll keep an eye out."

"Not always easy for someone like you to catch that kind of thing."

Someone like you.

Though Leanne knew he spoke of her ability to read horses, those three simple words had the power to make her shoulders hunch and her hands clench the halter rope.

Those three words held a weight of history behind them. George had tossed them at her when he discovered that she, a Rennie, daughter of one of the most hated and useless men in Cedar Ridge, dared to think she could date his favored son, Dirk Walsh, let alone marry him.

"I know enough about horses to see if one is lame or not," she finally returned. "And if you have any further concerns, we can bring it to see Tabitha or Morgan." Her sister held an equine specialist degree and her fiancé, Morgan Walsh, was a vet. Together they were starting a new vet clinic on some acreage Tabitha owned close to town.

"Morgan doesn't even have his clinic done yet," George groused.

"It will be. But for now they can still diagnose any problems Heart's Delight might have."

George's only reply was a slight curl of his lip and she fought the urge to defend her sister. Leanne knew it was only because of her marriage to Dirk and because of his grandson, Austin, that George tolerated her presence.

Which had made her even more determined to prove herself to him. Prove she was worthy. As a result she spent every available minute working on the ranch. Showing that she could ride and rope better than any hired hand they had, including their latest, Chad. She did the bookkeeping and dealt with the accountant.

"Is Chad coming again tomorrow?" Leanne asked.

Their new hired hand had started a couple of days ago but hadn't come to work yesterday and called in sick today. Which made her wonder if she would have to start looking for another hired hand all over again.

"He said he would. Though I don't know why you

hired him. He doesn't know much about cows or horses," George grumbled.

"He's willing and I think he can be trained." She wanted to say more but the sound of a truck engine caught both their attentions.

The ranch was nestled in a valley, well off the main road snaking through the hills. People arriving at the ranch had to drive along a switchback road that traversed the hill leading down to the ranch. If they didn't know the road, it could be trouble. And this person was driving far too fast.

"Idiot is going to overshoot the second turn," George muttered, pushing away from the fence, irritation edging his voice. "Probably some salesman who doesn't know how to drive his fancy truck in the back of the beyond."

But whoever it was seemed to know the road because, in spite of the speed of the vehicle, the truck easily made it around the corner and then down the tree-lined road toward the ranch. It suddenly slowed at the cattle guard, and as it rattled across, unease niggled through Leanne.

Though the driver seemed familiar with the approach to the Bar W Ranch, Leanne didn't recognize the black truck with the gleaming grill getting coated with dust.

It made the tight bend past the house, then came toward the corrals. As the driver killed the engine, silence fell again.

The door opened and a tall, broad-shouldered man stepped out wearing a cowboy hat over his collar-length hair. Sunglasses shaded his face and he dropped a cell phone into the pocket of a worn twill shirt, the sleeves rolled up over muscular forearms. Faded blue jeans hugged his hips and his boots were scuffed and worn at the heel.

He started walking toward them with the easy rolling gait of a man who had spent time on a horse. Definitely not a salesman.

"Can I help you?" George asked, the irritation in his voice shifting to aggression.

Leanne groaned. *Please, Lord*, she prayed as she led Austin and his horse to the rail fence, *don't let this be one of the officials from the association who promised to come and visit someday.*

Seeing George in full-on Walsh mode wouldn't help their cause. She was the temporary secretary for the Cedar Ridge Rodeo Group. For the past couple years the group had tried to get their town's rodeo to be a part of the larger Milk River Rodeo Association. They needed all the goodwill they could muster.

"This is private land," George continued as the man drew closer.

"Here, punkin, why don't you come down?" Leanne asked, tying up the horse and reaching for Austin. She had to intervene before George took a notion to grab the shotgun stashed in the barn behind them.

Leanne lifted her son over the fence, clambered over herself, picked Austin up, then hurried over to where her father-in-law stood, hands planted on his hips, head thrust forward in an aggressive gesture. "What's your business here?" George growled.

But the stranger was unfazed by George's belligerence. A slow smile crawled across his well-shaped mouth, shaded by a scruff of whiskers, and the unease in Leanne grew.

"Hey, George," the man said, sweeping his sunglasses off, tucking them in the pocket of his shirt and flicking his cowboy hat back. "Been a few years."

Leanne's legs suddenly went numb. Her heart turned to ice at the sound of that voice. At the sight of those brown eyes, crinkled at the corners.

Reuben Walsh.

Prodigal son come home.

And right behind all her initial reactions came a wave of anger so fierce it threatened to swamp her.

Reuben Walsh had known his father wouldn't throw out the welcome mat when he saw him nor kill the fatted calf when he arrived. And he had guessed Leanne wouldn't be thrilled either.

But the blatant rage in her narrowed eyes was unexpected.

The last time he'd seen her, she'd been lying in a hospital bed, her auburn hair tied up in a tangled ponytail he knew would have driven her crazy. Leanne always wore her thick hair loose, hanging halfway down her back. Always had her nails perfectly done. Always looked amazing even in the simple clothes she tended to wear.

But at that time she lay unconscious, her pale features slack as if she were as dead as her husband, Dirk, was. His brother, Dirk.

She and Dirk had been on their way back from their

honeymoon after a quick and unexpected wedding that happened before Reuben had flown back to Cedar Ridge.

To propose to Leanne himself.

He stopped in at the hospital to see her after his brother's funeral, stood by her bed, the angry questions swirling around his mind unable to be asked, and then he left. Taking his ring and his broken heart with him. He hadn't been back since. Nor had he and Leanne been in contact.

What could they possibly have to say to each other?

"Hey, Leanne," he said, surprised at the hitch in his voice when their eyes met.

To his surprise and disappointment, old feelings gripped his heart.

For years she had occupied his waking thoughts and drifted through his dreams. Now here she stood, Dirk's widow, with his nephew resting on her hip. Two reminders of the distance between them.

"Hey, Reuben."

Her voice was cool and clipped. He felt his own ire rise up, wondering what right she had to be bent out of shape.

"What are you doing here?" His father's gruff voice grated and once again Reuben fought the old inferiority his father always created in him.

When Reuben received the email from Owen Herne, chairman of the Cedar Ridge Rodeo Group, asking him to assess the unfinished arena for them, he'd been tempted to delete it. He had no desire to return to Cedar Ridge and face the woman he had loved, now the widow of his forever-favored older brother. And why would he deliberately put himself in the line of his father's constant disapproval? He had lived with that long enough when he was a teenager.

The last time he was in Cedar Ridge was three years ago to attend his brother's funeral. George had been so bitter, he hadn't acknowledged Reuben's presence. No personal greeting. No question about how he was doing. No recognition of Reuben's own pain at the loss of a brother.

As for Leanne, she'd still been unconscious and in the hospital. While seeing her so incapacitated had gutted him, in some twisted way it was probably for the best. Reuben wouldn't have known what to say to her after she'd left him for his brother.

But the tiny part of him that still clung to hope pushed him to come home.

"Owen asked me to come talk to the Rodeo Group. About the arena," Reuben said, determined not to let these two show how much influence they had over his life and emotions.

"He never said anything to me," George complained.

"You'll have to take that up with him," Reuben said, trying to keep his tone light and conversational. "But the ranch was on my way to town. I thought I would stop by and say hello."

"It's been a long time since you were here," George said.

On this point Reuben couldn't fault him, though he stifled a beat of resentment at his father's frowning disapproval. Didn't matter what he did when he was growing up, George criticized him.

Come home with good marks?

Well, he could have done better.

Ride the rankest bronc in the rodeo?

Could have scored higher.

Never as good as his brother. Never as good as Dirk.

"It has been awhile," Reuben agreed. He wasn't apologizing for his lack. As the son of the wife who had taken off, Reuben often felt his father held him to account for his mother's behavior. And Reuben had taken that on, as well, always trying to find ways to earn his gruff father's approval.

But it never happened. In fact George had made it clear Dirk would take over the ranch when he was old enough and that there was no place for Reuben in spite of all the work he had done here year after year. Reuben left home as soon as he graduated high school. He rode rodeo in the summer and took on any odd job to help pay for his structural engineering classes. He was determined to show his father he could go it alone. Now he had a degree and had already racked up some impressive jobs. Though his heart had always been here in Cedar Ridge, once he discovered that Dirk and Leanne had had a baby, he shelved any hope of coming back.

His eyes drifted again to Leanne, the woman who, at one time, he had dared to weave dreams and plans around.

"So, here we are," he said.

Instead of responding, she set his nephew, Austin, on his feet and clung to his chubby little hand. She adjusted the little cowboy hat he wore, then glanced over at George.

Looking everywhere but at him as a tense silence fell between them.

Since she'd moved here with her sister, Tabitha, and her father when she was in high school, Leanne Rennie had only had eyes for his older brother, Dirk. And he knew why. Dirk was the good brother. Steady. Solid. Dependable. A Christian.

Reuben knew exactly who he was. The irresponsible younger brother who could only worship Leanne from afar.

Though Leanne had dated his brother for years and been engaged to Dirk for four of them, Reuben had never been able to completely let go of his feelings for her.

But Dirk held off on setting a wedding date for four years. Then, as if she couldn't wait any longer, Leanne broke up with Dirk. His brother left for Europe, and he and Leanne met up at his cousin's destination wedding in Costa Rica. They'd spent two glorious weeks together. She'd confessed that, while she had always wanted the security Dirk could offer, she had a hard time denying her changing feelings for Reuben.

They decided they wanted to be together but she had said that she needed to tell Dirk first. Reuben couldn't figure out why, but he gave Leanne the space she asked for.

Then when Dirk came back from his trip, the next thing he heard, via his cousin Cord, was that Dirk and Leanne had eloped. Reuben was devastated, hurt, then the anger kicked in and he threw himself into his work.

He was determined to prove he didn't need anyone. That he could be successful.

And he had accomplished that. In two weeks he would be starting with a company that promised him prestige and financial independence.

He thought he had put Leanne out of his mind for good, but seeing her now, even more beautiful than he remembered, created an unwelcome hitch in his heart.

In the uncomfortable silence that lingered, a bird warbled, and the wind rustled through the trees sheltering the house beyond them. No one said anything more.

"Well, just thought I'd stop by and say hi." He looked away from his father and Leanne, then crouched down in front of Austin. "And I thought I would get to know you, little guy. I'm your uncle Reuben."

Austin pursed his lips, frowning slightly, as if he didn't believe he had an uncle.

The idea that his only nephew didn't even know who he was cut almost as deep as Leanne's chilly attitude.

"Wooben," Austin said finally. "Uncle Wooben."

"That's right."

Austin stared at him then pointed at Reuben's hat, then his own, looking proud. "My hat. I have my hat."

"It's a pretty cool hat," Reuben agreed.

But then Austin looked up at Leanne, no longer interested in his uncle. "Firsty, Mommy."

"We'll get something in a minute, sweetheart." Leanne hesitated, then glanced over at Reuben, her eyes barely skimming over him. "Would you like some tea?"

"He might not have time," his father said, as if Reuben was no more than a salesman whom George felt he had to be polite to.

Reuben pushed himself up, glancing from his father back to Leanne. He guessed her invitation was more a formality than anything. That his father could be so cool to him he fully understood. Nothing new there.

But Leanne? The woman he had, at one time, thought would be his?

"No. I should get going," Reuben said, fighting down his own resentment and anger.

Good thing the opinion of other people had never mattered to him. Otherwise this could have been a genuinely painful moment.

"Will you be coming by again?" his father asked.

"I'll have to see how things go" was all he would say. No sense in pushing himself on either his father or his sister-in-law if he didn't have to.

George turned to Leanne. "I'm going back to the house."

Then without another word to Reuben, he walked away, shoulders bent, head down.

He looked much older than the last time Reuben had seen him, and in spite of his father's lack of welcome and veiled animosity, Reuben felt the sting of remorse that he'd stayed away so long.

It wasn't your fault.

Maybe not, but he should have been the bigger man. Should have set aside the old hurts and slights. In spite of how George treated him, he was still Reuben's father.

He set aside his regrets for now and looked to Leanne, guessing he would get neither handshake nor hug from her. Not the way she stared daggers at him. As if she had any right.

"So we might see you around?" she asked. The chill in her voice almost made him shudder.

But then, to his surprise, she held his gaze a beat longer than necessary and once again the old feelings came back.

"I'm sure. It's a small town," he returned, then he turned to Austin and gave the little boy a quick grin. "So, I'll see you again," he said to his nephew.

"Bring a present?" Austin asked.

"Austin, that's not polite." Leanne gave her son's hand a gentle reprimanding shake.

"I should have thought of that," Reuben said with a light laugh. "After all, I am your uncle and uncles should come with presents."

"I like horses. My dad liked horses."

Reuben's heart twisted. Once again his and Leanne's eyes met.

"I never had a chance to tell you how sorry I was to hear about Dirk," he said, thumbing his hat back. As if to see her better.

"He was your brother too." Leanne's voice held a thread of sorrow and for a moment they acknowledged their shared grief.

"He was a good brother. And I'm sure he was a good husband."

Leanne released a harsh laugh. "I hardly had the chance to find out. We were only married two weeks." She pressed her lips together and Reuben took a quick step toward her. Before he even knew what he was doing he laid a gentle hand on her shoulder, tightening it enough to let her know that he understood.

She stayed where she was a moment, but then jerked back, her features growing hard. She turned to Austin. "I'll get you a drink, sweetie, but first we should put your horse away."

Then she left, Austin trailing alongside her, her head held high, back stiff, exuding waves of rejection.

"Bye, Uncle Wooben," Austin called out, looking back.

Reuben waved goodbye. It was time for him to leave but he waited, watching Leanne as she walked down the grassy path toward the corrals where a horse stood, waiting patiently. She told Austin to stay where he was as she climbed over the fence.

He wanted to ask her why she thought she had the right to be so angry with him when she was the one who'd run back to his brother as soon as Dirk came back into her life. Ask her what happened to those promises they made to each other in Costa Rica. When she had told him that she'd always cared for him.

Had they all been lies?

He spun around, striding back to his truck. That duty was done. He wished he had listened to the realistic part of himself and simply driven past this place and the two people who didn't want him around.

Reuben slipped his sunglasses on and climbed into his truck. He started it up and, without a backward glance, drove off the ranch that had been his home for years.

He and Leanne were over. He had to look to his own future.

And as he drove, he second-guessed his plan to work in Cedar Ridge for the Rodeo Group.

He glanced back at the ranch as it grew smaller in his rearview mirror.

Why should he put himself through this on purpose?

He would talk to Owen Herne. Tell him he wasn't taking on the job. He had no reason at all to stay in town.

Tomorrow he'd leave and Cedar Ridge would only be a memory.

Chapter Two

"I know I put you on the spot, but I don't have much choice." Reuben rolled his coffee cup back and forth between his hands, looking everywhere but at his cousin Cord and his Uncle Boyce sitting across from him at the Brand and Grill. "I can't do this job."

The muted hum of conversation and the occasional order called out by Adana, one of the waitresses, filled the silence that followed his pronouncement.

Cord Walsh lifted one hand, his green-grey eyes narrowed. "You said you were willing," he said. "We could have gotten someone else, but you said you could do this. We don't have much time to get this done."

"I know that, but I also know what I can and can't do."

"Did your other job get moved up?" Boyce asked, swiping his plate with the last bite of toast. "That why you changed your mind?"

"No. It still doesn't start for a couple of weeks but..." He hesitated, wondering what to say without sounding like some heartsick loser. "I don't think coming back was a good idea." He pushed his coffee cup away from him and sat back, as well. He didn't want to say any more than that in front of his uncle, George's brother.

Boyce was busy taking one last swig of his coffee. But Cord held his gaze for an extra beat as if delving into Reuben's thoughts.

If anyone knew Reuben's history, it was his cousin. Cord knew most of Reuben's secrets. Most, not all. The only other cousin who understood where Reuben was coming from was Noah. He also had to deal with a father who was never satisfied.

"Okay, then," Cord said with an air of resignation, glancing at his father. "I'm guessing we can't change your mind with our Walsh charm or appeal to your Walsh heritage."

Reuben chuckled. "Probably not. I'm immune to those tactics." Then he reached into the pocket of his denim jacket and pulled out a folded piece of paper. He pushed it across the table to Cord. "Here are the names of a couple of other guys you could get. They haven't made any firm commitments and they won't be available for a month or so. But they're good too." After his disastrous visit to his father's ranch, Reuben had made a few calls from the motel to some other engineers he knew. He got a couple of vague commitments from some old classmates. It was the best he could do under the circumstances.

"So tell us about this job you're starting," Boyce said, looking up as Cord pocketed the note. Clearly his uncle wasn't going to try to convince Reuben to stay. "I haven't heard anything about it from George."

Reuben wasn't surprised. He knew George didn't talk often about him. "It's a good position with a prestigious international engineering firm. I'd be my own boss, which is what I've been looking for since I graduated," Reuben said, thankful for his uncle's switch in topic. He didn't want to expound on the real reasons he was leaving. Leanne and Austin, the visible reminder of her betrayal of Reuben. "I'll be making good money and I'll be traveling around the world doing some big jobs. What's not to like?"

"And there's no one in your life right now who would object to all the moving around?" Boyce asked.

Reuben shook his head. "Nope. Haven't met anyone who created any sparks."

"I get where you're coming from," Cord said. "I think Ella and I had sparks the first time we met."

"Didn't help that Adana had just quit as your nanny and you were ticked off," Boyce said with a laugh.

"There was more than that going on." Cord grinned and then his phone dinged. He glanced at it, then back at Reuben. "I gotta deal with this. Are you leaving today?"

Reuben nodded. The sooner the better.

"Then I'll say goodbye."

"I'm heading out too," Boyce said, "Though I wouldn't mind sticking around and talking more, I sense you want to get a move on." He gave Reuben a rueful smile, which, more than anything either of them had said, made Reuben second-guess his decision.

But then he thought of Leanne's anger and his father's lack of affection, and he knew he wasn't ready to put himself in that vulnerable position.

"Much as I'd like to connect with some of the other cousins, I feel I should get going."

Cord got up the same time Reuben did and pulled him close in a quick, man hug then stepped back, holding his gaze. "You stay safe and don't be a stranger."

"I won't," he said.

Then Boyce dropped some bills on the table to pay for breakfast, got up and gave him a tighter hug than Cord had. "I've been praying for you," he said as he pulled back. "You and your father."

Reuben felt a twinge of guilt at the sentiment. After Dirk's funeral and Leanne's betrayal, he had kept his distance from God. Only in the past few months had he realized how much he missed his faith and started attending church again.

"Thanks. I probably need it," he said, keeping his tone light.

"You'll be back for my wedding, won't you?" Cord asked as they made their way out of the restaurant.

"I hope so. I'll have to see what my new work schedule is. I'll be needing to impress some big investors."

"This job sounds serious," Boyce said as he slowly made his way down the few steps out of the café. "And important."

"I've got a lot riding on it and the pay is amazing." This job was his chance to prove to himself that he had value. Worth.

"Well, you know, it's a cliché but money isn't everything," Boyce said.

"No, but it's a fairly universal measuring stick. One that your brother, George, understands."

Cord gave him a curious look but Reuben wasn't delving deeper into the past. He had a promising future ahead of him and in spite of feeling bad that he had let his cousin and his uncle down, he had to move on. Staying in Cedar Ridge wasn't an option.

"Well, you take care. Stay in touch and don't be such a stranger."

Reuben nodded as he buttoned his denim jacket closed. The wind still held a chill. It was cooler than yesterday and as he walked down the street to his truck, he shivered as he thought of California, where he would be headquartered.

It would be warm there. No snow and no winter. Just sun and warmth and work.

Boyce and Cord said goodbye and left.

Reuben watched them leave and felt a twinge of melancholy when they both laughed at something Cord had said. How often had he longed for a relationship like his cousin and uncle shared?

He shook off the feelings, walked to his truck, drove down Main Street, then headed to the highway out of town.

But as he drove away from Cedar Ridge, he tried not to think that he might not be back for a very, very long time.

His father's ranch was on his way out of town, and as he came nearer he was tempted to keep going. Drive on into his future and leave the past behind. But he knew guilt and second thoughts would follow him all the way back to Calgary, so he slowed as he came to the wooden and stone archway leading to the ranch. Hanging from the cross bar was the ranch's brand, stamped on a metal disc. The Bar W. And with it hung the weight of the Walsh legacy and their prominence in the community of Cedar Ridge.

This was driven home when he drove up to the imposing bulk of the ranch house once again. It was built to impress and easily fulfilled that promise. The house spread out and upward, two stories high. The main part of the house, directly in front of him, held the main living area. Kitchen, great room, family room, formal dining room, kitchen nook. Two wings stretched out from the main house. One wing held the master bedroom, a media room, an office and a guest bedroom. The other was where Reuben and Dirk had slept and also had an extra bedroom.

Reuben's mother had often said that the family rattled around in the large space. She was right, but the space also gave Reuben places to retreat to after his mother left. Away from George's steady criticism.

Reuben parked on the cement pad in front of the large, four-bay garage, guessing that Leanne and George's vehicles were inside.

He stayed in the truck a moment, taking a breath, readying himself to face them again. At least this time he was prepared.

He got out of the truck and strode to the house. But when he rang the doorbell no one answered. He put his head inside and called out, but again, only silence.

Puzzled he walked past the house and the gardens

Dirk's mother had started, surprised to see them all cleaned up and obviously cared for. His mother had never cared for them and they had been taken over by weeds and neglect.

Leanne must have revived the garden. He remembered how she had often wished she could fix it up when she and Dirk were dating.

He stopped again, listening for voices. Maybe they were all gone. He went a little farther and as he came over the rise separating the ranch house from the corrals, he heard the distinctive lowing of cattle and the bawl of baby calves.

He walked around the grove of trees between the garden behind the house and the cow corrals lying in a hollow tucked against the hill the house stood on.

The sound of shouting and the bellowing of cows grew louder as he got closer. Some cows stood in the pasture along the rugged fence, bawling for their calves, which had been separated from them in another large pen.

The rest of the cows were on the other side, milling about, creating a cloud of dust as they waited to be processed.

That's when he saw her. Leanne was mounted on a large palomino, wearing a down vest, her hair tied back. Her hat was shoved on her head and she waved a coil of rope as she pushed the horse into a crush of bawling animals, cutting some away.

What was she doing? That was dangerous work. She could be hurt. There were far too many cows in the pen. Why was she working with them?

An unfamiliar man stood by a gate connected to another smaller pen. Clearly his job was to open the gate when enough cows were cut out of the herd. A younger man sat astride a horse, a ball cap clamped over his dark hair.

"Devin, get over there," he heard his father yelling. Big surprise. Dad's default emotion was anger. "Stop being so ridiculously lazy and help out," he bellowed again from his position on the raised walkway by the fenced-in alley adjacent the pen.

He sounded so angry. If George wasn't careful, he would have a heart attack someday. Reuben hurried his pace to see if he could help out. Leanne shouldn't be doing what she was.

She was on one edge of the milling cattle, keeping them moving; Devin was working his way through the herd.

But when George yelled again, the young man pulled his horse to a stop, leaning on his saddle horn as if making a decision.

"Get in there," his father shouted, looking ready to climb over the fence and help out himself. "Get those cows moving."

The young man named Devin kept his horse where it was, then finally he made a move.

Only it wasn't into the cattle to help Leanne cut some out. It was in the other direction. Away from the cows.

Toward the gate leading out of the pen.

As he came closer, Reuben easily saw the angry set of the young man's jaw, the determined way he urged his horse toward the large metal gate separating the cows from one of the pastures. He dismounted and un-latched the gate, ignoring Leanne's cries and George's fury. His movements were rushed and jerky, the chain clanking against the gate. It was as if he couldn't contain himself any longer.

He had Reuben's complete sympathy. Reuben knew what it was like to be on the receiving end of George's demands. Never feeling like the job you were doing was good enough. Always getting pushed to do more. He wondered how long this young man had worked for his father.

"Devin. Where are you going?" Leanne called out, the concern in her voice evident from here.

"Get back here, Devin," George yelled. "Get back here or you're fired."

"You can't fire me," Devin shouted back, his voice filled with rage as he shoved open the gate, "because I quit."

Then Devin led his horse through the open gate.

But he hadn't looked behind him. Reuben could easily see what the young man, in his fury, had missed.

A group of cows and calves had followed Devin and his horse and were right behind him as he turned to close the gate.

Too late he noticed the animals and struggled to shut the gate on them. But by then the cows were already pushing past him to freedom. Devin jumped back, pulling his horse back, the cows now streaming out of the gate.

From what Reuben remembered, if the cows got away, they would run toward the open fields behind the ranch and from there up into the foothill pastures, which were spread out over hundreds and hundreds of acres. If they got too far out, it would take days to round them up again. Maybe even longer once the cows had gotten their taste of freedom.

"Devin, close that gate," George yelled, leaning over the fence, his face purple. "Close the gate, you useless twerp."

But Devin had given up and was leading his horse away from the herd flowing through the gate.

Reuben grabbed hold of a fence post and clambered over in his hurry to catch the gate and stop the rest of the cows from getting out. But it was hard to halt the press of all those large bodies and too dangerous.

"What did you do?" he called out to Devin, who was ignoring the herd racing past him as he walked along the fence.

"I quit." Devin muttered as Reuben tried to get by him. "George is a maniac boss."

"Is that your own horse?" Reuben asked as the cows, increasing in number, now thundered past them.

"No. Belongs to the ranch."

That's all he needed to know. Reuben yanked the reins out of Devin's hand, did a quick assessment of the young man's height. They were about the same. The stirrups should be okay.

Then he vaulted into the saddle, turned the horse around, nudged him in the flanks and galloped off to head off the cows before they got too far away.

It was a race and Reuben had to be careful not to get too close to the cows and get them running even faster.

He heard Leanne's shout and tossed a quick glance over his shoulder to see her following on horseback behind him, making a wide loop around the herd like he had.

All he could hear now was the thundering of the cows' hooves, the steady rhythm of the horse's, its hard breathing and Leanne shouting something indecipherable.

She needed to catch up to Reuben. Leanne gripped the reins of her horse, urging it on, fighting to stay in the saddle of the racing horse.

She shoved down a beat of panic as she galloped alongside the now running herd going faster than she thought possible.

She didn't have time to plan. All she could concentrate on was getting the herd turned around before they got too far ahead. Could they do it with two horses? She'd never handled a charging herd before.

Please, Lord, help me keep my seat. Help me not fall off.

Her prayer was automatic. She didn't want to disgrace herself in front of either Reuben, who seemed to be one with the horse he rode, or George, who had seemed on the verge of having a heart attack when the cows had surged through the open gate.

She was so angry with Devin, but right now she couldn't spare him much thought.

Slowly the gap between their horses lessened and, to her surprise and relief, Reuben managed to get his horse in front of the lead cows. He waved his hat at the herd as he pulled his horse's speed in.

Please don't split, she silently pleaded as she came behind Reuben, trying to gauge the correct distance between her and Reuben and the cows. Too close and she would spook the herd. Too far back and some of the cows might go right between them and they'd have two bunches to worry about.

Thankfully they stayed together, calves bawling, cows bellowing and dust rising up from the milling hooves.

Reuben made it to the front of the herd and slowly, slowly their forward momentum decreased. Reuben waved his hat again, yelling to get the cows turned. But the animals behind didn't know what was happening and kept running through, ramming into the cows in the front. This spooked them again and Leanne hurried to join Reuben at the front to hold the herd back.

But finally the animals seemed to sense they weren't going to carry on and the herd slowed its pace, Reuben and Leanne keeping up.

"Don't get too close," Reuben called out. "Stay far enough away that they can see you but not get scared again."

Leanne nodded, pulling her horse back.

Reuben waved his arm at the cows again and they stopped. "Get beside me but stay about ten feet away," he shouted to Leanne. "Turn your horse toward the cows and keep it facing them."

Leanne simply did what she was told. Reuben had herded far more cows than she had and knew what he was doing.

So she turned her horse around, her heart pounding

in her chest with a mixture of fear and anticipation as she faced down the herd in front of her. The cows had their heads up as if looking for a way out. What would happen now depended on the decision of the lead cows.

"Get along, you creatures," Reuben yelled, waving his hat at them again. Leanne had left her rope behind and her hat had tumbled off somewhere in the pasture so she waved her hands, praying it would help.

Then, together, they managed to get the front cows turned back toward the corrals and, thankfully, the others reluctantly followed suit.

The herd pushed and bawled as they made their way back, expressing their disappointment and confusion.

"You keep pressure on the herd, I'll make sure they stay bunched," Reuben called out.

Again all Leanne could do was nod.

A few calves made a break from the herd, heading for the upper pastures but Reuben quickly got them back, his horse easily stopping and turning them around.

Thankfully his horse was a seasoned cutting horse and Reuben knew what he was doing.

The cattle had their heads down now, plodding along the way cows should be moving. Leanne sneezed on the dust raised by the herd walking over the fields that were once green. She shivered as the worst of the drama was over.

Reuben was still working the one side of the herd as the animals headed back to the corrals. She knew they would face another challenge when they came to the gate, but hopefully the bale of hay she'd put inside the pen to lure them in the first place would draw them back again. The pasture they were riding on now was brown and chewed down so there was nothing to entice them here, though a few cows slowed to check it out.

As they got closer to the yard, she saw the gate was still open. George was on the other side of the fence, holding it with a rope to make sure it didn't swing shut. He also knew what to do.

Then, finally, the first cows went through the gate.

"Push them harder," Reuben called out, whistling at the cows. "We need to get them moving fast enough so the front ones get pushed farther into the corrals and don't decide to turn around when they reach the end."

Leanne clucked to her horse, urging the cows on, and then, finally, they were all back in the corrals and the large metal gate clanged shut behind them.

Her hands were shaking as she unclenched the reins and pulled in a long, steadying breath. They had come so close to a complete disaster.

If Reuben hadn't been there right when Devin quit...

She shut that thought off. She didn't know why Reuben had returned, but he had, and right now she was relieved to have the cows safely back in the pen. It had taken her and Devin and Chad two days to round them up the first time. She knew if the cows had gotten out to the far pasture, it would have taken them a lot longer to convince them to come back.

"Good job, Leanne," George said as she sat, her breath shaky, her pulse still pounding.

She acknowledged his rare compliment with a duck of her head, then grabbed her horse's reins and turned back toward the herd.

"What are you doing?" Reuben called out.

"Getting these cows processed." Time was wasting. George would be furious as it was, no sense making him angrier.

"No. You need to get your bearings. Your horse needs to rest a moment. Shift its mindset."

Leanne fought down frustration that she hadn't thought of that. Though her horse was breathing heavily, she knew the run hadn't worn it out. But it had put it in a racing frame of mind, as Reuben had said. She needed to settle it down.

So she nodded her acknowledgment of what he said, pulled in another breath and exerted a gentle but steady pressure on the reins to hold her horse in. He seemed to understand what she wanted and stopped its prancing and shifting, settling down and lowering its head.

Reuben brought his horse alongside hers, talking to it in a low voice, settling it down, as well.

Up until now Leanne's focus had been on the cows, on staying atop her horse, on keeping things under control.

But now that the crisis had been averted, she was far too aware of Reuben beside her, petting his horse, rewarding it, looking as if he hadn't just faced down fifty cow and calf pairs racing for the back of the beyond.

"So what's next?" he asked, shoving his cowboy hat back up his head with the knuckle of his forefinger, giving her a quizzical look.

She fought down a whirl of confusion, letting her old anger with him surface. How could he act so casual? As if they hadn't shared so much? Been through so much?

"What are you doing here?" she blurted out.

He looked taken aback, but then his features hardened, reflecting her own churning emotions.

"I came to say goodbye."

"You're leaving?" She shouldn't be surprised. It was what he did best. "What about the arena?"

"I told Cord he needed to find someone else to do the assessment." His horse did a turn away, restless now, but Reuben got it turned to face the cows. In the process he ended up even closer to Leanne and her horse.

"Why are you here?" George called out, joining them.

"So nice to be made welcome," Reuben muttered, his jaw clenched. He turned to his father. "Like I was saying to Leanne, I just stopped in to say goodbye and came into the middle of this mess."

"Sure. Yeah." George turned away from him and back to Leanne. "Chad is still here. Guess we should get going." He walked away from them, heading back to the head gate.

Leanne nodded, trying hard not to look at her watch. She had told Shauntelle to drop Austin off at suppertime. If it were only her and Chad and George, sorting these cows would take longer.

"You can't do this alone."

Reuben's tone rubbed her completely wrong. So full of authority. But his words were, unfortunately, correct.

"Done it before," she snapped. "Can do it again."

"Not without Devin."

She didn't need to be reminded of that particular betrayal. Though she didn't blame the kid, it was still lousy timing on Devin's part that he quit right now. This was only the first batch of cows they needed to work through. In the coming week they needed to get the rest of the cows down off the upper pastures, process and wean them. On top of that, she had committed to taking minutes at a meeting of the Rodeo Group. She had too much to do and not enough help to do it now that Devin was gone.

But she wasn't going to admit that to Reuben.

She turned to him, fighting a confusing mix of anger and loss as she held his dark brown eyes. Eyes she had once found herself lost in.

Focus. He's not the man you thought he was.

"So I guess this is goodbye," she said, turning away from him, determined not to let him see how he affected her. "I need to get to work."

"Not on your own."

"What do you propose I do? Run to the hired-hand store?" She couldn't keep the snappy tone out of her voice.

She'd heard nothing for the past three years from this man. A man she had given her heart to and so much more.

And now he swoops back into her life and tells her what she should and shouldn't do on a ranch he walked away from? A ranch he never showed any interest in?

"I could help out until you're done," he said.

All she could do was stare at him. Reuben? Working alongside her on the ranch?

She shook her head. "No. That's not happening. We'll manage on our own."

"You won't and you know it," he returned. It wasn't too hard to hear the annoyance in his voice.

Well, she didn't care. He had no right to be frustrated with her.

Leanne closed her eyes, trying to bring her focus back to what needed to be done and how she could swing it.

She couldn't have him around. She didn't want to live in the past with its pain and resentment. She wanted to move on.

Then she heard the jangle of his horse's bit and when she opened her eyes again he was already moving his horse into the herd, calling out to George.

"How many do you want at a time?"

"Send me ten pairs," George was saying. "But don't get too fussed if cows and calves get separated."

A chill shot through her as she heard George give Reuben directions.

"I don't think we need his help," she called out to George, anger blending with fear.

"Too late," Reuben tossed over his shoulder. "I'm not going anywhere until this job is done."

Chapter Three

"**S**end them through now, Reuben. Keep them moving."

Reuben ignored his father's barked commands and pushed the last of the cows into the pen keeping his horse right behind the last cow. He nodded for Chad to shut the gate. The poor guy looked exhausted, but then so did Leanne. She was slouched in her saddle now, wiping her face with a hanky. She had lost her hat in the race to get ahead of the cows. Her hair hung in a lank ponytail down her back, loose strands sticking to her flushed face.

"Chad, come over here and help me get these cows done," his father called out.

Reuben leaned on his saddle, watching poor Chad clambering over the fence and joining his father on the walkway to help finish needling the cows. Beyond them, in the second, much-larger pen, the cows and calves were finally settled, munching on the hay. Once the rest of the cows were through, the work was done for the day.

He arched his back, working out a kink, then slowly dismounted. He was going to feel every single muscle in his hips and legs tomorrow. He hadn't ridden in years and yet was surprised how quickly the old skills came back.

Leanne got off her horse, as well. She slipped the reins over the horse's head then walked her horse toward him.

Her expression was guarded as she trudged through the pen. Once again he struggled with her angry reaction to his presence. Where did that come from and what right did she have to be upset with him? She was the one who had betrayed him. Marrying his brother while he was giving her the space she said she needed.

"This is just the first bunch?" he asked as she joined him, her horse heaving a heavy sigh as if the day had been too long for him, as well.

"Yeah. We've got eighty more head up in the higher pastures."

"Shouldn't this have been done a month ago?" he asked, stretching his neck. "Time isn't on your side."

"We've been fortunate." Her voice held an edge of tension, which annoyed him.

"Considering your main hand just quit, I wouldn't say that."

"It's a glitch," she snapped.

"So you figure on gathering them tomorrow?"

"I can't. Your father and I have a meeting with the Cedar Ridge Rodeo Group tomorrow. It will have to wait until Friday."

"The weather is only going to cooperate so long," he said, struggling to keep his frustration down.

"I checked the forecast. We have a week of good weather ahead of us." The anger in her voice wasn't hard to miss.

"I'm trying to help," he said.

"Now?" Leanne's eyes narrowed. Then she seemed to gather her emotions. "I'm sorry. I appreciate what you just did."

He just nodded, realizing from the tension in her voice how difficult the apology was for her.

"I couldn't very well leave you hanging."

Reuben led his horse through a gate on the far side of the pen, trying to ignore his father's yelling at Chad.

"How many ranch hands have you been through in the past year?" he asked, opening the gate so she could lead her horse through.

Leanne's only reply was a halfhearted shrug. Which told him they'd probably been through a few.

He wanted to push the issue but he had already said enough. Besides, what did it matter to him what Leanne and his father were doing or the difficulties they were having? It wasn't his ranch and he had no skin in the game.

You should stay. Help.

On the heels of that thought came Leanne's anger with him. Why should he deal with that on purpose?

Daylight was waning by the time the horses were unbridled and released into their own pasture.

Leanne closed the door of the tack shed and arched her back, her eyes closed.

"You look beat," Reuben said, feeling a touch of concern.

"Just another day in paradise," she quipped. Then she walked over to a bale of hay and was about to fork some to the horses when Reuben stopped her. "I'll take care of that."

She nodded her thanks, then without another word to him walked toward where George and Chad stood. Reuben stabbed the fork into the hay bale, fighting his annoyance with her attitude. As if she had any right to be so cool with him.

Chad was cleaning up the syringes and George looked up when he joined them. "Good work" was all he said, but coming from George, that was high praise. Then he turned to Leanne. "Is Austin in the house?"

"Shauntelle texted me a few minutes ago. She just put him to bed but she brought supper. She's waiting at the house until I can leave."

"You go then, Leanne. We'll be right here," George said, then he glanced over at Reuben. "You should join us for supper. I'm sure Shauntelle made enough."

He heard Leanne's swift intake of breath but he didn't bother looking her way, sensing he would see the same anger he had when he first came. Her reaction made him want to turn down the invitation, but the fact that his father had asked was a small acknowledgment of Reuben's presence. A few crumbs tossed his way from his dad.

And right about now, he was ready to take something, anything, away from this visit. If it wasn't from Leanne then it may as well be from his father.

"Sure. That sounds good," he said.

"You can wash up in the house," George said, then turned to Chad. "When you're done here, you can go home." Then George walked away, leaving Chad with syringes and empty bottles to clean up.

"How long have you been working for my father?" Reuben asked Chad, who was gathering up the syringes and dumping them into a large plastic tub for cleaning.

"Few days. Not long."

"You ever work on a ranch before?"

Chad slowly shook his head, looking apprehensive. "No. But I need the work. Got a family to take care of."

"You ride at all?"

"I'm willing to learn."

Reuben held the man's eyes, sensing the desperation in them. He'd have to be at the end of his rope to want to put up with his father's abuse for the sake of a job.

However Reuben didn't give the poor guy another week. Chad seemed like a decent fellow but he needed someone who was able to take the time to help him out and show him the ropes. George would never be that guy. Leanne might, but he guessed any extra time she might have was taken up with Austin.

There was no way they could keep this ranch going.

This isn't your problem, he reminded himself. *You're on your way out of here. Stick to your plan.*

But as he walked back to the house, George and Leanne walking ahead of him, he couldn't shake the idea that the Bar W's time was done.

George and Leanne really needed to sell the place.

"So this job of yours. What will you do?" George was asking Reuben.

"I'll be contracting for a large engineering firm,"

Reuben replied, his voice even and measured in spite of the antagonism in George's voice. "This job will get me opportunities all around the world."

Leanne concentrated on her food, exhaustion clawing at her. The day had been emotionally and physically taxing. Devin's quitting had created a huge problem she wasn't ready to deal with. And while Reuben's help was appreciated, his presence wasn't.

She couldn't deal with all this right now. She wanted nothing more than to retreat to her room, but she was determined not to let Reuben know how much he got to her.

"I can see why you'd like that job. Moving around. Just like you've always lived," George put in, annoyance edging his voice as he scooped up some of the casserole Shauntelle had dropped off.

Leanne had never been so happy to see her friend. She wanted to fall into her arms, tell her all her current struggles, but she couldn't. Only Tabitha knew Leanne's secrets, and her sister had been so busy the past couple of days that Leanne hadn't had a chance to connect with her.

"Dirk liked staying in one place," George continued. "He would have stuck around. Helped on the ranch."

In spite of her own frustration with him, Leanne felt a touch of sympathy for Reuben. As long as she'd known Dirk and Reuben, it was obvious George favored the son of his first wife. His beloved Joelle.

Didn't matter what Reuben accomplished, it was either wrong or not as good as anything Dirk did. After Dirk died, George grew more bitter, railing against everyone and everything and, for some reason, Reuben most of all.

"So where is this amazing job based?" George continued.

"California. The company has contracts all over the world," Reuben said, pushing his food around his plate. "It's a great opportunity. A chance to make good money and be independent. And travel."

Leanne shouldn't have been surprised that Reuben would take this job. His constant moving around had been one of those important issues they had planned to discuss when they decided they would be together. She had hoped he would come and work on the ranch, but Reuben had been adamant that his father would never want him back or give him any share in the Bar W. Dirk was the favored son, he would be the one inheriting and Reuben had no desire to put himself through more humiliation.

"And no more rodeo?" his father asked.

Reuben glanced over at Leanne just as she looked at him. She ducked her head, focusing on the plate in front of her.

Leanne was thankful that in spite of George's antagonism to Reuben, he carried the conversation. She couldn't make idle chitchat with a man who had let her down so badly. Treated her so poorly.

A man she'd thought, at one time, she would be spending the rest of her life with.

And right now, sitting with him only a few feet away, with Austin sleeping upstairs, her own feelings were in such turmoil, she wasn't sure what she would say to him.

"Well, whatever works," George said, taking a drink of his water. "You're not in a saddle anymore but you're still running around, aren't you?"

"Haven't found a reason to settle down yet." Then Reuben turned to Leanne. "This is a great supper. Thanks so much for having me."

His polite smile and impersonal comment created a clench of dismay that surprised and frustrated her. All through the meal he'd been unfailingly polite, asking George questions about the ranch, the hired hands, the community. He didn't bother asking anything of her.

Or about Austin, which cut deepest of all.

"You're welcome," she said, keeping her voice cool. "It was the least we could do after you helped us out."

He shot her a frown, clearly picking up on the faint note of sarcasm that had crept into her voice.

"It was the right thing to do. So what are you going to do now that Devin has quit?" Reuben asked, his gaze fixed on Leanne, as if daring her to answer his question.

Leanne glanced at George, who glowered, tapping his fingers on the table.

"I don't know," George said finally. "Sometimes I think we should let it all go." Then he glanced at Leanne. "But then I think of Austin and know we should keep going."

His words created a low-level panic in her. Though Leanne knew, when it came right down to it, her father-in-law would never sell the ranch, he had floated the idea a couple of times. And she had simply let him talk, hoping he would change his mind.

He always did.

"We'll keep going," she said, giving George an encouraging smile. "We'll advertise for another hand. That's how we got Devin and he knew his stuff." She didn't add the fact that George had been the one to drive him to quit, but she lived in hope that they would find someone who was able to ignore George's bluster and do the work.

"This Chad guy. Where did you find him?" Reuben asked.

"Word of mouth," Leanne said, glancing over at George who had gone quiet, staring off into the middle distance. Leanne caught him doing this more often the past while. As if he was ruminating on life. Looking back into a past he couldn't change and the losses that had caused him so much pain.

"He seems like a good guy, but not too experienced," Reuben said.

"He'll learn."

"But you're still shorthanded. And you've got a lot of work ahead of you getting the rest of the cows processed and the calves weaned."

Leanne was wondering why he was giving her the third degree. What did he care about what was happening on the ranch? He never had cared about it before.

Or about other things.

"We are shorthanded," George said to Reuben, jumping into the conversation. "But you could help us out. You said you don't have to go back for a couple of weeks. You could help Leanne get the cows down from the upper pastures. Help us wean them."

"We can find someone else," Leanne chimed in. There was no way she could handle Reuben being at the ranch all day. "And besides, Reuben said he was leaving town."

"I can stay, help out around here," Reuben said.

Leanne could only stare at him. "Why?"

"My dad asked if I could, and I can," Reuben said, his tone even. Measured. As if he was challenging her. "And I know you won't find anyone to help on the ranch on such short notice."

Leanne pressed her lips together, struggling for self-control. She was the new secretary of the Rodeo Group. And when she'd found out Reuben would be doing the assessment on the arena, she figured it would only require seeing him for a couple of meetings and then he would be done.

But to have him here? Every day?

"Good. Then that's settled," George said. "We'll see you on Friday."

Leanne felt a headache crawling up her neck and had suddenly had enough of trying to sit through this visit. Trying to be polite to a man who had once held her heart and, instead, had pushed her away when she needed him most.

She couldn't struggle through inane conversation with Reuben for a single minute longer.

"Excuse me," she mumbled, shooting a glance at George, her eyes barely grazing over Reuben. She picked up her plate and carried it to the kitchen. She set her plate on the counter, gripping the edge as she tried to keep it together. In spite of her anger with Reuben, she was still disappointed to see how much he affected her. After all he had done, or rather hadn't done, he could still make her heart tremble. At one time in her life, she would have prayed about this visit, asking God to give her strength. But she hadn't attended church since Dirk died. The burdens on her shoulders weighed too heavily.

And now it looked like he would be here on the ranch. Every day until they were done moving and weaning.

She drew in a deep breath, then began scraping the food off the plate into the garbage can.

"Not going to feed those to Buster? I'm sure the old dog would love those leftovers."

Ruben's deep voice behind her made her jump. Why didn't he stay in the dining room? She just wanted this evening over and him gone.

"Buster's not around anymore," she said.

"What? Since when?"

"He died shortly after Austin was born." In spite of her feelings toward him, she softened her voice as she gave him the news. Though the old collie had been the ranch's dog, he had always been attached to Reuben and was always right at his heels everywhere he went.

"I was wondering where he was when we were working with the cows. I thought he was sleeping. Figured he was probably pretty old." Reuben released a heavy sigh as he set the bowls with the leftover food on the counter.

She didn't imagine the sorrow in his voice, and for the smallest moment she wanted to reach out to him and console him. But she stopped herself. He didn't deserve her pity.

George came into the kitchen, setting the last of the plates beside the sink.

"If you don't mind, I'm turning in," he said to Leanne. "Tell Shauntelle thanks for dinner."

He turned to Reuben. "So we'll see you again?"

Reuben nodded, then George left, his footsteps slow as he walked through the kitchen to the stairs leading to his bedroom in his wing of the house.

Reuben waited until he was gone, then turned back to Leanne. "He looks tired," he said, his voice quiet.

"He's getting older and he hasn't been feeling well lately." Leanne kept her tone conversational, wishing Reuben would just leave. She wanted nothing more than to go to her own bedroom, crawl into bed, pull the covers over her head and end this day. But she plugged on.

"Why does he keep going?" Reuben asked. "Why doesn't he sell this place? Sounds like he's talked about it."

"Sell the place?" Leanne couldn't keep the incredulous tone out of her voice as she finished loading the dishwasher. "This place has been in the Walsh family for generations. He can't do that. He *won't* do that," she amended.

Reuben gave her a surprised look. "You seem bothered by the idea."

"You don't sell land," she said, closing the dishwasher and punching the buttons, his nearness creating unwelcome feelings countered by his casual dismissal of everything she now held dear. "I can't believe you would even say that. You, a Walsh."

"C'mon, Leanne. Be realistic," Reuben said, frowning his puzzlement as he ignored her last statement. "It's just you and my dad now, and Chad who is a nice guy but no cowhand. And knowing my father, you've been through more than a few hired hands already. You can't keep going like this."

"I'm capable," she countered, leaning back against the counter, her arms folded in a defensive gesture over her chest. "I've spent the last three years learning how to handle cows, drive a tractor, work a horse. Prove my worth to your father. I can manage the work."

"I don't know why you would want to get into my father's good graces," Reuben said with a harsh laugh. "Those four years you and Dirk were engaged, my dad would have nothing to do with you. He fought with Dirk all the time about his dating you. And now you're working with him like he's a partner you can trust. How do you know he won't change his mind and cut you out?"

Leanne felt again the sting of that old rejection. When she was dating Dirk, she knew George's disapproval was one of the reasons Dirk kept putting off setting a wedding date. Dirk kept telling her it would take time and that he wanted everything to be just right before they got married. But he hung on for four long years, giving her excuse after excuse.

She finally broke up with him, realizing that it was probably for the best.

Because no matter how she had tried to convince herself that Dirk—safe solid secure Dirk—was the better man, it was the wild and unpredictable Reuben who had always held her heart.

And for a few blissful weeks, after she broke up with Dirk and she and Reuben found each other at that wedding in Costa Rica, she thought she had finally found her heart's true home.

Foolish, stupid, trusting girl.

But she was here now. Reuben was her past. Austin was her present and future. He was her focus now. Not this man who broke his promises to her and broke her heart.

"Land is an inheritance. A legacy. It's security," she said, repeating all the reasons she had dated Dirk. "You don't give that up."

"Security always was important to you, wasn't it?" Reuben's voice held a hard edge. "That's why you stayed with Dirk so long. That's why you went running back to him the first chance you could. After I thought we had shared something unique. Something I'd never had with anyone before."

His words dug into her heart, resurrecting feelings she thought she had dealt with, but the dismissive and furious tone of his voice stripped them all away. Laying bare the selfish man he truly was.

She felt her hands curl into fists and for a moment she wanted to hit him. Strike at him. Lash out in pain and fury and hurt.

"Dirk at least stood by me," Leanne said, pulling in a long, slow breath, trying to still her pounding heart, the old, painful tightness gripping her tired head. Always a sign of stress and sorrow. "He helped me when I needed him, which is more than I can say for you."

Silence followed this remark and she wondered what

he would say to that. If he would now finally admit to what he had done. Or hadn't done.

"I wish I had even the smallest inkling of what you're talking about" was all he said, sounding genuinely puzzled.

All she could do was stare at him.

"Are you delusional or are you really that insensitive?" How could he act as if he had no clue of what had happened between them? Did he think she would just forget those panicked text messages she had sent and his harsh, hard replies telling her to leave him alone? That he didn't want to have anything to do with her anymore?

"What's really going on, Leanne?" Reuben asked as she busied herself putting the leftovers away. "I can't believe you feel you have any right to be angry with me. Why?"

Where to start?

Leanne snapped covers on the leftovers and shoved them into the refrigerator, giving herself a chance to ease the fury clawing at her heart. She had told herself repeatedly that she was over this man and he didn't deserve one minute of her thoughts.

"Doesn't matter," she snapped. What she and Reuben had was past and gone. He'd had his chance and he'd tossed it away. That he would be working here was an inconvenience she would simply have to deal with until he was gone. Because if there was one thing she knew about Reuben, it was that his departure was inevitable.

"But it does matter. If we'll be working together for a while, I'd like us to not be circling each other." Then, to her dismay, he took a step closer to her and in spite of her obvious anger with him, he touched her shoulder. It was nothing more than the whisper of his hand over her shirt, but it was as if sparks flew from his fingertips.

She clung to the door of the refrigerator, as if to regain her balance, then turned to him.

"Why does this matter now? Why didn't it matter three years ago?"

"It did matter. What we had was everything to me. When we got together in Costa Rica, I thought we had finally come to the place you and I should have been years earlier. Instead you deserted me and ran to Dirk and married him."

All she could do was stare at him. "Deserted you? How… Where…" She shook her head, trying to settle her confusion. "You were the one who did the leaving. I sent you text after text and all I got from you was rejection." The old hurt spiraled up and she had to fight down the pain and, to her humiliation, the tears.

"Rejection? Texts? I have no idea what you're talking about."

The puzzlement on his face was almost her undoing. He seemed genuinely disconcerted.

"I feel like there's this gap between us I don't know how to bridge," he said.

Then, to her dismay, he took that one step separating them and fingered a strand of hair away from her face. She closed her eyes, her own emotions in flux. Her hand twitched at her side, longing to come up and cover his. To reconnect with someone she couldn't forget.

But then she heard Austin cry out and she was doused with icy reality.

"I should go check on him," she said, moving away from him.

"Can I come with you? I haven't seen him yet today."

His casual request was like an arrow in her heart. How could he act this way around Austin? How could he simply relegate him to one corner of his life? Like he didn't matter?

Her indignation and frustrated fury with him rose up. But behind that came a quiet question.

Maybe if he saw Austin face-to-face again he might relent. Maybe seeing him again would make a difference.

Really? If seeing him yesterday hadn't, why would it now?

Her mind did battle with herself as she recalled his coldhearted texts of rejection. The replies she typed out with trembling fingers on her cell phone, alone, pregnant and uncertain of her future.

"Please?" he asked, the pleading note in his voice easing away her resistance.

"Of course you can," she said, determined to be an adult about this, tossing out one last-ditch effort to make him own up to his responsibilities. "He's your son after all."

Chapter Four

Her words hung between them, echoing in the silent kitchen. Soft-spoken, but they rocked his soul. He felt like he was fifteen years old again and being tossed off the dock at Cedar Lake. Suspended in the air in disbelief, wondering what it would feel like when he went in.

"My son?" He choked the words out.

"Yes. Austin is your son," she said, her words sounded like they came from far away.

"My son?" he repeated, feeling like an idiot.

"I know I could keep him from you and not let you see him. That would be what you deserve, but I'm trying to take the moral high ground here. After all, you'll be here every day. You can't avoid him the entire time."

Reuben stared at her, trying to catch up one word, one phrase at a time as he surfaced to the truth.

"What are you saying? What do you mean?"

Leanne glared at him, eyes narrowed. "Please do me a favor and stop acting so surprised."

"But I am." He struggled to settle the information,

his mind ticking back, trying to think, to organize thoughts he couldn't pin down.

"I don't know why you are," she snapped. "This certainly isn't news to you. I still can't believe how casual you've been about the whole thing. You came flying onto the ranch and when you saw him, you acted like he was just some other kid, like he was—"

"My nephew," he interrupted. "Which he is. Dirk's son." Why was she saying Austin was his son? If that was true, why hadn't she told him before? Why wait until now?

Leanne shook her head, and her narrowed eyes latched on to him. "He's not Dirk's. He's yours. The same kid I told you about over three years ago. The same kid you told me you didn't want to have anything to do with."

He held his hands up, still trying to absorb what she was saying. "Whoa, what do you mean, I didn't want to have anything to do with him? This is the first I've heard about this."

"How can you look me straight in the eye and lie like that?"

"I'm not lying. How…when…" He caught himself. "Let's back up here. You got pregnant. Are you saying—"

"It happened at your cousin's wedding. The 'mistake' we both agreed we had made," she made sarcastic air quotes, hooking the air with her fingers.

He could only stare at her, trying to digest all this.

"You got pregnant then?"

"Yes. Except I didn't know at the time, obviously.

And then we decided we needed to think about what we were doing and the repercussions of what we had done—"

"You were the one who wanted space and time," he interrupted, struggling to follow where she was leading, his frustration edging into his voice. "I was all for keeping in touch. For making a commitment right then and there but you wanted to talk to Dirk first. But he was gone to Europe. When we came back, I respected that space and distance while you waited. I let you have your time alone and didn't bug you."

She held her hand up as if to stop anything else he might say. "And obviously you seemed to think that extended to responding callously to my texts when I told you I was pregnant."

"What? When? I didn't get any texts."

"I tried to phone you a bunch of times the night I found out but you didn't answer and I got sent to voice mail," she said, her arms wrapped around her waist, eyes narrowed in fury. "I was so distraught. So upset when I found out. Dirk was on his way back from Europe and I hadn't had a chance to tell him about us. So I sent you a text instead to tell you about Austin and that you were the father. And when you finally texted me back you told me that you were sorry but you couldn't take this on. That I was on my own." She spat the words out at him like venom. "I asked you if you were serious. You replied that you were and that you didn't want to have anything more to do with me. That you felt guilty about being with me. That I should go back to Dirk. That he was the better person." She listed off the reasons in a voice that both cut and accused simultaneously. "Then you told me not to contact you anymore. Then you blocked me. Or something. I never heard from you again."

"I would remember if I'd had that conversation. And I would never have said anything like that." He dug back into his memory, feeling as if his entire world had been shaken, unable to believe she would think this of him. "I was waiting for you to talk to Dirk so we could be together." If he had known he was a father on top of all that, he would have come charging back to Cedar Ridge immediately to make things right.

"Don't act so confused. I saw the answers you sent me. I even showed them to Tabitha because I couldn't believe you would say what you did. And she helpfully reminded me of other times when you were irresponsible."

"What other times?"

"You said you were going to take me to prom and you bailed on me. Then had the nerve to steal a kiss at prom after all."

What? Prom? They were going all the way back to that? Okay, he'd play along, if only to buy time to find his footing. "I didn't take you to prom because Dirk told me to back off. That you were his girlfriend."

"It wasn't true. Dirk and I had broken up."

"Just like you and Dirk had broken up before you came to Costa Rica?" He couldn't wrap his head around all of this.

"I broke up with him that time and you needn't look so surprised."

"That's all beside the point and in the past."

"Maybe, but to me it's all part and parcel of who you are. You don't keep your promises. And don't tell me it isn't true. You're bailing on the Rodeo Group."

In spite of his confusion and frustration with the information she had just dumped on him, Reuben knew how his quitting the Rodeo Group looked to her.

But he wasn't about to tell her it was because being around her and her unreasoning anger made it difficult for him.

"Never mind that. You need to know that I didn't get any of those texts you're talking about," he repeated.

"You can't argue with what I saw on my phone and what my sister saw. We can argue about the texts all we want, but the reality of it all is, whether you want to admit it or not, Austin is your son."

He felt like he was stuck in some maze trying to find his way out.

"Do you still have the texts?" It was a dumb question, but right now dumb was all he could manage.

She looked away, shaking her head. "I deleted them. It was too hurtful to keep the reminder of..." She paused, her voice breaking. Then she held her head up, eyes blazing at him. "It was the hardest thing I ever had to deal with. I felt alone and betrayed by you."

Reuben didn't know how else to tell her that he hadn't received any messages from her. "Okay. We can resolve this fast. I'll check." He pulled his phone out of his pocket, thumbed it on and hit the messages icon.

He scrolled through his message contacts, and as he did so, he realized something else and he stopped.

"Well? Did you find them?" Her voice was like ice.

He lowered his phone, pulling in a deep, heavy sigh as he shook his head. "I won't find them. I lost that phone and everything on it and I forgot to back it up."

"That's convenient."

"As convenient as your marriage to Dirk was, apparently," he snapped.

Leanne sucked in her breath. "That's a low blow."

"So was finding out that, after we had decided to make a commitment to each other, after we realized we should have been together from the beginning, you couldn't wait to marry Dirk when you got back home."

"I didn't have a choice," she said. "I was alone. Pregnant. I had no place to go. No job. No options. You had pushed me away. Rejected me—"

"According to you," he interrupted, refusing to allow her to shove him into that role.

"Dirk came back from Europe the day after I got your texts and told me he was sorry," she carried on, ignoring his interjection. "He begged me to take him back. He said he wanted to marry me right away. That he didn't care what his father thought. I had to tell him the truth about the baby. He was angry with me, but he didn't change his mind. I was scared and confused, and I could only think of my baby. So I said yes. He was being so kind and considerate. We flew to Vegas and got married right away. We had our honeymoon there. And you know what happened on our drive home from the airport." Her voice broke, and in spite of his frustration and confusion, he reached out to her.

But she pulled away.

They stood that way, staring at each other, at a stalemate.

"You're an engineer," she said, stone faced. "If you are still in doubt about Austin's parentage, you can do the math. Austin was born eight and a half months after Dirk and I got married. I think George assumed he was early when, in fact, Austin was overdue."

That still didn't prove anything to him. For all he knew, she had been intimate with Dirk before he and Leanne had gone to the wedding in Costa Rica, but he wasn't bringing that up right now.

"And I can see by the look on your face that you still doubt me." She shook her head in disgust. "You think Austin might be Dirk's child."

"It's a possibility" was all he could say in his defense.

"Why would I lie about this? How would it benefit me? George thinks Austin is Dirk's son. We both know what he thinks of you."

Which didn't precisely help her cause.

"So why haven't you told George the truth if Austin is, indeed, my son?"

Leanne's eyes flicked away from him and a flush tinged her cheeks. Which only underlined his assumptions.

"Dirk made me promise," she said, her voice quiet. "Just before the accident, on our way home from the airport, he made me promise not to tell George the truth about Austin. It was the last thing he said to me before—"

"Before the accident," he said.

She nodded and was about to say more when Austin

started crying again and she hurried away, as if glad of the distraction.

Reuben followed behind her, walking more slowly, still digesting everything she had thrown at him. If she had felt alone and abandoned, of course she would've turned to Dirk.

But he hadn't abandoned her, he reminded himself as he trudged up the stairs. Clearly more was going on here, and right now he couldn't put everything together from what she had told him.

Austin was sitting up in his bed, crying in the darkness of his room.

Leanne hurried inside, dropped on his bed and pulled him close, her one hand cradling his head. "It's okay, honey. I'm here. Did you have a bad dream?"

"I scared," he said. "I scared of da horse."

"It's okay, sweetie," Leanne said, as he crawled onto her lap, slipping his chubby arms around her neck. "You don't have to be scared. I'm here."

Austin looked over her shoulder. "Uncle Wooben," he said with a note of surprise.

"Hey, buddy." Reuben stayed in the doorway, watching as Leanne brushed the little boy's hair back from his face, studying the boy's features, trying to find any resemblance.

His hair was auburn like Leanne's. His eyes brown.

Like his.

Or like George's.

"You come here," Austin demanded, suddenly not so sad anymore.

Reuben pushed himself away from the door frame,

glancing around the darkened room as his eyes adjusted to the gloom.

This had been his room when he'd lived here. All traces of him were gone, however. All his awards, ribbons and plaques from competitions he'd entered and won.

Instead, cute prints now hung on the painted walls. A toy box was tucked at the end of the bed. A small rocking horse that Uncle Boyce had made for Reuben still sat in the corner of the room. One tiny remaining claim he could make on the house.

He was surprised his father had kept it.

"Come. Sit," Austin said.

Reuben hesitated, still not sure what to think of this child and where to put him in his life. Sure he'd known about Austin. The child had always been a reminder to him of Leanne's betrayal and her need for security. For Dirk.

"Come here," Austin said again.

It would look silly to keep standing there, so Reuben walked over to the bed, perching on the edge.

Austin grinned at him, his teeth flashing white in the half dark and Reuben grinned back.

He was a cute kid, that was for sure, but to him he was simply that. A cute kid.

Then Austin angled his head down and Reuben saw what he hadn't yesterday. A tiny, lighter patch of hair swirling out of the cowlick on the top of Austin's head. It wasn't large. You'd have to pay attention to see it.

But it was the same light patch of hair his mother had. The same patch of hair he had.

He felt his world shift yet again as the evidence in front of him, combined with Leanne's insistence, gave him proof he could no longer deny. Austin truly was his son.

His gaze shifted to hers. The look on her face showed him that she had seen his reaction.

Reuben reached down and fingered the patch of Austin's lighter hair, as if touching it would make it real. "My mom always colored her hair, but she had the same bit of differently colored hair" was all he could say, a confusing rush of feelings overwhelming him. "So do I. My mom told me it was hereditary. That her dad had it too."

Leanne said nothing as a heavy silence fell between them.

Then he looked up at her, still trying to sort everything out. "I don't know what to say."

Leanne's expression softened.

"So, do you believe me now?"

"I do. I have to."

"I'm sad that it took such hard proof. I was hoping you would have taken my word for truth."

He fought down a beat of frustration. Surely she had to understand he would have some doubts? But she seemed to think that he'd known and rejected her.

He blew out his breath, looking down at Austin again who was now yawning. Reuben crouched down, as if seeing him in an entirely new light. His son. He and Leanne truly did have a son. They were now bound with an unbreakable, undeniable bond.

And what are you going to do about that? Can you still leave?

Leanne pulled Austin close against her, tucking his head under her chin. As he watched Leanne holding Austin, remnants of dreams he and Leanne had spun those two weeks in Costa Rica returned.

The two of them, living on a ranch somewhere. Leanne had imagined it to be the Bar W ranch because she wanted their children raised in the same place he was. Reuben had said he wanted to live anywhere but the Bar W. They hadn't exactly fought about it—they were too in love at the time—but it had caused a moment of tension.

And now, here she was, raising Austin on a ranch with no future that he could see, clinging to it for Austin's sake.

Then Leanne lowered Austin onto his bed, tucking the sheets around him and brushing a kiss over his forehead. "Good night, sweetheart," she whispered. Austin curled up on his side, grinning at Reuben. "Good night, Uncle Wooben," he said.

Reuben gave him a forced smile, then left the room as Leanne switched on a nightlight. Then she closed the door behind her and led the way down the stairs back to the kitchen. She stopped there and turned to him. "So. That's your son."

"He's a cute kid" was all he could manage. "I forgot to give him his present."

"So, are you still leaving in a couple of weeks?" she asked.

Her question hung between them, unspoken ones hovering behind it.

"I don't know." One thing he knew for sure was that, in spite of his father's surprising request for help, he was moving on to that job. It was the opportunity of a lifetime as his future boss Marshall had said, and Reuben knew he was right.

She sighed heavily, which clearly told him what she thought of his evasive answer. "Okay. Then we'll play the situation by ear for now. And I guess you'll be coming here for the next few days."

"I'll be here until the cows are brought home and weaned," he said. "I know you need the help. Besides, how can I refuse my own father's request?" He couldn't keep the faintly bitter note out of his voice.

Leanne sighed lightly, resting her hands on a chair tucked into a corner nook of the kitchen. "I know you don't want to be here, and quite frankly I'm not crazy about your being here either, but for now we'll have to find a way to work together."

Reuben looked around the house he'd lived in for years and eased out a heavy sigh as echoes of old fights with George rose up and mocked him.

"You don't like it here, do you?" Leanne asked.

"It's my childhood home, but it doesn't hold lots of happy memories." He turned to her. "You always loved it here, though."

She nodded, a faint smile playing around her lips as she looked around the house. The first he'd seen since he arrived. That it was thoughts of the ranch causing it shouldn't surprise him. "I couldn't imagine why anyone would ever want to leave here," she said. "A place with roots and history."

Reuben knew firsthand how much she loved the ranch and wanted to be involved in it. Even when she and Dirk had dated, she'd learned to ride a horse so she could help with pasture moves and gathering cows. Dirk wasn't as enamored of the ranch as she was, and when she wanted him to teach her how to run the tractor, he'd refused. So she finagled Reuben into doing it. She was a natural, he had said, and then, of course, Dirk was jealous that Reuben had spent the time with Leanne instead of him.

"Depends on what type of history you have," he said, thinking of George and the treatment he'd doled out. He shoved his hand through his hair in frustration as he thought of the young boy upstairs. A child he had always thought of as his nephew and now had to think of as his son. "And no matter what you think of me, you have to admit I didn't have the best example of fatherhood."

"Are you saying you don't want to be a father to Austin?"

He easily heard the pain in her voice and he knew, once again, he had gone about this all wrong. He closed his eyes, praying for the right words, praying to a God he hadn't spent a lot of time with in the past. A God he had only recently come back to.

"I'm saying that I'm not sure how good a father I can be. George's blood runs through my veins too. And we both know what kind of a father he was."

"So you'll stick around to help with the cows but then

you're gone? Leaving your son behind?" Her fists were clenched at her sides, her eyes narrowed, her voice hard.

Her anger was like a wave, beating at him, dragging at the foundation of his life.

Please, Lord. Help me out here.

He forced himself to hold her angry gaze, drawing back into himself, pushing aside what Leanne wanted and what he wanted.

"I'm saying that I have to make the best decision for Austin's sake," he finally said.

She held his eyes a moment, then seemed to relax. "I'm sorry. You're right."

Then she dragged her hands over her face, her weariness suddenly apparent.

"You look tired," he said. "You should go to bed and I should leave."

"Thanks again for your help," she said, giving him a ghost of a smile. She hesitated a moment as if she wanted to say more. He wasn't sure what else there was to say right now.

Then she turned and walked away, heading back up the stairs that led to her wing of the house. He watched her go, then left himself, his footsteps echoing in the cavernous kitchen. Outside, the quiet and darkness seemed to enfold him.

The wide swath of stars overhead caught his attention. He looked up at the night sky and, in spite of everything that had happened, he smiled. He hadn't seen the stars like this in years. Bright, crowded, like a band of sparkling light. He watched them a moment, the utter quiet washing over him. Then, in the distance, he heard the gentle lowing of a cow, the nasal reply from a calf.

To his surprise he was swamped by a wave of homesickness. He had missed this more than he wanted to admit. Missed the silence, the utter majesty of the empty spaces around him. Missed working with his hands, riding horses. Being outside.

He had always known coming back here to live wasn't a possibility. That it would mean willingly putting up with George's derision and negativity and he knew, much as he needed Reuben now, George would never bring him back into the fold. Give him a share of the ranch.

He stepped into his truck, and as he did, his eyes were drawn to his old room where Austin now slept. The nightlight Leanne had turned on created a soft warm glow though the curtains. His son lay there. His and Leanne's son.

Knowing that made Leanne's marriage to Dirk even more difficult to get past.

Dear Lord, he prayed, *I have no idea what to think or what to do. I'm trusting You'll bring me through this because I'm so confused. I'm afraid of being a father because I don't know how that's supposed to look. I've got too many bad things in my past. I'd never be a good one.*

He let the prayer settle. Then he put his truck in gear and drove away. He would be back tomorrow and a few more tomorrows after that.

And then?

Then he had to go to California and start the life he had carved out for himself.

And Austin? Leanne?

He pushed those thoughts aside. He couldn't deal with that right now.

"So what did he say when you told him?" Tabitha leaned forward, her gaze intent. "Did he finally admit…" Tabitha glanced around the quiet restaurant, then leaned closer in, lowering her voice. "Did he admit the truth?" she asked.

"Only when he saw the lighter patch of hair on Austin's cowlick, the same as he has." Leanne stirred a large spoonful of sugar into her coffee and took a quick sip, resting her elbows on the wooden table tucked into the booth in one corner of Angelo's, one of the local cafés and restaurants in town. Prints of Italy and Venice hung on the walls, an incongruity in the cow town of Cedar Ridge.

"You look tired," Tabitha said, frowning.

"I am. My body aches and my head aches and I'm trying not to feel pressured about getting the cows down before the snow comes."

"There's no snow in the forecast."

Leanne massaged her temples, nodding. "I'm sure hoping they're right for a change. Reuben seemed to think I should be at the ranch today instead of at this meeting." The thought of all she had to do created a low-level panic, but behind that came an annoyance with Reuben.

"You're doing too much," Tabitha said.

"What else am I supposed to do now that Devin quit?"

"Not just with the ranch, honey. I'm also talking about this Rodeo Group you insist on being involved in."

"George asked me to help."

"And what George asks for, George gets."

Leanne chose to ignore the sardonic tone in her sister's voice. Tabitha had her own issues with George, but Leanne refused to make them hers.

"At any rate, it's good for you that Reuben is helping, though that can't be easy for you either."

Leanne sighed again. "Besides giving me advice—too little too late, by the way—he thinks we should sell the ranch."

As she spoke the words aloud, the idea lingered. And for the tiniest of moments she held on to it. Selling the ranch would release her from all the stress she'd been under lately. And the worst of it was, even once the cows were all brought home, the pressure wouldn't ease off. Then it was a matter of trying to find enough feed to get them through the winter and after that it was making sure the bulls got put out on time and after that—

"I can tell you're thinking about it."

Leanne shook her head, as if to dismiss the idea. "I have Austin to think of. The ranch is his security. I simply have to get through all of this. Keep pushing."

"And where does Reuben fit in all of this?"

"Where he did before. In the past."

"But he's Austin's father, and now that he's accepted it—"

"I didn't come here to talk about the ranch or Reuben." Leanne cut her off.

"Your cheeks are flushing though," Tabitha said, in a teasing voice. "He always was a big deal to you."

"Stop. Right now. This isn't simply a high school crush we're talking about." Though even as she denounced her sister's teasing, she had to admit that even the thought of Reuben could ratchet up her heart rate. Just the sight of him brought her back to those two glorious weeks in Costa Rica at his cousin's wedding. When she'd thought they could finally be together.

It had been just a dream.

She shook off the dead-end memories, focusing on her sister and her plans. "So how is work on the clinic coming?" she said, deflecting as quickly as she could. "I drove past to have a look the other day. Looks like the construction is going gangbusters."

"Morgan has been on the internet a lot," Tabitha said. "He wants to make sure his new clinic has all of the best of the best equipment, the latest of the latest." She shook her head in mock dismay. "He is determined to prove he can build and run a vet clinic better than his old boss, Anselm Waters, did." Then Tabitha grinned at her sister. "But I'm guessing you're not that interested in finding out about those fancy new rafters Morgan is ordering."

"I wanted to show support," Leanne said, smiling back at her sister.

"Speaking of. Reuben. If you want I can talk to him. Tell him what a jerk he was."

Leanne shot her a warning glance. "Don't you even think about it. Reuben has had his chance to redeem himself many times and he fell so far from grace, I still haven't heard the echo of the drop at the bottom."

Tabitha made a face, bobbing her head back and forth as if agreeing and yet not. "He admitted Austin was his," she said.

Leanne glanced around, worried someone might overhear. But the only other person in the café was Andy Rodriguez, Shauntelle's father, and he was on his phone.

"You stay away from Reuben. Sure he stepped up but only because I pushed it," Leanne said forcing herself to remember his heartless replies. "You saw those text messages he sent me when I told him I was pregnant. When he told me he didn't want to have anything to do with me. Or 'my kid,' as he so delicately put it."

Tabitha was silent, frowning at her half empty cup of coffee. "You still haven't forgiven him, have you?" Tabitha asked.

"Would you? Ever since I started dating Dirk in high school, Reuben borderline flirted with me. Telling me I was wasting my time with his brother. Constantly paying attention to me even though he knew I was determined to be faithful to Dirk."

"Never mind sneaking that kiss the night of the prom he said he was going to take you to," Tabitha interrupted.

Leanne ignored that comment, the memory of that night still able to create such a mixture of feelings even after all this time. "That kiss was a mistake I still feel guilty about."

"Why? Dirk broke up with you," Tabitha said, her eyes narrowing.

"He came back again."

"I'm sure it was only because he found out about Reuben. Then he waits a couple of years to propose to you, then he keeps you hanging another four years while he works up enough nerve to tell his father he wants to marry a Rennie."

"Well, he finally did," Leanne retorted, feeling she had to stick up for her husband.

"Only after you broke up with him and he took off to France." Tabitha's eyes narrowed, looking thoughtful. "Is there any way Dirk knew about you and Reuben getting together in Costa Rica? Do you think that's the reason he hurried back from his travels in Europe?"

Why was her sister determined to dredge up this old history?

"Doesn't matter if he did. Reuben said he didn't want to marry me and Dirk finally did. That was enough for me. And you don't need to diss my husband. At least he came through, unlike Reuben, who left me hanging in the worst possible way." Leanne stopped there, her cheeks growing even warmer at the resurrection of memories she thought she had dealt with.

Tabitha looked annoyed and Leanne felt bad. She reached across the table and curled her hand around her sister's. "I'm sorry. You're right. I'm just touchy and scared. Seeing Reuben again has been difficult."

"Because of Austin?"

"Partly." Leanne wove her fingers around each other, remembering how being with Reuben affected her. In spite of everything that had happened between them, he could still made her heart race. Could still create that trembling deep in her soul. A feeling she'd never had around Dirk. "I want everything done. He says he's leaving, which shouldn't surprise me."

"How are he and George interacting?"

Leanne shrugged. As antagonistic as always, yet George seems different around him. "I hope it continues. I'm just starting to earn George's trust and don't want anything to jeopardize that."

Tabitha frowned. "You're serious about working your way into the ranch?"

"Yes. You sound skeptical."

"Well, let's just say I don't one hundred percent trust George Walsh to follow through on his promises."

Leanne had her concerns about George, as well, but she had to believe him when he said he wanted to give her and Austin more security and give them a share of the ranch. "You know that I love working on the ranch. And for the first time in my life, I feel like I have something that's mine."

Tabitha nodded, showing her understanding. "But maybe someday someone will come into your life—"

"My husband is dead and the man I once saw as the love of my life has proven to be a major disappointment. I need to be my own boss and do what I love."

"But now that Reuben is back—"

"Stop. Now. He's only sticking around to help on the ranch, and in spite of how I feel about him, I need the help. But he'll be gone again."

"I thought he was going to do a structural assessment on the arena."

"He told me he wasn't going to, of course that was before he ended up helping us with the cows. I hope he doesn't. It would mean his working with the committee and right now I don't mind the break from him."

Then Leanne glanced at the oversize clock hanging on the wall behind her sister and gulped down the last of her coffee.

"Sorry. But I gotta go," she said. "The meeting will be starting soon and I want to get there before everyone arrives."

They said goodbye, but as Leanne drove over to the County Building, she felt as if her own thoughts were in a horrible tangle. Reuben. Austin. The past. The present. The ranch. Her future and Austin's.

Next job. Just think about the next job. The Rodeo Group meetings never went that long, thankfully, and she had to get groceries after that.

Another busy day but at least she would get a break from Reuben and the difficulties and questions he had brought into her life.

"So I'm sure you'll all be glad to know that Reuben has changed his mind about helping us, again," Reuben's cousin Cord said, glancing around the room and letting his eyes rest on Reuben. He gave him a quick grin, then turned his attention back to other members of the Rodeo Group. "So now that he's here, we want to put him to work as soon as possible."

"Sounds good to me," he replied with a forced smile.

"The sooner I get done, the sooner I can leave." He had felt foolish calling Owen and telling him that he'd changed his mind. Again, as Cord so delicately put it. But he figured as long as he was sticking around for a while, he may as well get the assessment done too. Or at least as much of it as he could.

"You've barely gotten here," Owen Herne, chairman of the group put in. "Can't believe you'd want to leave so quick. This is your hometown. Lots of people want to see you. Family, old friends."

"I didn't come for a reunion. I only came to do a job." Reuben shrugged away Owen's comment even though it created a mixture of guilt and sorrow deep within him. He would have liked to connect with all his cousins and friends, but between the work on the ranch and now taking this on, he wouldn't have time. Then he caught his father's glower at his flip remark but chose to ignore that, as well. "So what I need to know from this committee is how much do you want me to do?" he continued.

"We need to know as much as we can about the arena's structural integrity," Owen was saying. "Need to know if it's worth finishing what that weasel Floyd started." Owen flicked an apologetic look Leanne's way. "Sorry."

In spite of his mixed feelings toward her, Reuben couldn't help but feel sympathy for Leanne as her cheeks flushed. It couldn't be easy to hear people put down her father. He knew firsthand how difficult life had been for Leanne and Tabitha when they first moved to Cedar Ridge. He vividly remembered Leanne's first day of school. She was quiet, soft-spoken, wearing out-of-date clothes that looked worn and tired.

But she'd had a quiet dignity and a radiant beauty that struck him immediately.

Not only him but also his brother, Dirk. Trouble was Reuben knew who and what he was. A wild child who liked pushing boundaries and testing limits. A bareback rider who prided himself on being the toughest, hardest and baddest. A rebel who couldn't win his father's love no matter what he did.

Dirk was the charming golden boy, and while Reuben had held back, feeling undeserving, Dirk, who had no such qualms, had moved in. But Reuben could never shake the idea that on a deeper level Leanne seemed to be attracted to him, as well. It had never been obvious. A look that went on too long. A smile that became serious whenever their eyes met. But in spite of feelings he'd sensed they shared, he'd also known she would never break up with Dirk.

But then she did. When she walked onto the beach at his cousin's wedding, alone, barefoot, wearing a flowing pink dress, his heart had kicked into overdrive.

And they'd spent a glorious few weeks together.

Six weeks later she and Dirk eloped. Eight weeks later his brother was dead.

"We aren't entirely sure about the integrity of the building," Owen said, pulling Reuben's thoughts back to the present. "Given that Floyd didn't finish the work, we need to start assessing the building from the ground up. We have to decide if the structure is worth working on or if we should doze it and start from scratch.

What we want from your assessment is which direction we should go."

"I should be able to give you that information," Reuben said, dragging his gaze away from Leanne to the assembled members of the group who were looking at him expectantly. "It will probably take me about a week or more to cover all the aspects of the structure. Wiring, plumbing, anything that is in place. Make sure it's all up to code. I'll need to stop at the town office to see what the building permit looks like, whether we'll need a new one or if the old one is still valid."

"Could you give us an idea of what kind of money we're talking for your work?" Owen asked.

"I'll give you a discount on my usual fee," he said, keeping his comment deliberately vague. "It'll be a fair price."

"Leanne, you got that?" Owen said with a grin. "Make sure you mark down that he said a fair price. I know what kind of guy Reuben used to be. Left us hanging with the bar tab one too many times after a rodeo competition."

"Those were the old days." Reuben managed a feeble grin in response to the reference to his rodeo days. Leanne didn't need to be reminded of his former life.

"Anyone else have any questions for Reuben?"

Carmen Fisher, the manager of George's hardware store, sat back in her chair looking concerned but said nothing. Andy just shook his head. Cord was already tapping out a text on his cell phone as he got up, also shaking his head. George just shrugged.

"Okay. Then this meeting is adjourned," Owen said.

"We won't need to have another one until Reuben has some information to give us."

Owen gave Reuben a broad grin then got up.

"You're coming to the ranch again tomorrow?" George asked.

Reuben shot another quick glance at Leanne, who was still tapping away on the computer, then turned to his father. "I'll be there."

George acknowledged his comment with a tight nod. "Good." Then he pulled Cord aside as they walked out of the room with Owen, lowering his voice to talk to him.

Leanne was about to leave when Carmen got up. "Leanne, can you wait a moment? You too, Reuben? I have something I need to say to you both," she said, glancing over her shoulder as if to make sure no one was in the room.

"I don't have a lot of time," Leanne said.

"This will only take a few moments." Carmen sighed, then walked over to the door, opened it, looked around then closed it.

Reuben was officially intrigued as she walked back to where Leanne sat.

"So I need to talk to you about George," she said. "I feel like a traitor, but I'm concerned about his health. I don't know if you've noticed, but he's been smoking again. Tony, the young fellow who works at the store, caught him a couple of times out back."

Reuben wondered if his return had anything to do with his father taking up a habit that he'd indulged in too often in the past.

"I haven't noticed," Leanne said, frowning as she slipped her laptop into her briefcase. "He hasn't been sneaking out of the house for a cigarette that I could tell and I'm sure he hasn't been smoking in his room."

"Well, he's been doing it at the hardware store." Carmen sighed. "And he's also been short of breath lately. I think he's under too much stress."

"So do you think he should sell the store?" Leanne asked.

Carmen shrugged. "He's not that involved in the store's operations anymore, so I can't imagine there's any stress there. He only stops in to see what's going on and check on the books. If he stays it's to chat with the customers or putz around with the inventory. He likes rearranging shelves." She gave them a wry look. "However I don't know if the store is the problem."

It seemed to Reuben that Carmen didn't want to come right out and voice what needed to be said.

"So that leaves the ranch," Reuben put in, knowing Leanne would disagree with what he was going to say. "Do you think it's the ranch that's wearing him down?"

Leanne shot him an angry look. "The ranch is what keeps him going," she returned. "It's his life."

"His or yours?" he asked, his voice quiet.

This netted him another glare, but as their eyes held, he sensed a lingering doubt. As if on some level she knew, as well. But she couldn't admit it. She dragged her gaze away, turning to Carmen.

"What do you suggest?" Leanne asked. "What do you think we should do?"

Carmen glanced from Reuben to Leanne as if unsure

where and how to proceed. "I know he often grumbles about hired hands and all the work that ranch requires. I wish I had an answer, but like I said I just wanted to let you know what I've seen. I don't want to make it look like I'm going behind his back, but I felt you needed to hear my concerns."

"Thanks for caring, Carmen," Reuben said, giving her a smile. "I appreciate your letting us know."

She nodded, tucked her notebook under her arm and then left.

Leanne wasn't looking at Reuben as she slipped a sheaf of papers into her briefcase, then zipped it shut. He knew she wasn't going to address what Carmen brought up. So he would.

"So, what do you think of what Carmen told us?" he asked, pushing the issue.

Leanne swung the strap of the briefcase over her arm, her eyes looking everywhere but at him.

"Even if he isn't smoking that much, we both know he's not well," Reuben pressed. "So if there are other factors at play…"

Leanne closed her eyes, her hands clenched on the straps of the case. Then she turned to him.

"We might as well get to the heart of it. You think we should sell the ranch," she said.

Reuben lifted his shoulder in a half shrug. "I think you need to be realistic about what you and George can manage."

"You've never cared about that place at all," she continued, as if he hadn't even spoken. "You've never understood what your father has done to maintain it and keep it going without either of his sons around." Her eyes snapped as she looked at him.

"Why should I have cared or invested any more time in it? It was always going to go to Dirk, and it's not like he was that involved. You know that."

Leanne didn't respond to his assertion.

"Besides, you're wrong," he said, feeling an unreasoning desire to try to redeem himself in her eyes. "I cared more about the ranch than Dirk ever did. Worked harder on the ranch than my brother ever did. I loved my brother, you know that. But everything always came so easily to Dirk. He didn't value things as a result. He never had to work for the ranch or anything else in his whole life."

Including you, he wanted to say but he wasn't that dumb.

Leanne looked down at the table, the fingers of her one hand sliding up and down the strap. "I know that."

Her admission surprised him.

"I'm glad you're here," she said, adding to his shock. "I'm glad you're helping. George may not admit it, but I think he feels the same."

Reuben wondered if she was simply trying to make him feel good. But the lonely part of him that had always yearned for his father's approval and for Leanne's thanks was only too willing to take it all.

"Well, that's good."

"And I hope you know I appreciate the help, as well." This time she looked over at him and gave him a gentle smile.

Their eyes held, and old attractions, old emotions shimmered between them.

His breath caught in his throat and, to his dismay, he had to fight the urge to close the gap between them. To cup her face with his hand.

To kiss her.

He shook off the feeling, dragging his gaze away.

"That's good. I'll be there tomorrow," he said, fighting to regain control of himself.

She hesitated a moment as if she wanted to say more, but he kept his eyes averted.

Because he knew, if he looked at her again, he would do something supremely foolish.

Something he was sure he would regret.

Chapter Five

"So where's Austin?" Reuben asked, as he followed Leanne to the corrals.

It was late Friday morning and the sun shed weak warmth on the day, easing the chill that night had brought.

"George is bringing him to Tabitha's today. He can't take care of him and there's no way we can have him around." Leanne slipped a ball cap on her head, tugging her ponytail through the hole in the back, and zipped up the down vest she'd put on over her jacket. She hadn't wanted to admit it to herself but this morning, for the first time in weeks, she'd woken up with a sense of anticipation of the work ahead.

This morning she would have someone helping her who was competent and capable. That it was Reuben was unfortunate, but thankfully Chad would also be around as a buffer. She wasn't ready to spend an entire day alone with Reuben.

Yesterday, for just a moment, she felt as if she'd gone

back in time and the old feelings she had thought she had suppressed, forgotten, had come drifting to the surface. It would be too dangerous to acknowledge them now.

"He'll probably head to the hardware store and then the Brand and Grill for coffee," she continued, "so I don't expect him back for a while. And Chad called to say that he'll be here in about twenty minutes."

"I thought Shauntelle usually took care of Austin?" Reuben said.

"She couldn't today. She's getting ready for the farmers' market tomorrow." She walked faster than Reuben, trying to keep ahead of him and the unwelcome feelings being too close to him created. She couldn't allow herself to give in to them. Reuben was leaving. He'd made that very clear.

"So he gets bounced back and forth between Tabitha and Shauntelle?"

"Why does this matter to you?" She strode over to the tack shed off the main barn and slid open the large rolling door, taking refuge in annoyance at his questions.

"Because. He's my son," he said, following her. "I wonder if it's a good idea to pass him around like that."

Leanne spun around, her hands planted on her hips, thankful for the outrage flowing through her. "You haven't been a part of his life for almost three years and now you're going to get all parental?"

Reuben held her angry glare beat for beat, his own eyes narrowed. "Isn't that what you want? Or am I simply supposed to say, 'Okay, I acknowledge that he's my son. Here's some money—'"

"I don't want your money. I only want… I only wanted you to…" She paused there, suddenly in unfamiliar territory. She never thought she'd be confronting Reuben again. She thought his denial of Austin's paternity had put him out of their lives for good.

But he was back and, it seemed, had his own ideas about her son. correction, *their son.*

"Wanted what?" he asked, articulating her silent questions. "Me to be an involved father? Or am I just supposed to admit he's my son and walk away?"

Leanne held his narrowed gaze, suddenly unsure. Reuben admitted Austin was his. It was what she had hoped for forever, ever since she'd seen that faint line on the home pregnancy test.

Now she had a plan and a purpose. However, with Reuben, the man she had once loved so dearly facing her, it didn't seem like enough.

"I don't know," she finally admitted, stepping into the gloom of the shed, grabbing a couple of halters off their hooks on the wall and handing one to him. "I don't know what kind of father I want you to be."

Reuben released a sigh as he took the halter, his gaze fixed on her. "But you know what you want now, right? From life?"

She sighed, feeling the anger draining out of her. "I want a good life for Austin. I want security for him."

"I understand. And this is the place where that will happen." He looked around the ranch yard, a faint smile teasing his lips. "I remember sitting on a beach with you and talking about having six kids, a milk cow and chickens. I don't see a cow or chickens around."

"Someday." She held his gaze, memories floating upward. "I remember your saying you could only promise me the chickens."

"Because the milk cow required pasture, which meant land."

"Which, to you, meant settling down in Cedar Ridge. And you never wanted six kids." She struggled to keep her tone light but she remembered his comment hurting her at the time.

"Told you I never saw myself as a father."

"And here you are."

"Here I am." Then he shifted his cowboy hat on his head and sighed. "We could go round and round on this, but we've got cows to move. Which horse do you want me to use?"

She accepted his segue. It was probably for the best. Right now she didn't have the energy to look too far into the future.

"Mickey," she said. "The roan mare. I'll take Spud, the palomino. When Chad comes, he can take Pinto."

"I remember Spud," he said, hooking the halter over his shoulder and taking the second one for the horse Chad would be riding when he came. "I trained that horse."

"You did well with him," Leanne said as they walked out of the darkened shed into the light. "He's a good cattle horse. Not as good as Dickens, who I was using on Wednesday. He's a better cutting horse in tight areas, but Spud is good for long hauls."

"Listen to you, rancher woman," Reuben said, a lighter tone entering his voice. "Talking all horse and cow lingo."

She couldn't help but return his smile. In spite of

their history, talking with Reuben had always come easy. He could make her smile and laugh in a way Dirk never could.

"I've picked up a few things along the way," she said. "Your dad is a good teacher."

"He can be," Reuben admitted, opening the gate to the pen. "Not so good with hired hands, though."

"No. That's true. Dirk might have been better."

"I don't know," Reuben said, walking over to Spud and stroking his neck. "Dirk wasn't very patient either. Plus he hated cows."

"You're right about that." But as soon as she spoke the words, she felt a flash of disloyalty to her late husband.

Reuben quickly got the halter on Spud, Leanne not far behind him, but as he led his horse past her, he paused, giving her a look.

"Do you miss Dirk?" he asked.

Leanne wanted to look away; his eyes seemed to be asking for more than his question intimated. And for a moment the old attraction shimmered between them.

"Sometimes" was all she dared say.

"Did you love him?"

His question was heavy with portent. She wanted to lie, to tell him something that would keep the distance between them.

But there had been enough of that, so she simply shook her head, then tugged on Mickey's halter, opened the gate and led the horse through.

"That's the last of them, I hope," Reuben said as he nudged his horse to come alongside Leanne. He'd been scouring the gullies and hollows and hadn't heard or seen any other cows. He was sure they had rounded up all the cows and calves in this pasture. Now they were gathered up and plodding at a comfortably slow pace back to the ranch.

The wind was at their backs, which made the air feel less cold. He was thankful George hadn't been around to help. Having him elsewhere gave Reuben breathing space. A bit of peace. He could simply enjoy being on a horse out in the backcountry.

With Leanne?

The hills rolled away from them, brown now, the wind holding a promise of winter. And yet he felt a contentment he hadn't felt in a long time.

"I'm glad you could come along to herd them up," Leanne said, giving him a quick smile. "George doesn't have the patience and Chad doesn't have the skill."

Reuben glanced over at Chad who was riding up ahead, keeping his horse on the side of the herd as they moved along the fence line headed toward the ranch. This was the easy part, and unless some cows decided to make a break for it, they were home free.

"I know the lay of the land so that helps. And Chad did well, all things considered." He wanted to be positive, but the reality was Chad's main contribution to the roundup was to park his horse in a gully to prevent the cows from turning that way. Reuben could see it would take a while before Chad felt comfortable on a horse, let alone become an asset to herding and cutting cows.

Once again he felt a niggle of despair. How did Leanne even think she could carry the weight of all the work this ranch created on her own?

Leanne sighed, shifting in the saddle. "I'm glad this is the last of them. We'll just have to process them and then we can put them in the winter corrals."

"That's still a lot of cows to feed over the winter."

Leanne nodded and Reuben struggled to keep his comments to himself. It didn't matter what he thought of her trying to run a ranch with George and Chad—depending on how long he lasted—right now he had a job to do, so he might as well get it done.

"Did you get enough hay put up to feed them all?" he asked. He knew when he was working on the ranch, hay production was hit or miss. In a good year they had hay to sell. In a bad year, they'd have to buy.

This elicited another sigh. "Not really. I need to phone around. We'll need at least another hundred bales to get us through the winter. I'm thankful we could keep the cows on pasture as long as we could, otherwise that number would be higher."

He heard the faint note of tension in her voice and even though it wasn't his problem, panic flickered through him.

"Have you found a supplier?"

"Not yet."

"If you don't, you might have to sell some cows."

Leanne bit her lip in frustration. "Is that your solution to everything? Sell?"

"Just being realistic. You don't have dependable help and you're looking at a lot of work if you winter all the animals you have now." He stopped himself, wondering why he was even getting involved. He would only be around long enough to help, then he was gone.

"Did you ever like being on the ranch?" she asked, tilting her head as if challenging him. "Dirk always said you could never wait to leave, that that's why you spent so much time rodeoing."

"That's not true," he countered, nudging his horse to get closer to the cows at the back. "I loved working cattle, riding fences, training horses. I think I liked it more than Dirk ever did." He couldn't stop the defensive tone in his voice. It bothered him that she was quoting Dirk to him. Dirk, who had told him over and over again that he didn't want the ranch their father kept promising him.

She was quiet a moment, as if absorbing this information. "When Dirk and I got married, he talked about living here. Settling down."

Her calm discussion of plans she and Dirk had made when they got married dug like a hook into his heart. He and Leanne had made plans too. Though she had been angling for the two of them to live on the ranch, he knew he could never have let that happen because of his father. But he had hoped their love was strong enough that she would be willing to go with him wherever he wanted to go.

"Is that why you married him?" he asked suddenly, struck by an idea. "Because he wanted to live on the ranch and I didn't?"

She turned away from him, looking ahead, as if she couldn't face him. "I told you why I married him. I was pregnant and on my own."

The set of her jaw told him that until they resolved the issue of the mystery texts, they would always hang between them. And right at that moment, he was tired of the distance. He wanted to find a way to make things better before he left.

"It must have been difficult for you," he said. "To be in that position."

He looked ahead, his eyes on the cows as they moved along, but most of his attention was on the woman beside him.

"It was. Thanks for acknowledging that."

"Dirk was a good man," he said. "I'm glad he helped you out when…when you needed it."

"Ironic that he wouldn't marry me before. And when he finally did, we had only two weeks…" her voice trailed off and he realized that in spite of the history between them and how things had transpired, he should have guessed Leanne would be grieving the loss of the history she and his brother shared.

"I'm sorry," he said, moving his horse closer to hers. As he did, their legs touched and awareness flickered through him. Then, in spite of the voice in his head warning him not to not get too involved, to keep his distance, he reached over and put his hand on her arm, squeezing gently. "I miss him too."

To his surprise she didn't pull away, letting their shared grief connect them.

Then she turned to him. "I wish things could have been different. For us."

He held her gaze, shock and another, older emotion flowing up into his soul. Yearning.

For a moment, he wondered, the possibilities teasing him. He and Leanne and Austin. Together.

On the ranch? With George?

"I wish they could be different too," he said. Their eyes held a moment, and it was as if time wheeled back to a better place. When they were full of plans, focused on the same thing.

Not like they were now. Alone yet bound together by their son.

Then her horse turned its head, pinning one ear back, and Reuben recognized the signal Spud was giving his horse, Mickey, to keep its distance. As he moved away, reality doused any sentimental feelings he might have been harboring.

Stay focused on your plans, he reminded himself. *Leanne is a part of your past.*

And Austin?

Reuben pulled in a steadying breath. He felt as if he, Leanne and Austin were suspended in an uneasy limbo and he wasn't sure how to resolve it. He knew he couldn't give up on plans he'd spent the past four years putting together.

But could he walk away from Leanne again? Or turn his back on his son?

"So what did you think of what Carmen said. About George?" Leanne asked.

Reuben looked ahead as he shifted his thoughts to his father, swaying with the easy motion of his horse. The saddle leather creaked, the occasional lowing of the cows broke a silence he never experienced living in the city. "You've never caught him smoking?"

"No. And I'm sure he doesn't smoke in his room."

"You're in the other wing of the house," Reuben teased. "You wouldn't know if he was."

Leanne shrugged her reply.

"I have to tell you, though, that he's aged a lot since the last time I saw him," Reuben continued. "He looks tired."

"He's had a lot to deal with the past few years."

Reuben acknowledged that with a nod, but to him that didn't change the fact that his father seemed to have lost his will to keep the ranch afloat.

"You like working with my dad?" he asked.

Leanne looked away, hunching her shoulders as if in defense. "He's a...complicated man. But I also think he's lonely. Losing Dirk was hard on him." She looked over at him. "And you haven't been around much."

Reuben released a harsh laugh. "I doubt he's missed me," he said.

"I've never dared ask him, but maybe you can tell me, why is he still so upset with you?"

He paused, weighing his answer, trying to figure out how he was supposed to encapsulate all those years of stress and fighting and disagreement into a conversation that would end as soon as they got to the corrals.

"I know that part of it had to do with your mother," Leanne ventured.

"She was one reason. Dirk was the son of the loving mother and doting wife. I was the son of the woman who made George look like a fool. I was a reminder of the woman who left him."

"Could part of his treatment of you have been your behavior? You were quite the rebel."

"A rebel you were trying to avoid."

"Yes. I was, but it was hard at times."

Her admission surprised him, as did the flush that heightened the pink of her cheeks. His thoughts drifted back to those two weeks when they could finally admit to the feelings that had always hovered.

"What made you change your mind? When we were in Costa Rica? What made you think I was worth spending time with then, besides having broken up with Dirk?"

"I always thought you were worth spending time with, Reuben. And that was my struggle."

It took him a few moments to realize what she was saying. They had talked endlessly when they were together in Costa Rica. About how they had always cared for each other. How she had clung to her relationship with Dirk longer than she should have. When he found out she'd married Dirk, however, he had wondered if it was the exotic location and the distance that had made them both so candid about the feelings they both had kept to themselves for so long.

Now, here on the ranch, where life had always been complicated for both of them, she was saying the same thing she had then.

He took a chance and once again moved his horse closer, sensing a breaking down of the walls she had put up the moment she first saw him. "It was my struggle too," he said. "Watching you with Dirk when I felt that he was all wrong for you."

"Maybe he was." Leanne gave him a knowing look. "But I sometimes felt the same about you."

He held her gaze. "I knew I wasn't the best person for you either. Which was why I kept my distance."

"You didn't keep your distance at prom," she teased again.

"I couldn't help myself. Gave in to impulses I had always held back." He allowed himself a teasing smile, pleased to see her return it. "And you didn't exactly resist."

"I didn't want to then."

"And now?" The question popped out but he wasn't sad he asked it.

She turned her eyes forward, looking at the cows plodding ahead of them, her gloved hands clenched on her reins. "We have a child together. That changes a lot of things."

Which didn't tell him much. "We've had a child together for almost three years. Something you knew all along and something I just found out about."

She said nothing, her lips thinning. He knew she didn't agree and it annoyed him that she didn't believe him.

"Sooner or later we have to figure this out," Reuben said. "And I prefer it to be sooner."

"What's to figure out?"

"We've never compared stories. I think it might help to talk it through. Let me tell you my side and I'll listen to yours. They don't jibe and it bothers me that all these years you've thought so badly of me. I'd like you to give me a chance to tell you my experience."

She sighed, then nodded. "How about tomorrow night?" she said. "When we're done processing these cows."

"Tomorrow night it is," he said.

Then a calf broke away from the herd, heading off into a side gully and he nudged his horse in the flanks to deal with it. A couple of others tried to follow its lead, which kept him and his horse busy for a while. Once he got it all sorted, he and Leanne were on opposite sides of the herd and the open gates of the home pasture lay ahead.

He glanced at her over the shifting and moving bodies of the cows between them, surprised to see her watching him. Did he imagine the look of sorrow on her face? He gave her a questioning look, but then she looked away and the moment was gone.

He turned his attention back to the cows now flowing through the open gate ahead.

He hoped whatever they hashed out tomorrow would clear up the misunderstanding over her pregnancy once and for all. They couldn't resolve anything between them until they pieced together what she saw as his refusal to take responsibility.

And then? If they managed to figure out what happened, what would change between them?

Because no matter what, two things were very clear.

Leanne didn't want to leave this place.

And he would never stay.

Chapter Six

"You have a funny face, Uncle Wooben." Austin ran his hands over Reuben's chin, his soft, chubby fingers rasping over his whiskers.

"It's a prickly face, isn't it?" Reuben said, grinning down at the little boy.

He hadn't had a chance to shave or clean up after he and Leanne were done working with the cows. He felt grubby and dusty, and yet it felt so good to have his son sitting on his lap.

"I wike you here for supper," Austin said, returning Reuben's smile.

"I *wike* me here for supper too," he repeated, avoiding Leanne's slightly guilty look.

Yesterday, after bringing the cows in, he'd gone with her to the house to spend some time with Austin. But by the time Shauntelle dropped him off, the little guy was tired and out of sorts, so Reuben had only had about ten minutes with him before Leanne decided he needed a bath.

It had been a slightly awkward moment. George had escaped to his bedroom, which left Reuben alone in the kitchen unsure of his status or what was expected. So he left too.

But Leanne had promised they would talk tonight. So this afternoon, when they were done with the cows, he walked directly to the house with her. George had brought Austin home and he'd also brought pizza. Reuben stayed and helped set the table for four and sat down beside Austin as if he belonged there.

"And you have a dirty face," he said, rubbing away a smear of tomato sauce from the pizza he had gobbled down.

Austin just grinned, and as Reuben looked into the little boy's face, he was surprised at the sudden surge of protectiveness he felt. His boy. His son.

"I wuv pizza," he said, nestling into Reuben, tucking his head under Reuben's chin.

He held the boy close, enjoying the feel of him in his arms and at the same time fighting down a glimmer of anger that Leanne had kept this from him.

He caught her looking at them but he couldn't decipher her expression. It seemed as if she wasn't sure what to think of Austin sitting on Reuben's lap.

He struggled to sort out his own confused emotions. Where were he and Leanne supposed to go now? How were they supposed to deal with this little boy in a way that was best for him?

Could he truly be a father for him?

He pushed the troubling questions aside. Right now,

the next thing in front of him was sitting down with Leanne and sorting out the confusion of the past.

Then Austin yawned and Leanne got up. "I think it's time to put the munchkin to bed," she said, walking around the table.

She went to take Austin from Reuben but the little boy burrowed deeper into his arms. "No. Stay with Uncle Wooben," he cried.

Reuben had to admit, it did feel good to have Austin reluctant to leave him.

"You'll see Uncle Reuben again."

"See you tomorrow?" Austin asked Reuben, leaning back and grabbing his face between his hands.

Tomorrow was Sunday, which meant church. Reuben held the boy's trusting eyes and then nodded. He could do church. For his son's sake.

This seemed to satisfy him, so he crawled off Reuben's lap, took Leanne's hand and followed her out of the kitchen.

This left George and Reuben alone for the first time since he had come here.

"Thanks for having me over for dinner," Reuben said in the quiet following Leanne's departure.

"It was just pizza" was his father's gruff response. "And it was Leanne's idea."

As he had on Friday, George had stayed in town, supposedly working at the hardware store. Leanne had been frustrated with his absence, but George's being gone made things easier for Reuben. The work had gone smoothly and had been surprisingly peaceful. Chad seemed to be catching on and they got finished early.

Reuben was glad. He had checked the forecast and Sunday afternoon it was supposed to start snowing.

"Eating pizza here is a lot nicer than sitting by myself at the Brand and Grill listening to Sepp berate the newest waitress," Reuben said as he got up to clear the table.

"Sepp should never have let Tabitha go," George said in another rare moment of supporting a Rennie.

"She and Morgan sure seem happy." Reuben closed the boxes of pizza and stacked their plates.

"Yeah, but it won't be easy for them once they get married. Especially if Tabitha has to raise Morgan's kid. Sometimes you're better off staying single than putting yourself in that mess."

Reuben's hands slowed as what his father said set in. "What are you trying to say?" he asked.

George glanced past him, listening, but all they could hear was the muted sound of Leanne talking to Austin.

George turned back to Reuben. "You know, I didn't like the idea of Leanne helping out on the ranch, but she's a hard worker. And she loves the ranch. I want to make a place for her here. You need to know, most of the ranch and the store will go to Austin, but I want to give her something of her own. Because of Dirk. You're leaving soon for some job that sends you all over the place." George's eyes narrowed as he leaned forward. "I know you don't like it here. You're leaving and Leanne wants to stay. I want you to keep your distance. You can't give Leanne and Austin what they need."

Reuben held his father's gaze; the old familiar and unwelcome hurt spiraling up and clenching his soul. He wished he could let it slide off his back, but he was feeling defenseless and vulnerable. Spending the last few days with Leanne, then tonight, sitting at the supper table with Austin, his son, in a house where he'd never felt at home. All this had created a confusion he was tired of battling.

He had spent most of his adult life trying to prove to himself that he was worthy. All it took was a few words from his father to bring him back down.

He wanted nothing more than to tell George that the little boy he doted on so much was his. Not his beloved Dirk's. But he wanted to respect Leanne's wishes so, much as holding back the words almost choked him, he kept silent about that. But he couldn't leave the rest alone.

"Why do you think I'm such a bad person?" he asked. "What have I ever done to deserve such dislike?"

The questions jumped out before he could stop them, and anger followed the hurt his father could cause so easily. Anger that he let his father get to him. Again.

"You were always a hard kid. Always pushing, always trouble," George grumbled. "I gave you a home. A name and a place," his father shot back. "I gave you more than I should've. More than anyone else would have, and you tossed it aside."

"Was taking care of me such a burden? I'm your son," Reuben said.

George held his gaze and a flicker of something crossed his face. Remorse? Sorrow?

Or was Reuben simply projecting his own feelings onto the man who'd had such an influence on his life?

"I don't want to talk anymore," George mumbled, avoiding Reuben's gaze.

He got up and faltered, his hand grabbing for the back of his chair. Reuben was beside his father in an instant, catching him. He held him, surprised at his own response as he looked down at his father's stooped shoulders. His thinning hair. In that moment he saw his father's vulnerability.

George was getting old, and neither he nor his father had anyone else besides Austin and Leanne.

He doesn't deserve them.

Do you?

The question wormed its way into Reuben's own doubts and insecurities.

"I want to go to my room," George said, but to Reuben's surprise, he didn't push him away. He leaned on Reuben's arm as they made their way down the hall to the flight of stairs leading to his wing of the house.

They walked a few steps and Reuben couldn't stand it anymore. "You know, Dad, all I ever wanted was to be your son."

George said nothing, but when they got to the stairs, he grabbed hold of the large, ornately carved newel post and turned to him. His eyes were softer and Reuben wondered if he imagined the regret in them. Then George patted his hand and Reuben felt himself return to the young boy he once was who only ever craved his father's love.

"You were never like Dirk, that's for sure" was all he said.

Reuben's back stiffened and he pulled away as his father grabbed the banister and made his slow, steady way up the stairs.

He turned away and the first thing that came to his lips was a prayer to his heavenly father. *Help me, Lord, to know that you are my faithful Father,* he prayed as he walked back to the dining room. *Help me get through this with my soul intact.*

He returned to the dining room and finished cleaning up. As he turned the dishwasher on, Leanne entered the kitchen. Her hair was burnished like old copper by the light, and his empty heart was drawn to her once again.

And help me to get through this with my heart intact.

The prayer was one of self-defense. He knew that their son now inextricably linked him and Leanne. Yet many questions and mysteries were woven into their lives now, and he didn't know if they could draw them out without doing damage.

He knew he couldn't stay here with his father but Leanne was determined to make a life here.

And in spite of all of that, his foolish and hopeful heart still beat faster when she came closer.

"George gone?" she asked, looking past him.

"He isn't feeling well and went to bed early." He washed his hands and dried them on a towel hanging from the stove handle. "Is Austin in bed?"

"Yeah. He fell asleep right away."

He wanted to go up and see him, but right now the conversation Leanne had promised was hovering and he wanted that done.

"Did you want a cup of coffee?" she asked.

"Sounds good to me," he said, folding up the pizza boxes. He brought them to the recycling bin sitting on the deck outside. He pushed them in and looked out at the large fat flakes of snow silently falling onto the bare ground, thankful they had waited until now to fall. If this kept up, by morning everything would be covered, blanketed and softened.

He came back into the house, shivering in the warmth. "Good thing we got everything done today with the cows," he said as he came into the kitchen. "It's starting to snow out there."

Leanne was pouring coffee into mugs and looked up. "I guess it was bound to come. Thanks again for all your help. Couldn't have done it without you."

"I was glad to help. I enjoyed it."

"You did?" she asked as if fishing.

"I did," he admitted. "Even brought back some good memories."

"Really?" She shot him a disbelieving look.

"Really. Life with George wasn't all yelling and screaming. And no matter what Dirk told you, I always liked rounding up the cows. Working on my own in the back of the beyond, me and my horse." He gave her a grin and followed her as she went into a small sitting area right off the kitchen and other good memories came to mind. His mother sitting there, reading a book, opening her arm to him, inviting him to curl up beside her.

"You're smiling," she said. "What are you thinking about?"

"Just pulling out another good memory of my mom. Wishing I could have seen her one more time before she died and wondering if my mother truly was the horrible person my dad has made her out to be." Reuben looked at the chair opposite, then at Leanne who had dropped onto the couch. The smart move would be to sit on the chair across from her, but right now he was tired of being smart. He wanted to be close to her.

Leanne cradled her mug, watching him through the steam. "George does tend to hold a grudge, but he seems to have forgiven me for being a Rennie."

"I'm sure having Austin helped."

"He does love that kid."

"So when do we tell him the truth? I want him to know before I leave."

She gave him an anguished look. "Can you give me a few more days?"

"Doubts again?" Her hesitancy to tell George that he was Austin's father bothered him more than he wanted to acknowledge. Leanne choosing Dirk over him again. Putting her promise to Dirk over his own feelings.

"No. I just need to sort things out in my head," she said.

"Like our supposed text messages." Reuben leaned back and shoved his hand through his hair, forcing the conversation back to this difficult topic. "So tell me your side of all of this. From the beginning."

"From when we were intimate? And we agreed, the next day, that we had rushed into things too soon?" Leanne's questions held an edge of melancholy.

"We probably had," Reuben said. "But I think we both felt like we could finally be together without Dirk or anything else between us." He and Leanne had been so happy then. They had talked and talked and kissed and shared stories and secrets.

"Afterward, I often wondered if it was the atmosphere that led to what happened between us. That sense of being where no one was watching or judging," Leanne said.

"Maybe. But I also think we both knew we were meant for each other. Part of me is sorry about how things happened, but at the same time…" His voice faded away as he thought of his son, the result of that evening.

"Most people would say it was a mistake, but I don't want to think of Austin that way," Leanne said.

Reuben was quiet, not sure what to say.

She gave him a gentle smile and he was dismayed at how quickly his heart reacted. He was so easily falling back into his old patterns and behaviors around her.

"At any rate, in spite of what happened, at that time, I wasn't ready to quit on us," Leanne said. She looked away from him as if sorting her thoughts. "I wanted us to be together."

Her words rested in his worn-out, hungry soul and he wanted nothing more than to curl his hand around her shoulder, pull her close.

"I did too." The words came out before he could stop them.

She gave him a weary look. "Being with you was so much easier than being with Dirk ever was."

Her words wore away his resistance to her. He knew he couldn't give in, but he was sorely tempted as their eyes held and old feelings rose up between them.

"So why did you stay with him so long?" he said, dragging his gaze away from her.

Leanne clutched her mug. "He was safe. You were riskier with your rodeoing and running around."

"I know I wasn't the kind of guy any mom or dad would approve of."

"My dad wasn't exactly the kind of guy moms and dads would approve of either." Leanne released a short laugh but it held no humor. "And that's why I stayed with Dirk. Though I had to fight my feelings for you, my brain told me that Dirk was the wiser choice. That he would give me the security I so badly wanted and never had growing up."

"You never talked about your father," he said. He had asked, tried to find out what her life was like but she always brushed his comments off with a laugh.

Leanne took a sip of her coffee as if considering what to tell him.

"I feel like you've kept that part of your life separate from me," he pressed.

"I kept it separate from Dirk too."

"So what was Floyd Rennie like?" he asked, hoping that by finding out more about her father, he'd find out more about her.

Leanne kept silent, looking away as if going back in time to a place she didn't want to go again. "After our mother died, he fell into such a deep funk. Moved around as if trying to erase the pain. Always, he promised us the next place would be better but it never was. Often Tabitha and I were on our own, scrounging for food. Trying to make the best of what we had. We went to school hungry many times."

He had heard bits and pieces of her story, but this was

the first he knew of how difficult it had been for her. "I'm sorry," he said. "I didn't know you were ashamed of your life."

"Beyond ashamed," Leanne admitted. "It was hard not knowing, for so many years, if my dad would have work or even come home at night. It's a huge thing for two young girls to be worrying about where their next meal will come from, how we were going to get the money for clothes, let alone school supplies. We moved so much and each move cost us. Trouble was, Tabitha and I ended up paying the price more than our father ever did."

"I never knew it was that hard for you. I wish I had."

She shrugged away his concern. "I think my dad was dealing with the grief of losing our mother in his own way. We were grieving too but he didn't seem to acknowledge that. Anyhow, he finally seemed to snap out of it. Then we moved here and Tabitha and I thought this was our forever home. He settled down. Got work, but then, after a few years, he talked about moving on again. So when I met Dirk, I knew I had found someone who promised security in all the ways my father never had."

"So Dirk was your safety net."

Leanne gave him an apologetic look. "Even though I was attracted to you, some of the choices you made, the life you led, reminded me too much of my father."

Regret spiraled through him at her statement. "That bothers me because I know it to be true," he said. "If I'd been a better person, if I'd tried a little harder to be the person my father wanted me to be, maybe I'd have been the guy you needed me to be."

"I don't know." She set her mug on the low table in front of them, then sat back, resting her chin on her knees, twisting her head as if to study him further. "I think you had to find your own way through life. I know it wasn't easy being the odd son out. I know, from Dirk and from my own observation, how you and George got along. And it can't have been easy to see such obvious favoritism between you and Dirk."

"I always felt like I should dislike Dirk for that, but he was a good brother to me." Then he gave her a wry glance. "Except when it came to you. He was adamant I stay away from you. Especially when he heard I had asked you to prom."

"And then you didn't take me, yet you stole a kiss anyway."

"Like I said, Dirk had warned me away from you even though, as you said, he had broken up with you."

Leanne held his eyes. It didn't take much to conjure up the picture of her in that pink, gauzy prom dress. How her hair hung like a burnished cloud around her face. He'd had too much to drink, as usual, which made him bold and reckless. They'd been standing together outside and it had been a cool evening. She'd been shivering and he put his arm around her. She hadn't resisted and when he'd turned his head to find her face so close to his, kissing her felt so natural.

And with that one, simple act, he knew he could never simply be a bystander again.

But she'd stepped back, her eyes wide with shock. Then she spun around and ran away. Back to Dirk.

"I remember how angry he was when he found out

I kissed you," Reuben said, surprised at the breathless note in his voice. "It was a surprise for me how upset he was."

"He was jealous. Maybe he knew how I felt about you."

He wanted to pull Leanne into his arms again. But he knew they couldn't return to that innocent time.

"So let's go back to the timeline of us after Costa Rica," he said, focusing on what needed to be dealt with. "What happened when you got back home? I feel like I need to unravel this step by step."

"Well, you had your business trip to Dubai," she said. "And we decided that I needed to talk to Dirk before anything more could happen. We had agreed to give each other a couple of weeks of space. To find a way to fit each other, our relationship, into our normal lives."

"And how did that 'space' work for you?" he asked with a touch of irony in his voice. "Because it sure didn't work for me."

"I missed you. Wanted to talk to you, but I also knew I needed to talk to Dirk first. Clear that up before you and I could move on without any shadows of the past over our relationship." She was quiet a moment. "But I had my concerns about what we did so I bought a pregnancy test. As soon as I got the positive result, I phoned you but I got no answer. Then I started texting and only then did you respond."

He had thought about these texts many times now, but as convinced as she was that she sent them, he was that sure he hadn't received them. They couldn't both be wrong yet...

"Do you remember the day you sent them?" he asked.

"Yes. You had told me you would be back at your home in Montreal on the seventh of the month. I had it circled on my calendar. I didn't have your business phone number, so I thought maybe you left your personal phone at home and that was why you weren't responding."

"I did, actually. I remember being angry I forgot it because I was hoping you might call in spite of wanting your space."

She nodded. "So that's why you didn't answer. You had said you'd be home that day. So I tried again."

He dug back, struggling to reconstruct what had happened. "That was right around the time Dirk was coming back from Europe, wasn't it?"

"I think so."

"What did those texts I supposedly sent you say?"

Leanne bit her lip. Then she drew in a long breath and began. "I told you about the pregnancy. You asked if I was sure. I wrote back that I was and I asked what should I do. You didn't answer right away and then you said that this couldn't be right. You asked if this was because of Costa Rica, and I wrote back and said yes. Then you said…" Her voice broke, and Reuben struggled with his own feelings as she recited a conversation he had absolutely no recollection of. "You said that you weren't ready to be a father. That you didn't want to have any part of this. I wrote something back. I can't remember what, and then I read that you didn't think it was right for us to be together. That you weren't going to acknowledge this kid. And again that you didn't want to be a father. And then you told me to leave you alone. That you hadn't signed up for this and that you never wanted to see me again." She stopped, pressing her finger to her lips.

He felt his own anger rise as he heard her recitation of the conversation. He knew he hadn't participated in that and couldn't imagine what it had been like for her to be on the receiving end of it.

He had to fight his desire to refute everything she said. And he struggled between wanting to pull her into his arms and wanting to tell her that it wasn't true, but he kept his emotions in check. They needed to get to the bottom of this first.

"What time did you send those texts?" he asked, lowering his voice, keeping his tone gentle.

"I think it was five o'clock in the evening. I had just gotten off work and thought you might be back."

He nodded, slowly piecing her memories with his. "That would have been about seven o'clock my time. Half an hour before I got back to my place from the airport. I remember because an accident had snarled traffic. I had hoped to get back in time to watch the Jays game on TV, but I was running late and I knew I would miss the opening pitch. I was ticked about that." He gave her a shamefaced look. "Sorry. Sports fan. I really wanted to call you when I came back, but that whole 'space' thing you wanted prevented me. Then, when I got to my apartment, Dirk was already there. He had a key from the last time he'd stayed so he let himself in. He had said he might stop by on his way back from Europe but hadn't made any definite plans. I felt gross and wanted to clean up, so I told him we could go out for dinner after and catch up. So if you sent them at five, I wouldn't have been home."

He frowned as he thought back to that day. Then something teased his memory. Reuben turned to her and grabbed her hands. "Dirk was sitting on the couch reading the paper when I came into the apartment. He was acting all strange. Like he was upset. I remember wondering why. We hadn't seen each other for weeks and he didn't seem excited to see me."

Leanne stared at him, her eyes wide as if she was getting to the same place he was.

"I know he didn't stick around long after I got back," he continued. "When I got out of the shower, he had his coat on and said that he had changed his mind about staying with me. He was heading home to Cedar Ridge. He said that he missed you and needed to talk to you, which I thought was strange given that you had broken up with him. I didn't dare say anything to him, so we said goodbye and he left. I was confused by his strange behavior but also relieved that I wouldn't have to explain to him what had happened between us." He gave her a look. "Instead that fell on you."

"He came to my place early the next morning," Leanne continued. "He seemed agitated and I thought it was because he missed me, like you said. And I was feeling so distraught after I got your texts."

"So the day after you get these horrible texts, he comes over to talk to you and asks you to marry him even though you broke up with him. Didn't that seem odd to you?"

She furrowed her brow in confusion, as if trying to understand where he was going.

"You said you sent the texts at 5:00 p.m. here," he continued, things slowly coming together for him. "That's 7:00 p.m. Montreal time. I wasn't back until after that. After Dirk left, I went looking for my phone, to let you know what was going on. I was thinking I might text you to let you know Dirk was heading home but all our conversations on the message app had disappeared. I remember thinking it odd at the time and wondering if I had somehow done that by mistake."

She shot him a confused look. "You weren't picking up your phone when I called the first time."

"Because my phone was still in the apartment and I wasn't. So if you sent those texts right after you tried to call again, it couldn't have been me who replied to them."

Leanne closed her eyes, shaking her head as if processing the information.

Reuben moved closer, daring to touch her as things finally fell into place.

"I know what happened," he said, fighting down his anger as he realized his conclusion fit with everything Leanne had said and his own memories of that evening. "I couldn't have been the one who responded to your texts. But Dirk could have."

Leanne stared at him, her mind whirling as she tried to make sense of what he said.

"You think Dirk sent the texts?"

"I can't picture another scenario. I wasn't in the

apartment when you said you called or sent them but Dirk probably was."

Leanne looked away, feeling confusion at his replies.

"Why would he—"

"I think, deep down, he always knew how I felt about you. How important you were to me. Dirk was a great guy, but he wasn't accustomed to being second best. He'd always been Dad's favorite, he seemed to think everyone else felt the same about him. Can you imagine how he felt when he discovered you were probably pregnant with my son? Me? Mr. Second Best was your first choice?"

She looked at him then, too easily recalling the anger and fury and sorrow she'd felt at what she'd thought was Reuben's rejection of her.

"I think I always knew that about him," she said. Reality battled with the false illusions she'd created around both Dirk and Reuben, and a curious sorrow grabbed her heart. She had been wrong about both of them. And as she pieced together what happened, added it to her innate knowledge of Reuben and Dirk, she knew it was the only scenario that made sense.

And as it did, relief flowed through her. Relief and a realization that Reuben truly was the man she thought he was.

But behind that came a deep hurt.

"What has Dirk done to us?" she asked, her voice tight with anger.

Reuben moved closer, resting his hand on her shoulder.

"He played on your fears. And mine."

"What fears did you have?"

"That I would lose you after all. That I would come so close to complete happiness and have it taken away. Again." He reached up with his other hand and stroked a strand of hair away from her face, another small connection that wore away the restraints she had placed around her heart.

She looked into his eyes, and when she saw the raw pain there, all the desolation she had felt the past three years, all the misery and loneliness, rose up. And she realized he had been hurting too.

She released a sob, then another.

And suddenly she was in his arms, her head on his shoulder, her tears flowing. She held on to her anchor in this storm of sorrow and regret and missed opportunities.

"It's okay," he whispered, his arms now around her, holding her close. "It's okay. It's over now."

Her tears flowed awhile longer but when they subsided, she stayed where she was, feeling safe and protected.

She hardly dared believe that she was here, back in Reuben's arms. It felt so right. So good.

His arms felt like home.

Then he tipped her chin up and wiped her tears away with his finger, smiling down at her. "I'm sorry you had to deal with all of that on your own. I'm so sorry I couldn't be here for you. You have to believe that things would have turned out much differently had I known everything."

"I know that," she whispered.

He grew serious as his hand cupped her face, his eyes traveling over her features. "I missed you."

His words dove into her soul and took root. "I missed you too."

Then he lowered his head and his lips brushed hers. Gently at first. Then he pulled her close to him.

She wove her arms around his neck, her heart singing. This was how it should be.

He was the first to pull away as he cradled her head on his shoulder and leaned back, holding her close. His chest lifted in a sigh and she placed her hand on his chest, warm under the fabric of his shirt, his heartbeat as elevated as hers.

He traced gentle circles on the back of her head with his fingers.

"So now what?" he asked.

A great weariness drifted over her. A weariness created by years of anger and confusion that she could finally release.

She drew back to look into his beloved face, to take in features that had haunted her waking thoughts and nightly dreams. "We can't go back to where we were," she said.

"I don't want to," he said. "This, here and now, is how it should have been all these years."

Regret shivered through her at how long it had taken. At all the missteps along the way to here.

"I'm sorry," she said, but he stopped her.

Then he held her gaze, his own features shifting. "So what's next?"

The thought sent a faint chill through her, thinking

of the plans he had in place. Plans for a job that would take him away from here and keep him traveling. His idea that George should sell the ranch.

"Can we just enjoy being together? Here? Now?" She couldn't face those hard decisions. Not after they had finally found each other. She wanted just a few moments of her and Reuben. Together again.

"Sounds good to me." He gave her a careful smile, but she knew they were simply delaying what needed to be faced sometime.

Then he sighed. "And George? Do we tell him about Austin?"

She hesitated and he seemed to draw his answer from that.

"Okay. Let's give that a few days, as well."

She could tell he wasn't entirely happy, but she wasn't ready to see what George's reaction to the truth would be. Not so soon after she and Reuben had found each other.

"We will tell him," she promised.

"Okay. I'll leave it at that," he said. He bent over and brushed a kiss over her lips.

His response created a surprising relief. She wanted to have this uncomplicated time with Reuben for a little while longer. This moment of grace, so to speak.

"So will you be coming here tomorrow?" she asked. "After church?"

"Is this an invitation to Sunday lunch?" He grinned down at her, his fingers playing with her hair.

"Of course it is. Though Sunday lunch isn't roast and potatoes. I've scaled down considerably."

"I don't think my mom ever did roast and potatoes either," he said, with a teasing smile. "She always said it didn't make for a restful Sunday."

Leanne nestled closer in his arms, toying with a button on his shirt pocket. "You mentioned I never said much about my father, but you never talked about your mother," she said.

He shrugged, resting his head on hers. "She was a good mom in her own way. I think living on the ranch was difficult for her. Way more isolating than she thought it would be."

"She was from Calgary, wasn't she?"

"Yeah. Dad met her at the Stampede. She was working as a waitress in one of the venues. He had Dirk with him and she seemed to connect with both of them. Two months later they were married."

"That was quick."

Reuben's chest lifted in a sigh. "Too quick. My dad was struggling. He was lonely and trying to raise Dirk on his own, run the ranch and the store. So they got married and he brought her out here. She managed the first year but I think it was hard for her. I got the impression from George that she thought living on a ranch would be more glamorous than it was. Watched too many *Dallas* reruns maybe." He released a hard laugh. "And then I was born, and according to the stories in Cedar Ridge, things went from worse to worst. She was gone a lot. Then one day she just left. I was five years old."

"So what do you remember of her?"

"Bits and pieces. I remember her laughing, dancing

with me in the kitchen. I remember her helping Dirk with his schoolwork. He had stronger memories of her than I did. He was older. But I also remember her crying, and her and George fighting a lot. I don't think it was a happy marriage. Which is why, I believe, he's always had a hard time with me. I was the reminder of the woman who took off on him. Humiliated him."

"It wasn't your fault," Leanne said.

"I know it wasn't. But I wasn't the easiest kid to deal with after she left. I was angry and sad and I missed her, and I don't think George knew how to handle me. Plus he had to raise two boys by himself. And he was a firm believer in 'spare the rod and spoil the child.'"

"That must have been so difficult for you. Growing up like that."

"It wasn't all bad." He shrugged and looked away as if going back to another time. "I had some good memories. Dirk and I got along great and had a lot of fun."

"But you and George?"

He sighed. "More complicated. He always seemed to hold me to a different standard, and I fought it every step of the way. He wasn't the best father."

"I guessed that from things Dirk told me," she said. "I know he always felt bad for you."

"Some of it was my own doing, I'll admit. I pushed the boundaries."

"Do you think you'll ever find a way to reconcile?" Leanne put out the question tentatively. "I know George was a difficult father, but I also have seen a caring side of him. He's so loving with Austin."

She felt a shiver of apprehension at the way his mouth tightened.

"That's because he thinks Austin is Dirk's kid. I wonder how he'll react when he finds out he's mine."

Reuben grew solemn and Leanne drew back, feeling torn. She knew he was right and that was one of the reasons she held off telling George. But in that moment she felt as if she was betraying Reuben.

Just a few days longer, she told herself. She didn't want the drama yet.

"I still can't believe I'm a father," he said finally. "I didn't think that would ever happen. Don't know if I can do a good job of it given the example I've had. The father I have."

"I think you'll be a great father," she said, clutching his shoulder and squeezing her encouragement, fighting down her own concern about his reaction. "I don't think you'll be like George."

He said nothing to that, as if pondering her words.

"I guess I'll have to figure that out. Like I said, he wasn't the best example and it wasn't until I returned to God that I realized that I had another father who loved me unconditionally. That has made my life easier. I'm secure in my faith and that's been a blessing."

"That makes me feel ashamed," she said. "I wish I could say that I'm secure in my faith, as well."

"You used to be. What changed?"

She tried to figure out how to say what she felt. "Some of that has been keeping the secret about Austin. But after Costa Rica, I felt ashamed—"

He gave her a gentle shake. "It wasn't just you. It

was both of us. I know it maybe wasn't our finest moment, but I know I've confessed that and I know God has forgiven me and you."

"I thought, for a while, that you were too ashamed of it all and that's why you rejected me."

"Neither of us is perfect. I've made many mistakes but I also know that God is a loving father. I know that He forgives us if we ask."

"What about George?" she asked. "Do you think you can ever forgive him?"

Reuben's mouth grew tight and he got up, shoving his hand through his hair in a gesture of frustration. "Just a few moments ago I helped George up from the table. He wasn't feeling well. I asked him why he thought I deserved to be treated the way I was. I told him that all I ever wanted was to be his son."

Leanne heard the hurt in his voice.

"You know what he said to me?" Reuben asked.

She shook her head.

"He told me, 'You were never Dirk.' That was his answer." He released a harsh laugh. "So I don't know if it's a matter of forgiving him or letting go of the hold he has over me."

Leanne slipped her arms around him, holding him close. "I'm sorry I brought it up," she whispered. "I shouldn't have asked."

He said nothing. Instead he kissed her again and in that kiss Leanne felt his longing and his pain.

He drew away, his expression melancholy. "Can we check on Austin before I leave?" he asked.

She nodded then followed him as they walked up the stairs, her own feet heavy.

As she walked, she prayed that she and Reuben and Austin could find their way through this new place. She also added a prayer for George.

Because she knew that once they told him the truth, he would have much to deal with. They all would.

Chapter Seven

"But Joseph said to them, 'Don't be afraid. Am I in the place of God? You intended to harm me, but God intended it for good to accomplish what is now being done, the saving of many lives.'"

Pastor Blakely paused, looking down at the Bible in front of him, as if letting the words from Genesis settle into his heart as much as the gathered congregation.

"*Forgiveness* is a word that can get tossed around too easily," he said finally. "It can be something that is easier to tell other people to do than to do ourselves. Joseph had to forgive his brothers for what they'd done and that couldn't have been easy. His life was taken away as a result of their decisions."

Reuben sat back in the pew, his arms crossed as he listened to the pastor, the text hitting too close to home. The story of Joseph had always been a favorite, though he had often sympathized with the older brothers at times. He knew what it was like to watch a son being favored so heavily by his father, the son of the wife he loved more.

He glanced at Leanne who sat beside him, her hands folded on her lap. As if sensing his attention, her eyes slid sideways, catching his. The way her lips turned up encouraged him and he took a chance and slipped his hand in hers.

She slid closer and once again he was struck with the wonder of this moment. How often had he sat beside his brother fighting down his jealousy, wishing it were him with Leanne instead of Dirk?

Now, since he and Leanne had figured out what had happened with the wayward texts, he'd felt anger and disgust at what Dirk had done. How much he had destroyed for both him and Leanne.

He closed his eyes, fighting down the anger and trying to focus on being thankful that he and Leanne were back together again, instead of fighting his feelings about his brother. But no sooner did he feel as if he were in command of himself than he thought of Austin and all the time he had lost in his son's life.

You have him now, he reminded himself. And once they talked to George, then he and Leanne could make plans for their future.

Away from Cedar Ridge and George and the ranch and all the hard memories that clung to this place.

Can you do it? Can you take all this away from your father?

The thought lingered but behind that came what George had told him yesterday.

If he was to truly be himself, whole and complete,

then he had to leave this all behind. As long as he stayed close to George, his father would always determine his emotions and his sense of self-worth. He had fought too hard and too long to let his father have that hold over him again.

And Leanne? Can you take her away from this?

She couldn't keep working the ranch the way it was going. Nor could his father keep it up.

Can't you stay?

He pulled Leanne a little closer, turning his attention back to the sermon, pushing that question aside, as well. After what his father had said last night after Reuben had bared his soul, he knew he and his father could never reconcile.

"I think the biggest mistake we make in forgiving is thinking that it is an emotion," the pastor continued. "Forgiveness, like love, is often a decision. When you forgive someone, you release the power you have given them over you."

On one level Reuben knew what the pastor was saying, but he still felt hurt by his father's inability to apologize. How could Reuben forgive an unrepentant man?

He looked over at Leanne, feeling so confused. He'd thought being with her would resolve the hurt in his life, and while it had given him a tremendous sense of fulfillment, he still wasn't sure what to do about his relationship with his father. Would he ever find a place of peace with George? Would he ever feel he measured up?

And that's why you have to leave.

Half an hour later the service was over and he and Leanne were walking out. Together. The few curious glances he caught made him guess that this would be a topic of conversation over a few Sunday meals. He knew his reputation preceded him, but he didn't care what people thought.

George hadn't come to church this morning. According to Leanne, he wasn't feeling that well, so even that made him feel freer. Leanne was holding his hand, was at his side and they were going downstairs to get their son.

He clenched Leanne's hand a little harder at that thought.

"Is everything okay?" she asked.

"Yeah. Everything is great." He flashed her a smile.

They walked down the hallway to the nursery and, as Leanne signed the paper beside her name, the attendant opened the half door and Austin came bounding out. "Uncle Wooben," he called, his arms held out.

His son's pure joy at seeing him made up for the fact that his son still thought of him as his uncle.

Baby steps, he reminded himself.

"Reuben. Good to see you here," a familiar voice called out.

Reuben turned to see his cousin Cord walking toward him. His cousin's eyes flicked from Reuben to Leanne, who now stood beside him, a question in them. But thankfully he said nothing as his gaze slipped back to Leanne. "Did you get all the cattle moved?"

"Just in time," Leanne said.

"The snow is coming down now," Cord said. "Wouldn't be surprised if we get at least six inches today and tonight."

"We'll have a white Christmas after all," Leanne said.

"Which reminds me." Cord snapped his fingers. "Dad was thinking of having a Walsh family Christmas at the ranch. He wanted to have George and Leanne and Austin come, and now that you're here, you can come too. We're going to get together with Aunt Fay Cosgrove, as well. Not sure if cousin Noah will be around—who knows with him?"

Reuben wondered if they would be here at Christmas. He hadn't been home for either Thanksgiving or Christmas for the past ten years and he hadn't figured on being around this year.

But he could see that Leanne was considering the offer.

"Let me think about it," Reuben said. "I'll let you know by next week."

"Perfect." Cord nodded at the attendant behind them, then the door opened again and a chubby toddler with blond, flyaway hair scooted out and headed past Cord. He scooped the boy up before he could make his escape and shook his head at Reuben. "Kid does this every time. It's like he won't even acknowledge his own father."

Reuben, holding Austin in his arms, felt a moment of fatherly pride. Austin had come right to him.

"If you could let me know sooner than later," Cord continued, "Christmas is coming soon."

"I know. I've barely had a chance to get my shopping done," Leanne said. "If you have any ideas for presents for George, I would appreciate them."

"Or him?" Cord said, grinning at Reuben.

Reuben caught Leanne's blush and he felt like he was getting sucked into a whirlpool of obligations he hadn't expected.

Christmas hadn't been on his radar since he graduated college. Even the brief time that he and Leanne were together, they hadn't gotten further than figuring out how they were going to get through the next few months, let alone make concrete plans around family celebrations.

"I'm not a high-maintenance person," Reuben said, trying to find a way to end this conversation gracefully as he shifted Austin to his other hip. But no sooner had he spoken the words than he realized how it sounded. Like he was expecting Leanne to get him something, even it if was simple. "I mean, I don't expect anything for Christmas. Haven't for years now."

That made him sound rather pathetic. Time to head out before Cord asked him what he was buying for Leanne. Also something that hadn't even crossed his mind until now.

"We should go," he said to Leanne who was watching him with a faint smirk.

They navigated their way past a few more people who stopped to say hi to him and welcome him back. They also managed to avoid Tabitha, who stood with her back to them, chatting up a group of people. Leanne hadn't seen her and thankfully was already out the door. Reuben didn't want to deal with any more family plans or obligations.

Once they got outside, Austin held out his bare hands to catch the lazy flakes drifting down. "Snow. Snow," he called out, as if making friends. He wriggled in Reuben's arms. "Go down," he insisted.

"It's getting kind of deep, buddy," he said, holding Austin closer as he made his own way through the gathering drifts. "I don't want you to fall."

Leanne waited, smiling at him, her cheeks already pinking up in the cold, her face framed by the hood of her winter coat. "Isn't it beautiful?" she said, looking up at the sky, opening her mouth to catch some stray flakes. "And even more beautiful now that we have the cows all gathered up."

"Such practical enthusiasm," he teased, dropping his arm onto her shoulders, pleased at how easy it was to be with her. She grinned up at him and put her own arm around him.

"So, I hope you weren't put on the spot just now," she said.

"Well, I have to admit, I hadn't even thought about Christmas. The most important thing on my mind was getting away so I could do this."

Reuben stopped and gave her a kiss. Her lips were cool, damp from the snowflakes that had landed on them.

She pulled away, glancing over her shoulder, and Reuben felt a flicker of concern.

"Are you worried about who's watching?" he asked, trying to inject a teasing note into her voice.

She said nothing, confirming his suspicions.

"It's early for us yet," she said, pulling away from him and fussing with Austin's jacket, zipping it up, fiddling with his toque as Austin pulled away. "I'm still trying to get accustomed to the idea. We've got a lot of time to make up for."

He had to agree with that.

She gave him a conciliatory smile. "This is all new to me yet too," she said. "I have Austin to think of and how this all looks."

"So you're concerned what people think? Dirk's former wife now dating his out-of-control brother?"

"No. Of course that's not why," she said, shooting him a frown. "You just got here a week ago and we've already sat together in church."

"Which in a town like Cedar Ridge means we should be registering at Bed Bath & Beyond."

She laughed, which eased away the tension somewhat. "According to some, yes." She tucked her arm in his as they walked through the gathering snow to his truck. He had picked her up from the ranch, wanting to spend as much time with her as he could. "I want us to be sure of where we're going. And we have to think of Austin."

"I appreciate your caution," Reuben said, "but I've waited a long time for this to happen."

She stopped, held his arm and looked up at him. "Me too," she said, cupping his face with her hand, stroking his cheek with her thumb. "Me too."

The sincerity of her expression and the yearning he saw in her eyes eased his concerns.

But afterward, as he strapped Austin into his car seat, Reuben knew a lot needed to be resolved before he and Leanne found their happy-ever-after.

"Faster. Faster." Austin grabbed the sides of his sled, squealing his delight as Reuben, who had been pulling him around the snow-covered yard of the ranch at a more sedate pace, starting running. It was a beautiful Monday afternoon. After the heavy snowfall of yesterday, the sun was finally shining and it reflected off the snow, almost blinding Leanne. But it also created a stunning winter wonderland as the snow softened the spruce trees and laid a blanket of white on the mountains behind them.

Leanne took a photo with her phone, then simply enjoyed the sight of Austin with his father.

"You taking over anytime?" Reuben panted as he ran past her.

"Why? You're doing such a fantastic job," she called out as she snapped another photo. She looked behind her. George had come outside to watch for a few moments but headed back to the house again. Leanne knew that George was avoiding Reuben and, though it troubled her, it had also been a minor relief to spend yesterday with Reuben and Austin without George's disapproval washing over them.

After church on Sunday, he had sat with them all long enough to eat a bowl of soup and then had left for town to visit with his brother, Boyce. Today, however, he had no excuse. Shauntelle couldn't babysit, nor could Tabitha, but thankfully George had been willing to watch Austin while she and Reuben fed the cows this morning. Chad had to leave early for a dentist appointment. Reuben's work in town was done early, and he was able to help her out.

It had been fun working with Reuben. She could have managed on her own but it would have taken her much longer. It was nice to have someone cutting the strings of the bales and watching the gates while she went back for more hay. By the time they were done, it was still light enough for Reuben to take Austin out on the sleigh.

Reuben pulled Austin up to join her, chest heaving as he dropped his hands on his knees, bending over to catch his breath.

"This kid is heavier than he looks," he gasped.

"And you are a lot more out of shape than I thought," she returned. "You wouldn't last a minute in a snowball fight."

"Yeah. Says you." Reuben dropped the rope, got down and grabbed a handful of snow. He packed it together, then tossed it at her. However she saw it coming and dodged, squealing. She ducked down to make a snowball, as well, but before she could toss it at him, he hit her square in the chest with another snowball.

"Pretty quick on the draw," she teased, then lobbed hers at him.

And it hit him right in the face.

"Oh. I'm sorry," she said, covering her laugh with her mittened hand, taking a step back as the snow slid down his nose, dripping onto his chin.

He stared at her and she could see by the way his eyes zeroed in on her that revenge was on his mind.

Instinct kicked in and she turned and ran. But while her red ankle boots were warm and cute, they were made for walking, not running in loose snow. A few steps was all it took for Reuben to catch up to her and grab her by the waist.

The momentum threw them both off balance. Reuben twisted and cushioned her fall.

"You're going to regret that deadly aim," Reuben said with a laugh as she pulled away. He tugged her back, grabbing a handful of snow.

"What are you going to do?" she asked, pushing her hands against his snow-covered coat.

"You'll find out."

But she didn't have a chance to because right at that moment Austin started crying. "No. No hurt Mommy," he called out, trying to get off his sled.

She struggled to her feet to comfort him but Reuben was a few steps ahead. He picked up the crying little boy. "It's okay. Mommy and Daddy were just playing."

Shock jolted though her at his unwitting use of the term *Daddy* and Reuben glanced her way, as well, as if he realized what he had said.

But Austin was pulling away from him, reaching for Leanne, sobbing now, his toque hanging over his eyes, his mittens falling off.

Leanne took him from Reuben and cuddled him close, pushing his hat back so he could see. "Don't cry, sweetie. Mommy's okay."

She looked over at Reuben, who stayed where he

was, his hands on his hips, blowing his breath out in a surprised huff.

Austin's tears slowed, he sniffed a few more times and then he laid his head on Leanne's shoulder.

"I think we should take him in," she said, turning away.

He caught up to her, laying a hand on her arm as they walked. "Sorry about that. I didn't mean—"

She looked over at him, surprised at his apology. "It's fine. It's the truth."

"I wonder if George heard."

"We have to tell him sometime," he said. Reuben's hand slipped to her waist, pulling her close as he gently brushed a tear off Austin's cheek with one gloved finger. He looked so serious Leanne wondered what he was thinking.

"I know," she admitted.

She stopped, looking up at him, fighting with her need to find balance and his need to have the truth out.

"Every day I keep this to myself makes it harder for me too," she said, hoping he understood her own struggle. "You need to know I'm not ashamed of us. He knows we're spending time together. He said something about us sitting in church together on Sunday."

"Like I said, next stop Bed Bath & Beyond," he teased, as if trying to lighten the atmosphere.

"Is it?"

No sooner had the words slipped out than she realized what she had said. How it sounded like she was pushing him.

His expression grew serious and then, in spite of Austin in her arms, he bent over and kissed her.

His lips were warm and inviting, and when he drew away Leanne felt a sense of loss mixed with a feeling of utter contentment.

"I'm thinking a store that's more eclectic and local," he teased.

She relaxed a little, smiling. "I like being with you."

"And I like being with you. Even feeding cows. And you know how to run that old temperamental tractor my dad insists on keeping."

"It's the only one with bale forks on it."

"See, that's what I love about you. How many people would even know what a bale fork is?"

She laughed, then shifted Austin in her arms.

"Here, let me take him."

Thankfully Austin didn't mind going to Reuben. He even laughed when Reuben tweaked his nose. "Funny Uncle Wooben," he said.

"You like working on the ranch, don't you?" Reuben asked as he slipped his other arm around her waist.

"I do. I love the changing of the seasons and the different jobs that come with it. I feel close to nature. Close to God."

Reuben didn't respond, and she wondered what was going through his mind.

"And Cedar Ridge?" he asked.

"It's become home. It's the first place where I've ever felt like I belonged. Of course it's the first place I've ever lived longer than two years so that helps."

"And Tabitha is here."

"Yes."

"So you never thought of moving away?" he asked as he held the door to the back entrance open.

She stepped inside, temporarily avoiding the question. She sat down on the bench just inside the door and pulled Austin's knit hat off, setting it aside as she fought down apprehension.

"I've thought about it, but I've not had a reason to." She looked up at him, wondering what his reaction would be.

But he just nodded.

She knew this conversation wasn't over, and the thought of continuing it gave her a sinking feeling.

No sooner had she removed her son's boots than Austin was hurrying down the hallway to the family room and his toys.

Leanne took her time taking her own coat off, praying for the right thing to say.

"So, what did you think of the pastor's sermon on Sunday?"

Reuben hung his coat up, then he turned to her, a smile edging his lips.

"Are you wondering if I could ever forgive my father?"

"I guess I was being rather obvious," she said, pushing her damp hair back.

"It's hard to forgive someone who has never asked for forgiveness."

He gave her a soulful smile then walked away, following Austin into the family room.

Leanne stayed behind, dismay licking at her soul.

Please, Lord, help him to see, she prayed. *Help him to lose the bitterness that grips him.*

Because she knew that until he did, he wouldn't even consider staying here.

And the thought of moving was harder than she could bear.

Chapter Eight

"Maybe a little higher?"

Reuben leaned over, the ladder creaking precariously as he reached as far as he could, the red ball dangling from his fingertips. He slipped it over the spruce branch, then quickly retreated as the ladder wobbled.

He waited where he was, however, glancing over his shoulder at Leanne, who stood below him. She stared at the tree, eyes narrowed, tapping her chin with her index finger.

"Seriously? Do you think moving it a few more centimeters will make a difference?" he teased.

"Good is the enemy of best," Leanne returned. Then she nodded her approval, and with a sigh of relief he made his way down the ladder.

"Decorating the Christmas tree is not supposed to be a marathon," he joked as he pushed the ladder to one side. He wasn't putting it away yet. He had a suspicion he would be climbing up that ladder a few more times.

When Leanne had called yesterday and asked him

to pick up a Christmas tree in town after he was done working at the arena, he wanted to put her off. After all, Christmas wasn't for at least three weeks. And getting a tree felt like a commitment to a decision he wasn't sure of yet.

He didn't know where he would spend Christmas or how it would affect him and Leanne. He had tried not to feel pressured, but it was also unfair to put everything on hold while he and Leanne worked their way through this new situation. So he'd picked up the tree.

"I'm having fun," Leanne said with a wink. She turned to Austin who was running back and forth waving a branch they had cut off the tree.

Christmas music played softly in the background creating a festive atmosphere.

"That's a nice tree you bought there," George said. "Though we could have gotten a free one from the upper pasture."

"Snow's too deep to go wandering up there now," Reuben said, quashing his usual annoyance with his father's criticism, trying to focus on the rare compliment his father had given.

In fact, Reuben was surprised George had even deigned to join them this evening. Monday after his and Leanne's snowball fight, George had driven to town again. Yesterday he went directly up to his room. This evening, however, he must have gotten caught up in the spirit of the moment since he'd joined them in the family room, offering decorating advice from his recliner.

"Grampa, me got a tree," Austin crowed, waving the branch at George.

"You call that a tree, boy?" George said with a laugh, leaning forward and holding his hand out to Austin. "Don't go into the logging business, I think." The little boy climbed easily up on George's lap, looking content as his grandfather slipped his arms around him, holding him close.

The sight stoked a flicker of jealousy in Reuben. Had George ever held him so lovingly? Stroked his hair with a gentle smile on his face?

Austin quickly wiggled off George's lap and, ignoring his grandfather's protest, ran directly to Reuben, his arms wide.

"Do you like my tree, Uncle Wooben?" Austin asked, almost blinding him as he waved the branch around.

"I like your branch a lot," Reuben said, tickling him under his chin. Austin tucked his head in, giggling. Then he looked up at Reuben, his eyes wide.

"You buy me a Christmas pwesent?"

"Austin, that's rather rude," Leanne reprimanded.

"Of course I'll buy you a present," he said to Austin. "What do you want?"

"Horsies. Lots of horsies."

"Real horses?"

Austin giggled. "No. Grandpa got me a weal horse. I want horsies for my farm."

"Well, that makes it easier."

But even as he made his plans with Austin, he felt the pressure of the upcoming season. While he was still in town working at the arena, he'd gotten a call from Marshall, his future boss, asking if he was still coming to Los Angeles in a couple of days. Reuben had said yes.

While his time in Cedar Ridge had been a turning point for him, he still found himself eager to move on. More now that he and Leanne had found each other again.

He wanted a fresh start with her in a new place away from all the memories and unmet expectations. He wasn't sure how it would all play out, however.

"So I'm thinking we can hang this gold ball up by the red one you just put up," Leanne said, holding up another large ornament.

"I don't think Reuben should—"

"I'm not going up—"

He and George spoke at the same time.

"Looks like that's unanimous," Leanne said with a laugh. George and Reuben laughed, as well, creating a small moment of levity.

"We Walsh men have to stick together," Reuben added, grinning at George.

His father nodded, leaning back, a curious expression on his face.

"I think we should call it an evening," Reuben said, standing back to examine the tree.

The lights twinkled brightly, reflecting off the large gold and red balls, glittery snowflakes and gold ribbon woven through the branches.

"We're missing a couple of ornaments, though," George said, getting up off his chair. He picked up an old, worn shoebox that lay to one side and set it on the low table in front of the couch. "Austin, can you help me put these on the tree?" he asked. Then he looked up at Leanne. "If that's okay with you?"

"Of course. It's fine with me."

"We didn't put these on last year. Was a bit too soon after Dirk," George explained. "I kept the box back when you went looking but I think we can put them on now."

Curious, Reuben walked closer. Surprise flickered though him when he saw what lay nestled in the old tissue of the box.

"Your daddy made this ornament," George said to Austin, holding up a popsicle-stick sled. "And your Uncle Reuben made this one." He pulled out a wreath made of puzzle pieces spray painted green that framed a picture. "You remember this?" he asked Reuben, turning it to him.

Reuben came closer and took it from his father. A young version of himself grinned a gap-toothed smile back from the wreath frame. A much happier time. But he didn't take up the entire picture. In the background he saw a woman and looked closer.

His mother. She was laughing.

A surprising grief gripped him. He was five in the picture, which meant his mother had left shortly afterward. Why had she left him behind? Why hadn't she taken him along?

The old feelings of abandonment and loss drifted to the surface. He blamed the sudden ache in his heart on the music, songs he'd heard every Christmas he'd celebrated with Dirk and his father.

"I hang them up?" Austin asked.

Reuben nodded and handed him the ornament, pushing the unwelcome emotions back to the past. He glanced over at George just as his father's eyes met his.

George's expression softened and Reuben wondered if he imagined the look of pain that drifted over his face.

What would his life have been like if his mother had stayed? If his relationship with George had been better?

Futile questions he told himself. Life moved on and he had to, as well.

He turned back to Austin to help him get the two ornaments on the Christmas tree and as he did, he made a decision. Regardless of how she felt, he and Leanne needed to tell George the truth about Austin as soon as possible. Tomorrow at the latest.

He knew they were growing more serious about each other and it was time to take the next step.

And where will that step lead? Could you stay here?

Once again the question rose up, teasing him. But then he glanced at George and all the old pain and sorrow he had dealt with as a young boy returned. The only way he could be free from George was to get away from his influence.

"Are you okay?" Leanne touched his arm, getting his attention. He realized he was still kneeling down by the tree, looking at the ornaments Austin and he had hung up. He gave himself a mental shake and stood. Then, in front of George, he kissed her.

Leanne stiffened but then she relaxed and touched his cheek lightly.

"I want this done," Reuben said, keeping his voice low but determined. "He needs to know and we need to make plans."

Leanne held his gaze, a look of fear flitting through her eyes.

"What's the matter?" he asked.

She shook her head and he thought again about what she had said a couple of days ago when he asked her about staying in Cedar Ridge or moving away.

But he needed to know. He couldn't afford to spend more emotions and energy on this relationship if he wasn't sure where it was going.

"You know we have to do this," he insisted.

She looked up at him but even though she nodded he could see the fear in her eyes. "I know" was all she said.

"What are you two plotting over there?" George's abrupt question made Leanne draw back.

Leanne glanced over at Austin who was running around the room, laughing and hopping. Then he dropped against George's knee and the man's face lit up. He pulled Austin close and hugged him tightly, flashing the smile that he always reserved for his grandson.

Dismay flitted over Leanne's face, and Reuben understood where it came from. If they told George, how would he react to the fact that Austin, the child he so dearly loved, wasn't Dirk's, but was in fact Reuben's?

"It has to happen sometime," Reuben insisted while George was distracted, tickling Austin.

"Tomorrow, okay?" Leanne turned back to him, her eyes pleading for understanding.

"Tomorrow at noon," Reuben said. "I have to work at the arena in the morning so I'll come here after lunch."

She gave him a surprised look, then nodded again.

Then, as if to stake his claim on her, he kissed her again.

Leanne returned his kiss but he could sense she was preoccupied.

He tried not to worry. Tried to let go of his concerns. *Please, Lord*, he prayed. *I care for her so much. Help us to get through this. Don't make me give her up again.*

The revolving lights of the ambulance, the wail of the sirens piercing the quiet of the morning cut through Leanne's head like a knife.

She stood on the deck watching as the vehicle flew over the front yard, snow spinning from its tires, the red strobe light sweeping ominously over the snow-covered trees of the yard.

She clung to the doorway, swallowing and praying and trying to make her breath slow as she watched the ambulance's progress over the cattle guard, its lights bobbing as it made its way up the hill.

Her prayers were a tangle of petitions and fear. *Please, Lord. Watch over him. Please spare his life.*

George was in that ambulance on his way to the hospital in Cedar Ridge. He'd just suffered a heart attack.

Half an hour ago Leanne had been upstairs putting Austin to bed for his morning nap when she heard a puzzling thump, then a gasp coming from the kitchen. She hurried downstairs only to see George hunched over the sink, breathing heavily.

She had rushed to his side as he complained of chest pains. The next fifteen minutes were a blur as she stayed on the phone with the ambulance dispatcher, following his instructions, struggling to do CPR as the promised ambulance made its way to the ranch.

When the paramedics came, they made quick work of stabilizing him.

And then, as quickly as they'd come, they rushed him out of the house on a gurney and into the ambulance. Thankfully Austin had slept through it all.

The cold winter air slipped through her clothes, bringing her back to reality, and Leanne returned to the house, not sure what to do next.

Call Reuben. Arrange for someone to come and watch Austin.

She needed to go to the hospital to be with George.

She picked up the phone again and punched in Reuben's number. He answered it on the third ring.

"Hey, you," he said, the tenderness in his voice almost her undoing. "What's up? You miss me already?"

"It's George. He's had a heart attack." The words, spoken aloud sounded frightening and, for the first time since she saw her father-in-law hanging over the sink, gasping for breath, she started to cry.

"I'm coming over right away," Reuben said, sounding more alert.

"No. I want to meet you at the hospital. We should both be there." Her voice broke again and she drew in a few quick breaths to center herself.

"I don't want you to drive."

"I'll be okay. You should go to the hospital. Be there when your dad comes in. I'll meet you there once I call Tabitha. She can watch Austin for me."

Reuben protested again but she stopped him. "I don't know how serious this is, Reuben. I don't want you to miss out on seeing your father." As she spoke, the foreboding of her words dropped onto her heart like a rock.

She slowed herself down and eased the panic clenching her heart.

Be with George. Be with the paramedics and doctors. Don't take him yet.

The prayer helped her find firm ground, but even as she struggled to leave it all in God's hands, she caught herself jumping ahead and wondering what the implications would be for her, Austin and Reuben.

Don't go there. You don't know what will happen.

She pulled in another breath then hurried upstairs to change, waiting for her sister to come to watch Austin.

And as she did, another reality seeped in.

There was no way they could tell George the truth about Austin.

Not now.

Chapter Nine

"He looks okay." Reuben said the words as much to console himself as to encourage Leanne.

George lay on the bed, the tubes snaking out of him attached to beeping monitors. He looked as pale as the sheets covering his chest, his graying hair sticking out every which way. Leanne had tried to smooth it down, but it refused to be tamed.

George would be upset at how he looked, he thought. Much easier to focus on inconsequential things rather than think of how close they had come to losing his father.

The doctor had come by and told them they had caught it soon enough and that he was doing well. That he would only be in the Cardiac Care Unit overnight and then transferred to a regular hospital room tomorrow. He could, if all went well, be home by Monday.

This seemed improbable but encouraging at the same time.

"I'm glad he's sleeping." Leanne stood opposite Reuben, her hands clutching the bed rail, her gaze flicking from George to Reuben. She looked as concerned as he felt.

"He almost died." Reuben spoke quietly, still trying to understand what had happened.

"But he didn't," Leanne said. "He's going to be okay."

"For now." Reuben blew out his breath then picked up his father's hand. It was cool to the touch and hung limp between his fingers. He was still surprised at how panicked he'd felt when he got Leanne's phone call. How hard it had hit him. In spite of his feelings toward George, he was still his father.

"If he takes care of himself and does the rehab they lay out for him, it might not happen again."

Leanne's voice sounded strained. This was hard on her too, he realized. She had spent almost three years with George. Working with him, living in the same house. Watching him growing more and more attached to Austin.

His son.

"So I guess we won't be talking to George soon. About Austin," Reuben said.

Leanne released a short laugh, devoid of humor. "This definitely changes things."

As far as Reuben was concerned it didn't, but he kept that thought to himself. Austin was still his son and he still wanted to be with Leanne. Away from here.

But even as those last three words resonated through his mind, he looked down at George again. His father had never looked so vulnerable or helpless.

Somehow, at this moment, in spite of the anger and

the fights and the frustration that George and he had undergone, much of that was forgotten for the moment. Looking at George looking so pale and having come so close to death had given him another perspective on it all.

"You look troubled," Leanne said, coming around the bed to stand beside him. She laid her hand on his arm; her fingers warm through the fabric of his shirt.

"I've never seen him looking this weak." Reuben covered her hand with his. He turned to her, trying to articulate his confused thoughts. "He's always been so strong. Such a dominant force."

"He's not been like that the past few years, though," Leanne said, giving him a gentle smile. "He's definitely softened."

"Toward you and Austin."

Leanne shrugged. "Maybe, but there were times I caught him looking at old photo albums. Pictures of you, as well. I wonder if he didn't miss you too."

The part of him that had always yearned for a relationship with his father clung to her words. But the independent part of him, the one that had pulled away to protect himself, needed to reject what she was saying.

"You seem like you don't believe me," she said, her voice quiet.

"I want to, but I don't know if I dare." He paused, clinging to Leanne's hand like he was clinging to a lifeboat. "He scares me."

"Why?"

Reuben swallowed, wondering if Leanne would understand. He drew her away from George's bedside, just in case his father could hear.

He looked down at Leanne, praying she took his words the right way. "I'm afraid that I might be a father just like him."

Leanne held his eyes, her features impassive then he saw a sorrow drift over her face and she reached up and cupped his chin. "We make our own decisions in life. We're not only products of biology. I don't think you need to worry about that at all."

Threaded through her words of encouragement he caught a note of concern. As if she was worried that he was looking for an out.

"I want to be a father to Austin. A *good* father," he said, catching her hands and holding them to his chest. "It's just that I haven't had the best example."

Leanne entwined her fingers through his. "We don't parent completely on our own, you know. We live in a good community and we have our faith to guide and help us."

"There it is again," he said.

"What?"

Reuben glanced over at his father, still struggling with conflicted emotions. "That word," he said turning back to her. "*Community.* You want to stay here and nurture the roots you've put down. I feel like I need to leave and give myself a chance to be independent of… expectations. Be away from…well…my dad."

Leanne tugged on her hands to pull them away but he wouldn't release them.

"I don't want this to come between us," he said, lowering his voice, hoping she heard the urgency in his words. "We've waited a long time for this, and I want this to work. I want *us* to work." For emphasis he pressed a kiss to her lips. She lifted her arms and slid them around his neck, returning his kiss, easing away the tension that gripped him.

"I want us to work too," she said, giving him a tremulous smile. "And I want to give us the best possible chance to make that happen."

Reuben nodded as his cell phone vibrated in his pocket. He felt a flicker of guilt. The nurse had asked them to turn their phones off when they came into the room. In his haste to see his father, he had forgotten. However, he was expecting a call from Marshall.

He felt he was getting squeezed into a narrower and narrower space.

"I'm going to get a cup of coffee," he said. "Do you want anything?"

"Not vending machine coffee, that's for sure," she said with a grin.

He kissed her again, then he went out into the hallway. As he walked to the lobby, the sound of Christmas carols surrounded him. The nurses had strung lights and tinsel and hung paper bells by the nurse's station in an attempt to create a festive atmosphere.

Quite the challenge in a hospital, Reuben thought as he stepped out the sliding glass doors into the outside chill.

Flakes of snow sparkled and spiraled downward, adding to the layer they already had. Reuben took a moment to appreciate the beauty and peace of the scene. If the snow kept up, he and Leanne would have to put out more straw for bedding for the cows and weaned calves tomorrow.

He caught himself, tried to take a step back from the plans he was making. He was getting sucked into the day-to-day workings of the ranch. He knew from past experience that would only lead to disappointment and frustration. George would find a way to shut him out.

With renewed determination he pulled his phone out of his pocket and made a call.

"Hey, Marshall, how's it going?" he said trying to sound more jovial than he felt. He still had to wrap his head around the sight of his father looking so weak and helpless and what it meant for him and Leanne.

"Good. So, I just got a call from Dynac. They want to meet with you as soon as possible."

"How soon is that?"

"I've got a meet and greet set up for eight o'clock Sunday evening. Can you get here by then?"

"I'm not sure." Reuben fought down another beat of panic as events closed in. "My dad's just had a heart attack, and Saturday I have to make a final presentation to the Rodeo Group I've been working for here."

There was ominous silence on the other end of the line.

"Look, I'm sorry about your dad, but I can't shift it. This is an important meeting."

"Okay. I'll do what I can."

"No. You'll be here. That's it."

Marshall disconnected the call, and Reuben leaned his head against the wall, trying to plan. He could probably take the meeting. The doctor had said George's heart attack wasn't as serious as they'd initially thought. That he was in good shape and would recuperate. He wouldn't miss Reuben anyhow.

Twenty minutes later he had his flight booked for as late as he could possibly set it and still make the meeting.

As he walked back to the hospital room, the cold air still permeating him, his thoughts shifted to Leanne and her comment about wanting to give them the best chance to make their relationship work.

And he strongly suspected she meant staying here and not moving with him to Los Angeles.

In spite of what just happened with George, he still didn't think it was possible.

Chapter Ten

"Sit on Grampa," Austin said, trying to climb up on George's bed.

"Stay here, buddy. Grandpa is still not feeling good." Reuben caught Austin by the waist and pulled him up into his arms.

It was Friday afternoon, a little over twenty-four hours after his heart attack, and George was looking much improved over yesterday. Last night, as he and Leanne kept vigil, Reuben would not have thought that his father could be coming home in a few days. But now George's eyes looked brighter and he had more color in his face. His sister, Fay Cosgrove, had come by for a short visit, and Carmen Fisher, the manager of the hardware store, had dropped by with flowers. But for the most part they had tried to keep visitors to a minimum.

"I'm okay. He can sit beside me," George said, holding his hands out for his grandson.

Reuben wanted to protest, but Austin was reaching for George, and Reuben had spent enough time with

Austin that he knew when to stand firm and when to give in. Once Austin had fixed his mind on something, it was almost impossible to persuade him to change it.

He was exactly like his father and grandfather, Reuben thought with a touch of irony.

He set Austin on the bed; watchful of the cords that snaked to the monitors George was still attached to.

"How are the cows doing?" George asked, turning to Leanne.

"Good. Chad and I put out extra bedding this morning," Leanne said, fussing with George's sheet. Austin had tugged it down. "It snowed again last night though."

"Will we have enough straw or hay?"

"We'll know in a couple of months whether we'll manage or not."

"I contacted a farmer north of Calgary," Reuben put in, surprised how annoyed he felt at being left out of the loop. "He has a couple of hundred bales of hay he can get us for January."

Leanne shot him a puzzled look and he realized how he sounded. He was planning for the ranch past Christmas when he had been firm that he was leaving before that.

"You're talking about getting them delivered in January?" she asked, lifting her eyebrows, underlining her question.

He held her gaze, wondering how to approach this. "Chad can take care of unloading."

Leanne looked away and Reuben fought down a beat of concern. They really needed to sit and talk. Make solid plans. But how callous would it look for him to talk about moving away right after George's heart attack?

Take care of yourself, he reminded himself. *No one else will.*

Yet as he looked at his father, he was surprised how much it bothered him to see George so vulnerable.

Austin wriggled away, rubbing his eyes as he moved to Leanne's side of the bed.

"Stay here, son," George said, pulling Austin back to him. But Austin shook his head and held his hands out to Leanne.

"I think I should get him back home," Leanne was saying. "He's tired."

She looked tired too, Reuben thought.

"Did you have time to pick up those Christmas presents I got sent to the store?" George asked her.

Leanne shook her head. "I thought I could do that Saturday. We have a meeting with the Rodeo Group and Tabitha will be babysitting him."

"That'd be good." George glanced over at Reuben and gave him a surprising smile. "I'm glad I'll be here for Christmas after all."

Though Reuben returned his smile, the usual confusion and tension at the thought of the holiday season seized him. Once again he was torn between his future job and the possibility of a life here with his father.

Don't go there. You've been burned enough by this man. He's made you doubt everything about yourself. He's never lifted you up. He's even made you wonder if you could ever be a father.

Leanne bent awkwardly over and brushed a light

kiss over George's forehead. He reached up and caught her hand, giving it a gentle squeeze. "You're a good daughter," he said, his voice quiet, clearly moved by her action.

She gave him a careful smile then walked out. Reuben followed her into the hall, where the carols from the nurse's station filled the air, creating a curious counterpoint to the moment.

But she put her hand on his arm. "Stay with your father. I'm bringing Austin home and I might take a nap too."

She did look tired, he thought with some concern. Tired and worn. Too many things on her mind probably. He knew he was worn out from all the convoluted thinking he'd been indulging in.

"I guess I can stay for a while," he said, even though he wasn't sure he wanted to be left alone with George. "I should spend as much time with my father as I can."

His comment created a frown, underlining the shaky underpinnings of their situation.

"There's something else," he said. "I have an important meeting in Los Angeles on Sunday."

Alarm flitted over her features and she looked away. "For your job."

"Yeah. I can't get out of it."

"Of course. You should go."

She didn't sound excited about the idea and he didn't know what else to tell her.

"This is important to me," he said, keeping his voice low, his tone easy.

She looked at him, gave him a smile and then, to his

surprise, she leaned in and gave him a kiss. "I know. We'll be okay here while you're gone."

"I'll be back on Monday at the latest. For George's homecoming."

"That's good." She touched his cheek then left.

Reuben watched her walk down the hall, Austin on her hip, tamping down the fear that things were starting to get out of his control.

He came back to the hospital room and sat down on the chair beside his father's bed.

"Have you finished your report?" George asked Reuben. "On the arena?"

"Yes, I have. It didn't take as long as I expected. I managed to get hold of all the subcontractors right away and most of them were still in Cedar Ridge so that helped."

"And what did you decide?"

"It's viable. Worth fixing up. Say what you want about Floyd Rennie, he used good materials."

George huffed at that, but it was as if his reaction was more automatic than heartfelt. "He was still a shyster," George said.

"I hope you don't say that in front of Leanne," Reuben said, trying to keep his tone light.

George shot him a glare. "I say what I want about that man. Leanne knows he was a crook."

"But he was still her father. I know she cared about him."

"So you think that in spite of everything he did, she would love him anyway if he was alive?"

A curious tone had entered his father's voice. Reuben sensed he wasn't talking about Leanne and Floyd Rennie anymore.

"I think blood is thicker than water," Reuben said. "I think there's always a connection between a father and his child that can never be erased."

He spoke of Leanne and her father, but also of himself and Austin. Once he'd known, beyond a doubt, that Austin was his son, the feelings he had for the little guy had grown stronger every day.

George looked away, staring at the wall, but it seemed that he wasn't looking at it. Instead Reuben sensed he was looking into the past.

What did he see? Did he remember all the fights they'd had? The times George had physically punished him? The raised voices, the clenched fists?

Or was he thinking of some of the happy times they'd shared? Working together, going fishing in the creek?

"I still miss Dirk" was all George said.

The stark sentence was like a knife in his heart. Why did this bother him so much? Why did he spend so much time and emotion on this clearly one-sided relationship?

He couldn't be here anymore, no matter what Leanne said. He was about to stand when his father looked over at him. "But you're here now," he said, holding his gaze, his eyes intent on Reuben. "And you're all I have left."

Then George reached out to take Reuben's hand. The move was surprising. As his father squeezed, a reluctant joy suffused Reuben.

George clung to his hand, looking up at him. "I'm sorry, son."

Reuben could only stare, shock mixing with an older longing. This was the first time, ever, that he had heard those words cross his father's lips.

"You look surprised," George said.

"I guess I am," Reuben said.

George pulled his hand away and the gentleness on his expression was replaced with a downturn of his father's mouth. "Well, you should be. I don't like apologizing," he said, sounding more like the old George. He drummed his fingers on the bed, as his mouth grew tight. "I know I came close to dying, and it made me think about us and how things have been between us."

Reuben felt as if they were on the precipice of something different and unknown. He wasn't sure where George was going with this or what he would say. So he simply leaned forward, inviting his father to talk.

"I tried. You have to know that." George shifted his gaze to Reuben. "You were too much like your mother to make it easy for me. You were always a challenge."

So were you, Reuben wanted to say but again he kept quiet.

"But when your mother left, I had to take care of you. I should have done better. You were my responsibility in spite of everything."

"What do you mean, 'in spite of everything'?" Reuben blurted out.

George looked away, pulling his hand out of Reuben's. "I don't want to talk anymore." He closed his eyes and folded his hands over his stomach.

Reuben guessed the conversation was over.

Yet he lingered a few moments longer. His father's

confession, his moment of vulnerability, had shifted Reuben's feelings. As did the fact that he almost lost his father.

But as Reuben walked back down the hall and out of the hospital he wondered if it was enough to make him change his plans.

As his truck warmed up, he brushed off the snow that had gathered on the windshield, his thoughts jumping between the promise of his new job in a new place and the memories of his life here. He'd been away so long, could he come back?

He got into his truck, pulling off his gloves. As he reached to turn on the heater, he caught sight of an old scar on his wrist.

I'm sorry.

Reuben put his truck into Drive, backed up and spun out of the parking lot, snow spitting out behind him.

He didn't know if it was enough.

"Are you okay?" Leanne laid her hand on Reuben's shoulder. He'd been in a dark mood ever since he'd come back from the hospital.

"It's hard…seeing my father so weak." He dragged his hands over his face as if trying to erase what he had seen.

"The doctor said he'll be okay," Leanne said, tightening her grip.

"I know." He sucked in another long breath and Leanne sensed something else was going on.

But she left it alone. She couldn't force it if he wasn't ready.

The dishes were done and Austin was already in his pajamas, ready for bed, cheeks shining from his bath. Leanne had put Christmas music on the stereo and the twinkling lights of the Christmas tree should have made her feel more content. But Reuben's mood created a sense of unease.

Then Austin scooted over, carrying a book that Leanne had bought for him this afternoon and he dropped it on Reuben's lap. "Read it," he demanded.

Reuben laughed, seemingly letting go of his previous bad mood, and pulled the little guy up on his lap, snuggling him close as he opened the book and started reading. Leanne relaxed at the sight, watching Reuben, his head bent over his son's.

Father and son.

How often had Leanne dreamed of this moment? The three of them together in the ranch house, making it a home?

Austin looked intently at the story Reuben read about a colt that had gotten lost and was trying to find its mother by talking to other farm animals. Reuben changed his voice for each of the animals as he read, making Austin laugh.

When the book was finished, Austin turned to the first page again. "Read it again," he said.

So Reuben did, but when he came to the end again, Austin started yawning. Nevertheless, he flipped the book to the beginning. "Again," he demanded. "Read it again."

"I think someone needs to go to bed," Reuben said, closing the book.

"No. Read it. Read it. Read it." Austin's voice grew louder and shriller and Leanne saw his tears gathering as he tugged on the book.

"No, buddy. You need to go to sleep." Reuben tried to take the book from him but Austin wriggled in his arms, a small bundle of fury.

"No sleep. *Read!*" Austin yelled, his face red, tears of anger streaming down his cheeks. He swung the book around and hit Reuben on the face with the corner.

"Ouch. That hurt." Reuben caught Austin by the arms, staring down at him, eyes narrowed. Austin was suddenly quiet, as if sensing he had pushed things too far.

Then Reuben abruptly set Austin aside. He jumped up from the couch and strode into the dining room.

Austin started crying again and Leanne picked him up, wiped his eyes and then brought him upstairs.

"See Uncle Wooben," Austin whimpered as Leanne closed the door of his room behind them.

"No. You hurt him with your book," Leanne said, keeping her voice quiet. She was still surprised at the look of horror on Reuben's face when he had reprimanded Austin.

"I sorry," Austin said, hanging his head.

"That's good. I'll tell… Uncle Reuben." She faltered over those last words, a sense of dread tightening her abdomen. They had to tell Austin. It wasn't fair to keep this from him much longer.

But that would mean telling George, and now, with him just recuperating from the heart attack, when could they do that?

She tucked Austin into his bed, and as she sang his bedtime prayers with him, the door opened and Reuben stepped into the room. He stood by the door, as if uncertain what to do but then Leanne waved him over.

He came by the bed and Austin grinned up at him, everything forgotten. "I wove you, Uncle Wooben," he said.

Reuben dropped to his knees beside the bed and pulled Austin to him in a tight hug. "Love you too," he whispered.

Reuben pulled away. Leanne hugged Austin, then kissed him good-night. Reuben left the room, Leanne behind him. She kept the door open, following Reuben down the stairs. He walked into the family room but didn't sit down. Instead he turned to her, looking anguished.

"I'm sorry I got angry with him. I shouldn't have."

"He was being a little stinker," Leanne said, touching his arm to reassure him. He looked so distraught.

"But I felt… I thought I was…" He stopped, dropping his one hand on his hip, the other clutching his forehead.

She caught his raised arm and lowered it. "You thought you were what?"

He looked at her a moment, as if trying to get his bearings. Then he pulled his sleeve up and turned his wrist around. "This scar? Remember asking me about it all those years ago?"

She traced the puckered skin, remembering that afternoon, here on this ranch. Dirk had been inside the house, watching a football game with George. She and Reuben had been sitting on the deck. Just talking. She'd noticed the scar on his wrist and had taken his hand, had touched it. It was one of those forbidden moments, and it was then that she realized that she cared for Reuben more than she'd ever cared for Dirk. It was both exhilarating and frightening. "You told me you got it when you were putting up fencing with Dirk," she said, her voice quiet. "You said you cut yourself on a nail."

Reuben looked down at it, shaking his head and rolling his sleeve down again, buttoning the cuff. "I lied to you. I got into a fight with Dad over a horse. He hit me with the bridle, and the buckle cut my wrist wide open. I bandaged it and went back to work. He never spoke of it again."

Leanne couldn't stop her gasp of shock. Her eyes flew to his, but he was looking down at his arm, his expression grim.

"Dad had a horrific temper and he would let it fly anytime he got upset. I was on the wrong end of that temper too many times."

Leanne had known Reuben had it hard but she never knew that George had been physically abusive.

"I'm so sorry. I never knew how bad it was." She laid her hand on his chest, willing him to look at her. "I'm so sorry."

"It's in the past and Dad even apologized to me this afternoon." He released a humorless laugh. "Never thought I'd hear the words *I'm sorry* come from the mighty George Walsh."

He looked at her, and to her surprise he gave her a

gentle smile, easing her hair back from her face with his hand.

"Dirk never said anything" was all Leanne could manage.

"I asked him to keep his mouth shut. It was humiliating and I didn't want anyone else to know."

"I wish I had known."

"Would it have changed anything?"

"It might have."

"I wouldn't have wanted you to date me out of pity."

"It wouldn't have been pity—"

He stopped her there. "You know, deep down, there were other more important reasons we didn't end up together. I know I wasn't the best person for you. And I know that Dirk was."

"But he had it so much easier than you," Leanne insisted. "Now that I know what you dealt with, I think I might have been more understanding of who you were."

He shrugged. "We don't need to talk about that now. That's all in the past." He stroked her cheek, looking bemused. "Don't look so sad. It wasn't all bad. We had good times too. I remember trips to go fishing up in the mountains. Long drives to go to bull sales where we played road games. George taught me how to train horses." Then he grew serious. "But at the same time, my dad had a mighty temper and I've seen him go out of control too often. And that's why…that's why…" His voice broke, creating more confusion for Leanne.

"Why what?"

He shook his head and was about to turn away when

Leanne caught him by the arm, stopping him. "Please. No more secrets. Tell me."

Reuben swallowed, shaking his head. "When Austin hit me with that book, I got so mad… I was afraid I would hurt him. That's why I had to walk away. I've seen my father's temper boil over and I couldn't let that happen between me and my son. I can't let him have that kind of father."

"Of course you were angry," Leanne said, concerned at the sorrow in his voice and the anguish on his face. "He was being a brat. I was upset too."

"But you don't have my father's genetics. You don't have to worry what might happen."

"Nothing happened," she said, feeling a panicky need to encourage him. It was as if he was withdrawing from both of them. "You didn't do anything."

Reuben didn't look convinced and Leanne sent up an anxious prayer for wisdom and for him to understand. She grabbed him by the arm and gave him a small shake. "You said you can't let him have that kind of father, but you'll never be the father your dad was. I see you with Austin. You're loving and caring and kind and patient. Way more patient than I am."

He held her gaze and she was encouraged by the smile that slipped over his lips. "You sound convincing."

"I don't need to sound convincing. You need to believe that you are your own person. And that you don't have to worry about being like your father. Two-year-olds are annoying and frustrating, and there have been times I wanted to leave him in his bedroom with the door locked all afternoon so I wouldn't have to deal with him." She gave him a reassuring smile. "That's what being a parent is all about. And I'm not worried about what type of parent you are or will be."

Reuben shook his head and then, to her surprise, pulled her into his arms. "Because of you I want to make better choices than I have in the past."

"And you have. With God's help you have made good choices. Your own choices."

He kissed her again and she settled into his arms, his heartbeat reassuring.

But even as he held her close, even as they shared this moment of closeness, she knew those choices would take him away from her. She sent up a prayer for strength, knowing that they had come to the moment she had been anticipating but also felt apprehensive about.

It was time they talked about what lay ahead and what decisions they were going to make.

But before she could speak, his cell phone buzzed and he pulled away, glancing down at the number. He gave her an apologetic smile. "Sorry. I have to take this. It's Marshall."

She nodded, pulling away, wrapping her arms around herself. Reuben walked away, sounding animated and excited.

Leanne knew this man was Reuben's future boss and they were talking about his job. In California.

She looked around the room, trying to imagine herself away from this place that she had woven so many dreams around.

Trying to imagine herself sitting alone in the middle of a large city while Reuben traveled around the world, or moving from place to place like she had with her father.

Could she do it? Was her love strong enough?

Chapter Eleven

"Is the arena worth fixing up, in your opinion?" Owen asked as Reuben put a cap on the felt pen he had used to make notes on the whiteboard in the meeting room.

Reuben looked around the gathering of the Rodeo Group and nodded.

"I believe it is," he said, gesturing to the figures he had just written out on the board. "Like I told my father, Floyd used quality materials for the work he actually did." The smile he gave Leanne gave her a surprising sense of peace. Her father wasn't such a loser after all.

Reuben sat down beside her, giving her arm a gentle squeeze. They hadn't seen each other this morning. Reuben had been busy getting his presentation together and she had been cleaning the house.

She made a few notes on her laptop, glancing at her phone as she did. No messages from her sister, who was watching Austin.

She had left her son there because she had texted Reuben last night, after he left, saying that she needed to talk to him after she visited George in the hospital. The shadow of Reuben's new job was hanging over her and she was tired of the uncertainty. Discussing their future couldn't wait any longer and she didn't want the complication of Austin's being around, distracting them.

"Well, thanks so much for all your hard work," Owen said, looking around the room at the gathering. "And thanks, everyone, for taking the time out of your Saturday afternoon to come out here."

Owen had invited members of the Chamber of Commerce to the meeting, as well, so they could be kept in the loop. The small room was stiflingly full and Leanne felt a bit light-headed. She had missed breakfast and lunch, keeping herself busy with mindless tasks. Anything to avoid thinking of the conversation she and Reuben were going to have. Part of her dreaded it. It was so much easier to float along without making a decision when, no matter what they chose, it would be difficult for one of them.

I've made so many sacrifices for men, Leanne thought, memories of her father's pleading, Dirk's constant postponing of their wedding blending with what she guessed Reuben would soon ask of her. *Can I do it again? Should I have to?*

"Thanks again, Reuben, for doing this for us," Owen said. "I think I can say for everyone here that we're happy to know that we don't have to tear down the arena. We won't be having any more meetings until the New Year, when we can ask for contract bids to finish the arena." He glanced at Leanne. "And I understand that Helen is coming back as secretary then?"

Leanne nodded, giving Owen a cautious smile. "I can't juggle working on the ranch and taking care of Austin with this job." She felt a niggle of unease as she laid out her reasons. Her decision was more complicated and would be influenced by what happened after she and Reuben talked.

Please, Lord, help me to make the right choice, she prayed. *Show me what You want us to do. Show us what You want us to do.*

"I understand," Owen said, then turned to Reuben. "Will we be getting a formal report on this?"

"Complete with embossed folder," Reuben joked.

"Does anyone else have any questions for Reuben?"

"I wouldn't mind asking you about the possibility of adding to the building," Mr. Rodriguez said. "My daughter, Shauntelle, has spoken of starting up a snack bar and had hoped to start a restaurant there, as well. It wasn't in the original plans but she talked to an architect and can get some blueprints drawn up."

"That sounds amazing," Owen chimed in, standing up. "Why don't you come with me and Reuben to the arena right now? We can see what the possibilities would be in terms of where we could put it."

Reuben frowned at Leanne.

She gave him a reassuring smile. "I'll meet you at the hospital whenever it works for you," she said, gathering her things and standing. "Or at the back booth at Angelo's for supper."

The restaurant would give them more privacy than the Grill and Chill and it was quieter.

She slipped the laptop into her purse, and as she

stood, he laid his hand on her shoulder, giving her a gentle squeeze.

"I'll be there soon. But if I'm not at the hospital by seven, let's meet at Angelo's."

She felt a flare of disappointment but then, as he brushed her hair away from her face, she saw the scar on his wrist. Now that she knew the story behind it, her perspective had changed.

How could she expect him to even consider staying on the ranch with his father?

But how could she ever leave?

Later. Later, she told herself.

"Okay. It's a date," she said trying to inject a happy note into her voice.

He nodded then brushed a gentle kiss on her lips.

"See you there" was all she said, then she walked away, head down, avoiding the curious looks of the people gathered in the room.

"I don't want to be a burden." George was sitting up in bed, arms folded over his chest, looking determined. "The doctor said I can go home Monday so we'll have to see about getting help. I can hire a nurse to take care of me."

Leanne wanted to object but she knew it was a smart move. No matter what happened, it would be better if George had someone else taking care of him. She wouldn't have time.

"How are things going on the ranch?" he asked.

"Good in the minutes since last you asked," she teased.

He nodded, tapping his fingers on his arm. "I know. I'm sorry. I feel useless and I hate being away from the place."

"Well, no fears. The cows are doing well. This morning I talked to the guy Reuben mentioned yesterday about getting the hay hauled in and he said he could come in a week or so."

"We don't need it right away, do we? I thought we were good until January."

"No. But Reuben thought it was a good idea to get it delivered before the roads get too bad."

She saw his features tighten at the mention of Reuben's name, and her thoughts flipped back to last night. To Reuben's confession. To the scar puckering his wrist and the doubts he had expressed about being a good father.

So much of it was because of the man in front of her. A man she had come to care for in her own way.

"I'm glad Reuben has been around to help," she said. "He's done a lot."

"More than he used to," George grumbled. "Didn't always work so hard."

"He was only a kid then."

"So was his brother." George looked away then shook his head. "Too many memories I can't shed in my brain. Sitting in this hospital bed, I've had too much time to think about the past."

Leanne sensed an opening. "What have you been thinking about?"

George's lips tightened and Leanne wondered if she had gone too far. But she was tired of the unspoken words. The broken-off sentences. The things he refused to speak of.

He had pushed Reuben so hard and done so much harm to him. Reuben's revelation that he was afraid he would be a father like George was a blow Leanne still struggled with. She laid the blame for his fears square on George's shoulders.

"Dirk. I miss him," George said finally, giving her a melancholy look. "And I'm sure you miss him too."

Leanne didn't want to go there.

"And Reuben?" she asked instead.

"Well, he's here. For what that's worth."

And suddenly Leanne was tired of it.

"Why do you dislike Reuben so much?" The words spilled out of her, born of frustration and sorrow for a man she cared so much for. George glared at her and fear rose up at the sight of his widened eyes, the clenching of his jaw.

"Doesn't matter," he muttered, looking away. "It's in the past. Should stay there."

"I don't agree," she said, thinking of Reuben's expression whenever he talked about George. The fear that seemed to dog him, thinking that he could even come remotely close to being a father to Austin like George was to Reuben. If she and Reuben were to have a future, she felt she needed to deal with his past.

But by doing so, she knew she put her own future on the ranch at risk.

"Don't ask," he said in a gruff voice. "It's old history."

"What started it? Was it something he did? Because

if that's the case, then maybe we can find a way to fix it."

"Can't be fixed. Ever. It's done. Finished. Over."

"Please tell me. I want to find a way to bring you two together." Even as she spoke the words, she felt a flush of guilt.

Was she thinking of her own self-interests? Did she hope that if George and Reuben reconciled, Reuben would be willing to stay around the ranch?

She pressed her fingers to her lips, a prayer for wisdom and guidance winging upward.

Help me Lord, she prayed. *Help me to say the right thing for the right reason. Help me to think only of Reuben and Austin and what's best for them.*

The words the pastor read on Sunday slipped into her mind.

You intended to harm me, but God intended it for good. Could God use everything for good? Could he find a way to make good the things that George had done to his own son?

"All his life Reuben only wanted to be your son. I know he wasn't always the best behaved but some of it…was…well…because of how you treated him."

Surprisingly George didn't respond to that.

"He was a good son and I know he loves you. All he wants is that same love in return."

George blinked and Leanne wondered if she had imagined the glint of tears in his eyes. Or maybe it was wishful thinking.

"I know."

His simple admission ignited a spark of hope. "He

really cares," she pressed, sensing his softening. "All he's ever wanted was to be a part of your life and a part of this ranch." Was she overreaching? Superimposing her own yearnings on Reuben's actions?

And yet she sensed a peace about him as they worked with the cattle, as they rode the backcountry. She knew that, whether he wanted to admit it or not, the ranch was in his blood. In his soul. "I know it's hard to believe, but he's all you have left. He and Austin are the only family you have."

George shot her a narrowed glance. Did he, on some level, know the truth about Austin?

"I think we could have a good life," she pressed, making one last case.

"I don't know if it can happen," George finally said, closing his eyes. He looked tired today. More than yesterday and Leanne wondered if he would truly be able to come home on Monday.

"You know that we have been told many times that all things are possible with God," Leanne said, her tone quiet, gentle.

"Maybe."

Leanne waited, sensing that George wasn't pushing back at her anymore. That maybe, if she could find the right questions, he would tell her why he felt the way he did about Reuben. A man who had always been so important to her and who she was coming closer and closer to love with every day she spent with him.

"I've always had a hard time with Reuben. I don't think that's any secret," George said, his eyes still closed. "I've always had a hard time…accepting him."

That was confusing.

"What do you mean, accepting him? He's your son."

George opened his eyes, staring directly ahead, his hands clutching the sheets. "No. He's not."

He spoke the words so quietly Leanne wasn't sure she'd heard him correctly.

"I don't understand."

George's mouth grew tight, and for a moment Leanne thought the conversation was over. But then he drew in a shaky breath followed by a deep sigh. "I married too soon after Dirk's mother died. But I was lonely and Dirk was so young. I was lost on my own. Reuben's mother was beautiful and fun. But my sister, Fay, warned me not to be rash. I should have listened to her. Marrying Raina was a mistake. She was hard to live with. Hated the ranch. We grew apart. We…we weren't…intimate for the last six years of our marriage." He paused, pulling in a long, slow breath.

Leanne felt as if she was teetering on the edge of a chasm, but she had started this and she had to see it to the end.

"And she left when Reuben was five."

His words, so quiet, so softly spoken, fell like rocks into Leanne's soul. Hard. Uncompromising. Devastating.

"So you're saying that Reuben—"

"Isn't my son. That's why I've had a hard time with him. He was the son of the woman who cheated on me." He seemed to spit out those last words. "And she didn't even have the grace to take her son with her when she left."

Leanne fought down her panic, understanding what he was saying on one level but still unable to process it.

"Does…does Reuben know this?"

George shook his head. "No. I was too proud to let anyone know what had happened, how Raina had cheated on me."

"But you kept him."

George glowered at her. "Of course I did. He didn't have anyone else. Where could he go? His mother died while she was on some holiday in Mexico after she left and I was all he had."

Leanne held his gaze, hearing one thing, feeling another. George cared for Reuben in his own way and yet he had seen him as an unwanted responsibility.

And as all this fell together another, horrible thought came to mind.

Didn't I do the same? By staying with Dirk so long, wasn't I also unfaithful to Reuben? I am no different than Reuben's mother.

And behind that came another revelation.

Austin wasn't George's biological grandchild. In any way.

The room spun around her as she clung to the side of George's bed. Everything had changed.

"Are you okay, Leanne?" George asked, touching her hand with his. "Your hands are like ice, honey."

Leanne closed her eyes, praying one simple prayer over and over again.

Help me, Lord.

"Leanne. Tell me." George sounded frightened and Leanne had to fight down the nausea that threatened.

Her stomach roiled.

"Leanne."

She breathed in then out then squeezed his hand, trying to gain control of the emotions that swamped her. Trying to find solid ground.

"I'm so sorry to hear about Reuben's mother" was all she could manage.

"It was a long time ago, my dear."

The affection in his voice and the way he patted her hand loosened what little bit of control she had left.

She closed her eyes as a sob worked its way up her throat.

"Leanne, what's wrong? I'm calling the nurse."

She shook her head, tears slipping past her tightly squeezed lids. "Please. Don't," she managed.

"Where's Reuben? He should be here."

"I'm meeting him. Later." Slowly she regained her equilibrium but a deep grief and shame now wrapped icy fingers around her heart.

George waited while she dug in her purse and pulled out a tissue, wiped her eyes and drew in a steadying breath.

"What's wrong? Tell me," he demanded. His voice grew louder and she knew she couldn't put him off anymore. Though she and Reuben had agreed they would be together when they told him about Austin, Leanne couldn't hold the truth back from him any longer.

"I have something important to tell you," she said, her voice quiet now. She looked down at the tissue she had folded and refolded, unable to look George in the eye. "But before I do, you need to know that I always cared for Dirk. He was someone I had thought could give me what I didn't have growing up. Security. A solid support. He was a good man. But Dirk and I were engaged for so long I never thought he would set a wedding date."

"You know I never cared for your relationship with him at that time."

"I know."

"But I did come to care for you later."

He sounded apologetic and Leanne felt even guiltier. She wasn't worthy of even that small amount of consideration.

"Dirk and I fought over it so many times," she said. "And I got tired of waiting. I told Dirk that if he couldn't choose between you and me, then I didn't want to be with him. He didn't say anything, which, to me, was his choice. So I broke up with him."

"Was that when Dirk went to Europe?"

She nodded.

"And I went to Costa Rica for the wedding Dirk and I were supposed to go to," she continued. "I already had the tickets. Seemed a shame to waste them. And, well, Reuben was there. At the wedding." She stopped there, not sure how to carry on.

"And…" George prompted.

"We spent the whole time together. And we fell in love. Even though I'd dated Dirk, part of me was always drawn to Reuben. It wasn't right of me and I know that, but Reuben made me nervous."

"He should have. He was living a careless life."

Leanne nodded. "I know. That's why I kept myself

from him, but when I went to Costa Rica and saw him there, I knew I couldn't deny how I felt about him anymore. He felt the same way. While were there…we…we were together." She faltered, sucking in another breath. Sending up another prayer. Leanne kept her head down as she battled her shame. Her confession, coming on the heels of what George had told her about Reuben's mother, made her story sound tawdry and cheap.

But Austin came of that, she reminded herself. And she wasn't tarnishing the blessing he was to her. Nor was she going to deny her feelings for Reuben.

"We both agreed that it was a mistake, " she said, fighting for words past the thickness in her throat. "And then Dirk came back from Europe and he found out that I was expecting Reuben's child—"

"And he married you anyway?" His incredulity and the force of his anger sent her gaze flying to him. He was staring at her as if he didn't know her. "And after he died, you never told me the truth?"

"Dirk made me promise not to. He was so adamant about it. But the past few months I've wanted to, again and again. And then Reuben came back and I told him the truth—"

"But not me." His eyes were wide with anger, his lips white. His monitor beeped as his heart rate flew upward.

"Let me get a nurse," she said, concerned, wishing she had never told him.

George shook his head, breathing deeply.

"No. No nurse. I don't want a nurse." He took another breath and thankfully he looked more calm. Then he turned to Leanne, his eyes as hard as granite. "But you. You can leave. And never come back."

Chapter Twelve

"Can't meet you for dinner. Austin is at Tabitha's for the night."

Reuben stared at the cryptic text message he'd just gotten from Leanne, trying to figure out what to think. He had tried to call her but got no reply. So he had texted her back, asking her what was going on. Why did Austin have to stay at Tabitha's?

This was how it all began, he thought, hitting Send on his text message. Lost calls, misplaced texts. But he could see that she had read his text. And just to be on the safe side, he took a screenshot of their exchange.

Given their history, he couldn't be too careful.

He waited, watching the screen, waiting for her reply but there was nothing. He gave her a few more minutes but unless she was out of service, he didn't know why she wasn't returning his texts.

Or explaining better what she meant by "talk later."

He sat back, dragging his hand over his face, fighting down a sense of panic. He knew events had been converging the past week to a place of no return. His boss arranging for a meeting tomorrow, Leanne insisting they tell George the truth about Austin.

And, even more important, they had to make a decision about where they were going as a couple. California and the future? Cedar Ridge and his past?

The last thought created a surge of dread. He knew how attached Leanne was to the ranch and how involved she was. But he had to maintain his independence. He couldn't afford to let George take over his life and remind him of all he wasn't or couldn't be.

It doesn't have to be that way. He apologized to you. It could be the start of a new relationship.

It was an enticing idea that he had nurtured for too many years. He didn't dare indulge in it.

All his life Reuben had kept his own dream of working on the ranch tamped far down. It hurt too much to know that his father would, most likely, never accept him as a partner. In spite of that, no matter what he did, where he worked, his heart had always been here, in Cedar Ridge at the Bar W.

But now? Could it be different?

Reuben looked at his phone again, toyed with the idea of sending another text to Leanne but nixed it. If she hadn't answered by now, then something else was going on.

He shoved his phone into his pocket, fighting down an unreasoning fear that Leanne had done what his mother had. Left him.

His heart sank and his stomach roiled. No. He couldn't believe that.

Something else had happened and he needed to find out what.

He got into his truck and started driving. But his anger and disappointment with Leanne grew with each mile. Too many things going on. Too many things to deal with. Everything seemed to be converging into a situation he couldn't control.

Ten minutes later he swung around the corner of the gravel road leading to Tabitha's and his truck fishtailed, his lights arcing through the gathering dark.

He spun the steering wheel to bring the truck back onto the road, but rocked to a halt and sucked in a deep breath. Anger and driving were not a good combination.

Like father like son.

The thought chilled him to the bone. His mind slipped back to a time when he and his father had been fighting about something and George had turned to him, yelling as he lost control of the truck. When they plowed into the ditch, it had only served to make his father even more upset.

His father had a wicked temper and right now Reuben wasn't acting any differently.

He clenched the steering wheel, fighting down the fury that ripped through him. He wasn't going to be like his father.

But you are. You're his son.

The insidious voice rose up and right behind it came the memory of Austin hitting him with the book. His first response was anger, and it made him sick to his stomach that he could be mad at his son.

But what frightened him even more was that he was acting like his father.

Help me, Lord, he prayed. *Help me to make my own choices. To be my own person.*

He pulled back onto the road and at a more sedate pace, drove into Tabitha's yard. But that still didn't ease his panic.

He knocked on the door and Tabitha was right there, as if she'd been waiting for him.

"Come in," she said, stepping aside.

The mobile home wasn't large and Reuben felt as if he was filling up the space when he stepped inside the entrance, pulling his hat off his head.

"Austin is in bed already," she said.

"Kind of early, isn't it?"

"Early for bed, late for a nap." She shrugged. "Depends on how you spin it. Do you want a cup of tea?"

"I'm only staying long enough to take Austin home," Reuben said.

Tabitha's forehead creased in a light frown. "Home as in the ranch?"

Reuben blinked as he realized what he had said. "Yes. That's what I meant."

"I thought you meant the hotel you were staying at."

"That's no home."

"You're telling me. Anyhow, Leanne was quite specific that Austin stay here. She said that you were flying to Los Angeles tomorrow."

"Right," he said. "Then he may as well stay here."

"And you may as well have a cup of tea. Not to sound all dramatic, but you look like five miles of bad road."

"I feel like ten," he said, shrugging his jacket off and hanging it over the back of a wooden chair.

"So how's your dad?" she asked as she busied herself in the tiny kitchen, boiling water, setting cups out.

"The doctor said he could come home on Monday."

"That's early."

"He's a tough old cowboy, I guess," he said, drumming his fingers on the table.

"And how is Chad working out as a hired hand?"

"He's okay."

"I know he's never worked on a ranch before. Nice that your dad was willing to give him a chance."

Why she was chatting about stuff he didn't care about? Then as she set the mugs onto the table, he realized what she was doing. "You're going to make me ask, aren't you?" he said.

"Yes. I am." Tabitha returned to the counter, poured the boiling water into the pot then brought it and the mugs to the table. "Honey or sugar in your tea?"

"Neither."

"Ah. Manly man." Tabitha brought the teapot to the table and sat down. How could she act so casual when he felt as if everything was coming crashing down on him?

"Okay. So what happened with Leanne?" Reuben finally asked.

"All she would tell me was that she had made a huge mistake and now she was paying the price." Tabitha poured some tea into the mugs and set the pot down, folding her arms as she looked over at him. "What do you suppose she's talking about?"

"I have no idea. She hasn't said anything more to me than what I told you." Reuben massaged his temples with his fingertips, as if trying to draw out what might possibly have instigated this.

"Did you two fight?" Tabitha asked.

"What? No. We were supposed to meet at Angelo's after she visited my father in the hospital. I got her text while I was waiting there." Reuben pulled the steaming mug tea close, wrapping his chilled hands around its warmth. "Did she tell you if she stopped by to see my father?"

Tabitha shrugged. "She just called, asking me to watch Austin and saying that she needed some space."

That word again. That horrible word that had sent them off on this trajectory.

"Could she have had a fight with my father?" he asked.

"Maybe. She was crying and sounded too upset to say much, though I can't imagine what she would fight with George about. She's always gotten along with him."

"I know. That surprises me."

"Surprised me too. I know he hated her being engaged to Dirk, but since Austin was born, he's changed. He's crazy about that kid and would do anything for him. I think that made him more accepting of Leanne. Plus the fact that, for some reason, she loves being on the ranch and helping where she can." Tabitha took a sip of tea then sighed. "Are you still going to take that job in California?"

Her question came at him sideways. "I'm flying out tomorrow to meet with a prospective client." Was that why Leanne was upset?

"I understand the job means moving around a lot."

"At first, yes."

Tabitha looked reflective as she twirled a copper-colored strand of hair around her finger.

"You look like you're thinking about what you want to tell me," Reuben said.

"Sometimes I think before I speak." She flashed him a tight smile. "Did Leanne ever tell you what life was like for us? Living with our dad?"

"A bit. She told me it was hard. That there were times you were hungry because there wasn't enough food."

"Yeah. I also remember waking up one time and falling down the stairs because the house we lived in before didn't have stairs. Getting lost on our way to school because Dad was gone and Mom didn't have a car and we had to walk and had forgotten the way. But the hardest part was not feeling like a part of anything. I think that's what my mother struggled with the most." Tabitha was quiet as she released her hair. "Did Leanne tell you that our mom left our dad a couple of times?"

"No. She never did."

"She came back, but each time she did the next move was that much harder on her." Tabitha rested her chin on her hand and held his gaze, her eyes looking past him as if delving into her past. "My mom had a couple of potted roses. She always said that when we reached our forever home, she would plant them. She took them along every place we moved. After she died, Leanne and I didn't water them because we always thought it dumb that she put so much stock in those silly plants." Tabitha blinked and looked down at her tea, giving it a lackadaisical stir with her spoon. "I wish we had taken better care of them. We didn't have much of Mom after she died. Leanne and I often wondered if Mom died because she got uprooted so many times and her love wasn't strong enough to regrow. So I wonder if Leanne doesn't have the same fear. That her love wouldn't be enough to withstand the moving around that your job would entail."

Reuben felt a chill sneak down his spine. He and Leanne had faced so much, and now that they were finally together, he felt as if a huge part of what had been missing in his life had been restored to him. Did Leanne think she might not love him enough?

The thought gutted him.

"She loves the ranch," Reuben said, his voice quiet.

"It's security for her. She loves being rooted and grounded. Loves being a part of the cycle of life on the ranch. Loves her garden and seeing Austin growing up on a place his father grew up. But that's not everything to her." Then, to his surprise, Tabitha reached across the table and took his hands in hers. "I'm not telling you this about Leanne to change your mind about what you want to do or the decisions you need to make. I'm trying to give you some insight about my sister's life and her reasoning."

Reuben nodded, feeling as if his world was shifting. Realigning. The past few days had given him a different point of view. He wasn't sure he liked it, but he knew one thing for sure.

He wasn't letting Leanne go again.

Her head ached and her heart was sore.

Leanne stared out of the windshield of her car, not sure where she was going, but knowing that she had to keep moving. She'd been driving since she called Tabitha, aimlessly driving for the past few hours.

Reuben had sent her a text message when they were supposed to meet for supper. She had been tempted to ignore it but she didn't want him to worry.

So she had sent him a cryptic reply then turned her phone off.

Snow swirled in a cloud behind her car, blinding her to what was behind, and all she could see ahead was illuminated by the twin cones of her headlights, stabbing the gathering dark.

She slowed down as she came to a crossroad. One road led north to Calgary, the other south to the Crowsnest Pass.

Maybe she could find a hotel in Calgary. Stay there for the night. She would call Tabitha when she got there.

She choked down a sob as she made her choice, thinking of what George had told her. Of what had happened between her and Reuben the past few days. The truths that had come out.

With each step in Austin's growth, each change in his life, each stage he went through, she thought of Reuben and what he had chosen to miss. And each time that happened, her resentment and anger with him grew.

For so many years Dirk had been the hero, Reuben the villain and the ranch her home and safety net.

Now Reuben was back and she had discovered that she had been wrong about him and how he felt about Austin. Finding out that Dirk had created the circumstances of their estrangement had been the first tremor.

Discovering that her actions hadn't been any different from those of Reuben's mother, and seeing the condemnation back on George's face after she had worked so hard to gain his respect had shaken her. Then for him to demand she leave…

She felt as if she had lost her foundation.

Help me, Lord, she prayed. *I don't know who I am or where I belong.*

Living at the ranch had given her purpose and she felt as if she had finally found a place for herself and Austin. But no matter how hard she worked or how much she did, her future was always at risk because she had built her life at the ranch, on a shaky foundation.

She had built her house on sand and had not trusted in God. She had put her hope in living on the ranch to "save" her. She had put off telling George the truth about Austin because she thought it would jeopardize her position there.

And then Reuben had come back into her life, and for a while she clung to the hope that she could have both him and the life she had created.

He was leaving tomorrow to take the final steps toward a job that would mean a lot of moving. A job that would take them both away from the ranch.

And what will you choose?

She wanted to have things work for her. And yet she struggled to justify that the life she had built on the ranch would be best for Austin. But could she expect Reuben to live in a home where he'd been treated so poorly from the beginning?

"I love him. I love him and I want to be with him."

She spoke the words aloud in the silence of her car and they seemed to resonate. Fill the space. She waited, and slowly everything else slipped away.

She'd always wanted to be with Reuben. She had fought against it and tried to work around it. She had been selfish by putting her trust in the wrong place.

She needed to go back to Cedar Ridge and back to Reuben.

As soon as she made that decision, it was as if a deep peace suffused her. She had stopped fighting, trying to plan and arrange. Only one thing was necessary. That she and Reuben and Austin be together.

She peered through the dark, trying to find a place to turn off the highway so she could turn around.

Two small lights reflected at her. A dark shape suddenly appearing on the side of the road.

A deer bounded onto the road, racing to avoid her.

Leanne hit the brakes and swerved the car. The back end blew around and the front tires spun in the snow. She fought to regain control and then, a split second later, she slid sideways into the ditch.

It took a few moments to realize what had just happened. She inhaled deeply, her hands tingling in reaction.

Then the reality of her situation soaked in. She was

an hour from town, stuck in a ditch and who knows how long from getting a tow.

She grabbed her purse, yanked out her phone and turned it on. Her heart sank as the screen came to life and she could see that she had no cell service and how late it was. Which meant she had no way of calling Reuben or, even more important, a tow truck.

She dropped her head against the headrest, tamping down her fear and frustration. She had to get back to Cedar Ridge before Reuben left for Los Angeles. She simply had to.

Still nothing from Leanne.

Reuben shoved his phone into his pocket and turned his attention back to the breakfast he had ordered, wondering why he'd actually thought he'd be hungry.

Last night he stopped by the hospital after seeing Tabitha, but George was sleeping so he went back to his hotel and dialed Leanne's number. When she didn't answer, he sent a text message but again, nothing.

This morning he called Tabitha to see if she'd heard anything. All Tabitha would say was that Leanne had texted her early this morning saying she was okay. Nothing more.

Which only made him angrier that she hadn't bothered to get in touch with him.

He pushed his food around on his plate, then sent another futile text to Leanne.

In two hours he had to leave for Los Angeles, and once there he had to make the final commitment to the job. Once the contract was signed, there was no turning back.

A Christmas song came on the radio playing in the café. Christmas was two weeks away. Where would he celebrate it and what would it look like? Would he and Leanne and Austin be together?

He swallowed down an unwelcome knot of pain, and as took a sip of his coffee, he sent up yet another prayer for peace and for wisdom. He kept his head down, feeling rude as people walked past him, a few calling out a quick greeting. He looked at his phone, trying to look like he was a man with purpose.

If only he knew what that purpose was.

"Reuben, I thought you were leaving today." Owen Herne dropped into the chair across from him, making it impossible for Reuben to ignore him.

"I don't need to be in Calgary for a couple of hours yet," he said.

"Are you going to see George before you go?"

"Yeah. I'm picking up my…my…nephew to take him there." He caught himself. He had almost said his son.

He wanted so badly to tell someone. Wanted to make that declaration. Except he couldn't. Not until George knew.

"I stopped and saw George yesterday. After the meeting. He was pretty upset," Owen said.

"Did he say why?"

Owen lifted his one hand in a vague gesture. "Something about your mom and Leanne being the same. I didn't know where he was going with that, so I thought I would change the subject. So I asked him what he was getting Austin for Christmas. And then he started crying." Owen shook his head, still looking surprised. "Seriously, I never thought I'd see your old man do that."

"Crying?"

"Yeah. He just looked ahead, tears rolling down his face."

Reuben couldn't wrap his head around the idea and couldn't even begin to imagine his saddle-leather tough father crying.

"They say that people who have had heart attacks tend to be more emotional," Reuben said, still feeling shocked.

"Nah. This was more than that," Owen said. "It was kind of hard to see. I hope he's okay."

"I'm going there now so I guess I'll find out." He wiped his mouth and signaled to Adana to get him the bill.

"But you're not done with your breakfast."

"What are you, my mother?" Reuben teased.

"Just seems a shame."

"You can have it if you want it."

"Nah. I'm good." Owen got up and Reuben followed suit, still confused about what Owen had just told him.

Something about your mom and Leanne being the same...crying...

What had George been talking about?

But before he left the café, he pulled his phone out of his pocket and quickly dialed Leanne's number.

Once again he was sent directly to voice mail. Stifling a sigh of frustration he shoved the phone back into his pocket, put the truck in gear and went to pick up his son and visit his father.

Three generations of Walshes, he thought as he left Cedar Ridge. Hard to keep that out of his mind.

Leanne tried not to rush. She didn't want to end up in the ditch again. Fortunately she'd had enough gas in her car to keep it running while she waited for the tow truck to finally show up. The driver, who was the closest and most available, couldn't come for four hours.

She'd had to walk down the road until she came to a slight rise, and there she managed to get one bar of service. Enough to call a tow truck and give him her cell number, for what good that would do. Then she went back to her car, running it a few times, just to stay warm.

When the tow truck finally came, the sun was pinking the clouds on the horizon and her fuel gauge was flirting with Empty. It had taken him only minutes to pull her out of the ditch, which only served to increase her frustration and anger with herself. She'd filled up her tank up as soon as she could and kept on driving, surprised at how far she had driven last night.

As she drove she could still hear George's voice telling her to leave. Hearing the anger and betrayal in his voice. His rejection of her and her son.

She fought down a sob of despair as she finally reached the turn-off to Cedar Ridge. She glanced at the clock on her dashboard. Would Reuben be at the hospital or at the ranch by the time she got to town? She wished she could call him but her phone was dead.

As she played through the possibilities, she doubted Reuben would return to the ranch. He would be leaving for the airport this afternoon, so he would probably stop in to see his father.

His father?

Leanne shook off the confusion. One thing at a time. And right now that one thing was to get to the hospital. To see Reuben.

She prayed it wouldn't be too little too late.

Chapter Thirteen

George was sitting up in a chair when Reuben came into the hospital room, carrying Austin. The remnants of his father's lunch sat on a tray parked on a table and his father was staring out the window. Reuben couldn't read his expression but as soon as Austin saw George he called out, "Gwampa, Gwampa. Missed you."

George's head swiveled around and the smile on his face when he saw his grandson eased Reuben's worry. He still looked pale, however, and as they came closer, Reuben saw lines of weariness bracketing his father's mouth and eyes.

"Hey, little guy," George said, holding out his hands for his grandson, but Reuben held Austin back from climbing onto George's lap.

"Missed you," Austin said, leaning instead against George's leg.

"So, I understand Leanne came to see you yesterday." Reuben didn't have time to play around. He needed to get directly to what he wanted to talk about.

George's mouth narrowed and anger twisted his father's features. He readied himself to pull Austin back, but then George shook his head as if ridding himself of whatever reaction Reuben's comment made.

"I can't talk about it. Not in front of the boy."

Dread trickled down Reuben's spine. "Did Leanne tell you the truth?" he said, digging in the pocket of his coat for the toy car that Austin had taken from Tabitha's place. He handed it to his son to distract him, and thankfully Austin walked over to the other empty chair in the room and started running his car up and down the arm rest.

"The truth? About him, you mean?" George lifted his chin toward Austin who was making engine noises, engrossed in his play. "Yes. She did." George looked up at him and the dread became a deep-seated fear. "And I told her the truth about you."

"Me? What truth about me?"

"Your mother. She fooled around on me. I'm not your father any more than Dirk is his." He pointed at Austin, who had his back to them. "Didn't Leanne tell you?"

"Tell me what?" Reuben could only stare at his father, trying to sort out what he was saying. "I haven't talked to her yet."

George closed his eyes and rubbed them with the back of his hand. "The truth is… I'm not your biological father."

Shock. Surprise. Confusion. Reuben didn't know which emotion to deal with first.

"What?"

"Your mother cheated on me. She got pregnant by someone else."

He stared at his father as his entire world crumbled around him. Was God playing some cosmic joke on him?

In the span of a week he'd gained a son and lost a father.

"Who? Who is my father then?" he asked, his voice cracking, still trying to find the ground under him. Again.

George shrugged, then glanced over at Austin who was, so far, oblivious to what they were saying. "Some guy who came through town one day. Your mother said she didn't love him and that he didn't want to have anything to do with her or you. So she stayed with me. But I knew you weren't mine because, well, your mother and I hadn't been intimate for some time. She hated being on the ranch. Hated the ranching life, and it got to the point where she hated me."

Once again Reuben felt like his life had been rocked to its core.

"All these years, why didn't you ever tell me?" Frustration and anger edged his voice as he tried to find his bearings.

"I was too ashamed."

Which made sense to Reuben. His proud father wouldn't want to admit that the boy his wife carried, the boy born while he was married to his mother, wasn't his.

"So why didn't my mother take me with her?"

"She was selfish and she didn't want you from the moment she found out she was pregnant."

Reuben fingered the scar his father gave him, thought of the anger George had rained down on him. Thought of how concerned he was that he would be the same kind of father.

And in that moment he felt a curious untethering from this complicated man who had defined so much of who he was.

He wasn't his father's son after all.

He was his own person. He was a child of God first and foremost. But George Walsh's angry, at times vindictive, blood didn't run through his veins.

Reuben hadn't even realized how much it had haunted him until it was no longer there. As he looked at his father, he suddenly saw him in a different light.

"Is that why you were so hard on me?" Reuben asked. "Because I wasn't your biological son?" He leaned against the wall, looking for some support as he worked his way through this new place.

George looked up at him, his eyes narrowed slightly. "You were a difficult kid. Dirk was always easier. He was a happy, pleasant kid. He listened. Did what he was told. You fought me at every turn. Just like your mother did. But I was on my own with two young boys to raise. It wasn't easy. You weren't easy."

This was hardly justification for how he was treated but, in fairness to George, he had given a boy who wasn't his son a home. And, if Reuben were truly honest, some good memories.

Then George's expression softened. "But you did love the ranch—I'll give you that. More than Dirk ever did."

"Still do," Reuben admitted.

"Why didn't you stay?"

"Because of how you treated me. Because of how you were always favoring Dirk over me." Though now he understood better why, especially given George's temperament. In fact, if he wanted to be gracious, George could be given some credit for giving a home to a child that was no relation to him.

"I know I did." George sighed as he nodded. Then his eyes fastened on Reuben as if looking for something. "But I was trying. Believe me, I was trying."

Reuben wanted to believe him. "You were so angry with me when I came back last week."

"You made me feel guilty. About how I treated you." He sighed again. "Having Austin around made me realize how much I missed by being so hard on you. And now, after coming so close to death, I've been thinking. I know what I did to you was wrong. You were just a little boy when your mother left. It wasn't your fault, what she did." Silence followed this, broken only by Austin's jabbering in the corner of the hospital room. "I shouldn't have been so hard with you. I should have been more patient."

Reuben couldn't have been more shocked. But even as he processed this, another reality inserted itself.

"And how do you feel about him?" Reuben asked, looking over at Austin, who was still playing with his toy, seemingly oblivious to the emotional storm swirling around him.

George sighed, then looked over at Austin. "It was hard finding out that he wasn't Dirk's son." Reuben heard the confusion in his voice, saw the frustration on his face. "I had always seen him as a little bit of Dirk still with us."

"Do you love him less now that you know the truth?"

George's features altered, as he seemed to process this question. "He's such a sweet, dear boy."

Reuben watched the play of emotions on his father's face and felt a surprising flow of sympathy for George's confusion.

"I don't want you to take him away," George said. Then he looked up at Reuben. "Even though I know what I did, I don't want you to take him away."

"Why not? He's not your biological grandson. At all."

"But I care about him. I always saw him as…as a second chance. To do what I should have done with Dirk and with you. To do the right thing."

Reuben felt a mix of surprise and compassion for the confusion his father was expressing. For the feelings he was baring.

Then George caught his hand, his fingers tight. "You have some good memories don't you?" he asked, an imploring tone in his voice.

Reuben looked down at their entwined hands and as his shirt sleeve slid up he saw the scar on his own wrist. Painful memories intertwined with the ones that George was hoping he had.

"I remember going fishing. You, me and Dirk. We rode the horses up to that little lake up in Jackknife Basin. We had a fish fry and rode home under the stars."

"Yeah. I remember that. And the time we had that

roundup when that one kid we hired came along? He had a ukulele and insisted on taking it everywhere."

Reuben laughed. "I forgot about that one. He kept wanting to play while he was riding."

"He wanted to be Roy Rogers," they both said at once.

They fell quiet and then Austin, bored with his play, came back. "Gwampa still sick?" he asked, leaning against George's leg again. "You come home now?"

George smiled, curling his hand around the boy's neck. "Tomorrow. I'm coming home tomorrow."

"Uncle Wooben come home tomorrow?" Austin asked. "Stay at the ranch with me and mommy?"

Reuben looked down at his son, trying to imagine that scenario.

He suddenly felt less and less certain of the path he had chosen for himself. A path he had hoped to share with Leanne and Austin. The three of them away from Cedar Ridge and all the memories and pain. Starting over.

"You have to leave soon, don't you?" George asked. "Go to California?"

"I do." He folded his arms over his chest, thinking.

"Do you think Leanne will come with you?"

"I hope so."

George looked down at Austin, and Reuben thought of his father's earlier entreaty. Could he do it? Could he stay?

"You know, I was so proud when my dad transferred part of the ranch over to me," George was saying, rubbing Austin's shoulder as he spoke. "I still remember sitting in that lawyer's office signing the final papers.

He got up and shook my hand and told me to take care of it. To someday pass it on to my son like his father had passed it on to him. I knew early on it wouldn't be Dirk. He didn't love it like you did. But I didn't know if I could ever pass it on to you."

"Because I wasn't your true son. I wasn't a Walsh."

George nodded. "But I could see you loved the ranch," George continued. "It was in your blood even if it wasn't Walsh blood."

Reuben looked at the man he had always considered his father, and he thought of their past and wondered if they could write a new future.

It was what Leanne wanted.

He kept coming back to that. He thought of what Tabitha had told him about their life moving around with their father and how hard it was on their mother and on them.

Lord, show me what to do, he prayed. But even as he formulated the petition, he knew what he needed to do. What was the best decision for Leanne. For Austin. For George. And, if he was honest, for himself.

"Would there be room for me? On the ranch, if I stayed?" he asked.

Are you sure this is what you want? he asked himself. *You would be working with this man. Can you trust him?*

Reuben thought of the days he and Leanne had spent side by side, herding the cows, working with the horses. It had felt so right in a way that he knew that his job as an engineer, traveling around the world, leaving Leanne and Austin behind each time, never would.

George didn't look up at him right away, and for a heart-stopping moment Reuben thought he had made a drastic mistake by putting himself out there like he had with this complicated man.

"Yes, there would be room. I've wanted to sell the store for some time now. I can use the profits from that to expand the ranch."

"Sell the store?" Reuben was surprised. Walsh's Hardware had been almost as important to his father as the ranch.

George nodded. "I need to slow down, and I think Carmen could be talked into taking it over."

Then his father looked up at him and Reuben saw the sheen of tears in his father's eyes.

"Would you stay? Be a partner on the ranch?" George asked.

"We would have to trust each other," Reuben said, safeguarding his answer. "I'm not your biological son after all."

"I trust you" was all George said. "And to me, you are my son. The only son I have left."

"Then I think this can work. I want to stay and I want us to be a family."

George smiled gently, looking back down at Austin. "I want this too."

Even as they made this agreement, Reuben thought of Leanne, wondering where she was and what she was going through right now.

His heart twisted at the thought of her. But looking at Austin and his father, he knew that he had made the right decision.

* * *

Leanne parked her car in the parking lot of the hospital. Weariness clawed at her, but as she got out of her car, she saw Reuben's large truck and relief sluiced through her. Reuben wasn't gone yet.

She hurried over the snow-covered sidewalks, then into the blessed warmth of the hospital. She nodded at the attendant behind the counter and strode down the corridor to George's room, Christmas music following her. She almost faltered as she thought of Christmas and where she, Reuben and Austin might be sharing it.

Doesn't matter, she told herself. *The important thing is that we are all together.*

As she came near George's room, she heard Reuben's deep voice, Austin's sweet one and then George replying.

Then, to her utter surprise, the sound of laughter.

She paused outside the room, wondering what could possibly have gone on since George had sent her out of here with such anger in his voice.

Had he and Reuben made up? Had they found a way to bury their differences?

Would she even be a part of all of this?

She shook off her questions, reminding herself of what she and Reuben had shared and the feelings they'd always had for each other.

She loved him.

And with that resonating through her, she stepped into the room, shoulders squared, head held high. But she stayed in the doorway, still unsure of her reception.

George saw her first and she braced herself for his anger.

Instead, to her surprise, she saw contrition, not anger, in his expression.

"Leanne, I'm so sorry," he said, his voice breaking. "So very sorry."

Reuben spun around as Austin came running toward her. "Mommy, you here," he called out, arms held wide in welcome. She swept him up, holding him close as she tried to understand what George had just said, a complete contrast to the fury he had shown her a less than twenty four hours ago.

Then Reuben was beside her, his arms around her, holding her close.

"I'm so glad you're okay. I was so worried." He stroked her hair back from her face, his eyes holding hers as if to make sure.

She leaned into his arms, relief and love washing over him. "I'm sorry I left. I didn't know what to do. Where to go," she whispered.

"George told me what he said to you."

"Really?"

"Yes. So where did you go? Why didn't you contact me?"

"I was upset. George was furious when I told him the truth about..." She looked at her son who was running his toy car up and down her shoulder. Then she held him close, so thankful the three of them were back together. "He told me to leave and I did. Then I started driving. I felt like I was no different than your mother. I had done the same thing."

"You are nothing like my mother," he said, giving her a gentle shake. "Don't ever think that."

She gave him a watery smile, her emotions definitely shaky.

"You still didn't tell me where you went," he said.

"Nowhere. I just drove, thinking and praying, then a deer jumped in front of me, I hit a ditch and I didn't have cell service. Then my phone died."

"How did you get out?"

"Tow truck," she said, holding his puzzled gaze. "Thankfully I managed to get through to the driver before my phone died." She almost laughed. This wasn't how she envisioned their reunion. Talking about tow trucks and cell phones.

"I'm sorry I didn't get hold of you," she said, slipping her free arm around his waist. "After what George said, I needed time to think. To process what he told me and what I needed to do."

Then to her surprise and joy, Reuben bent over and kissed her.

"I love you," he said.

And in that moment every concern she had about her decision, every second thought was blown away.

"I love you too," she returned, laying her head on his chest. "And I want you to know that I'll go with you wherever you go. I'll live wherever you want to live. As long as we can be together."

"So you would move to Los Angeles with me?"

She nodded without hesitation. "Any place you want. I know that I love you enough. I know you'll take care of Austin and me. And I want us to be a family, wherever that may happen."

Reuben kissed her again, his arms surrounding her and Austin. "You are amazing," he whispered in her ear.

"We need to be a family," she repeated. "No matter where. No matter what."

Reuben drew back and turned to George, who was leaning forward as if trying to hear what they were talking about.

"What are you saying? What's going on?" he demanded. "Come over here and tell me."

Reuben, his arm still around her shoulders, escorted her to George's side.

"Leanne was telling me that she'll go with me wherever I go. Even if it's California."

Leanne could see the puzzlement on George's face and she thought of what it would do to him to have Austin move away. In spite of his anger with her only yesterday, she felt sorry for him. He would be losing so much.

"She's saying that we need to be a family." Reuben gave her a loving look, his arm firmly around her. "And I agree."

George still looked confused. "But I thought you were staying here. In Cedar Ridge. At the ranch."

Reuben brushed another kiss over Leanne's head. "We are."

"What are you saying?" Now it was Leanne's turn to be confused. "I thought we were moving. And don't you have to leave soon? For your interview in Los Angeles?"

"I'm not going."

"What? I don't understand."

Reuben looked from her to Austin then to George. "George and I have decided that I'm going to become a partner on the ranch. I'm staying here." He gave her a careful smile. "If that's okay with you. But if you have your heart set on Los Angeles—and given the snow we've been dealing with I wouldn't blame you if you do—we can still go."

All she could do was stare at him as the implications of what he was saying seeped into her sleep-deprived brain. "Stay here? On the ranch?"

"Together."

She didn't know whether to laugh or cry or shout out her thanks so she did all three.

"Happy, Mommy?" Austin asked, concern edging his voice as he grabbed her by the face, still holding his car. The wheel mashed into her cheek, which made her laugh even more.

"I'm happy, buddy," she said, giving him a tight hug.

She set him down and then slipped her arm around Reuben. She couldn't stay close enough to him.

"I can hardly believe this," she said. Then she turned to Reuben. "Are you sure this is what you want?"

He nodded, smiling down at her. "I'm sure. George and I have a few things to iron out but I'm confident we can make it work."

"So long as you learn to listen to me," George grumbled. Austin had come to stand beside him again and was now running his toy car up and down George's arm. Leanne was about to reprimand her son when George took his hand and moved it to the arm of the chair.

"Why don't you play with your car here?" was all he said.

"What happened while I was gone?" Leanne looked from George to Reuben, still puzzled at the obvious equanimity prevailing in the room. A far cry from the anger George had hurled at her yesterday.

"We can catch up later," Reuben told her. "For now, I think we have something more important to discuss. I think our son needs to be brought up to speed before we talk about another thing."

Leanne shot a glance at George, who was teasing Austin by putting his hand in the way of the car.

"You want to do this now?" George asked, his attention still on Austin.

"I don't want to wait any longer." Reuben looked to Leanne as if seeking her approval.

"I don't either," she said.

Reuben walked to the other chair in the room and brought it over, setting it down beside George. "Sit down here," he said to Leanne and, as she did, he picked up Austin, set him down on Leanne's lap and knelt down beside them both.

Leanne sent up a quick prayer for strength, wisdom and the right words and then brushed Austin's hair back from his face, her hand lingering on the lighter patch of hair so like his father's.

"Austin, honey, you know I love you," she said.

He nodded, his attention on his car, looking delightfully unconcerned.

"You know that I'm your mommy, right?"

Another casual nod.

"But you need to know something else. Uncle Reuben isn't your uncle. He's your daddy."

This caught his attention. He laughed. "No. Uncle Wooben."

Reuben took one chubby hand in his and curled his own hand around it. "No, sweetheart. I'm your daddy."

Austin looked puzzled but then nodded. "Okay" was all he said. Then Austin pushed Leanne away and slid off his lap, obviously done with the conversation.

Leanne looked from Reuben to George, puzzled. "Well, that was rather anticlimactic."

"I don't know if he fully realizes what just happened," Reuben said with a light laugh.

"He will. And when he does, it will seem normal to him," George said.

Leanne grabbed Reuben's hand for moral support then turned to George. "Yesterday you were angry with me when I told you the truth about Austin. If you truly want us to live on the ranch with you, I need to know that you are okay with all of this. His being Reuben's son."

George didn't say anything right away and Leanne wondered if she had pushed things too far.

"I am," he said finally, his voice quiet. "I was wrong to yell at you. But it was a shock."

Leanne acknowledged that with a nod. "I believe that."

"But I want us to be a family. You are all I have, and even though Reuben might not be my son through blood, he is my son in every other way. I want you all to stay with me. I can't imagine..." His voice broke. Then he regained his composure. "Anyway, I'm glad you're staying. All of you. Leanne, you've been a real blessing to me, Austin, as well, and I don't want you gone."

Leanne reached over and took George's hand, squeezing it gently. "I'm glad about that." Then she looked over at Reuben who was watching her, love in his eyes, and she felt a peace and joy that she hadn't felt in years.

"I love you," she said to Reuben, still holding her father-in-law's hand.

"I love you too," he returned, bending in for a gentle kiss.

"Okay. That's enough of that, you two," George said, his voice gruff. "We have plans to make."

Epilogue

"I think you must have cleaned out the entire stock of farm animals from your store," Reuben said to his father as Austin ripped open yet another box. The little guy squealed his delight at the sow with four little piglets nestling in the tissue paper. He set them up beside the barn that he and Leanne had painstakingly assembled, joining the herd of cows and the horses, chickens, dogs and cats already lined up.

George just laughed, leaning back in his chair, the lights of the Christmas tree playing over his lined face. "It's my duty as a grandparent," he said. "And it was the last chance to get the discount. Once I sell the store, I won't have that anymore."

Remnants of wrapping paper were strewn under the Christmas tree now empty of gifts. Christmas music filled the room and a fire snapped in the fireplace, all combining to create a feeling of warmth and home.

Reuben compared it to the Christmas he spent last year in a hotel room watching a forgettable Christmas

movie on television. It had been bleak and depressing
and lonely. This was light and love and peace. The contrast almost made him cry.

Austin got up and brought a handful of animals over
to Reuben. "Play with me, Daddy," he said.

Austin had been calling him that for the past couple
of weeks but it still sent a thrill through his soul.

"I don't know, sweetheart," he said. "I think it's getting close to bedtime, and tomorrow we are going to
Uncle Cord and Ella's place for Christmas dinner."

His son shook his head in denial and scooted back
to the farm he had painstakingly set up.

Leanne came in carrying a tray of mugs. "Hot chocolate for you," she said, handing one to George. "And
coffee for you," she said to Reuben.

Then she turned to Austin. "And bedtime for you."
She was about to pick him up when George stood up,
grunting as he did so.

"I can take care of that," George said.

"That's okay," Leanne protested, holding up her hand
as if to stop him.

"You've done enough. Besides I need some one-on-
one time with my grandson, and you and Reuben need
to talk."

He gave Reuben an exaggerated wink, which made
him groan. Nothing like being obvious.

Leanne shot Reuben a puzzled frown but he simply
shrugged as if he had no idea what his dad was talking about.

Austin protested, but only slightly, as George helped

him pick out an animal to take to bed with him. Then, together, they walked out of the family room.

"Sit here," Reuben said to Leanne.

She did, still looking puzzled. Especially when he got up and went to the Christmas tree and pulled a tiny box out of the branches. Then he sat down beside Leanne.

But he could tell from the way she was pressing her fingers to her lips and her shining eyes that she had some idea what lay inside the box.

He carried on anyhow, determined to do this right. He got down on one knee and opened the box to show her the ring inside. It caught the lights of the tree and reflected them over her face.

He'd had a speech all prepared but as he looked up at her, her eyes shining and his heart pounding, he decided to stick with simple.

"Leanne Rennie Walsh. I love you so much. I want to spend the rest of my life with you and Austin. Will you marry me?"

"Of course I will" was all she said, her lips quivering. Tears spilled from her eyes, leaving a glistening line down her flushed cheek.

He slipped the ring on her finger, and she held it up, making it catch the lights from the tree. "It's so beautiful," she breathed.

"Not as beautiful as you," he said. He stood up and gathered her in his arms, holding her close, a sense of utter peace and contentment washing over him.

They shared a soft, gentle kiss, then both drew back, looking deep into each other's eyes as if to cement their relationship.

"I love you so much," she said. "I don't know if I'll ever get tired of saying that."

"Me neither." He kissed her again.

She smiled, stroking his face with her hand, growing serious. "This was a long time coming," she said. "But I'm so thankful. So grateful."

"God has definitely worked in mysterious ways to get us here."

She laid her head on his chest, her hand on his heart.

"You know, after we figured out what Dirk had done, I was furious. I couldn't forgive him for what he did, but in the past couple of days I've realized that if Dirk hadn't done what he did, I wonder if we would have ended up here. At the ranch."

Leanne sighed lightly, then drew back smiling up at him. "Maybe that's true, but I'd like to think that we would have found a way to make our life wherever we would have ended up."

"I'd like to think that too, but I'm thankful that out of all of this, George and I have found a way to make peace and forgive each other. To be father and son at last."

Leanne held his gaze and her smile was like a bright beacon of love. "You are an amazing man, Reuben Walsh, and I'm so glad that we found our way back to each other."

"Me too. I'm so thankful and humbled that we've found a place where you and I can raise our own family. I will forever be grateful for that."

"Our family. I like the sound of that. I promise you that I'll always be there for you."

"And I promise that I'll always take care of you,"

Reuben said. "You and Austin and any other children we might have."

"Other children?" She gave him an impish smile. "How many other children were you planning on our having?"

"Let's take things one kid at time," he said.

She laughed then pulled him close, and as the lights twinkled in the tree behind them and the gentle music holding the promise of Christmas floated around them, their kiss became a seal on those promises and a hope for the future.

Together.

* * * * *

HARLEQUIN
PLUS

Announcing a **BRAND-NEW**
multimedia subscription service
for romance fans like you!

Read, Watch and Play.

Experience the easiest way to get
the romance content you crave.

Start your **FREE 7 DAY TRIAL** at
<u>www.harlequinplus.com/freetrial</u>.

"Oh, no," Mike whispered. "Not here, too."

A heavy stone of foreboding dropped in Julia's stomach as she slowly rose and pivoted to look at whatever Mike had just seen.

A fire was beginning to curl up the side of the cabin next door. It was maybe thirty yards away, separated by a dozen trees—and a pile of chopped wood that stretched between the cabins like one long dynamite fuse.

How could this have happened? There'd been no lightning. No one was staying in the other cabins. There was no reason a fire could spontaneously begin next door. There was only one answer—

The evil that had been setting Crooked Valley on fire had followed them here. Why?

"Daddy! There's a fire!" Ginny pointed at the orange flames eagerly running up the wooden siding of the cabin next door, inches away from the woodpile. Any hope Julia had that her eyes were deceiving her disappeared. The house next door was on fire, and their lives were suddenly in very real danger.

"We need to get out of here. Now." Mike grabbed Ginny's coat and started helping her arms into the sleeves. Julia bent down beside him and fastened the zipper, then grabbed Ginny's hat and tugged it on her head as Mike pulled back on his boots. Julia grabbed her coat just in time to see the flames leap to the pile of dried wood and race across the top like a hungry animal.

Heading straight for their cabin.

"Get in my car!" Mike shouted.

They ran for the SUV, but Julia stopped short just as Mike opened the passenger-side door. "Mike, look." The two front tires had been slashed. Julia spun to the right and saw the same thing had been done to her car. "Someone doesn't want us leaving," she said under her breath. Fear curled a tight fist inside her chest.

Mike quickly scanned the area. "He's out there. Somewhere."

Oh, God. Why would the arsonist follow them? Why would he target Mike and Ginny? Or Julia, for that matter?

A chill snaked up her spine as she realized the arsonist must have *watched* them stringing lights, singing Christmas carols. He'd watched them—and still decided to take the lives of two adults and a small child. What kind of evil person did that?

"Come on. We have to go on foot." Mike took Julia's hand in one hand, then scooped up Ginny with the other.

Even as he said the words, she could see the fire overtaking the small cabin, eagerly devouring the Christmas lights they had just hung. The sweet moment the three of them had was being erased.

It was a two-mile trip down the mountain. Another two miles back to town. On foot, they'd never make it before dark. How were they going to get back to safety?

Don't miss
Refuge Up in Flames *by Shirley Jump,*
available December 2022 wherever
Love Inspired books and ebooks are sold.

LoveInspired.com

LIMREXP1022